Please renew or return items by the date
shown on your receipt

www.hertfordshirc.gov.uk/libraries

Renewals and enquiries: 0300 123 4049

Textphone for hearing or   0300 123 4041
speech impaired users:

L32 11.16

46 390 991 3

Also by Abi Silver in the Burton & Lamb series:

The Pinocchio Brief
The Aladdin Trial
The Cinderella Plan
The Rapunzel Act
The Midas Game

THE
AMBROSIA
PROJECT

ABI SILVER

Lightning
Books (⚡)

Published in 2022
by Lightning Books
Imprint of Eye Books Ltd
29A Barrow Street
Much Wenlock
Shropshire
TF13 6EN

www.lightning-books.com

ISBN: 9781785633201

Cover by Nell Wood
Typeset in Minion Pro and Brandon Grotesque

British Library Cataloguing in Publication Data
A catalogue record for this book is available from the British Library.

For my father-in-law, John
who loved his food

To eat is a necessity, but to eat intelligently is an art
François VI, Duc de La Rochefoucauld

Ask not what you can do for your country.
Ask what's for lunch
Orson Welles

PROLOGUE

Nick Demetriou stood in the kitchen at Tanners' Hall preparing lunch and contemplating the considerable challenges posed by a life in the catering trade. As he would happily explain to anyone who would listen, he was not just a cook. Rather he was both producer and director of a touring, repertory culinary show, often tasked with a gruelling schedule. Sourcing fresh, high-quality ingredients was just the beginning. After that, every step had to be carefully choreographed to ensure they each reached maximum potential; the chopping, squeezing, chilling, mixing, warming, roasting and positioning. Using stalwarts he could rely upon and introducing newcomers for colour and excitement. It was only when they all peaked simultaneously that the accolades flooded in. Yes, providing a first-rate service was no mean feat for any chef on any regular day.

Today, sadly, was more than a little irregular. Andrew, one of his usual servers, had excused himself with 'flu' at 9am this morning, far too late to find a replacement. So Nick had been forced to step in and roll up his sleeves – the most overqualified of understudies – which had made him resentful. After all, he did own the business. He didn't want to be mistaken for staff.

Across the kitchen, a young woman was splitting cherry tomatoes with the tip of her knife, in the manner he'd shown her, and distributing the pieces evenly between individual salad bowls. 'Eleni,' Nick said. 'Finish the salad and get it out into the hall.'

The girl looked up and frowned. Her gaze bypassed Nick and settled on the face of the wall clock, before she pinched her lips together, turned back to him and nodded.

Clearly, she was cross at being hurried. He'd asked her to ensure the salad was laid out on the tables at the back of the hall by 12, and her silent protest told him she was still ahead of her deadline. Nick almost said something, something to remind her that he paid her wages, that there were still endless tasks to complete, that any boss could change his mind. He wondered, fleetingly, if the girl would have challenged his authority in the same way, if he'd still been the proprietor of *Giorgio's*, the best Greek restaurant in the whole West End. But then a crackling from underneath the grill forced him to check on the status of the halloumi and the moment to chastise Eleni was lost. Instead, he dabbed at his head with a freshly laundered handkerchief. He'd forgotten how stifling it could be in this kitchen.

He shifted the cheese to a chopping board, but before he began to slice it diagonally into narrow strips, he marched over to the back door, threw it open and took a deep breath. His young assistant didn't seem to be suffering from the heat. In fact, Eleni, who had started to hum as she worked, shivered, as the cooler air swept in from outside.

Nick left Eleni and went to survey the hall. The lines of chairs facing the front and the arrangement on the stage were of little concern to him. No, he occupied himself exclusively with the three trestle tables, placed end to end, on which the display of food – his food – was taking shape.

As Nick had envisaged, the beef carpaccio took centre stage: paper-thin, marbled strips of pure tenderloin. It looked bare on the plate without any garnish of any kind, but those were his instructions, and the bossy woman – Diana Percival, personal assistant to Brett Ingram – had made it very clear she wanted them to be obeyed. Even so, he'd slipped some watercress dip into a separate dish nestling beside it.

On either side were the sandwiches, still sealed with cling film, thickly cut with succulent fillings and interspersed with soft and floury wraps. Then, he'd left a space for the mini burgers, which were next on his list to heat up. He and his wife, Lisa, had cooked them last night at home, using a meatball recipe handed down from his grandparents, which he had modified and updated. Not that he expected Diana, or any of the guests, to appreciate the history, but Nick felt proud to continue the tradition.

At this end of the table, he would place the halloumi, which he planned to serve with acres of rocket and a red onion relish, and next to the cheese he would arrange the individual salad bowls: cucumber, avocado, edamame topped with pea tips and the cherry tomatoes Eleni had been faithfully dicing. The only other missing savoury dish was the sweet potato pakoras. Damn! There was probably not enough time to heat them in the oven after the burgers. He might have to resort to the microwave if they were really pushed. Damn Andrew and damn his flu!

But Nick's anger was extinguished when he viewed the creation

Eleni had set down at the furthest extremity of the table. This was his *exotic fruit platter (for sharing)*; a melange of the most desirable soft fruit on the market. Nick had purchased an orange-fleshed cantaloupe from Guatemala, a Cape pineapple, golden kiwi from New Zealand, mangos from the Caribbean and Chinese lychees. He had wanted Californian cherries too, to add drama, but they had been eye-wateringly expensive and now he looked, Eleni had worked wonders without them and the arrangement appeared enticing, sophisticated and most certainly exotic.

Nick returned to the kitchen and paused in the doorway to watch Eleni put the finishing touches to the salads. Sometimes, she reminded him of his sister, Maria. Not the Maria of today, but the vivacious youngster of happier times. Maria would have dry-fried the halloumi, two minutes each side until crisp and brown and then pressed the pieces into flat bread, with handfuls of fresh parsley and kalamata olives, drizzling her creation with freshly-squeezed lemon, laughing when the juice ran down her chin as she ate.

They didn't look so much alike, Eleni and Maria. It was more the way Eleni's eyes flashed with spirit when she spoke. That was classic Maria. And the gap between her front teeth, just like Maria's, a gap that would fit a penny. Their mother had advised it was a sign of good luck, that Maria would always be blessed with good fortune. Nick had joked that it meant she was destined to talk too much and she'd dug him in the ribs.

And of course there was the pixie cut which Eleni sported. Maria had experimented with shorter hair once. It had been a moment of rebellion, an outpouring of teenage frustration, and Nick knew she had regretted it bitterly, although she would never have let on. He'd heard her crying in the night, lamenting the loss of her beautiful hair, and he'd whispered to her in the darkness. 'No harm done. It'll grow back.'

'Mr Demetriou. Are you all right?' Eleni had noticed him standing there.

'It's still hot in here; that's all,' he said, tugging at his shirt and opening a button. 'And the clients will be arriving any minute.'

'OK,' Eleni said. 'I'll take these through now. I'll wait to unwrap the sandwiches until just before people arrive though,' she continued. 'What's next?'

'If I finish the halloumi, can you get the burgers in the oven?' Nick said, aware that he was still sweating, and hating himself for it. 'Then we're just left with the pakoras.'

'No problem.' Eleni treated him to her gap-toothed smile, as she picked up the tray of salad. 'Don't we need to label everything?'

Nick looked around him, then fumbled in his pockets. 'I must have left them in my car,' he said.

As Eleni left the room, he trotted outside to fetch the labels. He had thought he'd left them on one of the front seats, but he discovered that the pack had slipped down inside the passenger door. He had almost reached the safety of the kitchen once more when a shiny, black sports car drove into the car park and slid into the empty space immediately next to his.

***

Brett Ingram climbed out of his low-profile Porsche Taycan. He wasn't someone who usually purchased expensive items, even though he could, but with the Porsche, it had been different. On his first test drive, six years back, he had been enthralled by the growl of the engine, the rumble that shifted to the steering wheel, then the driver's seat and onwards through his entire body. He had bought one straightaway and driven it home via a circuitous route. There had been numerous occasions since then when he had manufactured a trip, with the sole aim of spending time behind the wheel of his extraordinary car.

These days, naturally, he had progressed to the electric version in which, despite valiant efforts, the manufacturers had been unable to replicate the authentic signature sound of its predecessor's six-cylinder engine. Or that original exhilaration-inducing vibration. But that was always the case with progress of any kind. No point fighting it. Sometimes you had to make sacrifices for the greater good. He reached out and stroked his fingers back and forth across the smooth paintwork.

Diana, his PA, was already crossing the car park. He'd averted his eyes as she clambered out of the car. But now, pocketing his keys, he could study her unobserved. Diana looked good today, Brett thought. She looked good most days but today, all five-foot-eleven of her, clad in that tight, pencil skirt and fitted jacket matched with heels that sent her soaring above six foot, and a shade of lipstick which reminded him of a bowl of ripe plums, he could hardly resist her. But resist her, he would.

Not that Diana wouldn't be willing. He'd tasted her disappointment when he had realised, halfway into today's journey, that he'd forgotten her birthday. He had heard the same tremor in her voice, the same flicker of her otherwise professional expression when, from time to time – only when he was snowed under with work – he had sent her out to buy gifts for his girlfriends or asked her to arrange taxis to or from unfamiliar addresses. Diana had been gracious about his forgetfulness today of course, but some things could not be hidden. He told himself he would make it up to her, show her how much he appreciated her. He just couldn't risk appreciating her in *that* way.

Brett looked around him. The front of the building had impressed him with its period red-brick façade and huge sash windows. Here at the back, the outlook was less inspiring. A large flat-roofed structure had clearly been added at some time in the last forty years, the painted lines of the parking bays were faint, the tarmac uneven and pitted and the sign announcing the venue to the world – 'Tanners' Hall. Since 1850' – had been knocked sideways by a stray vehicle.

And as the wind blew into Brett's face, he caught a faint whiff of decay. He noticed that one of the dustbins, around the far side of the building some twenty metres away, had been left open to the elements. That, then, was the most likely source of the unpleasant odour. How had Diana found this place? He couldn't recall now. She had insisted on somewhere 'low-key', which certainly described the place he was looking at now. He'd given in of course. 'As long as the right people come,' he'd said.

'With the cast you've invited, I can guarantee they'll come,' she'd replied.

He hung back, watching Diana walk towards a back door. She was right that they'd collected together an eclectic mix of speakers to suit their agenda. And what an agenda it was. He felt that familiar surge in his chest, the mix of anticipation and fear which preceded his greatest achievements. Any man who said he was never scared was a fraud and a fool. Yes, today, despite the inferior venue, marked the start of something huge, something with tremendous potential. Today heralded the beginning of the next phase for his company, Heart Foods, a phase which would catapult them into the food stratosphere.

'Mr Demetriou? I'm Diana Percival. How nice to meet you.'

Brett heard Diana introducing herself to someone inside the building, in the tone she reserved for new acquaintances. He smiled to himself as he imagined her extending her hand and nodding her head, in her inimitable fashion. He followed her inside.

Diana had laid a sheet of paper down on a metal table in the centre of the kitchen and was ticking off items one by one, using her Heart Foods' rollerball pen. A man with dark hair, grey around the temples, whom Brett assumed was the caterer, stood with his back to the door, leaning forwards to check on Diana's work.

'You won't forget the labels, Mr Demetriou, will you?' Diana said to the man, as if she was speaking to a schoolboy. 'Remember, I said how important they were.'

In the car, Diana had muttered to Brett something about how she hoped the caterer would do what she'd asked. She had rolled her blue eyes then to reinforce her frustration. Here in the kitchen, Brett pitied the caterer, as he had no doubt the man would feel the full force of Diana's wrath if he had not followed her instructions to the letter. You really didn't want to cross Diana.

'No problem,' the caterer replied. 'I was just getting them when you arrived.'

***

Once she had checked that Mr Demetriou had prepared everything she had ordered, Diana glided through to the hall itself. It was nothing like as imposing in real life as in the photographs, but that was always the way. Even so, the high ceilings gave a sense of space and, while the tiny windows meant there was little natural light in the hall, there were plenty of electric lights she could focus on the stage.

She sat down on the front row and spent a moment looking all around her. Yes. This would do. She hadn't wanted a plush auditorium for this event. She had wanted functional and plebeian and, in that respect, it was more than adequate. For a brief moment she wondered what it would be like to stand up on the stage delivering the main address herself – and receiving the applause – instead of helping out behind the scenes. What was the expression? *Always the bridesmaid, never the bride?*

'You must be Zoe.' She looked up at the sound of Brett's voice, echoing from the far end of the hall. He was greeting a young woman, no more than a girl really. She had pink hair, matching trousers and heavy, black-framed glasses. This was Zoe then, the carnivorous blogger, although Diana didn't remember the glasses from Zoe's avatar.

'I'm so delighted you could make it.' Diana heard the warmth in Brett's voice. 'Please help yourself to a drink. We have an assortment of fruit juices, wine and beer. Or is that not allowed?' He watched Zoe with interest as she reached for a glass of water.

'Do you know how many people are coming?' Zoe asked.

'I'm not sure, but at least a hundred. Diana can probably tell you.' Brett gave a half-nod in her direction, to show Diana he knew she was there, but Zoe did not turn around. 'She's my PA,' he continued, and Diana felt a surge in her chest at his words. 'We're hoping for press coverage and I'm sure you can help with the film too, and the feedback questionnaire I mentioned. How many followers do you have now?'

'I'm just short of forty thousand.'

'That's fantastic. And how often do you post?'

'Most days I put something out and I have my weekly podcast. But the main articles, they're like once every two weeks.'

'I'm sure a lot of hard work goes into them. You can tell that when you read them.'

Diana had to hand it to Brett. He knew just the right things to say. She was too distant to be able to read Zoe's expression, but imagined her blushing with pride. She wondered if any other CEO of a multi-million-pound business would take the time to make a nineteen-year-old girl feel comfortable and appreciated.

'Excuse me, just for a moment.' Now Brett beckoned her over. 'I have to attend to something, but I'll be right back. Oh…don't let me forget to talk to you about those diet recommendations you sent to me, before we finish up.'

As Brett left the hall, one hand reaching for his phone, Diana smiled her broadest smile and headed in Zoe's direction. She would ensure she continued the love fest, even though she didn't care much for the girl's work. Zoe ate only meat and derided virtually every essential food eaten the world over. She inhabited a shady corner of the online world, alongside conspiracy theorists and fake news. But blogs were the way of the future. Brett had made it clear that he wanted to engage with youth, and sending out Heart Foods' questionnaire to forty thousand of Zoe's followers was likely to be of considerable value to the company.

'Hello Zoe, I'm Diana.' She extended her hand to the younger woman. 'Brett was so delighted you could find time to come.'

'Thanks,' Zoe said, taking a sip of her water. 'A hundred in the audience is a bit smaller than I'm used to,' she said.

'Oh that's just here in the hall,' Diana smiled. 'There'll be exposure to many times that number with the film and the publicity drive Brett is planning.'

A few minutes later, Brett, his phone pinned to his ear, guided another guest towards them. Diana recognised her at once as Rosa Barrera, TV chef and the perfect guest for today, with its food-related theme. Rosa oozed love of eating – love of most things, in fact; big, round, epicurean love. Behind Rosa came a man whom Diana identified – through a process of elimination – as Mark Sumner, the farmer. The other man they had invited to speak was Adrian Edge, or 'Doctor Edge' to all Radio Two listeners, and Adrian she knew well, better than she would like, if the truth be told.

As Mark removed his jacket and slung it over a seat, Brett finished his call, apologised to them all profusely for his rudeness – *something urgent; sorted now* – and then greeted Mark with a hug and a slap on the back, which made Rosa's perfectly pencilled eyebrows lift and Zoe giggle.

'What a lovely welcome,' Rosa cooed and Brett turned to her, grinned and kissed her lightly on both cheeks. 'Now I know which of us is your favourite,' she said.

'Oh I'm sure it's not me,' Mark said, striding over to the table, on which Mr Demetriou had just placed a tray of sizzling beef burgers. Mark picked one up and popped it straight into his mouth. 'You can't beat eating them hot,' he said, by way of explanation.

Now Rosa appeared to be looking for someone or something herself, as her head turned this way and that. Diana was about to intervene, when Rosa caught the caterer's arm as he hurried by.

'Do you have oat milk?' Rosa asked him, her eyes skimming the drinks laid out on a table in the corner.

Mr Demetriou shook his head, as if he didn't understand.

Diana laughed to herself. He probably didn't. She couldn't imagine he had many requests for non-dairy alternatives, or for much vegan food either, among his usual clientele. His top-selling dishes, he had told her with pride the first time they had spoken, were moussaka and souvlakia, which she was pleased she had eschewed in favour of some less Greek alternatives, although she had agreed to the halloumi.

'Oat milk,' Rosa repeated, 'for my coffee. Or almond would do, but only without sugar.'

Mr Demetriou scuttled off with Rosa close on his heels and, now that more people had arrived, Diana decided to retreat and set up Brett's laptop for him on the stage. It was another twenty minutes before the scientist, Susan Mills, made her entrance.

Susan hovered at the extremity of the pack and Diana, sensing that she was shy, was about to step in once more and engage her in conversation when Adrian appeared. Diana could have predicted he would arrive last of all; he always liked to make an entrance. She had visions of him hiding out behind the bus shelter opposite the hall, spying on all the other guests, then waiting another five minutes before heading in, but only after checking on his appearance in the glass from every possible direction.

'I'm Dr Edge, but do please call me Adrian,' he declared, as he swept into the room, bowed low and then offered his hand to each of the others in turn.

There now. They were quorate.

***

Rosa Barrera had liked Brett when she'd first met him, some five years before, when his relaxed, genial manner had impressed her.

She'd had no idea then if his manner was genuine, but she hardly cared. It was refreshing to spend time with someone who was so easy to chat to and who understood everything you said and, importantly, remembered it the next time you met. One thing Rosa did not appreciate was being forgotten.

Brett's amiable nature was evident now, as he flitted between his guests like a butterfly, his jacket and top shirt button open, gathering praise instead of nectar, and throwing it back out to each of them. Although when she'd arrived, he had been distant – phone calls removing him from the action on more than one occasion. Naturally, she'd made a joke about it – he was the host, after all – but that was how powerful men were: always blowing hot and cold.

Her feelings towards Adrian were quite different. When she'd accepted today's invitation, she'd asked Brett outright who else was on the guest list and she'd queried Adrian's inclusion.

'We can't have a party and not ask Adrian,' Brett had joked to her, but she'd sensed that she might have hit a nerve and she didn't press the point. Brett was the host after all.

It was just that she couldn't immediately see what Adrian could contribute to a serious debate on what we should eat, given that his answer seemed to be absolutely anything. It was like offering advice on relationships and then advocating free love. It was lazy and unprincipled. That was why she had determinedly boycotted his show after a couple of episodes.

And Adrian had commented on her appearance. 'What a fabulous outfit,' he'd said, which might have been a point in his favour in different circumstances. She was not one of those women who was affronted when she received a compliment or someone held a door open for her. God knows, there were far more important things in the world at which to take offence. It was more that it had seemed mean-spirited of Adrian to single her out for approval when she was standing next to Sue in her dreary brown skirt and blouse, and Zoe in her pink trousers and zebra-stripe camouflage t-shirt. At least Adrian hadn't stared at Rosa's breasts. She had watched him to ensure he didn't, as it was something which most men she met invariably did.

In fact, it had already happened once today, as she exited her Uber outside the hall and took a moment to adjust her wraparound dress; she had spied the taxi man staring, not even trying to conceal his gaze. She had turned away from him, slamming the door shut with her bottom. It wasn't that she was embarrassed by the size of her breasts; she liked them and the curvy, sensuous shape they gave her. But they did tend to attract a lot of attention, not all of it welcome.

She couldn't remember now what it had been like before she had breasts. There were few photographs of her from her childhood. She would never have posed for any; *making memories* had to play second fiddle to *making ends meet* for her mother. And any taken surreptitiously, or ones she really couldn't avoid, like class photos, would have stayed pinned to the fridge in Mexico. So there was no easily accessible record of how her body had looked before she filled out. She had tried to diet once, in her late teens, when her mother's latest partner had shown a more than fatherly interest in her. Apart from feeling hungry all the time, and sometimes light-headed, it had made little difference; her defiant breasts had only protruded even further from her reduced frame.

Rosa looked around her. The third man in the room, Mark Sumner, intrigued her. He possessed the self-confidence which often accompanied those who cared little for how others might judge them, and that was unusual these days. And while she sometimes considered manliness a real turn-off, in his hands it was moulded into a physical strength and presence which she found reassuring.

However, for now, Mark could wait. Rosa approached Sue. It seemed like the best next move; starting a conversation with the least demanding person in the room. At the same time, she hoped that Brett or Mark might join them, but she would leave that to them.

'How is your research going?' she asked.

'I've almost finished,' Sue said, in a matter-of-fact way, not offering any further information. Now they stood close together, Rosa could see that Sue's fingernails were short and uneven and the skin around them red in places. What on earth made a grown woman – a scientist no less – gnaw at her nails?

'And after that?' Rosa tried again.

'I'm not sure. I don't plan that far ahead,' Sue said.

'Me neither.' Zoe had overheard them and joined in. 'That's the way with blogging. Every day brings something new, so there's no point. Listen, can I get a quick photo?' Zoe stepped towards Rosa, raised her phone up in front of her face and her glasses slipped right off her nose. She caught them with her free hand, folded them up and tucked them into the neck of her top. 'Brett asked me to take a few shots, for publicity.'

Rosa smiled her best smile and squeezed up close to Zoe to oblige, as Zoe took a selfie of the three of them – Sue visible on the tiny screen to Zoe's other side.

'Did someone say *lights, camera, action*?' Rosa hadn't noticed Adrian approaching. 'Actually,' Adrian continued, 'I was wondering if you'd like to come on my show some time, well, all of you.' He pushed his way into the centre of the frame and put his arms around them all before nodding at Zoe to take another photo. Zoe obliged and then lowered her phone and peeled away.

'I'm going to be running a series on influential women in the food business,' Adrian said, smoothing his hair. 'Apologies Mark, I'd have to leave you out, but the rest of you would be perfect.'

Mark approached, a beer in his hand and a faint smile caressing his lips. 'It's all women these days,' he said. 'Red-blooded white males can't get a look in anywhere. We're all out of fashion.'

He raised the bottle to his lips, took a swig and wiped the back of his hand across his mouth. Rosa saw him glance at her and sensed mischief in his words. She noticed he had not included Adrian in his comment and Zoe had evidently recognised this too.

'Adrian got *his* show,' she chirped.

Mark's wry smile lingered. 'You're right Zoe,' he said, pointing the top of the bottle in Rosa's direction. 'So he did.'

***

Sue wished she had arrived later. She was not nervous at the prospect of presenting to an audience; she had her speech down to a tee and was used to fielding the questions the public loved to ask, once they'd got over their initial distaste for her work, which involved a variety of insects. It was this *getting to know you* part of the day that she despised. *Networking.* That was what they called it. Except Sue didn't want to be part of a network, inextricably connected to people she neither knew nor liked. She couldn't think of anything worse. Disconnected, un-networked, alone. That was how she preferred to operate.

But, after a quick hello and introductions to everyone and Zoe's impromptu photoshoot, she found that host Brett and the farmer, Mark, with whom she might have found some common ground, had both disappeared from the hall. That left the other two women and Adrian. She wasn't, generally, good at talking to women, although she couldn't be sure why that was. Perhaps it was because she had found in the past that they wanted to identify with her simply because of her gender, which was ridiculous and often led to awkward exchanges.

She had first encountered Adrian outside the front door. She knew who he was; she sometimes listened to his show. But when she'd approached him and told him her name, he had made a low humming noise at the back of his throat. Sue had continued inside, thinking nothing of it, except to wonder if he had some kind of speech impediment, not apparent from his radio programme, or the beginnings of a nasty cold. Now that Adrian had proved he could speak clearly and without hindrance, and was in robust health, she wondered if outside he had been mocking her by making that noise in his throat, which had sounded rather like the buzzing of flies. If that was his idea of a joke – and now, she could think of no other explanation – then it was a pathetic and puerile one. And her humiliation was not lessened by his invitation to all and sundry to appear on his show.

Suddenly, a man in a loose-fitting suit came barrelling into the hall, his face contorted with concentration. As she watched, he began to apply paper labels attached to cocktail sticks to every tray of food, even the ones which were almost empty. But his hands were shaking so much that he kept dropping them or applying the wrong labels and the sweat from his palms had made the ink on the labels run so that when he wiped his hand across his face a black smudge traversed his cheek. Sue saw him glance up in the direction of a tall, elegant woman seated at the front of the hall, and then scurry away. But the woman had noticed him. She rose and headed off in close pursuit.

Sue's antennae began to twitch. This exchange promised to be far more interesting than any chat with this group of strangers. Phone in hand, she followed at a safe distance behind the tall woman, thinking she could always complain of lack of mobile reception for an important call, if challenged. But as the elegant woman was about to enter the kitchen, she was stopped in her tracks in the foyer by Mark and Brett, who were entering the building together, from the front.

Sue paused in the doorway and pretended to tap out a text on her phone. Tight-lipped, Mark continued into the hall, without acknowledging her or the tall woman. In contrast, Brett loitered, evidently waiting to speak to the woman, and Sue wandered on beyond and slipped into the shadows behind the staircase.

'What's up? You don't look happy,' Brett said and Sue agreed with him. She didn't know the woman so it was hard to tell for certain, but she was frowning excessively.

'Where've you been?' the woman replied. Sue concluded from her familiar manner that she was either Brett's wife or a colleague; she couldn't be sure which. Then she remembered that her invitation had been sent out by a Diana Percival, Brett's PA. This, most likely then, was Diana.

'I just needed some air. I'll…I'll tell you later,' Brett said. 'Look… Mark was bending my ear about…' He stopped, listened hard and Sue held her breath, even though she was sure no one could hear her. '*Walls have ears* and all that,' Brett continued. 'Anyway, I'm here now. Is *that* what's bothering you? That I was talking to

Mark. I thought you could hold the fort for five minutes.'

'It's that bloody caterer,' the woman said. 'One simple thing I asked him to do. I've a good mind not to pay him.' And now Sue was certain this was Diana. She smiled to herself at her successful powers of deduction.

'What heinous crime has he committed? Boiling the eggs for four and a half minutes instead of four?'

'I…I asked him to make sure he labelled the food and…'

'I'm looking now and there are labels galore on every tray,' Brett said, peering into the hall, although after he spoke he doubled over and leaned against the wall for support.

Diana touched his arm. 'Are you all right?' she asked.

'I told you, my stomach's no good today. Probably too much greenery for breakfast.' Brett laughed, although Sue thought it unconvincing. Then he straightened up. 'Better now,' he said.

'If you're really unwell, we could postpone things.' Diana appeared concerned but Brett seemed fine now, as far as Sue could see.

'When you're having so much fun?' Brett said. 'Not in a million years. I'll just wash my face again. The cold water should do the trick. Then I'll be straight back.'

Brett waved Diana away and disappeared into the men's bathroom, the door clanging shut behind him. Diana sighed, closed her eyes, frowned deeply and then re-entered the hall. After waiting a few more seconds and checking the coast was clear, Sue peeled herself away from behind the staircase and followed her.

Back in the main hall, Mark and Rosa were standing either side of the table, each holding a plate of food, separated only by the fruit platter. Sue watched them from two metres away as she began to select her own lunch from the various items on display.

'You're telling me you're more offended by that innocent mango than the beef burgers,' Mark said, raising one hand to his hair. His sleeve rode up and exposed the face of a cow, tattooed across his right bicep. Sue wanted to laugh at its flailing nostrils and jaunty expression, to show him she appreciated the humour of the image, but she stopped herself. Mark might think she was laughing at him. Better not to react at all.

'I've already explained,' Rosa said to Mark. 'I'm not easily offended. 'It was just a throwaway comment, that's all.'

'No, I'm intrigued,' Mark persisted. 'I want to understand. You look away when I guzzle the beef. I get that. But you hurl daggers at me when I approach the mango. What's the problem? No animals were killed in the making of this product, right?'

'It's come a long way, that's all. Look we all have to compromise sometimes.'

'I think if we asked our caterer over there, he'd tell us it came from the half-price section of Tesco by the underpass, that if he hadn't bought it today, it would have been thrown in the skip out the back.'

Sue turned around to see where Mark was pointing and saw the caterer hovering near the back of the hall. He still had the black smear on his face.

'You know exactly what I mean,' Rosa said. 'Whether it's grown in India or Thailand, it's still five thousand miles away.'

'Maybe not. Maybe they've found a way of growing them here?' Mark said.

'That's unlikely.' Sue spoke for the first time and everyone looked at her. The words had tumbled out, unchecked. Her hands began to tremble and she almost dropped the halloumi she had just added to her plate.

'Look,' Rosa said, turning her attention back to Mark and ignoring Sue. 'I really don't have a problem with the mango. I wish I'd never said anything.'

'Mango is the life blood of this planet.' Adrian had wafted his way over and interrupted the tiff, speaking in a voice like velvet. 'Mango improves your vision, your memory and your concentration. Mango does wonders for your libido and stamina. It's most certainly worth its cost in carbon terms.' He turned to Rosa. 'Do you really want to deprive us all of these potential benefits, quite apart from its glorious taste?'

'One thing I'm not, Dr Edge, is a puritan.' Rosa threw her head back and snorted through her nostrils. 'I like pleasure as much as any woman.'

Sue held her breath. She suspected Adrian might have met his match in Rosa. She did not seem the kind of person who would ignore his inflammatory mutterings and walk on by. Maybe Rosa would be an interesting person to talk to after all and she should have made more effort earlier.

'I'm just celebrating this wonderful fruit – nothing more.' Adrian picked up a particularly large slice of mango and held it between his fingers. 'I'm not having a go at you,' he said. 'Really.'

'It's so useful to have your wisdom and perspective,' Rosa muttered. 'Have you focused on mangos on your show yet? If so, it must have been an episode I missed.'

Adrian's grip on the mango tightened. 'If you're so anti-mango,' he said to Rosa, 'why are you pro-avocado?'

Rosa said nothing. Zoe had also approached and was watching the interaction in silence.

'That's what they make your vegan chocolate mousse from,

isn't it?' Adrian continued. 'You were happy to do the advert, as I remember, prime time, ITV3. In between *Vera* and the Omnibus edition of *Coronation Street*. What was it? *No one would know, it's av-o-ca-do*. They're hardly farmed in the Yorkshire Dales.'

'Hang on a minute,' Mark said. He had slid around the table and positioned himself between Rosa and Adrian. 'We were just having a bit of a joke, Rosa and me. No need for you to get involved. And Rosa didn't bring the food.'

Mark's hand had formed itself into a fist. Adrian seemed to notice this, and he dropped the mango back onto the platter he had taken it from. 'You're right,' he said. 'If the Mexican government is prepared to sacrifice its own people to murder, rape and poverty, and expose its landscape to devastation, to grow more and more of the *green gold*, then there isn't much we here in the UK can do to stop them. I'm with you, Rosa, my darling, selling out and making the ad; we may as well enjoy them and reap the benefits, while we still can, before the Greta Thunbergs of this world take all our fun away. *Eat avocado. Fuck Me-x-i-co*. That's what I say.'

'Adrian. Always the centre of attention.' Brett appeared out of nowhere and placed his hand on Adrian's shoulder, enveloping the whole group in the broadest of smiles. 'There's really only one way to resolve this argument,' he said. And then, as the three combatants awaited his judgment and Zoe eavesdropped, Sue marvelled as Brett picked up the largest piece of mango – the same lunar slice Adrian had subjected to considerable pressure a moment earlier – and popped it into his mouth.

'Hmm, delicious,' Brett said, wiping his hands and then his lips with a paper napkin.

It was Rosa who laughed first, throwing her head back, but then the others followed suit, even Sue, although in her case it was more instinctive than genuine amusement, as a wave of relief swept over her.

'Well, there was no point wasting it, was there?' Brett said.

He turned his head to look out across the hall as he spoke, as if he was seeking someone out. Sue looked too, but there was nobody there.

The arrival of Heart Foods' official photographer heralded a change of mood. Diana busied herself directing him where to set up his camera and lights and everyone – even Adrian, who naturally pretended that he didn't care about the next part of the event, but so obviously did – craned their necks to see what would be required of them. For Sue, it signalled that liberation from these forced social interactions was in sight and she comforted herself with that thought.

***

The moment Zoe had seen Rosa arrive, she'd wanted a selfie with her. Not only was Rosa a celebrity, so taking advantage of the opportunity was a total no-brainer, but she looked fabulous too, exuding natural beauty. Rosa clearly had the advantage of a few enhancements – no one's lips attained that shade of red without the painstaking application of a series of coats of the best quality lipstick and there was no way – NO WAY – her breasts were real. But Zoe was all for making the most of yourself. That was why she had dyed her hair pink a few months back – just a few strands at the front – when *Britney* had done the same. It had been part experiment, part solidarity with the Queen of Pop. Imagine your father having control over everything you did – even your boyfriends. Ew! Then everyone had said it looked so good that she had kept it.

The jury was still out, though, on whether she should ditch the specs. She didn't need them from a sight perspective. Well, she knew they were supposed to help with blue light and she certainly had plenty of that in her life, but not to see people or stuff like that. It was more that Zoe sensed, from time to time, some level of derision about her views, as a result of her relative youth; the addition of a pair of spectacles lent her some gravitas.

Zoe had also not been sure whether to include Sue in any picture. Then she remembered that Sue was a scientist and Zoe's blog was based on science – mostly. So, although the visual would be less dramatic, with Sue positioned on her other side, it would give Zoe the kind of authenticity she was often accused of lacking. And it wasn't a lie to say that Brett had asked her to take photos. He'd made it pretty clear that any publicity she could direct towards his company would be well-received.

Then, Dr Edge had to come along and force his way in. On one level, Zoe was fine with that. Dr Edge was famous too – famous-ish. It was just the way he'd done it, pushing in, not waiting to be asked; so impolite. And after he'd been weird about the mango. Although he had offered them a slot on his show – all of them except for Mark. And if Dr Edge meant it, she ought to grab the opportunity, even if it was Radio Two, which was, like, ancient. That was why she'd stuck up for him – kind of – when Mark had interrupted. But she had a feeling – and she was usually right about these things – that Dr Edge was the sort of person who made promises and forgot them later on, even if he owed you something. She'd already met a couple of men like that in the past.

Dr Edge walked away then, very deliberately, his footsteps

echoing around the hall as he headed for the stage and stopped to chat to the cameraman. That was a shame, but she'd make sure she reminded him of the invitation before he left. The others were pretending they weren't bothered by anything that had just happened. Mark said something about how the world was changing and that Sue might be surprised by the things they could grow in this country very soon. His tone reminded her of her teachers, when they made her stay behind after lessons and said it was 'for her own good'. Which was bollocks, of course. Not only did teachers know very little about the subjects they were supposed to be teaching in her experience, they also certainly didn't have a clue about what might benefit Zoe in the future, especially as none of them had ever taken the trouble to ask what she might want to do with her life after school.

Zoe was part way into her deliberation on the professed superiority of teachers when she saw Brett's face crumple and his hand grip his side, just for a moment. Then he straightened up and reached for some water. She wondered if he was ill but, whatever it was, it was over in a flash. Brett's eyes met hers. He nodded to her to reassure her that he was fine and she nodded back.

She was the only one who had witnessed Brett's distress; the others were too busy getting to know each other or looking but not really seeing stuff. Zoe was often the only one who saw things, things other people would never see. That was because she had *intuition.*

But that wasn't all. She also had *foresight.* Not the kind of foresight which meant you had a vague, random idea of what might occur at some point in time. Zoe saw things. She had visions and they often showed her exactly what was going to happen next. She had always experienced them, from when she was tiny, although she didn't often talk about them. They usually began with a pricking sensation in her fingers, or sometimes around her neck, and then, if she focused really hard and blanked out everything else, the image would come.

While some people were sceptical about these kind of powers, it was this, her sixth sense, which she had relied upon to advance herself and her own career so successfully, without anyone else to help her and it was that same instinct, that combination of intuition and foresight, which was telling her, right now, that something was not quite right.

She wanted a moment, a moment to concentrate on Brett, a moment to close her eyes, clear her mind and tune herself into the forces swirling around the auditorium, a moment to divine what it all meant. But she had no time. The audience had started to arrive; people her mum's age or even her Nan's. One man had a frame to help him walk. And as they filled up the rows, in random groups, Brett had begun to steer her and the other panellists towards the podium, to sit behind the name plates Diana had set out: *Dr Adrian Edge, Rosa Barrera, Brett Ingram, Zoe Whitman, Mark Sumner* and *Dr Susan Mills*. Zoe gave a low chuckle. She had predicted she would be sitting next to Brett and she was right again. She was the last one to slip into her seat.

'Do you have everything you need, Mr Ingram?' Zoe heard the caterer ask, as he brought them all fresh jugs of water, and Brett confirmed, with thanks, that everything was in order. She couldn't believe the caterer called Brett 'Mr Ingram'. Didn't he realise that no one did that kind of thing any more?

Zoe looked out at the audience, which was definitely skewed towards oldies and women. They were fidgeting with coats and bags and chatting to their neighbours. For a moment she wondered what point there was in talking to old people about the future of food, given they wouldn't be around for much longer, but then she remembered that some older people had influence. It was Paul McCartney's wife, for example, who began that whole line of vegetarian sausages some of her friends bought, despite her protests, and he was ancient. And Kim and Kanye were hardly young.

Anyway, as Diana had reminded her, Brett had asked all panellists, super-formally, by email, if they consented to the event being filmed. As if any of them would object. That provided the opportunity to share their combined knowledge and views more widely, even if the guests in the immediate vicinity were unreceptive. So Zoe planned to leave her phone on, at least during the introduction, and certainly when it was *her* turn to speak – that was a no-brainer. She checked through her messages one last time, muted her phone, then moved it to the top of the desk, waiting for the fun to begin.

Beside her, Brett tapped his microphone, then nodded to his PA – what was her name again? – in the front row. The PA, in turn, waved at the photographer guy, who had set up his camera in the central aisle. Zoe took that as her cue to begin the video on her mobile too, propping it up casually with her hand.

'Hello everyone,' Brett began. 'Thank you so much for coming. I'm Brett Ingram, CEO of Heart Foods, the third largest food supplier in the UK, sourcing food from all over the world. We aim to bring our customers the highest quality, best-value products and your feedback, as customers, is important too. Because, however good something may be for you, however reasonably priced, if you don't like the way it looks or tastes or smells, you're not going to eat it. So this is a partnership where we all need to agree, together, on what's good for us. And you vote with your pocket.'

Zoe thought that a sound introduction. She would use the partnership quote, unless something better came along.

'Separately – and I believe in this passionately,' Brett continued, 'just as my father did, just as I want the best for the next generation – you want to know where your food comes from, how it has got to your plate and that it was sourced in a responsible way. The days where we expected to buy coconuts all year round, for no good reason other than that we could, are long gone. We have a responsibility to look at the journey to the plate of everything we eat, for so many reasons.'

But when Brett said the word *coconuts* Zoe thought she saw his face squeeze up, just for a second, on one side only. She saw it through her phone screen and by the time she had looked up, and repositioned her joy-riding spectacles, everything had returned to normal. Again, she seemed to be the only one who had noticed Brett's discomfort. Everyone else was gazing out at the audience, with that smug look that guests often wore on their faces at this stage of an event.

'We have a really excellent panel this afternoon, representing vastly different views across the food industry,' Brett was still speaking. 'Beginning on the far left, we have Dr Adrian Edge. Dr Edge practises as a GP in Ealing. But most of you will know him from his long-standing weekly show on Radio Two, which focuses on foods from around the globe, how they define people and how we can enjoy them over here. Next to Dr Edge, we have Rosa Barrera, chef extraordinaire, known for putting vegan cookery well and truly on the map.

'On the right, next to me, I'm delighted to welcome Zoe Whitman, author of the staggeringly popular blog "meat and no veg", who will tell us all the opposite: why meat is best and how we should avoid all the other staples – like rice and potatoes – we've been eating for the last hundred years. Perhaps I'm in a dangerous position, *sandwiched* between the two of them.' He laughed at his own joke and Zoe made sure she joined in.

'Then, Mark Sumner, a key figure in the campaign for sustainable British beef farming. We can probably tell what he's going to be promoting. And last but certainly not least, it's Professor Susan Mills, an academic and scientist, currently working on a ground-breaking initiative to feed insects to our livestock.'

Brett broke off for a moment and kneaded his left side with the heel of his right hand before continuing. 'I know that this is going to be a fascinating debate, with so many different points of view on the future of food in the UK. And so, without making you wait any longer, I'm going to kick off with Professor Mills, I think, as she...'

Brett fell silent, his face changed colour, from pink to red to almost purple. He clutched at his side, and, emitting a loud groan, he wrapped both hands around his abdomen. Then, without further warning, he tipped forward from the waist and landed with a crash on the table.

Adrian jumped up, overturning his chair, and ran to Brett's side. Diana leaped forward too. Mark reached across Zoe to switch off Brett's microphone, so that the crowd would not have to hear the spluttering and wheezing coming from the stricken man. What was wrong? Was it a heart attack? Wasn't he too young to have one?

Mark spoke calmly to the confused spectators. 'Ladies and

gents. I'm sure it's nothing to be too worried about, but maybe you could all move back and give Mr Ingram some space, please.'

'Call an ambulance,' Diana shouted in Rosa's direction, but Zoe was already on her feet and dialling the emergency services as she watched Adrian attempt, without success, to lift Brett up and spin him around. Brett appeared to be resisting, the muscles in his neck bulging grotesquely. If it was a heart attack, shouldn't he be all weak? Mark had now sidestepped Zoe and he helped Adrian slide Brett on to the floor of the stage and turn him over onto his back. Diana knelt down close by.

'What's wrong?' she shouted into his twisted face. 'Tell me what's wrong.'

As Adrian leaned over Brett, Diana shoved him away, pressing her cheek close to Brett's mouth and talking into his ear. Brett raised his hand and caught hold of Diana, pulling her down towards him. His lips moved once or twice. And then he ceased his convulsions and lay still.

'Oh God,' Adrian said. Now he thrust Diana out of the way, straddled Brett and began pounding at his chest, slowly and rhythmically. Zoe had watched the TV adverts, like everyone else. The ones with the footballer who used to foul people a lot.

She checked the screen of her phone and found the call had dropped. She dialled 999 again, and this time she heard the operator's voice almost immediately. She moved to the far side of the stage and provided full instructions, conscious of the dryness of her throat and of her own heart pounding in her ears.

As she finished and turned her attention back to Brett, Adrian took a break from pummelling his friend. 'How long?' he called out to her.

'Twenty minutes.'

Adrian frowned. It sounded pretty quick to Zoe. You always heard of these ambulances taking hours to arrive, but it seemed like Adrian didn't agree. 'See if there's a defibrillator,' he ordered no one in particular. And then, to Brett, he whispered, 'Come on buddy. Don't do this to me. Who'm I going to play golf with if you've gone?'

Zoe looked around. The hall was almost empty. Mark, who had shepherded most of the audience out, was now scuttling around opening doors and scouring walls and skirting boards. Rosa stood by the window, looking out for help. Sue appeared rooted to her seat, her arms folded in her lap, her face pale. Slowly but surely Zoe backed away from them all, mobile phone in hand, placing one foot behind the other.

When she reached the doorway, she saw Adrian sit back on his heels and shake his head. No! It couldn't be true! Not Brett, who'd just said all those nice things about her work, and who was not even all that old. Then Diana draped herself over Brett again, screeching and crying, tears streaming down her face. Could there be a miracle? Zoe wondered. Like in one of those fairy-tale-ending films, where some impossibly beautiful woman's tears had dramatic effect, healing a lover's wounds, restoring his sight or even his life. But those were only stories and Brett's face did not regain its familiar hue, nor did he sit up or smile or take Diana in his arms and thank her for saving him. Instead, he lay still and silent.

And, try as she might to remain upbeat, Zoe was as certain as she had ever been that the head of Heart Foods had breathed his last breath. And, without boasting or anything, she was usually right about these things.

PART ONE

TWO DAYS LATER

1

CONSTANCE WALKED along Gosset Street, stopping to adjust her skirt as she crossed from one side of the road to the other. It was a bright morning and she strode out purposefully, trying at the same time to reflect on the conversation which had led her to make this journey.

Usually when she spoke to relatives of suspects, as she had today, the conversation followed a similar pattern: a panicked general enquiry about her availability, a barrage of specific questions (some sensible, some less so), tears and protestations of innocence (often at the same time) and an entreaty to pass on words of support and keep the concerned family member updated.

The call she had received this morning had been subtly different. The woman had provided basic information – the name of her husband, his profession and a request for Constance to meet him at Hackney police station at 2pm – but no detail about why he had been detained, which Constance would have to pick up from the officer on duty when she arrived. And the caller had seemed calm and composed. But Constance had detected the quiver in her voice. Despite her words, the woman had clearly been concerned.

After five more minutes of walking, she stood opposite the station, a cheerless building in need of modernisation and a place where she spent more of her life than she would ideally like. But that was the lot of a solicitor working in the criminal law field: hours on end spent in police stations. Even so, she had to admit that there was never a dull moment and her hefty and varied workstream was unlikely to dry up any day soon.

After a brief conversation with the duty officer, which provided scant details as to why Nick Demetriou had been brought in, Constance entered the interview room to find him seated at the table, his handkerchief covering his nose and mouth, his elbows splayed wide.

'Mr Demetriou?'

'Yes.'

'I'm Constance Lamb, your lawyer. I spoke to your wife this morning.'

'Oh.'

The handkerchief was folded and pocketed. Constance sat down, unpacked her tablet and switched it on.

'Did I surprise you?' she asked.

'No, I…you look so young. And Lisa didn't tell me you were coming.'

Constance accepted Nick's explanation gracefully. She couldn't be certain that his hesitant manner on her arrival, his exclamation of surprise, had anything to do with the colour of her skin. And even if it did, he would be in good company. She had been practising for almost ten years now, and she would be a wealthy woman if she had a pound for every occasion on which she had been mistaken for a member of the public or a defendant when attending court. This included errors made by other lawyers and court staff, even when she was formally dressed or carrying the relevant papers under her arm. She had learned to live with it. And Nick was clearly upset. No. She wouldn't hold this against him.

'Can you tell me what happened on Tuesday afternoon, in your own words?' she asked, hoping this open and straightforward question would help Nick find his voice, particularly as she knew very little about why he needed a lawyer.

Nick shook his head. 'I can tell you what happened on Tuesday afternoon, what I *saw* happen, but the rest is what I am worrying about. This is all such a big mistake.'

'Why don't you tell me about it? Then I'll see what I can do to help.'

This was Constance's customary follow up, if her stock starter for ten did not succeed; to emphasise that she was there to provide assistance. She wanted to instil trust in clients, so that they would relate all the salient points to her, including those they were worried about. Sometimes, they told her too much – information which could get them into trouble. Other times, although she stressed that she was on their side, they said little or nothing at all. On this occasion, she seemed to have found the right formula, as Nick began to talk.

'I do most of the catering for Tanners' Hall, near Haringey,' he began. 'Someone rents the hall from the manager, June, and wants food, June calls me up and asks me if I'm interested. If it's

46

something really special or a big event and I'm pressed elsewhere I say no, but most of the time I can help and it's easy money, to be honest.' He sighed. Clearly, this time around, things had been far from easy. "Then, about two months ago, June calls me and asks can I do a cold lunch for this week – Tuesday – says there's going to be an event for around a hundred people. "Light lunch" is what we call it, how we price it. It sounded fine, so I agreed.'

Constance was pleased that Nick was being so communicative and, as his words came tumbling out, she struggled to keep up with her notes.

'Then, after I agree, she tells me it's only food for ten guests, that the others are coming to hear a talk *after* lunch and we're not feeding them. I had to think hard, but I didn't have anything else on that day. So, it was only ten people. I accepted it. But then, every week, I got a message that they wanted this and that and it started getting more complicated,' he continued. 'I have my usual suppliers, you see, and now they wanted all this special stuff: vegan and beef and some things hot and some grilled. And I offer Greek food. It's my speciality. But no. She didn't want Greek. She wanted "British" – whatever that is. In the end, I asked the customer to contact me direct and this woman – Diana Percival, was her name – she called. She seemed very nice at first, very polite. Anyway, I almost said no, because everything had to be this and that, but in the end I didn't want to let them down. It's important to me to keep my word.'

'I understand,' Constance interrupted, partly to slow Nick's flow.

'Usually, I just order the food from one supplier, or maybe two, and get it delivered,' Nick said. 'This time, I had to buy the food from all different places and I collected it up, prepared some dishes at home and I took it all to the hall myself. I employed staff – both kids I've used before, well only one in the end. So, *they* arrive. Brett Ingram – he introduced himself – Diana and the others; around ten of them altogether. They have lunch and then they go up on the stage. He's talking when he gets ill, in front of everyone. Then he stops talking and he dies, right there. It's crazy. People are screaming and crying. They all start running out and the ambulance men are pushing to get in. They said it was a heart attack, like that, so sudden. Just…chaos.'

'What happened next?'

'They put him, Brett Ingram, on a stretcher and took him away. The police came. I gave them my name and address. They were filming when he died – Brett's people – and the police took the film away. Then they said I wasn't allowed to clean up. I said I would be in trouble with June – it's in my contract – but they said they would explain and that it was a "crime scene". I didn't really listen then, only when I got home, I wondered what they meant.'

'What did you do when you got home?'

'I called June myself, and good thing, because the police hadn't. She was pretty upset. There was another booking for the evening, but she said she would cancel it. I was about to head off there to meet June today and see if I could get the rest of my stuff – not much, just a few knives and boards. Suddenly the police show up at my home, tell me I have to come here. Then they ask me lots of questions, saying that Mr Ingram was poisoned and that it was my fault! Saying that my food was no good, that I killed him with my food. That I could go to prison. That's not true, is it? I have a wife, a sister, a family…'

Constance smiled at Nick.

'You haven't been charged with anything, for now,' she said.

'The police officer who brought you in told me they are doing more tests to establish how Mr Ingram died.'

'So it's not true then?'

'It depends what the tests show.'

'I *bought* the food. How can it be my fault if it looked all right, but it turned out to be bad?'

'Didn't you cook it?'

'Some things, OK. Not the sandwiches. Or the fruit and veg. It's just crazy. All of it.'

'You were still responsible for serving the food to Mr Ingram. If, for example, you mixed together raw and cooked food, that could be a problem. Or, if you bought food from a supplier and you knew – or should have known – that they didn't have a good hygiene rating.'

'How'm I supposed to know what they do in *their* kitchens?'

'You're right, but you should check out your suppliers, on a regular basis.'

'It was just a *light lunch.*' Nick's voice became strained and he reached for a cup of water on the table and gulped down the remains. 'I only get paid £30 a head,' he said. 'After paying the staff, I make pennies.'

'I can see that.'

'What happens now?' Nick slumped forward, resting his frame heavily on the table.

Constance contemplated her response. Nick was clearly agitated and she didn't blame him. And she understood a little more now why Lisa, his wife, had been vague when they had spoken. She had probably not understood why the police were interested in her husband. And as for Nick, Constance appreciated that most caterers would not consider there was any risk of killing someone when going about their usual business. But Nick would have been well aware of the importance of good hygiene practices. That went without saying.

'We'll need to see what the results of the further tests are,' she said, 'but can you give me a list of all the food you provided that day – everything: names of suppliers and invoices and where it was stored? Also, who handled the food, the names of your staff?'

'I don't have that here.'

'You can go home and send them on to me.'

'I can leave?'

'You're not under arrest, but you need to stay around, at home, at work, not go on any trips.'

'Who would go on a trip with all this hanging over their head? Look. What do you think? Will this come back to me?'

Constance wanted to reassure Nick, but she wouldn't mislead him, especially not at this early stage. And she wanted him to take her request for information seriously and do as she had asked. She cast her mind back to her long-ago student days to locate the relevant information.

'If the police are advised that your food killed Mr Ingram, however that happened, then you will be charged. It could be a health and safety offence, it could be an offence by your company. Both of those would result in a fine. But if the police feel that you were directly responsible for Mr Ingram's death because you were grossly negligent in how you stored, prepared or served the food, then you could be charged with manslaughter.'

'*Manslaughter!*' Nick's eyes were wide. 'This is a nightmare. You know cooking is my dream. Food is my dream. Now a dream becomes a nightmare. Whatever happens, I'm done for. I'm a *man-slaughterer.* Or, if not, I'll lose the contract with June and no one will ever want to eat my food again. We will lose everything.'

'My advice is to go home and get some rest. Then send me those lists and invoices. And call me if the police ask to see you again.'

After Nick stumbled off down the road in the direction of the Underground, looking back over his shoulder more than once, Constance retraced her steps to her office, but with less enthusiasm than on her outward journey. Halfway back, she bought a sausage roll – she'd missed both breakfast and lunch – and sat down on a handily placed bench at the side of the road to eat it. The traffic slowed ahead of the nearby lights and she felt comforted to be a mere spectator, observing the vehicles passing by, transporting people to wherever they wanted to go. That was London: always moving. She felt a light touch against her leg and looked down to see a crop of miniature daffodils, blowing in the breeze, the last of the spring early birds.

Daffodils were not her favourite; there was something vulgar-looking about their trumpet shape, like the whole flower was tipping back its head and shouting. What was the message it was broadcasting today? *Why help a man who values his livelihood above another man's life?* the diminutive blooms chorused. And Constance inclined her head to one side as she listened and the cars continued to pass her by.

2

EARLIER THAT SAME DAY, Susan Mills had set off for work at her usual time of 7am. In an email she had sent last night to a colleague, she had declared that her return was prompted by the desire to save her 'stand-in' from an early start. The truth was that after a day spent at home, reflecting on Tuesday's awful events, she was keen to get back to her research project and her 'babies' as she affectionately termed them.

No one in the world had ever lavished so much love and affection on black soldier fly larvae as Sue had; monitoring their temperature control like a hawk, reviewing and moderating their food quantities and sources, even addressing them on a range of topical subjects. Once she had sung to them – 'Diamonds Are A Girl's Best Friend'. She had watched *Gentlemen Prefer Blondes* the night before and had even thrown in some Marilyn Monroe puckering and shimmying, out of sight of the security cameras. However, that day's yield had been three per cent down, so she couldn't afford to repeat her performance, however liberating she had found it.

And she was better off at work anyway. Sitting at home as she had yesterday, attempting to write up her recent results and catch up on academic papers, had been difficult. All she had thought about was Brett Ingram, his easy charm over lunch – he was the kind of man who really made eye contact with you, made sure you knew he was looking at you, spoke *to* you, not *at* you. Only some men could carry that off without making you feel uncomfortable. People assumed it was connected to how good-looking he was, but Sue thought it was linked more to his integrity and professionalism. She didn't dwell on the fact that, when one of the lab helpers had made similar eye contact with her some weeks back, she had felt compelled to have him replaced. That was justified. After all, *he* had a body odour issue and an unfortunate twitch.

But the incident with Brett had been so upsetting that Tuesday's events seemed jumbled in her mind; the lunch, his introduction of the speakers, then his collapse and prompt demise. And, even after the paramedics had confirmed that his heart really had stopped, Brett's eyes had continued to focus on her. She was sure of it. It was an unfortunate twist of fate, his head having finally settled itself to one side, his face and, therefore, *those eyes*, open but unseeing, pointing in her direction.

In the foyer, Sue went through the security measures to enter her place of work; she swiped her pass, entered her personal code, washed her hands thoroughly and covered her hair with the regulation net, before repeating the process at the second set of doors. These stringent requirements were more than a little ironic, she thought, as she scrubbed away at her hands and nails. They were soldier fly larvae she was tending, not, despite her nickname for them, premature babies. In nature, there would be no sanitised environment – quite the contrary. And more than that, here they were deliberately exposed to a wide range of 'dirty' products for their nourishment. Some days, it was blood or unwanted body parts from a range of animals sourced from the local abattoir, other days organic household waste and, only occasionally, used coffee grounds from local cafés. Even so, she had to be squeaky clean, to ensure she did not contaminate their surroundings or invalidate her own experiments.

As the second door slid back and Sue glided through it, she felt a sense of peace; memories of Tuesday receded as everything appeared in order, the machines containing the larvae, laid out in neat rows, emitting their usual low-pitched hum, the floors clean and clear of any equipment. She had been away for almost forty-eight hours, but nothing had gone amiss.

Sue went through her usual morning routine, checking on every container. One of the most important aspects of her role was to monitor the temperature to which the larvae were exposed; the optimal conditions from previous research suggested this was around thirty-five degrees Celsius and seventy per cent humidity, although part of her testing regime was to find the best combination. And so, as she walked the lines like a sergeant major, she checked that each vat was set with a slight incremental increase, when compared with its neighbour. Although she set the temperatures herself, even she had been known to make mistakes, albeit rarely, so it was always better to check. Then, when she selected her samples for testing in the lab upstairs, she could plot the results with confidence, by reference to the precise circumstances in which the larvae had been encouraged to develop.

Today was a significant day for batch 5061 and 5062 and she paused longer to stare into the vessels which housed them. After fourteen days and, having increased their body weight five thousand times over, the fat wriggling, burgeoning larvae were to be chilled and dried, before their final incarnation as poultry or fish food. Sue was to be the one to administer the coup de grâce, the flick of the switch to lower the temperature to between ten and sixteen degrees. With that downward dip, she would ensure that each one of those larvae never developed into an adult fly, never acquired glistening thorax or tapering abdomen, never grew gossamer wings or sweeping antennae. Did that make her a killer? If so, she was a killer of thousands – hundreds of thousands. Was there even a term for that?

Some people, some sentimental people, who equated the life of an insect with that of a human, or even another mammal, might assume that she preferred not to think about the consequences of her actions, as the smallest movement of one digit condemned the larvae to death. On the contrary, this was the point at which she felt the biggest sense of achievement. Her offspring had been raised successfully, passed all relevant milestones under her care and were now dispatched to fulfil the next part of their journey. They had value only because of their position in the cycle; they had been created in the first place only to fulfil this role. In this sense, Sue was playing God and she rather liked it.

Around midday she picked up a message that the police wanted to speak to her and could she make herself available tomorrow? Not unexpected in the circumstances, but still unwelcome. There wasn't anything she could tell them. She'd sat down and Brett had died. It was nothing to do with her. What more could she say?

Then, at 5pm, just as she was preparing to send 5061 and

5062 to their final resting place, a message arrived on her phone. She read it through, then frowned, rested one hand against the nearest container, the gentle, rhythmic motion helping to restore her equilibrium. After a moment, she read the message again, before putting her phone back in her lab-coat pocket.

Normally, she liked to say something – inside her head of course – to help the larvae on their way, but now, today, this moment, the words wouldn't come. Instead, she pushed her glasses up to the top of her head, leaned in close, peered at the dial and then lowered the temperature on the first vat, repeating the process with its neighbour. She emailed the lab technician to ask him to come by in thirty minutes and bag up the larvae.

Then, murmuring 'Sweet dreams,' she removed her lab coat, dropped it into the nearest bin for washing and padded out of the building.

3

CONSTANCE HAD BEEN invited out on a date – the first for a while. In part, that was why she had worn a skirt this morning, to put herself in the mood for something new. Instead, every time the waist band shifted or the wind caught underneath it, making it billow up and out like a sail, she regretted her wardrobe choice. As soon as she returned home, she discarded the skirt and stood in her underwear, flicking through the possibilities for her evening attire. Eventually, she settled upon some black jeans and a lacy top, which she would match with her favourite ankle boots; casual enough to reflect her preference for informality, but demonstrating some effort had been made before coming out. Then she went into the bathroom to look for a lipstick.

There had been various drink and dinner invitations since Mike, her actor boyfriend, had moved out, almost four years ago. Mike had objected to Constance defending a Syrian refugee on a murder charge and she had not appreciated being told who to represent. And later, much later, she had realised that their differences went deeper than politics, and had been grateful to her client, Ahmad Qabbani, for saving her from making a longer-lasting commitment to Mike, a man she didn't love. That would have been an even bigger mistake than the eight months she had wasted trying to please him. But the consequence of dumping Mike had been many evenings spent alone; on only two occasions had she felt inclined to allow things to progress with anyone else. Both liaisons ('relationships' would be overstating things) had ended quickly; one with a minor disagreement for which neither would apologise, the other just petering out.

She found the lipstick at the top of the cabinet and set it down on the shelf above her wash basin. Then she laid her phone next to it and called Judith Burton.

'I've got a new case in. Thought you might be interested,' she said, hitting the speaker button as she put the finishing touches to her hair.

'Have you now? You do know that there are seventeen thousand barristers in the UK. You don't always have to come to me.' Constance could sense Judith's teasing down the phone. She must have caught her at a good moment.

'I wasn't thinking of giving this one to you,' Constance replied. 'Just telling you the best bits, so you're jealous when it hits the News. And I know how you like to keep on top of what's going on in the criminal underworld.'

'Go on, then.' Constance sensed rather than heard Judith's low laugh.

'Brett Ingram, CEO of Heart Foods. He collapsed and died on Tuesday, during a speech he was giving.'

'I saw that,' Judith said. 'I assumed it was a heart attack.'

'They think it might have been food poisoning.'

'How interesting. I've never been instructed on a poisoning case.'

'I said *food poisoning*. I'm not sure it's anything deliberate.'

'Then why come to you?'

Constance picked up her phone, walked back into her bedroom, sat down and laid her comb on her dressing table. She caught sight of herself in the mirror and made a mental note to remember to put on her lipstick.

'They think the caterer might have messed up; that's all,' she said, determined not to say too much to Judith yet. 'He's our client – potential client.'

'Ah! That's disappointing. I was thinking more arsenic, cyanide, ricin even. Or what did they use for poor Alexander Litvinenko?'

'I don't know.'

'You do. Something radioactive in his tea. Polonium, that's it!'

'They're doing more tests. Look, I can't chat now, but I thought you might have some ideas to persuade the police to go with a health and safety offence, you know, something where the caterer gets off with a fine.'

'I always have ideas. But a *gross negligence manslaughter* trial would be much more fun, wouldn't it?'

Judith was not one to be coy about her enthusiasm for her work.

'Not for the caterer it wouldn't,' Constance said. 'Although his reputation is ruined whatever happens.'

'We shouldn't just discount a sophisticated poison, you know,' Judith persisted. 'Look at Salisbury. No one thought about Novichok at the start.'

Constance had known it was a risk that Judith's imagination would begin to run riot. 'Brett Ingram ran a food company,' she said. 'He wasn't some kind of spy. And if they suspected one of *those* poisons, wouldn't everyone be in quarantine?'

'I'm just keeping an open mind, that's all. What kind of meeting was it, where Mr Ingram met his maker?'

'Public meeting about food, titled "What should we eat?". That's all I've discovered so far.'

'Other speakers too?'

'I don't have a list from the police yet. But there's a clip on YouTube doing the rounds; you can see who was there. I recognised Dr Edge, from the radio. It stops short of showing Brett's death, but only just. I'll send you a link. So, you'll think about how to get the prosecution to go for a health and safety offence, then? I've got to go.'

'And where might you be off to so early on a Thursday night?' said Judith.

'I have places to go, people to see.'

'Do you now? You just give out orders and then go gallivanting off. I hope he's worth it.'

'I hope so too,' Constance said, as she grabbed her jacket and bag, before realising what she had just given away. There was a moment's silence, in which she could imagine Judith congratulating herself on forcing this admission from her. Then Judith spoke again.

'Don't tell him you're a lawyer till you're sure he likes you.'

Constance laughed. 'Now you sound like my mother.' Better to forgive Judith's intrusion into her private life than to take offence. After all, they had shared a few personal experiences, even if they both tried to maintain some professional distance. That had to be right when you spent so much time together.

As she headed for the Underground, Constance remembered

more of her mother's advice on matters of the heart. *Never trust a man who makes you wash his clothes. If he's like that at the beginning, just think what he'll be like later on.* She giggled. She had only met her date, Chris, once before, but she was fairly sure he owned his own washing machine. Then she thought back to Judith's words of wisdom and wondered what profession she should admit to: *church organist? Primary school teacher? Midwife?* 'How about hired assassin?' she whispered to herself, as the wind gusted around her neck and she pulled the zip on her jacket higher. It was only then that she remembered she had forgotten to put on her lipstick after all.

4

ZOE WHITMAN WAS SITTING at her laptop, tapping away at its keys, reading the latest questions sent in by readers of her blog. From time to time, she would check her phone – swiping up, frowning and murmuring to herself – put it down and continue to type. It was difficult to focus after Tuesday. That was her excuse anyway; someone dying right next to you, especially the way *he'd* died, arms and legs all over the place, spitting and gurgling, clutching and tearing at his chest. If someone had behaved like that in an audition, they'd have been rejected for over-acting. It wasn't something you could easily forget.

But Zoe didn't have to rely on her memory. She had it all on film. She hadn't meant to record everything – not the bit where he died. She'd just wanted to film the intro, then she was going to switch off and start recording again, when it was her turn to speak – Brett had told her that was OK and she'd cleared it with his assistant – but that wasn't what happened. So now she had this sensational, could-see-his-eyeballs-bulging footage of his death, recorded on her phone, and she wasn't sure what to do with it.

'You *have* to post it,' her best friend, Sophie, had said when she'd confided in her. 'It's like…an exclusive.'

'No way,' her joint bestie, Amy, joined in. 'I mean, it's someone dying. It's like, gruesome. And people will hate you for it.'

'That's true,' Sophie reconsidered. 'Major backlash potential. Forget it, babes. But such a shame. Think what it could have done for your ratings.'

Whenever Zoe had re-watched the film, as she had over and over throughout Tuesday afternoon, it had felt strangely personal; Brett's gasps and splutters, sweat soaking through his shirt, his last murmurings to his assistant. But also, the things he'd said when he first stood up, the way he'd stretched out his arm in her direction, said her blog was 'staggeringly popular', made that joke about sandwiches. It was as if he was executing all of it just for her. And the more Zoe watched it, the more she became convinced that this was true. She felt that there was a reason why she, alone, had this footage. There must be. She just couldn't be sure what it was, yet.

Then, in the middle of Tuesday night, after at least a dozen viewings, that tickly sensation had returned, this time beginning at her fingertips and spreading through her torso. When it reached her head, she had closed her eyes and focused on an image of Brett's face. After a few minutes, she had sensed his presence in her bedroom, viewing him in her mind's eye, with his index finger pressed firmly against the lips of his pallid face. She understood, then, that he had entrusted the film to her, to keep intact and private, not to hand over to the police to poke and probe, not to share with strangers, and she was pleased she hadn't published it.

Anyway, now it was too late. The guy with the tripod at the

hall, the official camera guy –he'd given the police his version and someone had leaked it. In the twelve hours before its removal from YouTube, it had notched up 36,000 views. There was no point her coming forward now – second place was for losers.

Zoe returned to her blog and answered some incoming messages. After that, she would prepare for her podcast. Last week, she had achieved more than a thousand listeners and ten times that via YouTube. This week it was bound to be more. True, she'd balked at sharing the video of Brett's last moments – and decided against it – but nothing had stopped her downloading to her audience that she had been there, at Tanners' Hall, replete with sad-face emojis and a photo of Jackie at JFK's funeral, and the sympathy and the followers had flooded in, salvaging something worthwhile, after all.

It was funny the things Zoe recalled from that afternoon, aside from Brett's death. She remembered Sue, the mousey scientist woman, had been nice to talk to – well, a good listener anyway. She'd have really liked to hear more about her work. She could ask Sue to do a feature on the insect stuff for her blog. Insects were meat, right? She knew they weren't like real animals, but that could help draw new people in, people who were a bit 'on the fence' about eating things with fur and eyelashes. She'd message the prof in a day or two, ask her if she'd like to write a guest post.

And Dr Edge – *Call me Adrian*. He was a riot! Who'd have thought he could be so sarky, when he oozed *Mr Nice Guy* on his radio show?

Who else had she chatted to? Oh, yes. She'd asked Rosa about her dress – more to be polite than anything else, because, to be honest, it was just a tiny bit tight on her. Rosa had explained it was made from 'discarded orange peels'. Apparently, someone went to all these cafés where they squeezed oranges for juice and shit, collected the skins, boiled them up and out came these fancy clothes. When Rosa wasn't talking about that, she was coming out with all these stupid buzzwords, the kind of words that celebs think will help them get noticed: *lifestyle choices* and *sentient beings*. It was all so transparent, so 2019.

Zoe paused her stream of consciousness. Was she imagining it, or had she heard a noise coming from her bedroom? She stopped scrolling, sat very still and, when all seemed quiet, she held her breath. There it was again, a light tapping noise, as if someone or something was knocking on her bedroom window. Her face became hot and, although she was forced to start breathing again, otherwise she would probably have died, she remained very still, straining her ears. The tap, tap, tap continued now and, with a lump of lead in the centre of her stomach, weighing her down more and more with each step, she tiptoed towards her bedroom and peered around the door.

She saw it almost immediately. A giant bumblebee, knocking against the pane over and over in a bid for freedom. Zoe crossed the room, opened the window and watched it fly away, smiling to herself at her act of kindness. But, as she turned around, she caught sight of an image in her mirror, an image of a face that was not her own, a face contorted and strained, skin stretched tight, muscles labouring, expanding even as she watched, spreading out to fill the opposite wall: Brett Ingram, struggling for breath. He had come to her again, this time when she was awake.

Go away, she whispered, covering her eyes and repeating the command inside her head, willing him to leave. *Go away.* She repeated her entreaty, peering through the gaps in her fingers. When she finally lowered her hands and looked around her, swaying a little from side to side and resting against the bed to steady herself, Brett's ghost had left the room. She took a deep breath, returned to the kitchen and downed a glass of water. Then she climbed up onto a chair and dug around at the back of the highest cupboard till she found a bar of Dairy Milk. She bought her chocolate by mail order in plain packaging; she couldn't risk anyone seeing her with it in her supermarket trolley, in case she was recognised – chocolate was not officially permitted on her carnivore diet. This was her last bar, reserved for emergencies only.

When she'd eaten most of the chocolate, and her heart rate had finally returned to normal, she began to wish she hadn't willed Brett away after all. It had just been a bit of a shock, seeing his face superimposed over her Peaky Blinders poster. First the film on her phone and now him appearing like that; he must have something he wanted to tell her. That was how it worked in all the books she'd read and docudramas she'd watched. Next time, she'd be ready for him. Next time, she would listen to what he had to say.

5

ON FRIDAY NICK CALLED Constance and told her the police had asked him to attend at the police station again and intimated he was going to be charged with something serious. The man could hardly get the words out and she was forced to wait patiently for the message to be delivered, in between gulps and gasps. After she had provided as much reassurance as she could, she cleared some space in her diary and made an appointment to visit Diana Percival, Brett Ingram's PA. She wanted to see Diana before her memories faded, and to find out as much as possible about who was at the Tanners' Hall meeting and why.

Heart Foods' head office, where they agreed to meet, turned out to be a sprawling, unassuming building, just off the Hanger Lane gyratory system. Given Brett's reputation for innovation, Constance had expected a modern design, or displays more obviously associated with food. The only indication that the company had any food connection at all was in the reception area: a series of posters hung on the wall behind the receptionist's head, each displaying the motto 'food with heart' above an appetising image of a food group (fruit, nuts, bread and pastries, fish) arranged in the shape of a heart.

Then, in the lift, as she headed up to the fourth-floor meeting rooms, a strong scent of freshly baked bread with no obvious source filled her nostrils. Perhaps she was just above the canteen, she thought, although the smell persisted as she continued along the corridor to meet Diana.

Brett's assistant turned out to be an inordinately tall woman, hardly short of six feet. Diana's hands shook as she poured them both tea, adding a lump of sugar to her own cup. Constance sat down on the nearest chair, pulling it in towards the table. Then she dug out her laptop and lifted the lid, but paused when she saw Diana watching her.

'I'd like to make some notes, if that's all right,' she said. 'Or we could just talk and I can record us on my phone. Whatever's easier.'

'I'm not sure what I can tell you,' Diana said, sitting down opposite Constance and stirring her tea. 'It all happened so quickly. Brett was up there introducing everyone, then he was dead.'

'It must have been an awful shock.'

'It was.'

'Was there no warning? Mr Ingram wasn't ill?'

'Look, this is what I told the police,' Diana said. 'Not long after we arrived at the hall, he started to feel ill. He disappeared off to the men's room a couple of times. I asked him if we should call the meeting off, but it had been such a bugger to organise, he said he was fine. He drank some water, said he felt better. Look. I don't want a recording. You asked to talk. That's what I'm offering.'

'Of course,' Constance said, closing her laptop and reaching for her own cup of tea. She would have preferred to have an accurate record of their conversation, but she could make a note as soon as she got back to the office. 'You know the police believe it was something Mr Ingram ate?'

'It didn't come from the police,' Diana said. 'When he collapsed, we all thought it was a heart attack, including the paramedics.'

'Because it was so sudden?'

'And he was breathless. Then I started to think about how he'd felt ill earlier. And then, well, when they were examining him, one of the ambulance men said he had a rash on his chest. I looked it up on my phone. I wanted to do something useful, with Brett just lying there. And then I read what it said – that it could be linked to his allergy.'

'His allergy?'

'Yes.'

'I thought the police said it was food poisoning.'

'Brett has…had an allergy – shellfish. I'd told the caterer. When Brett wasn't feeling well, I went into the kitchen, checked all the food. There wasn't even any fish; no prawns or anything. So I didn't make the connection. Just when I saw the rash, I thought… I don't know. I'm just telling you what I told the ambulance men and the police.'

'The police didn't say anything about an allergy and I haven't seen the results of the post-mortem.'

'Why should a healthy man die just like that? I keep asking myself that question.'

Diana covered her eyes with both hands and her shoulders heaved up and down. Then she looked at Constance again.

'Is there anything else you want to know?' she said.

'I'd like to know a little about Mr Ingram, what kind of man he was?'

'He was a man who knew what he wanted from life and how to get it.' Diana stirred her tea some more and stared out of the window. 'That's how he managed to build this business in only twelve years. We're up there with the most well-established household names: Heinz, Bird's Eye, Premier Foods. Brett is... *was* the youngest CEO of any UK-based top 100 company.'

'You're saying he was ruthless?'

'Not ruthless. That makes him sound evil. He was focused, very focused. And extremely hard-working. No down time. Everything he read or watched or wrote was about food. And quality was important to him; not price – quality.'

Constance noted that this approach had clearly engendered considerable loyalty in Diana. 'Does he have a successor?'

'The board will decide. He didn't have anyone lined up. At forty-one you wouldn't usually, would you?'

'And the meeting, what was that about?' Constance asked.

'What? What do you mean?'

'Is it usual for food companies to organise events like that?'

'Brett liked to be different.'

Constance nodded. 'All right. But why these particular guests?'

'He liked to know what was going on in the world of food, so he invited speakers on all different topics. It was the first of a series of similar events he was planning across the country.'

'Why a public meeting, if he just wanted to be informed?'

'Gosh.' Diana frowned and tapped her teaspoon against the side of her cup. 'You really are asking a lot of questions.'

'I...I'm sorry. If you don't want to answer, that's fine.'

'No,' Diana said. 'Look, Brett knew what these people were like: a blogger, a radio star, a TV chef.'

'You mean they wanted publicity?'

'Exactly. They were not prepared to give up their time to explain their philosophy on life to him, even though… Well, even the other two – the insect woman and the farmer. All interested in promoting their products, their processes, but isn't everyone these days? So, he gave them a platform. Or he would have done, if he hadn't died.'

'And the camera?'

'Depending on what they said and how it turned out, Brett wanted to make a film, something informative, about the future of farming and food. I told you. He had big ideas.'

'And you were the one who arranged the meeting for Mr Ingram?'

'Can you stop calling him Mr Ingram? It makes him sound like someone's grandfather,' Diana snapped, before taking another deep breath. 'I arranged the meeting, yes. Just like I did everything for him – and I mean everything: diary, meetings, hospitality, travel, events, gifts for family and clients, even laundry and dry cleaning. But he trusted me with more than arranging things; he asked for and valued my input.'

'What was your role at the meeting?'

'I booked the hall, liaised with June, the curator, and Mr Demetriou. On the day, I was there to ensure everything ran smoothly. Brett had decided to get the panel in for lunch before the event, kind of breaking the ice – he worried that some of the personalities might clash, and he thought he might get some useful intelligence too. He always believed that people give more away in informal settings.'

'What time did everyone arrive?'

'The panellists came from twelve onwards, the public at two.'

'And what was the atmosphere like?'

'It was fine. I mean, apart from the scientist – she was pretty quiet – the rest of them were all busy talking, expressing their opinions.'

'What were you doing?'

'I was mingling and listening out for anything interesting, and making sure they all got fed.'

Constance paused before continuing. It was a trick Judith had taught her. Sometimes, people gave things away during a silence. But Diana just sipped at her tea and stared at the carpet.

'Did you talk to Mr Demetriou?' Constance asked, eventually.

'Of course – when we first arrived, then I returned to the kitchen a couple of times to chase food and, like I said, to check there was no shellfish. And he stood at the back of the hall when the panel went on stage. I think he wanted to hear what they had to say too.'

'Was he helpful?'

'I…he was…nervous. I thought maybe it was me. I can be a bit pushy, people have told me. And I had given him lots of dos and don'ts, but, you know, he was fine. The food was passable. What did I expect? It wasn't Nobu.'

'Where was the food kept?'

'There was a big metal table in the centre of the kitchen. Some food was laid out there on trays when we arrived and some had already been carried through to the main hall ahead of the guests arriving.'

'The kitchen was clean?'

'It looked clean to me. There was a waitress, wearing gloves, hair tied back, that kind of thing. Nothing stood out as worrying.'

'What did Brett eat?'

This time Diana's shoulders rose up to meet her ears and she pursed her lips.

'I don't know,' she said. 'I can't remember. Those scientists carving him up will tell us though, won't they?'

'You didn't ask him, when he said he felt unwell?'

'I didn't make the link then – not till after.'

'And you? What did you eat?'

'Oh, I never eat lunch. Especially not when I'm working.'

Constance had a few more things to ask – Diana had been informative, despite her apparent reticence – but better to leave without overstaying her welcome. That way she could return more easily another time. She drank her tea and placed her cup and saucer down on the table.

'Is that it?' Diana said.

'Yes, except...'

'What?'

'This will sound a bit strange, but I thought I smelt bread in the lift, but now it's in here too. Is there a bakery on site?'

'Mondays it's bread, Tuesdays coffee, Wednesday lemons, and so on.'

'What do you mean?'

'That was Brett all over. He read an article on an aeroplane which said that when we smell bread, we're kinder to strangers. He has it coming in via the air con.'

'I can see that the coffee smell might perk you up,' Constance said, 'but lemons?'

'I can't remember now. If it's important, I can look for the memo he sent around?'

'No,' Constance said. 'It's not important. Just my own curiosity, that's all.'

6

ON MONDAY AFTERNOON Constance met Judith for a coffee in Gail's bakery at South End Green. Whenever she walked along Pond Street, as she had today, Constance remembered Judith explaining that it dated back more than five hundred years and that the whole area had been created by filling in a deep pond – hence the name. Constance didn't usually get too hung up on history, but this was a fact which resonated with her; the progressive drive of the human race to transform its surroundings, coupled with a parallel need to commemorate what had come before. And since then, whenever she noticed other roads with similarly descriptive names, as she marched around London – Cornhill, Fish Street, Poultry – she made a mental note to look up their provenance too, when she found the time.

Judith had arrived first and selected a table in the far corner of the artisan café. Constance sat down opposite her and slung her bag around the arm of the chair.

'Well? What's new?' Judith asked.

'They've charged him, my caterer, with manslaughter,' Constance said. 'Sergeant Thomas told me just now. She was surprised, I think.'

'I'm not,' Judith replied. 'Since you called me, I've been digging around, as you expected I would, and I'm sorry to disappoint. There's this big push on food hygiene post-lockdown. You know the government was worried about all those people setting up takeaway businesses from home. There's been a slew of health and safety prosecutions and they probably came under pressure to find a big one to make a splash, and Brett Ingram was big enough.'

'Poor Nick.'

'Is that the caterer's name? A sacrificial lamb, I fear.'

'I do get it, though. You don't expect to die from a buffet lunch.'

'Is that what killed him?'

'They don't know for sure, but Diana, his PA – I went to interview her – she told the police he'd felt sick earlier. She thinks it might have been an allergic reaction to shellfish, but they're checking everything.'

'Hmm, not many allergy cases are fatal, but let's keep an open mind. I've been looking into some of the major food poisoning scandals of the last few years.'

'You know that wasn't why I called you.'

Judith smiled and Constance followed suit. Perhaps that wasn't entirely true. Constance had known that Judith was likely to overstep any narrow instruction she gave her – she just couldn't help herself, especially if she didn't have much else to occupy her time. And now Constance examined Judith more closely, she thought how relaxed Judith appeared, her hair longer than usual, her face fuller. Perhaps the Hampstead Ponds had been closed through the Covid-19 pandemic and Judith hadn't been able to exercise as much as usual. Or maybe it was Greg's influence, now they were back together, sitting down to more regular meals, eating out, the odd treat.

Greg Winter had acted as an expert witness in the first case that Judith and Constance had collaborated on, and he and Judith had started seeing each other, before Judith abruptly broke things off. Constance had tried to encourage their reunion and Greg had told her recently that they were back together. Whatever the reason, Judith appeared to be thriving.

'You can't blame me and it can't harm us to know what's out there,' Judith said. 'The big ones we all know about; those three hospital deaths from listeria, numerous *e coli* outbreaks – do you remember that one linked to bean sprouts? I haven't touched them since. And I also read that nine members of a family in China died from eating noodle soup.'

'I didn't know that.' Trying not to interrupt Judith's flow, Constance asked a passing waitress for coffee.

'Some kind of toxic acid from fermented flour,' Judith continued. 'They ate it for breakfast and they all died – three generations. Most of the unusual food-related deaths are not from *eating* bad food, though. They're more related to accidents in food manufacturing, like falling into sausage mincers or, in one case I read last night, a man was crushed by an avalanche of beans – pinto beans they were; good in stews apparently.'

'This isn't helping.'

'It's showing me how much I need another case to focus on, if nothing else. After I read about that poor man – the death by avalanche – I spent thirty minutes researching pinto bean recipes... Anyway, enough of that. We'll need to know who supplied our man, Nick, with all the food, then, and all the ingredients.'

'I'm working on it.'

'Tell me what you know about him.'

Constance took a moment to think back to her encounter with the caterer. 'There's not much to tell,' she said. 'He's in his early fifties, runs a small business. He's desperately worried about his livelihood, if things progress, as you'd expect. A bit excitable – I could hardly stop him talking. I haven't gone further than preliminaries so far.'

'And what's she like? Diana, the PA?'

'It's hard to say. She was hesitant, edgy even, especially at first, wouldn't let me make notes or record the session. She was one of the people there when he died. She seems...well-organised, efficient. I think they might have been more than work colleagues.'

'Oh?'

'She said she did *everything* for him, even his laundry. And she bigged him up to be some kind of superhero in the food industry.'

Constance's coffee arrived and she took a sip.

'I read a couple of obituaries from less partisan people and they would probably agree with her,' Judith said. 'Apparently, he paid dairy farmers twenty per cent more per pint than anyone else, for supplies to one or other of the businesses he owns. Said they deserved it. Anything else useful from her?'

'Not really. She couldn't even remember what he ate.'

'That's disappointing.'

'Oh, and I nearly forgot. At their offices, they have this food smell piped through the air vents, a different one for each day of the week. Monday was bread day.'

'Hmm. Do you think they ever do "hotdogs and onion" or "smoked haddock"?'

'Those weren't on the list,' Constance said.

'You don't seem impressed?'

'I thought it was a bit weird, like Mr Ingram was trying too hard to remind all his employees that it was a food company. Not letting them breathe their own air, even. You hear about employers like that, don't you? Ones who want their staff to live the business.'

'Maybe he just liked the smell,' Judith said. 'Freshly baked bread is near the top of my list.'

'He's taking away people's choice.' Constance could see Judith frowning at her, thinking her strange to be bothered by something so inconsequential.

'And the others, the panellists?' Judith said. 'The YouTube video you mentioned had disappeared by the time I got around to looking, although there were bits and pieces online still.'

'Five people from the food industry.'

'I saw one of them was Rosa Barrera.'

'You know her?'

'She has a Saturday morning TV show,' Judith said, 'jumping on the vegan bandwagon, but good luck to her. She's quite good. Keeps things simple, which is a challenge with only vegetables. Who else was there?'

'Some farmer and a blogger. I'll get the names and send them over to you.'

'That would be wonderful, and dig around them also, if you can. Remind me where the venue was?'

'Tanners' Hall in Haringey.'

'Hardly the Ritz. Did the PA say why they chose that venue?'

'I didn't ask, but they were planning to film it too, so maybe they were just keeping costs down.'

'That's plausible, I suppose. Can I also have the other things we just discussed – the list of food and some background on our client and on Mr Ingram?'

'No problem.'

'Now we've got the work out of the way, how was your date on Thursday night?' Judith uncrossed and re-crossed her legs and leaned forward onto the table.

Constance had hoped that Judith wouldn't ask, not because her evening had been a disaster – quite the contrary – but because she didn't feel ready to share her experiences with anyone yet. In fact, although she knew she had enjoyed her date with Chris, she hadn't analysed things any further. She wanted some quiet time by herself, without pressure of work or anyone else's expectations, to reflect before she could decide how she really felt.

'It was nice,' she said, hoping that would be sufficient.

Judith finished her drink. 'That's good,' she said.

'Would you like another coffee?'

'I don't think so. I must go. I promised Greg I'd check out the new exhibition at the Tate Modern. He's thinking of taking some clients, so I'm trekking into London and I need to be back by seven, although if it rains I won't stay out long. And I can see you don't want to chat.' She stood up and tucked her chair underneath the table.

In fact, Constance didn't want Judith to go. Their conversations always left her with plenty to reflect upon. Constance would never have thought of researching food poisoning outbreaks, or suspected any of the panellists. Judith was always one step ahead. And their meeting place was not exactly local – not that it would cross Judith's mind that Constance might want a little more attention, after a forty-five minute journey here. But she couldn't think of a way of persuading Judith to stay without answering her question, at least on a superficial level.

'His name's Chris,' she said. 'The man I saw last week. I'm seeing him again. He's an engineer.'

Judith tapped her on the arm. 'Chris is a good name,' she said. 'My first love at kindergarten was a Chris.'

Was that really true? It was the kind of thing Judith might say to wheedle information from her. The sharing of what sounded like something immensely personal and significant when, even if it was true, meant nothing at all. But two could play at that game.

'How're things going with Greg?' Constance asked.

'Good,' said Judith, without drawing breath or any change in her facial expression.

'I'm…so pleased you got back together.'

'It's early days.' Judith released her hold on the back of the chair and faced the exit. And Constance knew that was all she would impart, at least for now.

Judith slipped out between the tables and hovered in the doorway, peering at the sky with a doubtful air. And then, without looking back, she marched off along the road, her umbrella swinging from her arm.

TWO DAYS LATER

7

PERCHED ON A HIGH STOOL in the lab, Sue stared down the microscope at sample 5604/3, one of the flies she had allowed to hatch from its pupa, and then chilled the life out of, in the interests of research and for the benefit of mankind. She had already been through the formalities of its measurements: length, width, wingspan, weight. Now she was taking a closer look inside.

Dissection was always enjoyable, even when there was more blood, tissue and guts involved than with an insect. Getting inside the creature to see how everything worked; the satisfying first cut, the parting of the skin to reveal the organ systems, then organs, tissues and blood vessels. She felt a kind of religious gratitude towards her subject, wherever it sat in the food chain, for dedicating its corpse to science. This in turn motivated her desire to maximise the opportunity to learn, so that her volunteer had not died in vain. Today's exhibit was no different, although it had had little choice in its destiny.

Sue had always been fascinated by insects; two hundred million of them for each one of us, conquering every part of the planet, from the Saharan silver ant, to the synchronous fireflies of the Great Smokey Mountains. The diminutive desert ant was the world's fastest sprinter, capable of running its own body length in less than one hundredth of a second. 'That's the equivalent of four hundred miles an hour for a human,' she had told one man on a first date – and watched his eyes glaze over.

And the synchronicity of the fireflies? They flashed repeatedly in time with their peers, as part of their mating ritual. In May 2019, after a successful bid for a viewing spot, and armed with a fold-up chair and gallons of insect repellent, Sue had travelled to Elkmont, Tennessee, to watch their dazzling foreplay. And of course there was her current area of interest: the protein- and calcium-rich, natural decomposer, the black soldier fly.

She checked her watch and switched on the radio, an early noughties relic from her predecessor, who had maintained that the insects liked the human voice, and who had played them radio programmes incessantly, to fill the gaps of human absence. He hadn't approved of Sue's other nurturing theories but, on this point, at least, they had agreed. Sue tuned the radio from music to talking, turning the volume down low, so that she could listen in or zone out, according to her preference.

She had just reached a tricky bit of the dissection, opening up the stomach, when Dr Adrian Edge's voice broke into her thoughts: 'Good morning and welcome to my show,' he said, his silky tones more muffled than in the flesh, as they winged towards her from the speaker.

Sue paused, knife in hand. She had tried to shrug off her interaction with Dr Edge outside Tanners' Hall. She had always possessed a sense of hearing at the extreme end of the human range, but it was less what she'd heard and more his attitude; the way he'd dismissed her with his puerile humming before they'd even been introduced. Women working as scientists often found men responded in this way, disparaging their achievements, decrying them as unfeminine for their interest in clinical things. Marie Curie's solution had been to marry another scientist. Sue had found her scientist acquaintances tended to prefer less serious partners, presumably as an antidote to their day job, but perhaps that observation was skewed – a result of her own self-preservation mechanisms kicking in.

'This morning's programme is the first of a series,' Dr Edge continued, 'in which I'll be speaking directly to women, all over the world, who work in areas relating to the science of food.'

Sue dropped her scalpel and slapped her hand down on top, to prevent it from rolling off the desk and the blade caught the skin of her palm, nicking it and drawing blood. She swore, more at the radio than at the knife, and lifted her hand to her mouth, before hesitating and, instead, watching the red liquid bubble and pool. There had been no blood with Brett Ingram. No. He had died a sudden, violent death, but without any external injuries – or none visible. The others might have been more shocked than she was to discover he was really dead; Sue knew about death without blood.

There wouldn't be any blood now either, not even inside his veins. The pathologist would have drained it all away and returned his body to his loved ones, empty, a dried-out husk; less weight for the coffin bearers.

She looked down her microscope again – at the incision she had made into the fly's stomach cavity – and the whiff of putrid organic matter reached her nostrils, but there was still no blood.

Insects do have blood, just not the same as ours. She'd explained that to one of the technicians only last week, when she was eating her lunch and he'd come in to collect some equipment. Insect blood wasn't red though – just a yellowish liquid that transported nutrients, hormones and waste products around their bodies. She'd joked to him that horror films wouldn't be quite so terrifying if humans had watery yellow blood. He'd nodded and left.

'Today's guest is...' Dr Edge, on the radio, was still speaking. Sue grabbed a tissue, pressed it onto her palm and closed her fingers tightly around it. But any thought of Dr Edge and his rudeness automatically led back to Brett, and Sue was determined not to allow herself to think about him. *No way.* Because if she did... She tried to focus on her specimen and on her work, cutting carefully down from the stomach and watching its contents ooze out onto her slide. *That was better. Keeping occupied was the best way to forget.* And Sue had plenty of things she wanted to forget about.

8

CONSTANCE HAD NEVER VISITED a working farm. She'd been to a children's petting zoo, where she'd stroked a guinea pig and fed a goat and she'd been on one or two walks across fields which were probably farmland, on a long weekend in Yorkshire. But she hadn't ever met a real farmer before – not one who drove a tractor or worked a sheepdog or milked a cow. Now her curiosity and Judith's request for answers had brought her to Mark Sumner's smallholding, in the wilds of Hertfordshire.

She found no one at home when she rapped at the door of the house, a quaint but unassuming stone-built property, with huge sash windows and a short gravel drive. She checked her watch and then the message she had exchanged with Mark only this morning, which confirmed they had agreed on a 2pm meeting. She looked around her. To her left, the road became narrow as it progressed towards the open fields, but without any indication of how far it continued. Following her instinct, she skirted the house and found herself standing in a small, neat walled garden.

There was a low gate leading into yet more fields, the closest of which was filled with an extensive glass structure. She was about to turn around and try the road when a woman came out of the greenhouse, noticed her and waved.

'Hello, you must be the lawyer,' the woman said, hurrying towards her. 'I'm Rachel, Mark's wife. He's out at the barn; said to send you down.'

'Thank you,' Constance said. 'Looks like you have your hands full with all this.'

Rachel nodded. 'Who wants to be idle?' she said. 'And Mark needs the open space. He'd drown in the city.'

She led Constance back to the front driveway and pointed along the road. 'Over there,' she said. 'Just keep going and you'll see the barn on your right. But...' she looked down at Constance's feet and tutted. 'All that rain we had last week. Why don't you borrow some boots? I have a spare pair in the hallway, just inside the front door. It's a shame to spoil your shoes.'

Two minutes later, Constance found herself waddling along the single-track road in the Sumners' Wellingtons, remembering that the last pair she had worn had been at least twenty years earlier. Those had been shiny and red, with a chunky blue sole and she'd cried when she'd outgrown them and been forced to hand them on to her brother. This pair was quite different; matt olive green with a deep, beige tread and gaping at the top. Constance found herself thrusting her hands into her pockets and lengthening her stride, as if she were a farmer herself, stepping out for a quick once-over of her estate.

As she trudged along, she inhaled the smells of the countryside, noticing for the first time the complete absence of noise. Except that not all noise had been removed. She heard a bird tweeting from a hedgerow to her left, only to be answered by another in a tree further ahead, a loose fence post creaked in the wind and the low whine of a train was just audible in the distant background.

Constance reached the barn quickly, but entering it involved navigating a boggy morass, which began near an overflowing water trough. She could see a man, whom she assumed was Mark, shifting hay from one side of the barn to the other. He wasn't overly broad, but his arms were well-muscled and his tightly-fitted t-shirt revealed a similarly taut chest. He wore airpods in his ears and she heard him singing to himself, as he drifted across her field of vision.

She called out 'Mr Sumner. I'm Constance Lamb. We spoke yesterday. You said to just come along.' She waited, reluctant to leave the shiny world of birdsong behind and to intrude on him. He didn't respond immediately but then, as the sun came out behind her, catapulting her shadow into the space between them, he noticed her. He removed his earpieces and Constance repeated her greeting.

'You're right,' he said. 'And then I completely forgot. There's been a lot going on recently.' Mark exited the barn, trampling through the stinking stream of water. 'I'm going to check on the cows. Walk with me and we can talk at the same time.' And he gave Constance little choice, as he headed through a gate and took off across the next field.

Mark didn't particularly look like a farmer, Constance thought. First of all, he was much too young. And then she had imagined wavy hair and a hat. But he did have a beard, albeit closely cropped, like his hair. And, as he passed by, she noticed an inking on his wrist, some words she couldn't quite make out.

'You want to talk about last Tuesday?' he asked, as he strode on and Constance struggled to keep up. The ground was soft in places, even away from the barn, and her boots were large and unsupportive. She didn't want to turn her ankle.

'Whatever you can tell me,' she said, swinging her arms, so the momentum would help propel her forward and maintain her balance.

'You're the lawyer for the caterer?'

'Yes.'

'I thought it was a heart attack. Not that I know about these things. But so sudden like that. Adrian said that's what he thought and, I mean, he's a doctor. Now they think it was the food?'

'You sound sceptical?'

Mark slowed down, indicating to Constance that he was pondering her question and she slotted in next to him.

'I can't answer that,' he said. 'But the reason we have autopsies is to find out what kills people, isn't it? Anyway, it isn't good for any of us who were there, for *food* to have killed him. Food is what we're all about.'

Another one trying to protect his pocket. Constance was transported back to that East London bench, with the daffodils bellowing their sanctimonious message in her ear. 'What did Brett eat at the meeting?' she asked.

'I wasn't really watching.'

'And you?'

'That's easy. There were trays of beef burgers with all the trimmings. I wasn't so keen on the raw meat. I left that for the blogger. And I had some fruit, although that led to a big debate.'

'How do you mean?'

'Rosa, from the TV, she started on about the mango, said

maybe we shouldn't eat it – carbon footprint and all that. I wasn't bothered, but in the beef industry, we're trying so hard to make people see the benefits of eating *British* beef, not importing it, so I had to agree with her. To be honest, I was just trying to be polite.'

'Then what happened?'

'Oh I don't know. Adrian waded in, you know, *Dr Edge*. He was a bit of a dick, really, excuse the expression. Out of order. Maybe he didn't realise Rosa's family's from Mexico. Not that that should matter, but he started on at her, saying she was a hypocrite for eating avocados. He was a bit of a dick all through lunch, actually. Luckily, Brett smoothed it over. I'm probably making more of a big deal of it than it really was.'

Mark slowed down again, as they reached another field, all the time walking parallel to the narrow road, just visible over the low bushes. This time he held the gate open for Constance and they continued towards a small herd of cattle. Constance began to lag behind, eyeing the cows warily. Mark turned around and waited for her, clearly sensing her reluctance.

'They won't hurt you,' he said. 'I promise. Come,' and he seized her hand.

He led Constance slowly on, until they were within a metre of the animals. Then, just when she thought she was going to have to make a fuss, to make him let her go, he released her and stroked the nearest beast along her flank. The cow turned her head towards him and licked his free arm. He whispered in her ear and her tail flicked one way and then the other, swatting the flies off her back.

'See how beautiful they are. And how happy,' he said. 'This one is Klara, my personal favourite, although I don't tell her that often, so that she doesn't get big-headed.' He smiled for the first time.

Constance didn't reply. The cows were even larger, close-up, than she had imagined – absolutely huge. How much must they weigh? Twenty, thirty stone? Before embarking on her journey today, as part of her customary research, this time into farming methods, she had read a story about cows trampling a man to death. In an interview, all the locals had said how docile the cows usually were, that it was out of character, that the man's dog must have scared them. That didn't reassure Constance for one moment, now she was in close proximity to a dozen of them, although Mark's presence helped, as well as the fact that he was located between her and the herd.

'I get it. Beef has had a bad press,' Mark said, as he moved from one cow to the next to greet each one. 'First it was Mad Cow Disease, but we survived that – just – although that was before my time. My dad had to navigate that. Then the environment stuff and, yes, we can't stop them altogether, but scientists have proved that *grass-fed* cows produce far less methane and that it does decompose eventually. We have to tell people that they're buying British beef; then they'll have confidence in what they're eating. You can't say the same about the fruit we import. It's double standards.'

Constance kept her distance. 'I don't know much about it,' she said, 'but I imagine it's quite hard to grow mangos here, or avocados.'

'Then we should do without. That's what the campaigners say,' Mark said. 'Eat mangos when we're in Barbados, although if the climate change lobby have their way, we'll never be able to get to Barbados in the first place. Funny world, isn't it?'

'Is that what you were going to talk about, at the meeting?'

'I…I was going to try to explain to the doubters, not just the animal rights brigade, that we do things right here in Britain. Our cattle have lovely lives roaming free, as you can see. They eat a healthy diet and enjoy life.'

'How do you know that?'

'What do you mean?'

'How do you know they're happy?'

'Come,' he beckoned to her and she shook her head. 'I'm not answering any more questions till you've had a go.' He stood with his hand outstretched and Constance could see his tattoo more clearly; the words travelling away from her, up his forearm in looping script: *God made me a farmer*, she read. She laughed to herself at the joke.

Still wary but determined not to give up on her interrogation yet, she took Mark's hand again, then leaned forward and allowed her fingertips to graze Klara's side. The cow's hide felt warm and soft and reassuringly solid. Klara turned her head a fraction in Constance's direction, blinked heavily, then moved away. Constance withdrew her hand.

'Not so bad, eh?' Mark said, and Constance thought that now he was with the cows, stroking them, whispering to them and tickling them around the ears, his manner was softer than before, his rough edges smoothed away, like a pebble washed by the tidal stream. 'To answer your question,' Mark continued, 'I was reading this week, there's a guy in Holland who reckons he knows from their expression.'

'Their expression?' Constance couldn't keep the scepticism from her voice.

'I'm not saying I agree with him, but he claims he's filmed thousands of cows and he can tell if they're relaxed just from their faces. He's not totally wrong. I mean, that's the kind of thing I look for too, but for me it's the whole package, how they're moving, the noises they make. Sometimes they stare and they open their eyes really wide, so you can see the white rim. Then they're scared. I know that. Anyone who keeps cows knows that. These ladies right now? I can guarantee, one hundred per cent, they're calm, they're healthy, they're happy.'

Constance registered how Mark's face lit up as he spoke and she was almost convinced. Almost but not quite. At that moment, a lorry drew up on the road, with a clatter, the driver wound down his window and leaned out, brandishing some sheets of paper.

'I'm looking for the farmhouse. Rachel Sumner?' he called out to them over the hedgerow.

'You drove right past it,' Mark said. 'You can turn around just ahead, then you'll see it on your left, before the main road.' The lorry trundled off. 'You think they'd send the same delivery man,' Mark complained, as it disappeared around a corner. 'Every week it's someone different and they always get lost.'

'What are they bringing?'

'Oh…some things for Rachel. That's all.'

'Do you grow crops here too?'

'Uh…yes. Mostly behind the farmhouse, where we have more land. Shall we head back?'

Constance noticed Mark's hesitation. Had she used the wrong terminology? Did people only say 'crops' in textbooks or on the News? In any event, if the conversation was coming to an end, she had one more question to ask. It had been on the tip of her tongue when the lorry had interrupted them. Instinctively, she took a step back and lowered her voice, as if the cattle might understand. 'If you love the cows so much, isn't it difficult to kill them?'

And right on cue, Klara let out a loud moo. Mark laughed out loud and patted her head, before waving Constance onto the lane leading back to the house.

'Of course,' he said. 'You know, I heard Marco Pierre White talking on the radio the other day. Rachel likes to listen to Radio Four when she's cooking. Bit over my head, but it keeps my well-educated wife happy.

'Anyway, some of it I couldn't follow – Michelin stars and all that and lots of French. But then he was talking about how they kept rabbits when he was a boy and how, when his mother used to cook one, she would use fresh herbs and spend hours preparing it and then serve it to them all with a smile, but with tears in her eyes. You know, they had to do it; they had to eat. But she'd at least make sure she gave the rabbit a good send-off. That's kind of how I feel with my girls, although I don't kill them myself and I'm not eating Klara here. But someone has to do it, if we're all going to eat. Feed the world and all that.'

As they followed the muddy tyre tracks of the wayward lorry back towards the farmhouse, Constance thought about Mark's response; that he accepted his role was to nurture his animals, only to give them up to myriad strangers' dinner tables. She had meant her question as a direct challenge, picking up the gauntlet he had thrown down, when he forced her to touch the cows. But Mark seemed unmoved as he tramped along at her side.

**

Constance had left the narrow lane leading to the Sumners' farm and walked another thirty metres along the road towards the railway station before she remembered she was still wearing the borrowed boots. Chastising herself for her carelessness, she retraced her steps and, as she turned into their driveway, she could see Mark and his wife, Rachel, in profile, through the kitchen window. Rachel, her back to Mark, appeared to have her hands inside a basin and Mark had wrapped his arms around her waist. As Constance watched, Rachel turned around and waved flour-covered fingers at him. When he didn't retreat, she touched one to his nose. He laughed and held her even tighter.

Constance swallowed hard. This was awkward. Should she just leave and post the boots back? Or she could reverse a few metres and make a loud noise, out of view, then wait a few seconds to make sure they had heard her and disengaged. But she was also conscious that the next train to London left in twenty minutes and, if she missed that, it would be another forty minutes to wait. In the end, she did neither. Instead, she crept slowly towards the front door.

She opened it a few centimetres, reached around it and grabbed her shoes from the hallway. But the door into the kitchen must also have been open, because she could immediately hear Rachel questioning Mark, with a light, playful tone.

'What did she want, the lawyer?'

'Just asking about last Tuesday,' she heard Mark reply. 'If everyone got on, what Brett said and did, what he ate.'

'And you told her?'

'What I remembered, most of it, yes.'

'You didn't tell her...'

'No, of course not.'

Constance should just leave now, but she found herself continuing to listen.

'Do you think she'll find out, digging around Brett?' Rachel asked.

'I doubt it. She just wants to know whether her guy fed him something that killed him. I don't see why she'd be interested in us.'

'She came out back, into the garden, saw the greenhouses.'

'So what?'

Constance heard a scraping noise, then a shuffle of feet, then the sound of a cupboard door opening and closing. She held her breath, her shoes still dangling from her fingers.

'Nothing,' Rachel said. 'It's just that we've kept things quiet this long.'

'And with a bit of luck, we won't have to do it for much longer.' Mark sighed. 'You worry too much.'

'We're just so close and we haven't had much luck so far. And who knows what will happen now Brett's dead?'

'It's fine, all of it. You know, it might even be a good thing that he's gone.'

'Don't say that.'

'Sometimes you have to just get on with things yourself, you know, take things into your own hands.'

There was a silence then, during which time, Constance pulled off the boots and put on her shoes. But she couldn't resist eavesdropping one last time.

'Brett wasn't always so good at that,' she heard Mark say. 'He was trying to juggle too many balls.'

Constance closed the door, left the boots on the outside step and tiptoed away from the house, but once she reached the road for a second time a feeling of dread seized her. She had thought Mark had been cooperative and open. Now that it turned out he had a secret, she realised her judgment had been poor. But, worse than that, she couldn't tell anyone about this last revelation, not even Judith, because she had not discovered it by legitimate means. She couldn't possibly confess to listening in on what was plainly a private conversation. She turned it over and over in her mind without resolving her dilemma. On the journey back into London, she found the solution. Until she could determine what Mark's secret was in an open and transparent way, she would keep what she had overheard to herself. That had to be right. It was probably nothing important anyway.

9

ROSA WASN'T KEEN ON ZOOM. She understood that it had allowed her to keep in touch with her nearest and dearest over the past year, when the option of hopping on a plane was just not available, but now the practice of spending time with others virtually had become embedded in her daily life and difficult to throw off. Despite all formal travel and socialising restrictions having ceased, friends who would never have turned a hair at an hour's trip across London to sample a new tapas bar or a three-hour round trip for crêpes in a country pub, or a day out in Eastbourne to appraise the dinner options, were still offering her this digital alternative instead.

And it seemed churlish to even begin to explain that her invitation had not been just about company, that an in-person hook-up could not be replicated by chit-chat exchanged on a small screen, even if accompanied by alcohol and a suitable backdrop – The Maldives appeared to be the most popular one among her crowd recently. Rosa lived to smell and taste and feel – seeing and hearing were fine and she would never take them for granted. But to experience the splendour of life, you had to stimulate the more emotion-charging, evocative senses.

So, even though she had been forced to accept that most days she would find at least one – and more often two or three – of these online sessions slotted into her diary, she faced each one with an attitude of bitter regret for what might have stood in its place.

Today, unexpectedly, she found herself invited to a call chaired by Adrian Edge. A reminder had popped up on her screen fifteen minutes earlier and it had jolted her back to the events of last week, which she wanted to put behind her. She also had no recollection of having accepted the invitation or what it might be about, but she could see now that Mark, Zoe and Susan were also scheduled to participate.

Her finger hovered over the 'join meeting' button and the various options beneath it – with or without video camera or microphone. She smoothed her hair and prodded at her cheek bones before enabling them all.

'Hello Rosa,' Adrian called out to her from across the ether, as if they were the best of friends. And, yes, just as she would have predicted, had she known about the call in advance, he had some kind of sun-baked amphitheatre superimposed behind his head and held a glass mug containing a purple concoction. She smiled half-heartedly.

'We're just waiting for Mark and then we'll start,' Adrian continued. 'Probably mucking out the pigs or whatever he does for fun.'

No one laughed, although Rosa noticed Zoe waving, so she waved back. Zoe appeared to be busying herself with a series of tasks involving shifting items around, reading and typing simultaneously. In contrast, Sue, who had only appeared for a moment, had moved off camera, leaving a large, empty room with whitewashed walls in shot. But the mention of Mark's name, aloud, had thrown Rosa into a spin.

'Sorry I'm late.' A clatter and the appearance of an additional box on her screen confirmed his arrival. 'I'd double-booked. What's this all about?'

Adrian nodded to all of them. 'I can see you want to get on, so I'll try to be brief.'

Mark continued, grinning. 'You don't have a full hour, like you do on the radio.'

His beard was fuller and it suited him. That was one positive attribute of Zoom. You could examine people closely without appearing impolite. His eyes darted around. Was he seeking her out? Rosa reached up to check her hair a second time.

Adrian was speaking again. 'Can I just begin by saying that I appreciate all the help and support you provided last week when…when we suffered the terrible loss of our mutual friend.'

Zoe groaned, Mark's mouth set into a grim line and Sue reappeared momentarily, then promptly also switched to mute. No one said anything.

'The funeral arrangements are in hand, and I'll make sure they're shared with you all, so you can pay your respects.' Adrian emitted a prolonged sigh. Sue turned her camera off.

'After I'd gone back to my flat,' Adrian continued, 'and cried and reminisced and all those kinds of things – I'm sure you all did the same – I thought that the best thing we could do to honour Brett would be to carry out his wishes. That's the purpose of today's call.'

Zoe's mouth hung open, Sue remained both silent and invisible, Mark frowned. Rosa focused solely on Mark. If she held her own breath, she could hear his gentle breathing, amplified by the microphone on his laptop. It was the same gentle breathing she had heard, when she'd sat next to him in his car last Tuesday afternoon, when they'd left the hall together. Only later it had turned to faster, more laboured gasps, as Mark had pressed her up against the back wall of her house.

'Not here,' she'd said, before she'd pushed him off and fumbled for her keys.

Then they'd both fallen through the door and into the kitchen, her mouth finding his, her hands loosening his clothes, unbuckling, unfastening, untucking, him tugging and wrenching, seeking a way through to the softness of her flesh before lifting her up onto the granite worktop and pushing himself inside her.

Once they'd finished and he'd withdrawn and released her and Rosa had pulled down her tight, red dress and slid off the counter, she had seen Mark looking around the room. He'd laughed, even as she placed one hand against his chest and felt his heart still racing. 'I recognise this place,' he'd said, 'from the TV.' And the magic of the moment, if it had ever existed, was gone, just like that. Rosa sensed his disengagement; the association with her public persona leading his mind elsewhere.

Back on the Zoom call, Adrian coughed, clearly expecting a response to his opening remarks which had not been forthcoming. Rosa collected herself.

'Brett's wishes?' she queried, the sound of her voice helping ground her in the present.

'Brett was going to make a film of the event,' Adrian said. 'Use it for marketing. 'We could still do that, dedicate it to him.'

'But he was going to use the film to promote his company, wasn't he?' Rosa pressed on, wondering what Mark, the current, brooding version of Mark, would think about this. 'I don't have a problem talking on screen about my cooking, about the enormous, proven benefits of a vegan diet, like I would have done last week, if that's what you mean. But doesn't the company have to confirm things? Have they asked you to contact us?'

Adrian squirmed. 'As you can imagine, they're a bit all over the place at the moment, without a CEO or anyone else to step into Brett's shoes – not that they'll be easy ones to fill. But I know they'll endorse whatever we do.'

Everyone was silent again. Rosa did not dare look at Mark, but he was the first one to speak this time.

'Just so I'm clear,' he said, 'you want us to agree to be in a film, where we talk about our work. Then you're going to give it to Heart Foods, but you haven't asked them about it yet?'

'Well, I...'

'Why don't you ask them first and then come back to us, not waste any of our time?'

'I thought you'd all want to honour Brett's legacy, but if that's not the case...'

'Just out of interest,' Mark interrupted, 'what were you going to talk about? I know it wasn't about your radio show, because Brett told me.'

Adrian smiled again. 'Well,' he said, 'Since you ask, I have this fabulous idea, and Brett liked it too. Last week's meeting was an opportunity to share some of the underlying themes with the audience.'

'What's the idea?' Zoe asked, finally zoning in. Rosa noticed she had ditched the glasses she wore at the meeting.

'I…I would need you all to agree to keep it confidential, before…before I tell you.'

'What!?' Mark shouted, his face the personification of righteous indignation.

Everyone, Rosa included, stared at him. And as the dopamine surged from her brain, flooding her body with longing, she wished she could keep a freeze frame of that image forever.

'Mate,' Mark continued, 'I don't know about the others, but I think this is nothing about Brett and all about you. I'm out.' And, with that, Mark had gone.

It seemed he was good at that – leaving places in a hurry. Zoe remained, but she also switched to mute now. It was left to Rosa, again, to say something.

'Adrian,' she drew his name out to give herself time to formulate her words. 'What do you mean by keep it confidential?'

'I have this brilliant idea, which Brett knew all about, but we were worried that someone else might steal it. I know it sounds strange, but we talked to a lawyer. You can get people to sign up to say that they won't steal your idea. Then if they do, you can take them to court. My idea is so radical and so brilliant that, before we tell anyone about it, they need to agree to keep it confidential – not tell anyone else about it – and not use it themselves either.'

Rosa tried to understand. 'If you talk about your idea on the film, then it won't be secret any more, will it?'

'I wasn't going to say too much on the film, just enough to get people interested. But, if *you all* knew about it, you could help spread the word at the right time, when we decide to go live.'

Zoe unmuted. 'I understand I think,' she said. 'You mean you tell us about it now, but we keep quiet. Then we make the film, like Brett would have done, and we give it to Heart Foods. Then you get feedback on your idea and, if it's looking good, we can tell everyone all about it then.'

Now that Mark had gone, Rosa could focus on Adrian and on this call, on his stupid backdrop, his pretentious drink and his 'confidential' idea. Had Mark been right to call him out though? In her mind, Rosa was rubbing non-dairy fat into flour. Now she was shaking the bowl from side to side, so that the lumps came to the surface and she could squash them between finger and thumb. It only took a moment more for her to locate the 'lumps' in Adrian's explanation and, in Mark's absence, it was up to her to expose them to the others.

'Mierda,' she said aloud.

'I'm sorry?' Adrian said.

'I said mierda...bull...shit.'

Adrian sniffed and said nothing.

'Will you make money from your idea?' Rosa asked.

Adrian blinked twice.

'You said "steal",' she continued. 'It's confidential because you want to sell it, make money from it, and you're worried that if you share it before you sell it, then someone else will "steal" it. You mean the thief makes all the money instead of you?'

Adrian jabbed his finger at the screen. 'What's wrong with that? None of us does what we do for free – you included.'

Oh Adrian could be so confrontational, brimming with the conceit of the privileged, white male. And this time Mark wasn't there to defend her, so Rosa would have to take him on herself.

'Maybe,' she said, 'Zoe doesn't mind helping you to promote yourself and your idea – whatever it is. Maybe if you'd come out and asked me direct, I wouldn't have minded either. We all need a bit of support in this world, to help us on our way. But you didn't do that. You called us all together, you said this was about Brett, about remembering him.'

Rosa knew she was beginning to raise her voice, shake her head, wave her arms around, but she couldn't help it. The more she talked, the more wound up she became. 'You even talked about his funeral, when all the time... Ah. And now I remember. Zoe? Sue? You asked us on to your show – *women in food*. OK, you need guests. I get that. But that wasn't why you asked us. It was all about this. All about you and your big, con-fi-den-tial idea and selling it to the highest bidder. You know what? Total fucking mierda.'

Rosa pressed the red cross on her screen marked 'leave meeting' but not before she saw Adrian's face turn scarlet with fury.

10

JUDITH HEARD THE CLICK of the oven door opening. Greg was most probably checking if dinner was ready. He had arrived at her apartment an hour earlier, found her engrossed in online research, kissed her cheek and then disappeared into the kitchen. Judith hadn't expected him to cook tonight, but if he hadn't, she would probably have just skipped the meal, as was invariably the case when she was following up on any line of interest.

'Is now good for you to take a break?' He leaned around the door, a pair of oven gloves dangling from his shoulder, bringing with him the delicious smell of roast pork.

Judith smiled and nodded. It was certainly handy having Greg around, and not just for his culinary skills. She closed her laptop and cleared it away, then gathered cutlery and napkins from the kitchen and hastily set the table. Greg brought the plates through and Judith followed, with a bottle of Pinot Grigio and two glasses; the fruity flavours would complement the pork. She muttered a *thank you* to him, before sitting down and tucking in.

'What do you think of veganism?' Judith asked, waving a forkful of meat in the air and making appreciative noises. 'Not a comment on the marvellous meal you've prepared,' she added, just in case. But she needn't have worried. Greg poured them each some wine and picked up his knife and fork. Then he sat all the way back in his chair, the way he always did when he was mulling things over.

'As a lifestyle choice?' he asked.

'As anything you like,' Judith said. 'Let's brainstorm. Isn't that what you do with your troops at work?'

Greg lay his knife and fork down on the side of his plate.

'Can't you speak and eat at the same time?' Judith asked.

'I was always told that was rude.'

'Oh come on. Don't be a spoilsport. I'm not eating alone. And if I can't ask you anything till after dinner, think how much time we will have wasted by then.'

Greg retrieved his cutlery and smiled. 'I don't know a lot about veganism,' he said. 'I think it must be a difficult regime to follow, especially the *no eggs* bit; dairy we've got lots of substitutes now. But I've always believed there were potential health benefits.'

'Me too,' Judith said, delighted to engage on her topic of choice. 'I mean Novak Djokovic seems to have done pretty well on it. How many grand slams has he won now?'

'You have to be careful to get enough iron – isn't that the main problem?'

'And the time it takes to prepare the food. I mean, *you* could just throw this together, whereas a lentil curry might take hours.' Judith smiled again and placed her hand on top of Greg's, before he could protest. 'I'm joking…about the *thrown together* bit. You know, reading about it – veganism – it made me think of a Roald

Dahl story from years back. I have it over there on the shelves somewhere.' She waved at the groaning bookcases behind her. 'I don't remember all the details, but it's about a man who builds a machine which can hear trees screaming.'

'Trees...screaming?'

She could sense Greg's mockery, but this made her more determined to explain the relevance of her story.

'It's like an old-fashioned gramophone. Some big wooden box with an ear trumpet and he, the inventor, he takes it out into the woods and cranks it up and it magnifies the sounds of the trees. It can tune into their natural frequency – something like that – and most of the time he hears this gentle, flute-like playing, all very Edward Elgar. Then comes the awful part when someone arrives with an axe.'

'That's where the screaming comes in then,' Greg said.

'You got it,' Judith said. 'Even when he's walking on the grass, this man, carrying the box, he hears the individual blades protesting, each one crying out, as they're crushed underfoot. I forget what happens in the end, but it's not happy. Most of his stories aren't. Anyway, it got me thinking and I did some research and guess what?'

'You're going to tell me that he was right all along.'

'Not exactly, but there's information online about *sentient trees* and it's fascinating.'

'Sentient trees? You're telling me they exist.'

'They nurture communities, they look out for each other, they're acutely aware of everything going on around them and they adapt to their environment. It reminded me of that time-lapse photography of ferns – their fronds unfurling. Have you ever seen it?' Judith made a fist and then allowed each finger to uncurl in sequence. 'When you see *that*, how lithe and sensuous those ancient plants are, it's easy to believe they have feelings. It's rather lovely.'

'They're just responding to stimuli,' Greg said.

'Might that not mean they can feel?'

'So do solar panels,' he added.

Judith huffed out her irritation. She liked logic more than most people but, every now and again, she wanted permission to be vague and creative. 'I'm just saying that the idea of living, breathing, sensitive plant communities, looking out for each other is…appealing.'

'Maybe.'

'But it must come as a blow to vegans,' she added. 'Then again, it's grist for the mill for Zoe Whitman, carnivorous blogger extraordinaire.'

'Who is she?'

'She was one of the speakers at the event where Brett Ingram died. She writes about how vegetables are the hidden killers of Generation Z.'

'Ah,' Greg smiled.

'What?' Judith asked.

Greg lingered over his last piece of cauliflower. 'I just haven't seen you this animated about anything in a while, that's all,' he said. 'So this…research – ferns and bloggers – it's all a result of your coffee with Connie a few days ago? Her briefing you on the Brett Ingram case?'

'Yes. But I'm not telling you the rest for now.'

'OK?'

'You'll only start trying to help me, before I even know I want to be helped.'

Greg threw back his head and laughed. 'That's the best way, isn't it?' he said.

Judith sipped at her wine and said nothing.

'All right. I give in. You know me too well,' he replied. 'Cards on the table? I admit to digging around your dead man a bit already. Want to hear what I've discovered?'

'If it's about his desire to support dairy farmers, I already know that.'

'Not that, no, more generally. He was very outspoken, apparently. That's what I've been reading. All in the pursuit of better quality food.'

'Oh.'

'He was against preservatives and E numbers, anything artificial, and intent on bio-degradable packaging. And very pro-consumer, providing lots of details on products, to keep everyone well informed.'

'Was that profitable?'

'Heart Foods was doing very well, but I'm not sure how much of his rhetoric had been implemented yet.'

'And did they make him popular – all those eco-warrior, friend-of-the-consumer objectives?'

'With staff and customers, definitely. There's feedback on their website which makes that clear. But not with competitors. Nobody likes to be rubbished for what they produce, told it's unhealthy or harming the environment. I'm going to wade through the company's annual report and accounts. There might be some useful detail there about what he was getting up to, in the months before he died...just out of my own interest, that is. Nothing to do with your case.'

Judith reflected on Greg's words. It really was nice having him around, she thought, even if he did insist on getting involved in her work. He began to clear their plates to the kitchen.

'Is there any dessert?' she asked.

She heard the clatter of crockery in the sink, and wondered if Greg might also do the washing-up.

'Maybe,' he replied, 'but the tree huggers might not approve of it.'

'I think we can live dangerously,' Judith called out to him. 'Just this once.'

11

ZOE SAT AT HER KEYBOARD, writing a new piece for her blog. This time she had chosen pomelos as her theme. She knew they weren't exactly mainstream, that avoiding pomelos wouldn't necessarily be a hardship for most people, but there were only so many times she could write about potatoes. And she had a gap to fill; she'd messaged Sue, the insect professor, and had no response – not yet, anyway – but she was certain Sue would reply. Everyone wanted free publicity, didn't they? Although there was a chance, now she thought about it, that the Zoom call with Adrian might have put Sue off. If she didn't hear from her in a day or two, she'd try again, but maybe include a link to her blog. Just so Sue could see how much real science she used in it.

'Citrus Maxima,' she cooed aloud, as she began to write. Who'd have ever thought she'd get good at Latin, a language only spoken by dead people? She'd been prompted by Rosa's pomelo salad, her latest TV creation, which was trending on Twitter, a salad which also included brussels sprouts, shallots and star anise, all ingredients with lurking secrets Zoe could reveal. Zoe had also noticed that Rosa prided herself on not wasting anything. She had this crass mantra, *Be a user not a loser*, which she would roll out at least once per episode, replete with her trademark toss of the head. On this occasion, that honour had been bestowed on the pomelo seeds, which Rosa had advocated using to thicken jam, stringing together to make an impromptu necklace or enclosing within two bio-degradable yoghurt pots to form a shaker.

Many people who had watched the show were lauding the pomelo's health benefits – *boosting the immune system, aiding weight loss* – and its *anti-ageing properties*; the 2021 triumvirate of the food sector. Of course, they tried to distance it from the grapefruit – devil of the diabetics – in a number of ways. They maintained 'it's less sour' or 'it's the natural citrus fruit, genus Maximus, where grapefruit is the sub-tropical hybrid,' or they highlighted the very obvious difference: 'its sheer size' – a feature which Rosa herself had mentioned, with a suggestive pout. But it was all semantics. They were pretty much one and the same.

When your doctor tells you not to eat grapefruit, because it will interfere with your blood thinners or your blood pressure medication or your cholesterol-busting statins, he ought to mention these critters too. And if you're pregnant? Don't even peel one! Zoe wrote, admiring her ability to acknowledge, but deftly recalibrate, the discussion.

But how to move on from this? She'd targeted ill people and pregnant women, two of her most vociferous support groups. Now she needed another focus. Lips pursed with concentration, she trawled the internet. After a few minutes, she paused, her eyes widening. 'Gotcha,' she murmured.

Research proves that menopausal women who eat pomelo, are at 25% higher risk of developing breast cancer, owing to its ability to increase oestrogen levels.

The study she found had been conducted on grapefruit, but no one would know if she substituted one for the other. And 'menopausal women' was a huge potential target audience, except, as she began to write the word 'menopausal' her fingers froze. People weren't comfortable with that word, she decided, with its negative connotations. She could substitute 'women over forty' pretty safely, she thought. Although maybe she shouldn't limit it to just women, given all that JK Rowling row about menstruation – another word to avoid at all costs. Funny that the two words had 'men' at the beginning, but they were both about women. There, she'd just use 'over 40s'. If she could only find something negative for children now, then her work would be complete. Another half hour and she had decided on the next bullet point.

While pomelo is a good source of dietary fibre, more than one cup (when you don't want too much scrutiny, always use the cup measurement. No one has a clue what size that is, she thought) *can cause bloating, stomach cramps and diarrhoea, particularly in children and young adults. This, in turn, can lead to dehydration and nutrient deficiency.*

Phew. Done!

Zoe stretched out her shoulders and stiff back. She stood up, went into the kitchen and drank two glasses of cold water in rapid succession. Writing her blog was seriously hard work. Picking up her messages was less taxing and, on occasion, rather good fun. Settling back down on the sofa, she began to read her incoming mail on her phone. It began well enough.

Dear Zoe, I have IBS and I've always thought that vegetables made my condition worse. I've been following your diet suggestions for three months now and my symptoms do seem to be less...

Dear Zoe. I'd like to know what you think about coffee? I know it's a bean and all that, but as we all drink so much of it, maybe it deserves its own post. And tea too? Do I really have to give them up?

Hiya. I loved your article on beetroot. I always think you should trust your instinct and I never liked it. It stains your hands red – think what it's doing to your insides. And they eat it in Poland.

Then the troubling messages began.

Hi there. Your article on berries was riddled with inaccuracies. It's not true that blueberries are unsafe for breastfeeding women (or lactating women as you insisted on calling them, making it sound like we're all dripping milk everywhere!) and it's totally irresponsible of you to peddle this dangerous nonsense. In fact, fibre is particularly good for post-partum women. All the problems you describe are associated with excessive use and research shows time and again that the advantages of blueberries far outweigh any possible downside. Just maybe, there is a kernel of truth regarding people who have recently undergone surgery, but that's it. Get your facts right!

Closely followed by:

Hello Zoe. I checked with Dr Emil Traynor, whose research you cite. Together we tried (but failed) to find the quote included in your article on nuts and seeds, which you attributed to him. He does talk about cashew nuts, but he says that you make a leap from the poison ivy material and it's very rare to eat raw cashews anyway. He will be writing to you directly, but he wants you to remove any mention of him or his research from your article – immediately. Otherwise, he will be contacting his lawyers.

Both messages were from the same person: @truthwarrior79. Zoe's fingers hovered over the keys. Most days, she would soak this kind of stuff up. She might not reply at all or, if she was feeling generous, and depending on how many views the negative material was collecting, she would send a holding message first, carefully worded. 'I'm so delighted you've taken an interest in my blog. It's incredibly important that my articles are well-researched and I always check and double-check my sources. However, as you've asked, I will go through your points and make sure I respond to each of them. That may take a day or two, but a promise is a promise.' That kind of thing.

But today was not most days. Today represented the end of a very difficult period, a week in which Brett Ingram had died on the stage right next to her and then he'd appeared to her, like a ghost in a Shakespeare play – she couldn't remember which one now, but it had been nasty when she'd seen it with her GCSE class; blood and shouting and more blood – not real blood, she knew that, but not ketchup either; some pretty realistic substitute.

Simon Jenkins, the boy who always sat at the back of the class and had once followed her home and hung around outside, until Amy – or was it Sophie, or maybe it had been both of them? – had told him to piss off, he'd said actors used pigs' blood on stage, to make it convincing. Ew!

But even that unsettling experience of her formative years was nothing compared with this; a week in which there'd been the death thing she'd just remembered, which came top of the list – obvs, then the opportunity to go viral with her video, which she'd had to relinquish, all the supernatural stuff, and finally she'd been interviewed by the police, for hours and hours, without a break or a snack or a lawyer. It was too much to bear, really too much. She ran to the toilet, flung up the lid and was violently sick.

After she'd flushed and downed more water, she returned to her screen and read the messages through once more. Then she did something usually reserved for perverts and paedophiles, of whom a number had bothered her in months gone by. She blocked the sender and deleted the messages. Once that was done, she took a deep breath and refreshed her page. *Gone. Better now.* She wondered if Truth Warrior really had consulted Dr Traynor or if he was just saying that to scare her. It was a while since she wrote the piece about cashews and she had been fairly careful.

Then another message came in, this time from @sonoftruthwarrior. Zoe gasped.

'The Truth will out!' it declared, before descending into a diatribe on sunflower seeds, which became increasingly strident. Words leaped out at her, in between her hyperventilation, like 'unfounded' and 'baseless' and 'scaremongering' and 'charlatan' – she had to look that last one up. Each one wounded her deeply.

Zoe blocked this account also and, too distracted to focus,

she darted into her bathroom, lit a scented candle to help mask the residual odour from her bout of vomiting and began to run a bath. She told herself to just leave things alone, relax and, afterwards, once the soothing water had calmed her, to change tactics and respond. But when her bath was almost full, she changed her mind. She grabbed her phone and, one eye closed, she accessed her messages. There were three new ones, each from a different sender: @notburningpants, @tellingporkiesiswrong, @majorendanger.

And they were beginning to spark responses, including from some of Zoe's most loyal followers. She bit her lip, cried out and then she began to type the holding message she'd begun to draft in her head earlier. As she was writing, another missive came in. 'You can't handle the truth!' it read, replete with wild red-haired emojis. Zoe knew now what she had to do. This wasn't right, it wasn't fair and it was against all her principles, but there was a limit to how much a girl could take, especially in her fragile state. She sat down at her laptop, in her underwear and, within thirty seconds, it was done. *Taken down; off air; bye bye all.* She'd put a message on her site which would do for now. 'Zoe's blog is undergoing an upgrade. Back in a few days with some fabulous new material and easier to navigate hub.'

What else could she possibly have done in the circumstances? she thought to herself, as she slipped off her clothes, tucked up her hair and immersed herself in the steaming tub.

12

JUDITH AND CONSTANCE SAT in the front room of Nick's house, an unassuming semi with a large bay window, while his wife, Lisa, brought them tea. Nick was 'running a bit late' and would be 'down in a second', Lisa announced, with a glassy smile and a quivering bottom lip.

'How has your husband been?' Constance asked, as she saw Judith begin her usual, visual inch-by-inch sweep of the room, through half-closed eyes. Honestly, Judith was like one of those super trawlers, the kind that hoovered up anything and everything from our oceans, leaving them barren and empty. Most of the time, she kept her catch for herself.

'I know he wanted bail,' Lisa said, 'but he doesn't go anywhere and he won't see anyone except for our kids, and he hasn't much to say even to them.'

'I can understand he doesn't want to see many people,' Constance said.

'I told him he had to get fresh air,' Lisa continued, 'how important it is for his mental health, but he doesn't listen. Maybe if I said it in Greek, he'd listen. What do you think? But I never learned much…Greek that is. I mean, if you go there, they all speak English.'

Constance looked at Judith, who remained impassive.

'Then, last night, suddenly, he went out in his Parka,' Lisa said, 'with this great big hood, maybe five minutes and he was back, went straight to his room. Today, he stayed in bed till two o'clock. How long is this going to go on?'

'The trial will be in August,' Judith said, 'which is quick by today's standards, but not so quick if you're counting every day. You'll need to find a way to keep your husband motivated until then.'

'Even if he wanted to work, no one will do business with us. After thirty years. I'm not sure what we're supposed to live on.'

'What about insurance?'

'We asked. They said if Nick was *negligent*, there's no cover. I said no one had decided that yet, but they said it doesn't matter. They're not going to pay us and then have to get it back later on when we've spent it.'

'I thought you also had a food importing business?' Constance jumped in.

'We do. Our son runs that. It's not an income for two families though.'

A shuffle outside the door signalled Nick's presence and he entered the room and slumped down next to his wife. His wet hair stuck up in all directions, he wore an untucked polo shirt over some chinos and a pair of Adidas flip flops adorned his feet. Constance had the impression he had shrunk since their last meeting; his head was bowed and his shoulders hunched.

'Sorry to keep you waiting,' he mumbled.

'No problem,' Constance said. 'This is Judith Burton. She's helping me with your defence and will represent you at your trial.'

Nick nodded in Judith's direction but said nothing more.

'I was just telling your lawyers that it's thirty years since you started out – more than that if we count what you did when you were a boy.' Lisa continued her monologue. 'When I met Nick, he and Maria – that's his sister – they used to run *Giorgio's*. You've probably heard of it?'

Constance shook her head.

'No matter. It was named after Nick's dad. What a character he was, wasn't he? Tall, good-looking, smooth. And such a chef! Best Greek food in London. It's where Nick proposed to me. Shame it had to close down. His dad would have been so upset. Anyway, then we set up the catering business.'

'They didn't come to hear all that,' Nick said, without looking up.

'We came to update you both,' Constance said, 'but it is useful for us to know about your work. And it helps to show you're a professional.'

Lisa acknowledged Constance's support with a nod.

'The post-mortem on Mr Ingram is not certain,' Constance continued, 'but it concludes that the most likely cause of death was an allergic reaction to shellfish.'

'There was no shellfish. I sent you the list,' Nick protested, looking up at Constance for the first time.

'The prosecution case is based on traces of shellfish, most likely in the sandwiches, not a whole item.'

'How would I know that? You don't buy a cheese sandwich and expect it to have shellfish in it.'

'Mr Demetriou, you told Constance the sandwiches came from a local shop, but she called in there and they have no record of an order from you on the 13th of April. Can you recollect or perhaps check and let us know where the sandwiches *actually* came from?' Judith skipped the niceties and got straight to the meat of their visit.

Nick looked across at Lisa, who removed the lid from the teapot and prodded at the steaming liquid inside with a spoon.

'He didn't want to say, because people get funny about it,' Lisa said, her focus all the time on the tea, which she began to pour into cups and hand around.

'What didn't you want to say, Mr Demetriou?'

Lisa stared at her husband, whose hands were tightly clasped in front of him. Still he didn't speak.

Judith continued in an even tone, but Constance sensed her impatience. 'You do understand,' she said, 'from what I just explained, how important it is that we have precise details of the origin of the sandwiches?'

'Costco,' Lisa said and Nick gave a low grunt of disapproval, but she ignored him. 'Their food is very good. Lots of caterers use their products, pretend they made things themselves, even. But Nick didn't want to say. People think it's too cheap, or even cheating, especially with sandwiches. The other things we made ourselves.'

'I see.' Judith looked at Constance and then back at Nick.

'I had ordered the sandwiches first from the local shop. That's why it was on the list I sent to you,' Nick answered now. 'But this woman, this *Diana*, she was driving me mad with all her changes.

So, when she changed again, I just cancelled and picked up some trays from Costco. I forgot, with all that's been going on.'

'You can let us have the receipt for the sandwiches, then? You must have it, for your accounts?'

Nick shrugged. 'I think so,' he said.

'And Costco should list any allergens in their food.'

'Maybe.'

'Mr Demetriou. This is serious,' Judith said. 'You had a responsibility to read the ingredients of any food you purchased before you served the food to Mr Ingram, who had a known allergy.'

'No, he didn't,' Nick replied.

'What?'

'He didn't have a known allergy.'

'His PA, Diana, says he did.'

'No, I mean, she never said. All those emails, back and forth, "British beef", "local tomatoes", "vegan pakora". She never said; no allergy.'

Constance and Judith exchanged glances.

'Is that important?' Lisa asked.

'There are other defences we can raise, but if your husband can convince the jury that he was never told about the allergy, that is a key point in his defence.'

Nick nodded his understanding and rested one hand on the arm of the chair.

'I'll get more water for the tea,' Lisa said and exited the room.

'How does she – Diana – how does she say I knew?' Nick had visibly perked up at this glimmer of light in the darkness which his life had become.

Judith looked at Constance.

'We'll check, like you said,' Constance said. 'Your emails and messages will need reviewing.'

'If she did send my husband a message and he didn't see it, what then?' Lisa had returned, twisting her wedding ring around on her finger, the sound of the kettle firing up again, in the background.

'That depends,' Judith said, 'but if she took reasonable steps to bring the allergy to your husband's attention, the court will say he should have known about it.'

'She didn't.' Nick was adamant. 'No emails, no message, no allergy.'

Constance and Judith exchanged glances once more. This was good. This was why coming to see Nick today had been worthwhile. Not only what Nick had said, but his conviction, his clear denial. Constance was pleased Judith had seen it first-hand.

Suddenly, an emaciated woman appeared in the doorway, although Constance had not heard her approach. She had white hair, cascading onto her shoulders, one side shorter than the other, as if it had been chopped away with a pair of large scissors. A navy, polyester blouse hung off her scrawny frame and her eyes were sunken deep into her head.

'This is Maria, who I just mentioned,' Lisa said, standing up, more to bar the woman's way, Constance thought, than to welcome her in. 'These are Nick's lawyers,' Lisa continued, 'here to advise us.'

The woman nodded, one of her bony hands resting on the door handle.

'Nice to meet you, Maria,' Constance said.

'I don't want to intrude,' Maria replied, her voice low and gravelly. 'I just heard visitors.'

Lisa fiddled with her ring again. There was space on the two-seater sofa next to Constance, but no one offered it to Maria. Constance wasn't sure if Nick had mentioned a sister when they had first met. She would consult her notes later on.

'I'll just check on the washing,' Maria said, after a moment, 'and not bother you.' She turned on her heel. 'Nice to meet you too,' she said, as she closed the door behind her.

Lisa sat down, her bottom lip working extra hard to keep itself under control. She appeared to have forgotten her promise to bring hot water to refill the teapot.

'She's living with us, just for a while,' she said, by way of further explanation of Maria's presence. 'She's not been too well, recently.'

There was a loud noise from the kitchen, as if someone had dropped something made of china and it had shattered. Lisa flinched, shifted her weight forward as if she might stand up, then remained seated. Nick's eyes darted up towards the wall adjoining the kitchen and he let out a deep sigh.

Judith ignored the interruption and pressed on, clearly keen to see if they could uncover anything else useful.

'Did you see what Mr Ingram ate that day?' she asked. Nick shifted his head slowly around to face her again.

'I was so busy with everything,' he said. 'This Diana, she came into the kitchen and said everything looked so nice. She even said it tasted nice.'

Lisa patted her husband's hand. 'Are they sure it wasn't something else?' she said. 'I mean, so many people have things wrong with them and they don't go to doctors, you know, especially men.'

'We'll check that out too, as much as we can,' Constance said. 'Did you see any evidence that Mr Ingram felt unwell, before his collapse?'

Nick looked at her again. 'When he got up to speak, you mean?'

Constance thought back to her conversation with Diana. 'Before then. Over lunch? Did you see him go to the bathroom a lot, for example?'

'I didn't have time for that, watching bathroom trips. I was preparing the food, with that Diana standing over me.'

'And what was the issue with the fridge?'

'Ah!' Nick rubbed his eyes with the fingers and thumb of one hand. 'It's such a nothing.'

'What is?' Judith asked.

'Them saying it should have been in the fridge, the food.'

'Shouldn't it?'

'When I arrived the fridge wasn't clean. Not terrible, but not as clean as usual. The guests were coming, Diana wanted the food out by 12.15. So I had brought it in cool boxes, with freezer packs. It was better to keep it there than start trying to clean out the fridge.'

'How did this even become an issue?' Judith asked.

'The police were obviously looking for something – a fallback,' Constance said. 'I think one of your staff mentioned it to them.'

'They never asked me. And I have the freezer packs still. I put them back in the car, after the food was served.'

'You're right,' Judith said. 'It's a nothing issue.'

'But we need to make it clear that Mr Demetriou was following good hygiene practices, when he gives his evidence,' Constance said and smiled at Nick and Lisa, so that they knew she was listening to them.

A door slammed shut somewhere upstairs and Lisa scowled.

'I'd better check that she's all right,' she said, pointing at the ceiling.

'Don't worry. We'll leave now.' Judith drained her tea to the bottom and returned the cup to its saucer. 'We'd finished anyway. Anything else, Constance will be in touch.'

'Thank you,' Lisa replied. Nick said nothing.

Constance felt for Lisa. It must be hard trying to pretend that everything was fine, when it really wasn't. And looking after Nick's sister on top of everything else was clearly a strain. 'It's nice you have such a close family,' she said, collecting up her bag from the floor and heading for the door.

***

Outside, Judith took off at a pace which might have made the Olympic scouts take note. Constance had to hurry to keep up with her. 'Running a bit late?' Judith spat out the words, once they had turned the corner at the end of the street.

'Sorry?' Constance replied, not following Judith's drift this time.

'I might expect Bill Gates to be "running a bit late" – you know, someone who's at the helm of a multinational conglomerate and a charity with responsibility to eradicate world poverty – not our client who, on his own admission, has nothing to do, except provide an inaccurate account of where he bought his sandwiches.'

'He apologised, didn't he?' Constance said. 'And he's depressed. You heard what Lisa said. You're just cross because the case isn't as exciting as you imagined.'

'What?' Judith said.

'You were expecting radioactive poison and MI5 spy rings, as I remember.' Constance looked over each shoulder. 'And instead you got journeys to the men's toilet and freezer packs.'

Judith slowed down, then laughed. 'You're right, not about the lack of excitement – that doesn't bother me, really it doesn't. It's just…clients. They dig themselves into these holes, then they expect us to get them out and they don't often appreciate how much effort that involves. I mean, if he loses, he faces a long spell in prison, but he's more interested in covering up key evidence because he's embarrassed he shopped at Costco!'

After five years of working together, Constance expected these outbursts from Judith, from time to time. She didn't mind, as it was just her way of letting off steam and it was usually short-lived. Constance had learned that a change of focus was the best way of calming Judith down.

'He's told us now,' Constance said. 'And he's certain Diana didn't tell him about Brett's allergy. That's good isn't it?'

Judith stopped walking and looked around at the neat rows of semi-detached houses, each side of the street a mirror image of the other.

'All right. I was just having a moment. Now it's passed,' Judith said. 'Anyway, this is far safer than foreign-sponsored assassination.'

'You don't usually like safer.'

Judith laughed and began walking again, this time side by side with Constance.

'There aren't many gross negligence manslaughter cases these days, or many successful food allergy prosecutions,' Judith said. 'It's good for my CV to have a niche area of expertise. Anyway, I am fairly sure this case will be more interesting than it sounds, once I get my teeth into it. Ah – unfortunate turn of phrase in the circumstances. Have you seen the prosecution's witness list?'

'It's long.'

'It's very long and that tells me they're worried.'

'It does?'

'If they were feeling secure, we'd have the expert and Diana Percival showing whatever message she sent Nick to tell him Brett had an allergy, and that would be it. OK they'd have to argue it was grossly negligent to ignore the warning, but there's precedent for that: the case last year with the takeaway in Bradford, where the chef went to jail. No, I'll bet they don't have an email from Diana and they're worried the forensic evidence is equivocal. And I'm sure we can have fun with some of their witnesses, especially if they're all celebrities.'

Constance nodded. Judith could never resist a challenge. 'What do you think is wrong with the sister?' Constance asked.

'She really didn't look well, did she? Mind you, at least she doesn't have to run a business with her sister-in-law any more.'

'You don't like Lisa? I thought she might make a good defence witness.'

'What?' Judith said. 'So she can tell everyone how little Greek she speaks. People never cease to surprise me with their capacity for laziness.'

'You don't know that.'

'Oh come on. She marries a Greek man – all right, a British man whose family hails from Greece, but who is clearly in touch with his Hellenic heritage, running a traditional restaurant, part of an ancient civilisation which brought us philosophy, science and art, dating back thousands of years – and she can't be bothered to learn one word of his native tongue.'

'She didn't say that and I think you're being harsh. You don't know what else they had going on. Not everyone has…leisure time. Anyway, some people aren't good at languages.'

Judith sighed, which Constance took as part-acceptance of the arguments she had put forward. 'I'm digressing again. Where were we?'

'What would you like me to do next?' Constance asked.

'I hardly know where to start. Check on the sandwiches, now we know where they came from, including any warnings on the packaging and re-check all the other food sources. If Nick got one of them wrong, there may be more smouldering "mistakes" – let's be charitable and call them that. We need to find them now and extinguish them. I want the list of what was in the food waste left behind at the hall. I'd like the forensic expert report. And most important, what concrete evidence is there that Diana told Nick anything at all about Brett's allergy?'

'I had that one.'

'Oh, and Brett's medical records. And dig around Diana a bit.'

'The usual no stone unturned, then?' Constance said.

'Yes, the usual. Nothing more nothing less.'

13

CONSTANCE AND CHRIS MET at an Indian restaurant on Wardour Street that evening. They selected the buffet option, partly because the food set out behind them on a series of hot plates appeared colourful and appetising, but also because it meant neither of them had to spend time navigating the extensive menu. Constance, for one, was delighted not to have to process one more word that day.

Instead, she gathered various pickles and dips set out in steel bowls while Chris brought over paratha and bhajis. Constance was first back to their place so she could watch him, leaning forward over each hotplate to read the description of its contents, considering all the alternatives and, after choosing a few, finely balancing saucers on his wrists when his hands were full. He must have felt the heat of her gaze, as he turned around and smiled.

He sat down opposite her. 'What have you been working on this week?' Constance asked, as she spooned chutney onto her plate.

'The floods in Bolton have kept me pretty busy, now you ask.'

'I saw that. Those poor people. What could be done for them?'

'Some were evacuated. But I was there to look at the river, see what we could do to stop it overflowing.'

'And what did you do?'

'We put up some temporary barriers along the bank and fortified the existing ones. And we installed a temporary pumping station to take water out of the river and bring the level down.'

'Did it work?'

Chris shrugged. 'It helped. We certainly saved some homes which were borderline.'

'Sounds like a lot of hard work.'

'It was. But if we can protect people's property or make the clear-up process quicker, then it's worth it.'

Chris helped himself to some sauces, took a paratha from one of the plates in the centre of the table and dipped it into them.

'It seems to be getting worse every year,' Constance said, 'or is it just me noticing it more?'

'You're asking the right question. Essentially everything begins and ends with rain, if that's not too obvious an answer, and we are getting more of it. In some parts of Scotland, as much as an additional two hundred millimetres of rain per year, every year.'

'Why doesn't it just drain away?'

Chris smiled again. Clearly, he was enjoying holding forth. 'Well, with extra rain, the rivers become swollen and burst or overflow, but you also get groundwater flooding when the ground is so saturated it can't absorb any more water, or flash floods too, at low levels. Throw into the equation that the systems we have in place have been deprived of cash for years. It's inevitable. Do you know they've said 5.2 million UK properties are at risk this year?'

'What would you do with the extra money?'

'The things I just mentioned. Build up the existing defences, install permanent pumps. We're always being reactive, which means people suffer before we get in there. It would be so much better to do the work first and prevent the flooding in the first place.'

'Wow. You spend a lot of your time in waterproofs then?'

'Not all the time. I'm heading out to Sicily next month to advise on a water treatment plant. I don't expect much rain there.'

He took a bite of his paratha and Constance helped herself to some chickpeas, balancing them, a few at a time, on her fork.

'Do you go abroad often?' she asked, once the spiced pulses were safely transferred to her plate.

'We tender for projects all over the world and, if we win, then I go. I was in India for a year – that was quite an experience. I've also worked in New Zealand and Greece.'

Constance pricked up her ears at the mention of Greece. Here was her chance to expand her knowledge. 'Are there problems with flooding in Greece?' she asked.

Chris chuckled. 'They wanted us to update their sewage system. I don't know if you've been to Greece ever, but their plumbing is pretty archaic. It's a throwback to the original watercourses, built thousands of years ago, when everything was channelled into the bay of Athens. Anyway, they finally got some funding back in, ooh, 2017, to replace their tiny pipes and I was out there overseeing the project for three months or so.'

'And what was it like?'

'Crazy, haphazard, scorching hot. One day we found this ancient sculpture in one of the sewers – complete it was – a lifesize man: beard, curly hair, the works. They think it dated back to the fourth century. They just dug it up, took it to one of the museums, then we carried on. It's a bit like that out there. You never know what you're going to find when you go beneath the surface.'

'But they don't have any problems with flooding in Athens?'

Chris shook his head. 'The Acropolis, the highest part of the city, has flooded more than once. It's climate change. We can't fight it. We just have to do the best we can to protect everyone.'

Chris suddenly grabbed his glass of water and downed it, tipping his head back until he had drained every last drop. He pointed at the innocent-looking tomato paste Constance had brought to the table. Then he dabbed at his eyes with the serviette.

'That hot?' she said.

Still unable to answer, Chris grabbed a teaspoon and began to ladle the yoghurt dip into his mouth.

Constance began to giggle. 'I'm sorry,' she said. 'You do look funny. Are you all right?'

'I think I just became the first fire-breathing human,' he gasped. 'You did that on purpose.'

'No, I promise. It just said "chutney".'

'I think it's a sign we should stop talking about my work and talk about yours instead.'

Constance pushed the offending paste to the far end of the table. 'My work? All right. You asked for it. This may be worse than the secret chilli though, I'm warning you.'

'That would be difficult.'

'Well,' Constance began, 'I've just had a new case in. You might have seen Brett Ingram died last week?'

'I was fairly preoccupied.'

'He was the head of Heart Foods. They're saying it was food poisoning, or maybe a food allergy. You know, let's not talk about that one.'

'You're worried I might tell someone? Leak it to the press?'

Constance laughed. 'I'm more worried it might put us off our meal.'

'Good point. Is there anything else you can tell me about? Not talking about food but just to give me a *flavour* of your work?'

Constance laughed again. How good that felt.

'Sure. Last week, we also had a heady mix of shoplifting, criminal damage and drink-driving. The shoplifting was committed by a pregnant girl of fifteen. And, yes, before you ask, she did hide the two pairs of joggers and a tiara under her extra-large jumper covering her baby bump. She got off with a warning, given a series of background circumstances I won't relate, but I could see from the magistrate's face that he couldn't get his head round the tiara – if you see what I mean.'

Chris nodded. 'And the criminal damage?'

'You'll love this one. You might have even seen it on YouTube – a woman went crazy in Aldi, destroyed their entire wine and spirits section.'

'What do you mean destroyed?'

'She walked in and just started smashing all the bottles. At first, she knocked them off the shelf, ten, twelve at a time. Then, as more and more people watched, she started picking them up one by one and hurling them around the store.'

'Didn't anyone stop her?'

'No one wanted to get hit by flying glass. The police were there in twenty minutes but by then the whole lot was destroyed – £10,000 worth. You should have seen the mess.'

Chris began tentatively to nibble on an onion bhaji. 'Why did she do it?' he asked.

Constance hesitated before responding. This case had upset

her, despite her making light of it. 'She was out of work, lonely, struggling with bills, forgot to take her medication. She had a total meltdown. She got a suspended sentence, which was probably the best we could have hoped for. No point putting her in jail. Whether she'll get any help is another matter. And then today, like I said, a drunk driver, insisted his orange juice was spiked, which was just about believable until the footage came through from the pub showing him necking pints.'

'What did you do?'

'I told him to plead guilty.'

Chris offered Constance the remaining paratha and she broke it in half. 'Are you ever scared of the people you advise?' he asked.

Constance thought for a moment. 'No. If they're in the police station, I feel safe and often, whatever they're accused of, I see them the day after or the day after that, when they're usually calm and reflective...and sorry. What's more scary is seeing them in normal life.'

'How do you mean?'

'Oh I don't know. I got a kid – seventeen-year-old – off an assault charge – quite serious, involving a knife. I showed it was mistaken identity. Then I saw him a few days later, with a group of boys, on the corner of a street near where I live and they were all packing knives. I could see. I went the long way round to avoid them. Then I was scared.'

'Why do you think people commit crimes?' Chris asked, leaning one elbow on the table.

Constance noticed a dimple in his left cheek. 'There are loads of theories,' she said.

'I know that. I wondered what you thought.'

Constance smiled. It was nice of Chris to be interested in her opinion. Most people preferred the gritty real-life details of the cases. 'There are some people who have very difficult family circumstances,' she said, 'and the odds are stacked against them. That's definitely true. But others I see? It's just a moment. A crazy moment. An insane moment, you know. I'm not sure I even think of what they've done as a deliberate act. It's more that most of their lives they're prevented from doing things they might want to do, by rules and conventions and morals and fear of punishment. Then, for that one moment, they forget all of that and just…go with the flow, whatever that may be.'

'Then…you must think we're all capable of really awful things?'

Constance pursed her lips. 'You don't want to hear this?'

'You can't stop now.'

'All right,' she nodded. 'Yes. I don't believe the world is divided into good and bad people. I think we all have the capacity to do really bad things, once in a while.'

14

WIDE AWAKE, SUE SAT IN her office chair, surrounded by vats full of sleeping black soldier fly larvae; slumbering, snoozing, dozing. It was funny how all those expressions associated with sleep seemed so peaceful, even the sounds of the words with their extended vowels, like they were stretched out on a couch. She so preferred those words – the more colloquial ones – to their scientific, harsher counterparts; latent, inactive, dormant, but she would keep that to herself. Her mother had advised that she was too sensitive for the life of a scientist, too emotional and easily distracted. Well, she had proved everyone wrong, hadn't she, making professor at twenty-nine years old?

She laughed a manic laugh and it rang out across the empty room and bounced off the part-full vessels. Then she ran to each container in turn, pressed the palm of her hand against the glass and duplicated that laugh, trying to remember its exact pitch and tone. Once she had interfered in this way with one vat, she had to repeat the process at each and every one, ensure all the insects were treated the same. She knew that any observer would think she was crazy, but it was so important to be thorough and accurate and true. She couldn't allow her research to be invalidated.

She ground to a halt at the last container, when she spied unexpected movement. Two flies had hatched, unexpectedly, prematurely, inconveniently. It was the first time this had happened. She checked the temperature on the container and it was exactly as she had left it, but clearly these specimens were defying protocol. One of the outliers was moving, rubbing its front legs over the top of its head. Then, as Sue pressed her face close to the glass, it paused its grooming session and its great big V shaped antennae – like a miniature, water-divining rod – twitched twice in close succession.

Sue's breath steamed the glass and she lost sight of the insect. When the mist cleared, she saw that the other one was only minutes behind, its body shivering with the anticipation of being brought to life, although it probably really was shivering. Regaining consciousness at those temperatures must be the equivalent of waking up in the Arctic without a sleeping bag for those two.

Sue watched them for a few seconds more, then she removed the cork from the vessel and snatched the two flies out. At first, she allowed them to bask in the palm of her hand, its heat only accelerating their awakening. Then, when the more mature of the two took a step to straddle her life-line, she felt a constriction in her throat and she closed up her fist, tight. She counted to five, then released their crushed bodies to the floor, grabbed a brush and swept them away.

***

Rosa waited on the line, listening to the phone ringing out. It was the third time she had called Mark at home this week. She counted the rings – ten, eleven, twelve – on thirteen it clicked to answerphone. She rang off. What was the point in leaving a message? She'd already sent three texts and a WhatsApp and had no response. Mark knew she wanted to talk; clearly he didn't.

She rose from the sofa, went into her kitchen and selected a lemon from her fruit bowl. She washed it carefully under the tap, rubbing at the skin in rapid circular motions – her practice ever since she'd read that seventy per cent of all citrus fruits sampled in bars had substantial bacterial growth on the peel – then she slid a chopping board out from beside the microwave, grabbed the largest of her collection of knives, lifted it high above the worktop and...bang!...brought it down smartly on the unsuspecting lemon, cutting it cleanly in two. She poured herself a glass of water and squeezed the juice from one half, jabbing at the flesh with the knife. Then she sliced the remainder into thin strips and dropped them into her drink, where they fizzed around before settling just below the surface.

Rosa turned through 360 degrees, returning to lean on the counter. She loved this space. It had taken two full months of work and nearly £35,000 to get it exactly as she wanted, but it was perfect. And apart from the state-of-the-art appliances, some of which had been donated by sponsors keen to see their products on her show, she had delighted equally in kitting it out with the best quality equipment. She ran her fingers over the shiny, copper-bottom pans, lined up on the hooks to one side of the oven, which played such a prominent role in her cooking. Then she tapped with her shiny nails at the two enormous woks into which she had grated endless cloves of garlic, throughout her most recent series. Finally, after washing and wiping it with care and with a deep breath, she slid the awe-inspiring knife back into its slot, in the carved Green Oak block.

Then she returned to the living room, collected her phone and tried Mark again. This time, after only four rings, someone answered. Rosa listened hard but no one spoke. It must be Mark, as surely his wife would have said something by now.

She'd sat in that same spot and sipped at a whisky – neat, no ice – right after their coupling. He'd refused to join her for a drink. That should have warned her that his interest was already on the wane. Instead, he'd stood in front of her, shifting his weight from one foot to the other. Rosa had known what was coming before he opened his mouth.

'I should probably be going,' Mark had said.

'Home to the farm,' she'd replied, trying not to sound bitter.

'Will you be OK?' he'd asked, finally meeting her eyes. She had obliged him with an insipid smile and a casual nod.

And that had been it. Nothing more than many of her encounters with men and considerably less than others. Usually she was content to move on, especially if they weren't interested in anything more long-lasting. And yet, here she was, messaging and calling him, like some smitten schoolgirl. She tried to imagine how Mark would view things: just sex; a moment of weakness in a time of emotional turmoil; animal instinct had taken over; they had lost control of their senses; they'd been incapable of making rational decisions; certainly not the precursor to a relationship of any kind. Perhaps he believed Rosa had tempted him – she'd heard that one before – by her helplessness as she struggled to fasten the seatbelt, when violent spasms had taken over her fingers.

'Hello,' Mark said into the phone.

Rosa pressed the disconnect and stared into the distance. Why had she called him? She wasn't entirely sure now. She probably wouldn't have done so, if he had answered her texts or perhaps if she hadn't sensed his curiosity, when she'd seen him on the Zoom call. She imagined him now, bristling with anger and running himself a cold shower or thumping at a punch bag. She knew men like Mark; they had to get rid of their rage. It wouldn't dissipate by itself.

15

ONE EVENING, SIX WEEKS after Brett's death, Greg and Judith met at the top of Primrose Hill. Judith had spent the best part of two hours wandering around Hampstead Heath and its environs, Greg had come straight from the Underground and work, bringing two bottles of craft beer with him. They sat down together, shoulder to shoulder on the grass and gazed out over the London skyline. This was one of Judith's favourite places. 'Every time I come up here, I see something new,' she said, inclining her head towards his.

Greg opened one of the bottles and passed it to her. 'I was looking for the blog of your panellist – you know, the one you mentioned,' he said.

Judith wiped the top of her bottle with her handkerchief. 'You mean Zoe Whitman?'

He nodded. 'Who knew lentils could be so lethal?'

'Did you find it illuminating?'

'It's been taken down…maintenance, it said, the last three or four weeks. And she's suspended her Twitter account.'

'She's giving everything an overhaul then.'

'That's how she wanted it to look. But when I dug around, I could see it was in response to some incoming messages she wouldn't have liked. I could still get the gist of what it's all about from elsewhere – articles she's posted and things other people have picked up and shared.'

'What did you think then?'

Greg gave a low laugh. 'I think you can say anything you like online these days.'

Judith took a sip of the beer and smacked her lips together. Greg made her do these things to test her; sit on the grass, swig from a bottle. Next he'd be suggesting she take off her shoes and socks. She wondered if he sometimes mistook her for someone half her age.

'I know but what's so...intriguing about Zoe's blog,' she said, 'or was, when I read it last, is that it has this ring of authenticity. I mean, she begins by setting the scene – humans living for thousands of years as hunters, eating meat with the odd morsel of leafy greens on the side. Then she reminds us that the last *hundred* years, when we've started to manufacture our staples – rice, wheat, potatoes – are just an evolutionary blink. She says our bodies would need centuries to evolve to be able to eat the food we're packing them with today.'

Greg clinked his bottle against Judith's and took a drink himself. 'Does she have any real evidence these things are harmful?'

'Now you're beginning to sound like me.' Judith gave a low laugh. 'She does, but not quantifiable. I mean, you know people tell you not to eat apple pips because they contain cyanide. The sceptics say that's true, but you'd need to eat a lot of apples to feel any ill effects. Then I read that a dog died after eating five apples, so there is something in it, after all.'

'It's anecdotal then.'

'She explains what chemicals vegetables contain, how they're bad for us, and references the occasional study. I found the information about wheat the most powerful; there are, after all, around 700,000 coeliac disease sufferers just in the UK – one per cent of the population. The link between red meat and heart disease, which most people accept as gospel these days, is really no more evidence-based. It's just we've been talking about it for longer.'

'What about the moral angle; eating animals is wrong?'

'That I understand – and the environmental impact too. But what if Zoe's right? What if pulses and seeds and nuts are no good, and if we just ate an old-fashioned diet of fresh meat with a side of broccoli every day. No, scrap broccoli – she says that's cancer-inducing – iceberg lettuce, we'd all be better off. I mean the Japanese, they live the longest don't they? I can't see them troughing panini or potato gnocchi.'

'But they do eat a lot of rice.'

Judith drank some more beer. It was actually quite pleasant once you got over the initial bitter assault on your taste buds. She was pleased Greg took their discussions seriously and responded when she asked for his input. And, she told herself, even though she sometimes made light of his contributions, he knew, deep down, that she valued him.

'Doesn't your Zoe have a fundamental PR problem with all this?' he asked.

'What's that?'

'I don't see how anyone is going to buy the idea that we have to kill more animals in today's climate. Even if personal health is in jeopardy, the younger generation will say they're willing to take that risk, when the alternative is more dead living creatures.'

'At least they'd be informed, give informed consent. I'd certainly be interested in learning more about all of this – explosive broccoli and satanic seeds – when she's up and running again.'

'So now those touchy-feely plants you were learning to love have gone over to the dark side, have they?' Greg laughed at his own joke and Judith dug him in the ribs.

'Just because I'm willing to be receptive to new ideas...'

'You're right and I'll stop, but it's so out of character that I'm wondering if I'm here with Judith Burton or some clone with a woke implant in her brain.'

Judith fell silent. She could tolerate light teasing, but sometimes Greg went too far. Just because she was cautious about innovation did not mean she was a Luddite.

'Lab-grown beef might sort out the problem, don't you think?' he said, reinforcing the question with a jaunty tilt of his head. Judith had to hand it to him, he didn't give up easily. And he was clearly waiting for her to respond.

'I can't imagine it tastes any good,' she said, and left a long enough pause before replying for Greg to realise he had upset her, but also to appreciate that she was prepared to be magnanimous and forget about it. 'Maybe for burgers, hardly for Chateaubriand,' she added.

'Listen, I don't want to impose, but I did some more digging on Heart Foods.' A change of subject. Judith decided to go along with him and see where they ended up.

'Did you now?' she said.

'There was some fuss at their last AGM when a shareholder

asked about spending and didn't get a straight answer.'

'What kind of fuss?'

Greg tipped his head back and took a large mouthful of beer, then he drew his knees up tight and crossed his hands around his legs.

'The company spent over £4m last year on something called "Ambrosia",' he said.

'Ambrosia?'

'Yep. The accounts list it. They say something high-level about "a food revolution" and how it's part of their five-year plan for the company. This man – presumably a shareholder – he asked if Brett could tell him what it was all about.'

'And did he?'

'Brett said it was a number of initiatives to improve the quality of food and that shareholders had to trust him to invest wisely.'

'And that didn't go down very well?'

'Apparently, the man shouted and the share price plummeted, but only for a couple of days. There was speculation over what Heart Foods might be doing with all that money. Interesting choice of name, though. *Ambrosia*. Whatever it is.'

'Isn't it?' Judith said.

'Anyway, I've also discovered that a fairly large shareholding – thirty per cent – is held offshore. I'm not really sure what that's about – some tax dodge, most likely, but I'll see what I can find out about who really owns it.'

Judith nodded. 'Hog all the best work, why don't you?'

Then Greg drew her close to him and kissed the top of her head and they sat in silence, as the sky went through the artist's palette from fiery orange, through salmon pink, fading to grey.

As the last sliver of sun disappeared below the treeline, Judith stood up and dusted down the back of her trousers and Greg followed suit.

'Does she say we have to give up alcohol?' Greg asked, 'your "meat only" blogger? I didn't see anything on that topic.' He examined the label on his beer can, as they wended their way down the hill. 'I mean it's all made from grain or fruit.'

'I don't think she's tackled drinks yet.'

'I bet she hasn't. Maybe she has good sense after all. I'll look out for when she's up and running again and keep you posted.'

He took Judith's empty bottle from her and dropped it into a nearby bin, followed by his own. Then they linked arms and began to walk home to Judith's flat, past an array of restaurants and bars, just beginning to come to life.

16

Rosa cleared away the last of the plates from the day's trade at the Sweetpea café. She only came in three or four times a month, usually on different days, so that customers would never be sure she was going to be there. That was the best way to keep them keen, she found, even though it was harder than people might think to arrange to appear randomly, rather than to have a routine.

She had opened the café in 2009, at a time when money had been tight. It wasn't a grand or smart venue, but that had suited the clientele of the time – mostly women with or without young families. Back then, she had waited tables every day, with only one additional helper. Her nights had been spent 'batch-baking' at home, her mornings, rising early after only four or five hours of sleep, to package and transport her fresh produce to the shop, until she earned enough to install a full kitchen at the back.

And she'd worked hard on the design scheme too, painting the walls in warm hues, fitting the raffia-shaded, low-hanging lights which everyone remarked upon and installing her favourite Mexican tapestry by the counter. Designed and executed with love and care by her mother and sisters as a leaving gift, its coloured squares had remained vibrant through the years, each one embroidered with a bird or animal, surrounded by marigolds, hibiscus and morning glory. If she felt sad, which happened from time to time, she would run her fingers over its intricate stitches and think of her beloved family and how proud they would be of how far she had come.

Then, in 2015, not long before her big TV break, Darren Jason, an actor whose star was on the rise, came in for tea. It happened purely by chance; he was filming around the corner and fancied some cake. But he'd been so friendly and complimentary that she had plucked up the courage to take his photograph and asked permission to hang it on the wall. That was the beginning of a series of visits from famous guests, whom she had similarly won over. So now Rosa's café offered a curious juxtaposition of décor; by the till, her old life was represented by charming, rustic flora and fauna, fashioned by hand from coloured yarn. Opposite, on the wall against which most of the tables were arranged, was a montage of images of the great and the good, in various states of joyful indulgence of Rosa's cuisine.

Now that she was a celebrity, albeit a relatively minor one, Rosa was fortunate that the café remained in fashion. Even the most well-heeled customers, visiting from further afield, appreciated its shabby-chic vintage overtones, or at least they said they did. So she had eschewed the invitation to move or expand or modernise. This place represented her culinary journey, her navigation of English culture. It had encouraged her to capture memories in a way she would never have done, if she had stayed at home. Even when she was tired from her other far more lucrative engagements, she enjoyed coming here; baking, waiting tables and chatting to customers. She loved this place to death.

Rosa picked up the last piece of aubergine tart from inside the refrigerated counter, slid it onto a metal tray and placed it in the mini oven behind her. The dish had been a wonderful seller this month, although she liked to ring the changes and keep things seasonal. She clicked through on her iPad to her list of suppliers, selected three and then emailed them enquiring about asparagus and other vegetables she might introduce now the days were long. Asparagus would also work well in her tart. Then she cleared the rest of the items from the counter and into a bag to take home.

After twenty minutes of stocktaking, reordering and then checking on the day's takings, she munched her way through her dinner and collected a broom, bucket and mop from the storeroom. She always allowed the staff to go home early on the days she was on site. It was a nice perk for them and it also meant she had the place to herself, time to sit and reflect and enjoy being there, in the space which had grown from nothing into this cheery part of the local scene.

Rosa swept the floor, beginning near the door, where she spent a few extra seconds looking out at the street. Then she added a few squeezes of eco-friendly cleaner to her bucket, half-filled it with water from the barrel outside the back door and began to clean. The process itself was soothing, the side-to-side motion involving a shallow rotation of the hips, the swishing of the mop, the lifting and twisting to wring out the excess water. She moved slowly, and by the time she had finished the light had begun to fade.

She lifted the nearest chair from the counter where it was stacked, carried it into the tiny back yard and sat down. There was just enough room for a bistro table out here, among a wide variety of herbs, a selection of fiery chillies and the one pot reserved for non-edible greenery, currently full of crimson tulips, just past their best, their petals splayed wide, their blackened centres edged with yellow. As she rubbed one of the flowers between finger and thumb, she thought about Mark again. She had found him attractive from the outset, she wouldn't deny that – the haunted look he wore, as if some constant need to outwit danger was wearing him down. She had always liked men on the edge, although only as lovers. They were too unreliable to make good friends or business partners. But she also knew that she would never have instigated or accepted any advance from Mark if Brett hadn't died. She closed her eyes, folded her arms across her body and before long she was asleep.

Rosa couldn't be certain what caused her to wake up – the crackling noise or the smell. In her mind, she was at home in the village of her youth, preparing for a pig party, helping her mother and sisters roll the tortillas, collecting up the muslin bags for sausage making, slicing cucumbers, squeezing limes and watching the pig skin curl up along the sides of the black iron cooking pot. Except the sounds and the scents were not in her head.

She opened the back door of the café, only to be met by thick black smoke, which poured past her, escaping into the night air. Grabbing a towel from next to the sink and holding it over her mouth, she advanced through the tiny, fog-filled kitchen and into the café. Here flames licked across the floor and up the left-hand wall, leaping from one picture frame to the next. For a second, she failed to understand what she saw. Yes, it was a fire, but how? A stray candle? A faulty wire? There was no time to piece this together now. Instead, she snatched up the fire extinguisher from the corner of the room, pointed it at the flames and set it to work.

Fifteen minutes later, when she was certain the fire was out, she returned to her seat in the yard, her face blackened and streaked, her lungs aching. How had the fire started? She was still uncertain. She had checked the oven and all the dials were in the 'off' position, and in any event the fire had originated in the shop itself. No electrical appliances had been switched on, as far as she could tell. True, the microwave and coffee maker, situated behind the counter, were both badly burned, but the area most damaged appeared to be nearest the front door.

And this was where Rosa felt vulnerable. At closing time, she had turned the sign around to indicate the café was closed, but now it appeared that she hadn't locked the door, a matter she had remedied just now, after only a few seconds of risk assessment. No one no way was going to pin the blame for this on her.

In her hands Rosa held the charred fringes of her precious tapestry, almost completely consumed by the inferno. She reflected that many things in life were surplus to requirements or could be substituted with little trouble or emotion, if you had sufficient funds. Very few items were irreplaceable. Only then did she call the police and tell them what had happened. As she waited for them to arrive, she drew the scorched material close to her cheek and, for the first time in a while, she allowed the tears to flow.

17

ZOE SAT IN HER FLAT WITH the curtains closed. She didn't have any blinds, so she'd waited till now for it to be properly dark outside, although she had not been able to entirely block out the street lamp opposite. In front of her, on the low coffee table, was a scrabble board. She'd tipped all the letters out into the centre and inverted them, even the blanks. Next to her on the floor, close to her feet, was a gin and tonic, nestling by the wrapper of a Mars bar (double size). All dietary restrictions had been shelved as she prepared herself for this moment.

First she took out her phone and played the video of Brett's last moments, forcing herself to watch it right to the end, even though her eyes filled with tears part-way through. Then she skimmed her playlist until she located the Native American Indian flute music – perfect for what she had in mind. She'd found it when she'd written a piece on their diet – caribou, moose, bison – plenty of meat, making them the healthiest people alive, at the time.

Then she closed her eyes and began to breathe deeply, in and out through her nose, her ribcage rising and falling more with every breath.

'Brett,' she allowed herself to speak his name. And, as she did, she focused on an image of his face, as he had stood up to speak at the meeting weeks before. She concentrated so hard that she ground her teeth against each other. She allowed her jaw to slacken and tried again. 'Brett,' she said, 'are you there?'

A cool breeze swept around her ears, the music entered inside her head and her breathing slowed. She stretched her hands out over the table, then reached down and took one square scrabble piece, dropping it onto the cushion beside her. She focused again and suddenly she sniffed. There was an all-pervading smell of mango. She leaned over and took a second tile. 'Yes,' she whispered. 'I'm listening.'

Inside her head, she heard a voice say 'I'm here'; a third square selected.

Nothing happened for a while, then she sensed a bitter taste at the back of her throat. She took a fourth letter from the pile. Was that it? Just four letters? Not much to go on to solve a mystery. She opened her eyes. Across the room, the TV screen flickered to life then died again. Without even noticing, she found she had collected a fifth piece. 'Is that all?' she asked, closing her eyes again, waiting. You had to be patient with spirits. They had all the time in the world.

Just when Zoe thought it might be over, she felt a sensation inside her head, not unpleasant, like a tap of honey had been turned on and it was pouring all over her brain. With a gasp, she opened her eyes and found the sixth and last piece in the palm of her hand. She sat back, exhausted. Then she ran to open the curtains and switch on all the lights.

Wiping her face with the towel hanging in the kitchen, she shifted all the untouched pieces back into their bag, collected together the six chosen ones and laid them out, face up, on the board. 'B, Y, T, E, O, H.' She spoke their names aloud. God, she needed her friend Amy. Amy was brill at anagrams. Amy would have gone on *Countdown*, if there'd been no maths. But what would she tell Amy anyway? She couldn't tell anyone about this. They'd think she'd cracked.

Zoe set herself a target – five minutes to solve the puzzle; if not she'd Google it. No-brainer; someone out there would have done this before. She began to shift the letters around each other, trying different permutations; 'T, Y, O, H, B, E', followed by 'O, B, Y, E, T, H'. Then she saw it. 'Oh God,' she said. Rearranging the letters and separating them out, she finally read the message Brett had sent to her. 'THE BOY' it said.

PART TWO

AUGUST 2021

18

Judith sat in Constance's office on the morning of Nick's trial, her shoes kicked off, strands of fair hair escaping her loose ponytail.

'Do you know how much the food industry is worth, in the UK alone?' she asked.

Constance marvelled at how relaxed Judith was, given that in less than an hour they would be in court. Instead of poring over her notes, as many other barristers would, Judith wanted to chat about big-picture themes which were, at best, loosely connected to their case.

'You're going to tell me,' Constance said, pausing her review of her notes. She had learned that with Judith it was preferable to join in and roll with whatever she wanted to discuss. There was absolutely no point in trying to shut her down or persuade her to focus on something else.

'It contributes £30 billion to our economy and employs

almost half a million people.'

'That sounds like a lot. And I bet that's not including celebrity chefs or radio hosts.'

Judith smiled. 'You're probably right.'

'Why are you thinking about that now?' Constance asked.

'I was just wondering why anyone might want to kill Brett Ingram and I suppose there's only one place to start – and that's money; hence my question.'

'Money?'

'Most people are killed by someone they know and often by someone they love or loved. But when you're killed by a stranger, it's usually about money. I mean it may be about drugs, but that's about money. Or it may be about who's going to win a huge contract, but that's about money or who's going to be president, which is about power, which is about money.'

'Hang on. Why are we talking about *murder*, exactly?' Constance asked.

'Don't worry,' Judith laughed. 'I have read my brief. I know that Nick is not up for murder and I know our plan of action. It's just that…well, you've seen the pathologist's report. It's not exactly robust. So we have to be receptive, keep our minds open right till the very end.'

'I always do that. You usually prefer focusing on getting our client off.'

'Ah, but look what happened with Liz Sullivan?' Judith pointed a finger at Constance.

Judith was referring to the last case they had worked on together: a psychiatrist had been found dead at home, a local gamer had been the prime suspect and, for the first time in their partnership, Judith had been the one expanding the parameters of their investigation.

'There's no point in having experience if you don't put it to good use,' she said. 'And you're always telling me to evolve, to move with the times.'

Constance sighed and pushed away her tablet. 'You think one of the others – the panellists – killed him?' she said, knowing that this was precisely what Judith wanted her to say, to engage with her, to chew the fat by batting around alternative theories. Little things Judith had said, since their first coffee back in April, had indicated that this was nagging away at her.

Constance could refuse to play the game, but she would certainly lose and she also risked upsetting Judith – two reasons why this was inadvisable, especially given the close proximity of the trial. 'What, with one of those secret, sophisticated poisons you keep going on about?' she said.

'I think they're a colourful bunch and they know more than they're letting on. You know Zoe took her blog down in the aftermath of Brett's death and she was offline for almost two months.'

'So?'

'I thought it was just to give it an overhaul, but Greg did some digging. Turns out she'd received nasty messages, questioning the authenticity of her material.'

Constance raised her eyebrows. 'Is that such a surprise?'

'And Rosa Barrera's café was set on fire not long after. Luckily, she was there and put it out or it could have been much worse.'

'What has any of *that* got to do with this?' The words were out of Constance's mouth before she could stop them. But she did feel that Judith was getting distracted. And Judith always said she respected Constance challenging her. Even so, she held her breath while she waited for Judith's response.

'I'm not sure yet,' Judith said, her voice remaining even. She hadn't taken offence. 'It may be nothing. But that's two people who were there, when Brett Ingram died, having…professional difficulties, shortly afterwards. And you know I don't believe in coincidences.'

'Maybe it's Brett taking revenge on them, from beyond the grave?' Constance giggled.

'I don't know why I bother explaining myself to you,' Judith said, but her eyes were smiling and Constance knew she had judged her responses perfectly – on this occasion.

But Judith hadn't finished yet. 'Of course there's also the *Ambrosia* stuff Greg turned up,' she said.

Constance frowned. 'Ambrosia?'

'I told you – the big spend in Heart Foods' accounts, which the shareholders didn't like.'

'I'm not sure you told me the name. Why *Ambrosia*? Isn't it some kind of custard?'

'I think you'll find the rice pudding is still their bestseller. Some people eat it cold from the can, or so I'm told,' Judith laughed at her anecdote. '*Ambrosia* was the food of the gods, in Greek mythology,' she continued, more serious now. 'Legend has it that it was brought to them by doves and anyone who ate it would live forever. Presumably that's why the dairy company decided to use the name for its products.'

'How do you know these things?'

'You know I'm the product of an expensive private education. But a quick Google search will tell you the same in twenty seconds, for a fraction of the price.'

Constance shifted in her seat. It wasn't just about attending a superior school. Judith was interested in so many different things, her mind worked remarkably fast and made links Constance would never begin to contemplate. 'So what did Heart Foods spend the money on?' she asked.

'Greg couldn't find out very much. It was definitely a project associated with improving food quality, though. Diana Percival didn't mention it, did she?'

'No. But then she didn't offer much; just answered my questions, and even then a bit reluctantly.'

'I could ask her – Diana – I suppose, when she's in the box,' Judith reflected.

'Ask a question, when you don't know the answer?'

'I'm not sure I can see the harm in it on this occasion. If it's totally unconnected, there'll be no damage done.'

'Whatever you think's best,' Constance said, concluding that if Judith was prepared to contemplate breaking her own cardinal rule then there was really no point arguing with her this time around.

'I'm not sure I know entirely with this case.' Judith reached for a glass of water and drank it down. 'What I do know is that a man is dead and nothing will bring him back and that's very sad,' she continued. 'I also think I need to close my eyes for five minutes and focus on my opening speech.'

***

As she headed for court, Judith spied Andy Chambers seated in the corridor, his head buried in papers, his hair flopping over his eyes. Some years back, she had defended a case which Andy had prosecuted. Then, only last year, he had been selected as the legal brain to analyse cases filmed in the *cameras in the courtroom* pilot scheme. He had ended up commenting heavily on Judith's performance and that of the presiding judge, Judge Nolan, in a high-profile murder case. Judith had not enjoyed the experience or the associated fame, which had dipped, at times, towards notoriety. Thankfully, any interest in her had settled down within a week or two of the next case to receive the Court TV treatment. But Judith was not one to forget disloyalty, which was how she viewed Andy's conduct, even though she acknowledged that he had also suffered at the hands of the bulldozing media machine.

'Hello Andy,' Judith said, pausing next to him. 'You decided to return to the real world, after all?'

As Andy looked up, his report slid down his knees and almost fell to the floor.

'Judith? Nice to see you again,' he stammered, attempting a smile. 'Well, the pilot finished. You know that. A man has to work.'

'They'll call you back, when it finally goes live?'

'I'd like to think so. I did receive lots of positive feedback and quite a lot of fan mail, actually. But I'm told they're fickle in television. You know, they follow fads.'

'I see. So you returned to the more mundane arena of criminal justice. I should warn you. I heard that our judge is a great friend of Judge Nolan. I believe they studied together for their Bar exams.'

Andy's smile weakened.

'Only joking,' Judith said and she tapped his elbow lightly and headed into court.

***

Judith sat down in her allotted place in the wood-panelled courtroom and glanced around her. The public gallery, only a few metres away, was almost full and the low hum of conversation from its occupants spilled over to her. Nick's wife, Lisa, was seated in the front row. She kept turning around, evidently seeking out Nick, who had not yet arrived.

Judith could not begin to guess who the rest were. Most likely at least one reporter, a law student or two and there would usually be members of the family of the deceased. But there was no one there who resembled a grieving relative, which was unsurprising, as Constance had told her that Brett's parents were both dead and he had no siblings or children. She immediately felt the imbalance of the situation and it bothered her; that there was no one there for Brett.

Then she noticed two gentlemen sitting behind Lisa, wearing smart casual clothes, talking quietly to each other. Both were white and middle-aged, one with a prominent, aquiline nose. Often, strange as it may seem, members of the public, without any connection to a case, came along, purely out of interest. While these two men might fall within that category, Judith preferred to imagine that they may have some association with Heart Foods. It was important to her that justice was seen to be done.

Judith pulled her notebooks from her briefcase and arranged them next to the files her clerk had already set in her place. This was the worst moment, just before the case began; wondering if she had prepared sufficiently, if there was anything obvious she had missed, even some tiny clue she might have picked up. At the same time, she was hopeful that her plans for the other side's witnesses would be successful, the jury would be receptive, that her own witnesses would withstand the considerable pressures and perform as she hoped.

This wasn't just a one-woman show; for success in a trial, she had to rely on a whole host of complete strangers, some of them hostile, to behave in the way she desired, but with no guarantees; a show she had scripted almost entirely alone, but now sought to put on for the viewers, without even a dress rehearsal. Anyone who said 'don't act with children or animals' should try this, she thought.

Sometimes, perversely, it helped Judith's concentration to take a few moments and switch off from the case completely, just before the start of a trial. As long as, at the moment of truth, she could switch back on, which she invariably did. So when thoughts of Greg, his face, his hands, his voice came into her mind, she didn't push them away. She was pleased he had been content to pick things up again without looking back; she hadn't wanted to revisit her reasons for ending things last time around and if Greg wondered, he had the good sense not to ask. This was what she required – a partnership of equals and without regret for things already past; *co-existence not dependence*, although she was happy to accept more support than usual sometimes.

Take this morning, for example. Knowing how preoccupied Judith was and how she was unlikely to eat again till the evening, Greg had prepared an array of breakfast choices, laid them out and not so much as coughed when she eschewed most of them and plumped for toast and jam. He had simply collected up the rejected pancakes, muesli and raspberries, smiled and said that what he didn't eat himself, he would take in to work for his staff. He really was too good for her. Maybe, once the trial was over, they would go on holiday. That would be nice.

Judith couldn't remember the last time she had taken a

holiday. Not a real one, where you packed a suitcase with clothes you would never wear in the UK – tops with spaghetti straps, floaty dresses and open-toed sandals – and looked forward to a day stretching out without deadlines, supplemented by irresistible ice cream and exotic cocktails. Where to go? She would usually plump for Europe, probably Italy. Then she could dip into some real culture at the same time. She suspected Greg might prefer somewhere further afield and perhaps it wouldn't be too awful for her to try something new, but she mustn't give in to him too much. So, Italy first perhaps, then somewhere else of Greg's choice.

Someone touched her shoulder.

'Everything OK?' Constance mouthed, as she settled herself in the row behind.

Judith nodded. Of course she was OK, with Constance there: dependable, determined, indefatigable. Constance opened up her laptop and although Judith couldn't see the screen, she knew Connie would have everything relevant to hand and be ready to step in and prompt, should Judith falter.

Just then Nick, their client, entered the courtroom, flanked by two police officers. After a brief exchange of nods with her and Constance and then with his wife, he sat down and looked around at his surroundings. Judith knew from Constance that his mood had not improved since they had visited him, and Lisa had said she could hardly persuade him to eat. The pleasure he had previously taken from preparing and eating food had been completely destroyed by the allegations against him and this was apparent from his hollow cheeks and gaunt frame.

Judith rose to her feet, together with everyone else, as Mr Justice Linton entered. The learned judge had recently been censured for criticising the evidence of a young woman who had accused her boss of sexual assault in a case which came before him. Judge Linton had described her as 'a sensationalist' with an 'overactive imagination'. The boss had been acquitted but the newspapers had gone to town on the story, declaring that the judge's comments would only prevent other genuine victims from coming forward.

'Is that good for us?' Constance had asked, when they discovered that Judge Linton would be in the driving seat, and Judith had shrugged. She disliked being in front of judges whose views had been publicly denounced in the recent past. In her experience, they were either unduly sensitive, and so allowed anything and everything to pass unchallenged for fear of more condemnation or, as she suspected might be the case with Judge Linton, they hunkered down and took every opportunity to demonstrate that they were unrepentant and unchanged.

'This case is very different from that one,' was all Judith managed, reflecting that the powers that be, those unseen scribblers who allocated the cases, had probably decided that an accidental poisoning case was a relatively safe forum in which Judge Linton could begin his rehabilitation.

Andy Chambers introduced himself and Judith, then launched into his opening speech and Judith finally switched off any and all diversionary thoughts and tuned in to his words.

'My Lord. This is a tragic case,' Andy began, 'tragic because the death of Brett Ingram was so easily avoidable. If the defendant, Nick Demetriou, had only taken the most *basic* level of care with the food he provided on the 13th of April, then Mr Ingram would be with us today and his company, Heart Foods, one of the biggest British success stories of the last decade, would still have its founder and CEO at its helm.' Andy let out a sigh, which Judith considered might have been more suitably delivered in an episode of *Bridgerton,* and Mr Justice Linton's raised eyebrows hinted that he shared her view. But Andy continued unabated.

'It's not disputed that, on the afternoon of 13th April 2021, Mr Ingram attended a public meeting at Tanners' Hall in Haringey. He had arrived there late morning and Mr Demetriou had served Mr Ingram and a number of other guests a light lunch. Shortly afterwards, Mr Ingram felt unwell. Even so, he insisted to his assistant, a Miss Diana Percival, that he would keep going. But, shortly after 2pm, as he introduced the meeting, he collapsed and died. The prosecution will show some film of Mr Ingram's last moments, captured by a video camera which was recording the event.

'Now, Mr Ingram had an allergy to shellfish and had been very clear in his instructions regarding food for lunch. Mr Demetriou, the defendant, paid scant regard to those instructions and the expert you will hear from, Dr Leigh, will explain that traces of shellfish, in the sandwiches served by the defendant, killed Mr Ingram. In addition, the fact that all the food had been kept without refrigeration for at least two hours before it was consumed, may have contributed to the terrible consequences and, in any event, constituted a clear breach of health and safety regulations.

'When Mr Ingram writhed around, in terrible agony, Mr Demetriou did not go to his aid. Instead, realising what must have happened and seeking to cover up the part he had played, he left Mr Ingram dying on the floor and ran to the kitchen to destroy as much evidence as he could, throwing the remaining food into black bags and pouring boiling water over all the exposed surfaces. When police on the scene asked him what he was doing, he said "I'm cleaning up". That is exactly what he was doing, members of the jury. He was *cleaning up*, in order to cover his tracks!'

Judith watched Nick while Andy was speaking. After his initial limited interest in his environs, he had bowed his head, and now his eyes were half-closed too. Constance had given him a notebook and pen and urged him to jot things down if he heard anything controversial, but his hands were empty and she could see the top of the book peeking out from his pocket. *Innocent until proven guilty.* That was what the law said. But you had to be resilient to withstand the pressure, not only of the trial, but also the finger pointing, the absent friends, the ostracism which all accompanied such a serious accusation. As Constance had pointed out, he was fortunate he had his family to support him through this challenging time.

Lady Justice understood how hard it was to stay strong in the face of adversity. A statue in her honour stood tall on the roof of the Old Bailey, sporting a spiky crown, the scales of justice in her right hand and the sword of retribution in her left. Other iterations of Justice existed of course – other portraits and carved effigies. Many of them wore a blindfold to indicate imperviousness to outside influences like politics or celebrity culture. A well-intended but poorly thought-out metaphor, in Judith's opinion. It was so much easier to interpret the blindfolded image as the law being unable to find its way through to the truth. No, if statues had any value at all – and they seemed to be coming in for a lot of criticism these days – then their symbolism had to be crystal-clear and, for Judith, the Amazonian version of Lady Justice, standing 200 feet above their heads, said it all.

It was funny though, Judith mused, that we had no problem with the embodiment of justice being female, centuries before women were allowed to practise as lawyers, although, from her infrequent visits to church, as a child, she remembered that the

169

Hebrews had many women judges.

Judith watched Andy sit down, the judge finish making notes and the faces of the twelve jurors turn in her direction. Even as she admonished herself for day-dreaming further than her rigid discipline regime would usually permit, she reflected upon the women who had come before her and fought so hard to sit in her seat: Ivy Williams, Helena Normanton, Stella Thomas. Harnessing all of their energies, she stood up to begin.

'My learned friend was absolutely right to describe Mr Ingram's death as a tragedy; the death of a healthy man at the tender age of forty-one, a man who had given so much to society, a man destined for a long and distinguished career in business. We should take note of this and remember the man and his achievements. However, this should not detract from the need to search dispassionately for the truth through the evidence provided in this courtroom, and to reach a decision consistent with that evidence. Mr Demetriou, the defendant, a caterer and food importer by trade, is also a pillar of the local community. He belongs to the "Just Call Us" network, a charitable venture where services – food, drink, entertainment, flowers – are supplied free of charge to deserving families, to allow them to have the celebration of their dreams when they would not otherwise be able to pay for it. He is a man of modest means, a family man, a man who takes pride in his work.

'It is accepted that there were the tiniest traces of seafood in the kitchen at Tanners' Hall, totally unsurprising for an establishment which sees a large footfall. The hall had been hired out the night before Mr Ingram's death and there was another booking for 6pm that evening. We say that the prosecution cannot establish beyond reasonable doubt that those minute amounts came from food

Mr Demetriou provided or that they were linked to Mr Ingram's death. In fact, there is no evidence that Mr Ingram's allergy, if it existed, triggered his death. The pathologist's report is unclear on both counts.

'It is also perfectly right that we should be able to rely on cafés, restaurants and caterers to feed us in a safe and responsible manner, ensuring they comply with good hygiene practices and any instructions from customers regarding allergens. But Mr Demetriou did exactly as he was asked. He is here today not because he did anything wrong, but because we don't like deaths which go unexplained, especially when a high-profile person is involved. I urge you, therefore, to listen to the evidence and evaluate it and I am sure that when you do you will agree that Mr Demetriou was not even negligent, let alone grossly negligent. In those circumstances, he cannot be held responsible for Mr Ingram's death.'

During the break, before the first witness was sworn in, Andy leaned over towards Judith.

'I heard you tried to run *the blame culture* argument in your last case. Then you abandoned it, because it was never going to work.'

Judith said nothing. She wasn't going to share any intelligence with Andy, especially not after he had spilled so many secrets on national TV last year.

'I should be pleased, then. It will make my job so much easier,' he continued. 'And thanks for confirming that your client never made any money from his work, although I noticed his wife had a rather nice ring – bit gaudy, but some people like these things – and a dazzling necklace. Much easier, then, to conclude that he cut corners.'

Judith ignored Andy, but once he had shifted back to his side of the bench she stole a glance at Lisa. As Andy had pointed out, and Judith was cross with herself for failing to notice, Lisa wore a long, sparkly heart-shaped pendant, encrusted with what appeared to be a number of precious stones. Although there was no reason, in principle, why Lisa's choice of jewellery – or clothes, for that matter – should make any difference to her husband's prospects, and there was no way of knowing if the necklace had any value, Andy's comment hit home.

Sometimes the reason a case was won or lost turned on impressions the jury formed, especially of the accused. In circumstances where she hoped to present Nick to the court as cautious and abstemious, this was an unwelcome expression of glamour and frivolity by his wife, and Judith made a mental note to take it up with Lisa at an appropriate moment.

19

JUDITH WATCHED THE FIRST witness for the prosecution, Sergeant Thomas, stride across the courtroom and take the stand. In textbook how-to-address-the-jury fashion, the police officer angled her head and shoulders towards them, as she prepared to speak. Before her promotion, Sergeant Thomas had helped investigate some of Judith and Constance's previous cases, but their paths hadn't often crossed, as Chief Inspector Charlie Dawson had usually been in charge and given any necessary evidence in court. Dawson had confided in Judith that he was unwell some months back, so she wasn't surprised to find another police officer in his place. But Sergeant Thomas was an unknown quantity. Assessing how this witness responded to Judith's opponent would be invaluable to her in gauging how best to approach Sergeant Thomas in cross-examination.

'Sergeant Thomas, you attended at Tanners' Hall around 2.30 on the 13th of April,' Andy began.

'I did.'

'What did you find when you arrived there?'

'There was an ambulance outside and a large crowd exiting the hall and congregating – more than fifty people, I'd say. Inside, the paramedics were lifting Mr Ingram onto a stretcher. He wasn't moving and they had a defibrillator with the pads on his chest.'

'Was he still alive at that point?'

'I understood that his heart had stopped, but they hadn't given up trying to resuscitate him.'

'What happened next?'

'There were a few people still inside the hall. I learned afterwards that they were all speakers for the event. I asked one of them, a Mr Mark Sumner, what had happened. He directed me towards Dr Adrian Edge, one of the other guests.'

'What did Dr Edge say?'

'It's all in my statement, but if you want me to be accurate about the words they used, then I need to check my notes. I have them here.'

Andy turned to Judith, who nodded her agreement and Sergeant Thomas consulted a small notebook, which she pulled from her pocket. 'Dr Edge said Mr Ingram had collapsed suddenly.' She read for a few seconds before looking up at the jury again. 'He said that he'd thought it might have been a heart attack, but he wasn't sure. I asked for more details and he told me that Mr Ingram had been breathless. Then Miss Diana Percival – she was Mr Ingram's assistant – she said he had an allergy to shellfish.'

'Brett Ingram's PA came forward and told you that he had an allergy to shellfish?' Andy asked.

'Yes.'

'Did she say anything else?'

'She repeated it a few times, until she saw I made a note. She seemed very upset.'

Judith observed the jury, watching Sergeant Thomas. They were all focused and listening hard, as they should be at the beginning of any trial. But the police officer was making it easy for them.

'What did you do next?' Andy asked.

'Once I'd checked that no one was in any immediate danger, I went into the kitchen, where I found the defendant, Mr Demetriou.'

'Just Mr Demetriou?'

'Yes.'

'No other staff?'

'No.'

'What was he doing?'

'He had a black plastic bag in his hand – a bin bag – and he was carrying it out of the back door of the building.'

'What did you do?'

'I called out to him, "Excuse me, sir" – something like that – but he didn't answer.'

'He didn't answer?'

'He carried on walking. I asked him to stop, but he didn't.'

'What happened then?'

'I followed him outside and I asked him to stop again. And this time he did.'

'You spoke to him on three occasions before he acknowledged you?'

'Yes.'

'Was there any chance he didn't hear you?'

'No.'

'He wasn't wearing headphones, for example?'

'No, nothing like that.'

'And you were wearing your uniform?'

'Yes. Same as today. Well, I would have had my hat on too.'

Andy nodded and pursed his lips, to reinforce the significance of Sergeant Thomas' answers.

'Once Mr Demetriou had stopped,' he continued, 'what happened then?'

'I asked what he was doing and he said he was throwing the rubbish away. I asked if he knew that Mr Ingram had been taken seriously ill and he said *yes*. I told him to leave everything in the kitchen, as it was.'

'I see. Did the defendant say where he was throwing the rubbish?'

'No, but his car was in the car park. I believed he was taking it to his car.'

'To his car?'

'Yes.'

'Were there no dustbins on site?'

'I looked around the exterior later on and I noticed there were bins around the side of the property, but that was not the direction the defendant was walking in when I approached him.'

Judith made some notes, her pen moving slowly and laboriously. Sometimes the physical act, writing out the words on the page, led her to make connections inside her head, with other parts of the evidence.

'What happened next?' Andy asked.

'The defendant came back inside, put down the bag, then picked up the kettle and began to pour boiling water over the work surfaces. I asked what he thought he was doing and he said he was *cleaning up*.'

'Cleaning up?'

'That's exactly what he said. I made sure I wrote it down.' Sergeant Thomas pointed to her notebook to emphasise the point. 'I took the kettle from him,' she continued. 'I said something like, "Didn't you hear what I said? We must leave everything alone".'

'And then?'

'He…left the kettle where it was and followed me back into the hall.'

'How did Mr Demetriou seem?'

'He was…jumpy, is how I'd describe him.'

'Jumpy. Might that have been because he was worried that Brett Ingram's collapse was connected with his allergy to shellfish?'

Judge Linton slammed his hand down on his desk and fixed Andy with a ferocious stare. Judith had begun to leave her seat to object, but it was clear that her own protest was unnecessary.

'The jury will ignore that last question please,' the judge said. 'It is not permitted or, in fact, possible, for Sergeant Thomas to know what was going on inside the defendant's head. Mr Chambers, you are an advocate of considerable experience, or so your résumé would have us believe. On what possible basis could you justify breaching the rules so comprehensively, by asking the witness such a completely outrageous leading question?'

Judith almost felt sorry for Andy, as he faced the judge's ire and struggled to find a suitable answer that would assist his own position but not give more offence. In the end, he gave up attempting the former and settled for 'Forgive me, My Lord. I was carried away. It won't happen again.'

'Good,' the judge said, nodding to Sergeant Thomas and returning to his notes.

'Did you interview Mr Demetriou at any time about the events of the day?' Andy returned to his questions, with only the slightest tremor in his voice.

'In the hall, when he followed me, like I asked,' Sergeant Thomas said, 'he told me that he had seen Mr Ingram collapse. He asked me if he was going to be all right.'

'Anything else?'

'He didn't say much else.'

'Did you ask Mr Demetriou about the food he had served?'

'My priority was to secure the kitchen,' Sergeant Thomas said, 'to make sure no one else touched or removed anything, so I sent another officer to keep guard. Then I was keen to get back to continue my investigation.'

'What happened to the bag Mr Demetriou was holding?'

'It was given to forensics. There's a list of exactly what they found inside in one of the reports.'

'Thank you. No further questions.'

Andy smiled at Judith as he relinquished control of Sergeant Thomas. She knew this was part of the show, designed to shake her up, by indicating he was more than content with the performance of his witness, despite the judge's intervention. And it was true that Sergeant Thomas had given her evidence, so far, both clearly and coherently, and she had an air of earnestness, which would appeal to the jury. If only Judith could use that intensity to Nick's advantage. She took a moment to read through the notes she had written, then, with a nod to Andy to acknowledge him handing her the metaphorical baton, she stood up and faced Sergeant Thomas.

20

'SERGEANT THOMAS, HELLO,' Judith began. 'I'm going to start at the end, if that's all right, but sometimes that's the best place to start.'

The police officer nodded but Judith could immediately see that she was on her guard. There seemed little point, then, in taking things slowly or gently. She may as well dive right in.

'You've just said,' Judith continued, 'that my client told you, back in the main hall, *after* your conversation in the kitchen, that he had seen Mr Ingram collapse and he asked if he was all right.'

'Yes.'

'And when you arrived a few minutes earlier, Mr Ingram was on a stretcher. You said the paramedics had the defibrillator out, his heart had stopped, that they were trying to resuscitate him, to bring him back to life?'

'Yes.'

'How many people have you seen die, close up?'

Sergeant Thomas gulped and her cheeks flushed red.

'A few,' she said, after a short pause. 'Maybe ten.'

'I'm not talking about coming along *after* they're already dead. I mean, watching someone who's alive one minute and then they're dead.'

Sergeant Thomas thought for a moment. 'Just two, I think,' she said.

'How did that feel?' Judith asked.

Andy leaped up. 'My Lord, this is clearly distressing for the witness and completely irrelevant.'

'I'm sure Sergeant Thomas has faced many difficult challenges as a serving police officer,' Judge Linton said, without even looking at Andy, 'and is robust enough to answer the question, although it seems to me to be on the far periphery of relevance. Answer the question Sergeant, please.'

'It was difficult,' Sergeant Thomas said.

'Difficult?' Judith repeated.

'Upsetting.'

'Did it shock you?'

'Yes.'

'Did it stay with you afterwards?'

'Yes.'

'And, as his lordship said, you're a trained police officer; you're told to expect that death may arise as part of your working day, any day?'

'You hope not but…yes.'

'The behaviour you just described from Mr Demetriou – that he was "jumpy" heading outside – if I told you that he had just seen Mr Ingram die in front of him, as you say, he admitted to you he had seen Mr Ingram collapse and feared the worst, hence the "Is he all right?" question to you. Do you accept that might have caused my client – someone who is not used to dying or death – that might have caused him to be upset and jumpy and shocked?'

'I accept that's possible, but then I would have expected him to be sitting down somewhere quietly, not cleaning the kitchen, not trying to dispose of evidence.'

Oh Sergeant Thomas was good. Not just sincere; she had an answer for everything, was willing to explain and extrapolate, not just stick to the facts. But that could be her undoing.

Judith moved on. 'Now you've accepted the possibility that Mr Demetriou's jumpiness, his desire for fresh air to breathe, could have been caused by seeing the dramatic demise of Mr Ingram, let's examine the rest, shall we? What was in the bag he was carrying?'

'Like I said, it's in one of the reports. It was the leftover food from lunch and the containers it came in: trays, plastic bottles – that kind of thing.'

'When a caterer works at Tanners' Hall, do you know what the policy is for clearing up?'

'No.'

'If the usher could hand Sergeant Thomas a copy of the first document in His Lordship's bundle? Thank you. Sergeant, these are the rules of hire of Tanners' Hall, and Mr Demetriou was familiar with them, as he often provided food at the hall. Can you read out rule number five please?'

Sergeant Thomas frowned down at the sheet of paper. 'All food, packaging and waste must be removed from the site at the end of the rental period,' she read.

'Could you read it a second time for me, please – a little slower?'

Sergeant Thomas looked up. Judith smiled and nodded. She could sense Sergeant Thomas' frustration at having to go through this process, but also that she would stick with it. The system provided for her evidence to be tested and she would do what she must to assist.

'All food, packaging and waste must be removed from the site at the end of the rental period,' Sergeant Thomas repeated, although she rattled it off even quicker than the first time.

'That wording is very clear, wouldn't you say?'

'Yes.'

'Do you know why they have that rule?'

'They want to keep the place tidy?'

'Anything else?'

'Maybe they don't want mice?'

'Good guess. Mrs June Grant, the manager of the hall, has advised – and will come here and say, if this is in dispute – that to avoid problems with pests, all rubbish must be removed completely, not even placed in the on-site bins. When rubbish is placed in the on-site bins, they quickly overfill and overflow, attracting some rather nasty pests. Mr Demetriou accepts that he was walking towards his car with the rubbish, as you, eagle-eyed, had spotted. He will say he was taking the rubbish home, as he always did when he catered at Tanners' Hall.'

'I can only report on what I saw.'

'Of course. Now you testified that when you came across my client, he was in the process of leaving the kitchen through an exit leading to the car park, so he had his back to you?'

'Yes.'

'And you mentioned that you asked Mr Demetriou to stop three times, twice inside the kitchen, the third time outside the back door, and he only obliged on the third occasion, and my learned friend Mr Chambers asked you a very sensible question next. He asked if Mr Demetriou was wearing anything in his ears, so that he might not have heard you, and you said no.'

'That's right. He wasn't.'

'And I know you said the contents of the black bag were listed in a report. I don't want to go there now. I can later on, or if Mr Chambers insists, but do you remember if there were any glass or china items listed as being in the bag?

'I don't believe there were.'

'Now I want you to think hard about my next question, really think back to that day in the kitchen in April. Close your eyes if you like and picture the layout of the kitchen – everything in that room. Think hard. Was there any reason you can think of, leaving aside for a moment that a crowd of people – you mentioned at least fifty – were pouring out of the building – "congregating" you said – and the paramedics were running about... In that kitchen, clearing up after lunch, can you think of any reason why my client – no headphones but he had his back to you – might not have heard you on the first or indeed the second occasion you called out to him?'

Sergeant Thomas looked across at Nick, and Judith held her breath. She had her own answer to this question scribbled on her pad, but it would be so much better for Nick if Sergeant Thomas got there herself. *Come on*, she whispered under her breath. *Come on, remember.* Sergeant Thomas was fair. Sergeant Thomas was trying to tell the truth. She looked back at the jury and then coughed into her hand, but she didn't say anything.

'Sergeant?' Judith was itching to supply the response she was seeking but she held on just a fraction longer.

'I think maybe the dishwasher was on,' Sergeant Thomas said.

Judith hid her delight with a low cough. 'You think?' she said.

'I believe so. I remember later on that I opened it up and there were glasses and plates inside and they were clean.'

'The dishwasher was switched on. Thank you,' Judith repeated. 'And was it an old model or one of the new, silent types?'

'I couldn't say but it was making some noise, a small amount. Not enough that he wouldn't have heard me, though.'

'All right. That's your opinion. But there was something else, wasn't there?'

'No. I don't think so.'

'In your evidence to Mr Chambers, you mentioned that my client heard you speaking to him once you were both outdoors. Then you returned inside and my client "picked up the kettle and began to pour boiling water over the work surface". Is that correct?'

'Yes.'

'How did you know the water was boiling hot?'

'There was steam coming out of the kettle.' Sergeant Thomas hardly moved her head as she spoke now. She wants to tell the truth, Judith thought, but she also has to think of her own reputation, to defend evidence she had set down in writing some weeks back and had sworn was true. She was a police officer, after all. And as she gave her answer, Sergeant Thomas allowed her shoulders to rise ever so slightly. Only now, too late, she understood the reason for the question. Judith decided not to confront her head on, this time around, not to make her choose between the truth and her good name.

'Is it possible,' Judith said, 'and I put it no higher than this, that when you first entered the kitchen – you've accepted Mr Demetriou had his back to you – you spoke to him, there was noise in the background from the people exiting, noise from the paramedics, you've now told us the dishwasher was running… Is it possible that the kettle which, one minute later you say was steaming, could the kettle also have been switched on? And we all know how noisy some kettles can be.'

Sergeant Thomas looked at Andy for the first time and her lip trembled.

'I don't remember the kettle being on, but it's possible,' she said.

Judith was more than satisfied with this exchange in the circumstances, but she was careful not to give away any emotion. She moved on. 'If we could go back to your evidence one more time to pick up on another point, to clarify things for the court, for the jury. You said just a moment ago that Mr Demetriou was "trying to dispose of evidence". When you asked Mr Demetriou to give the bag of rubbish to you, what did he do?'

'He gave it to me.'

'He didn't object or try to remove anything from the bag?'

'No.'

'Given what you now know: that Mr Demetriou was upset, shocked, shaken from seeing Mr Ingram's collapse, but knew that the manager of the hall was a stickler for cleanliness, and that he was *contractually obliged* to remove all refuse from the hall, and that it is possible – your words – he did not hear you speak to him, do you still say that Mr Demetriou was trying to *hide* the contents of that bag when he walked outside into the fresh air?'

'That was how it seemed to me, at the time.'

'Do you accept now that the impression you held at the time, might have been the wrong one – the impression that Mr Demetriou was being secretive, trying to conceal something.'

'I trust my instincts. That was what they told me then. The other stuff you're telling me now, how do I know it's true?'

Judith paused. Sergeant Thomas' expression was less guarded now. Her shoulders were drawn back, her head held high and her eyes were wide. Now she was prepared to fight. But Judith could deal with that, she was prepared to engage and see where that led.

'All right,' Judith said, 'So, sticking with your instincts then – important attributes for any police officer – at what stage during your time at the hall did you form the view that Mr Ingram had been unlawfully killed?'

'I didn't…I didn't form that view.'

'What did you think had happened to him?'

'I thought he had probably had a heart attack, but then, with Diana Percival talking about allergies, I was keeping an open mind.'

'Let's say that, for example, you had arrived and Mr Ingram had been lying on the ground with a knife in his chest, what steps would you have taken then?'

'I would've moved everyone away from Mr Ingram's body, I would have called for forensic examination and done what I could to secure the crime scene.'

'What does that mean "secure the crime scene"?' Judith asked, knowing it was a gift of a question for Sergeant Thomas, but that was fine. Judith wanted her to feel at ease.

'Making sure people didn't come in and out,' Sergeant Thomas replied, 'to ensure there's no contamination of evidence.'

'That didn't happen here, did it?'

'He wasn't lying on the floor with a knife in his chest.'

'No, he wasn't. If you can answer my question, please. No criticism is being levelled, but you didn't "secure the crime scene" when you first arrived?'

'No.'

'Because you didn't believe it was a crime scene?'

'That's right.'

'Your…instinctive reaction, you could say, was that this wasn't a crime scene – Mr Ingram's death was from natural causes.'

'That was before I had investigated.'

Judith had to hand it to Sergeant Thomas. She would not give an inch. And she just had to keep on explaining. But a little more probing and she might regret being quite so expansive.

'What happened once you had the opportunity to investigate?' Judith asked.

'I found out, like I said, that there was this allergy thing.'

'Do you now believe that Mr Ingram died because of a food allergy?'

'I…it's not my place to believe.'

'You're a witness for the prosecution, on behalf of the police, in a case against Mr Demetriou for gross negligence manslaughter.'

'I'm not a lawyer…or a doctor.'

'All right, I'll put it another way. If the prosecution case is correct, then your instinct was wrong, wasn't it? And if it was wrong regarding the circumstances of Mr Ingram's death, then it could just as easily have been wrong about Mr Demetriou's motivation for cleaning up. That's all I'm saying. We're all human, Sergeant Thomas. Sometimes, we judge things incorrectly, especially in the heat of the moment. It would be wrong to send a man to prison solely on the basis of *your instinct*, which you have just accepted has, in the past, sometimes been wrong.'

Sergeant Thomas was silent. She knew that she had said too much, but, more than that, Judith could sense her confusion. She could not work out how she had reached this place, where she had taken a wrong turn, how she could have navigated differently. Judith allowed sufficient time for the silence to take on meaning, before continuing.

'From the auditorium where Mr Ingram died, how did you get to the kitchen?'-

'There's a door at the back leads out into a hallway and then there's another door to the kitchen.'

'And was the door to the kitchen open or closed?'

'I can't remember.'

'Was it locked?'

'No.'

'And the hallway – that was where the public entered and exited?'

'Yes.'

'So members of the public could also have entered the kitchen, the way you did?'

'Yes, but I didn't see any of them in there.'

'What did you say to the other eyewitnesses – Mark Sumner, Dr Edge and others? We'll be hearing from them later in the trial.'

'I asked them all to provide contact details. Dr Edge was interviewed then and there. The others were too upset. Their statements were taken later on, mostly the following day.'

'Is it true that one of the eyewitnesses had already left the building?'

'Zoe Whitman had gone. We caught up with her, maybe on the Thursday.'

'So, you accepted that *those* witnesses, the panellists who had been appearing with Mr Ingram, might be shaken up and need time to recover before you spoke to them?'

'Yes.'

'Did you search any of them?'

'What do you mean?'

'Let's take Dr Edge, for example, who had been sitting close to

Mr Ingram when he collapsed, and who ran over to help him. Did you ask him to turn out his pockets?'

'Of course not.'

'Or Rosa Barrera, who was seated right beside Mr Ingram, their arms almost touching. Was she asked to empty out her handbag?'

'No.'

'But Mr Demetriou?'

'I thought he was trying to hide evidence.'

'You've already said that. Let's leave aside your perceived justification. What did you ask Mr Demetriou to do?'

'Like I said, he had to leave the bag of rubbish behind and stop pouring boiling water over everything.'

'Did you ask him to turn out his pockets?'

'I...'

'It's a simple question, yes or no.'

Andy jumped to his feet. 'My Lord, the defence is not maintaining that any evidence was improperly obtained, so this questioning is simply irrelevant.'

'My Lord,' Judith countered. 'The prosecution is asserting that Mr Demetriou behaved in a furtive manner, when confronted at the hall, to support their theory that he was covering something up. My questions are designed to challenge that and explain his behaviour, and it's perfectly proper I should be allowed to do so.'

'Continue, Ms Burton,' the judge said. 'Sergeant Thomas, please answer the question.'

Sergeant Thomas fiddled with the buttons on her pristine uniform. 'I asked to see what he had in his pockets,' she said.

'And he obliged, he emptied them out?'

'Yes.'

'Did you find anything of interest?'

'Just a handkerchief, wallet, car keys.'

'No whole lobster or crab sticks or seafood flavoured sweets?'

'No.'

The sergeant was no longer standing upright. She had turned to face Judith and her chin had sunk towards her chest.

'What else did you ask Mr Demetriou to do?' Judith asked.

'To provide details of the staff working with him.'

'Which he did?'

'Yes.'

'Did you take a statement from him?'

'I asked him some more questions, but he didn't reply.'

'He didn't reply.'

'He said he felt unwell. I brought him a chair and he sat down at the back of the hall.'

'Until you told him he could leave?'

'Yes.'

'When was that?'

'Around 3.30.'

'3.30?'

'Yes.'

'You made Mr *Demetriou*,' Judith emphasised Nick's surname, 'sit at the back of the hall for a further hour before you allowed him to leave?'

'Yes.'

'Were any of the other eyewitnesses kept until 3.30?'

'No.'

'Mr Demetriou was the last?'

'Yes.'

'Thank you. No more questions.'

***

'What did you think?' Constance asked Judith. They had returned to her office after court. Judith kicked off her shoes, downed her second glass of water and tucked into a packet of salt and vinegar crisps.

'I don't know,' she said. 'I'm the one busy talking. However proficient I am at multi-tasking, I draw the line at talking, listening and analysing my own performance simultaneously. What did *you* think?'

Constance smiled. 'I thought the judge was on our side.'

'It's early days and I think he might only have been on our side because I was being pushy. On the basis of today's performance, I could've asked Sergeant Thomas for her bra size and he would have made her answer.'

'Pushy, you?' Constance laughed.

'I was racking my brains through Andy's questions,' Judith said, 'trying to remember who Sergeant Thomas reminds me of, and I finally got there as I stood up.'

'Who's that then?'

'There used to be this police drama on TV, well before your time – *Juliet Bravo* it was called – fictional police force headed up by a very principled, no-nonsense woman.'

Connie nodded. 'Sergeant Thomas impressed you then?'

'She looks like the actress, that's all I meant.'

'Oh. And I thought *you* thought she was a racist.'

Judith looked at Constance then. With another solicitor, she might have said something sharp or made a joke, but not with Constance, not with someone who lived and breathed the consequences of having a skin a different colour from most of her colleagues.

'Is that what *you* thought?' Judith asked.

'Yes,' Constance said. 'Maybe? She didn't make Rosa stay.'

'That's true, although I suspect it would be difficult to make Rosa Barrera do anything she didn't want to do. I am worried that, despite the possibility that the jurors will have been with me, as you are, they will understand that Sergeant Thomas might have been a tiny bit overenthusiastic and targeted Nick because she felt she could – he wasn't a celebrity, he isn't middle class and of course he has a foreign-sounding name. Even so, her upright conduct in court – she was impressive, you must agree – will help justify what she did at the scene, even if they accept that was not so honourable.'

'Which bit of *what she did at the scene*, do you mean?'

'Oh come on,' Judith said. 'I can just see it now, in my mind's eye. April 13th, Brett Ingram being stretchered out. He's already dead although the paramedics won't give up. There's nothing for her to do, but she doesn't want to waste the opportunity of showing what a great police officer she is. So she hovers behind the kitchen door, peering around it, and there he is, our second generation immigrant client, scrubbing down the work surfaces. Is he just a caterer trying to clear up? No! He's covering up a crime and has to be treated accordingly. Hand on holster, she bursts in. By then, Nick is half way out of the door, bin bag in hand, so now he's a suspect fleeing arrest and she points her weapon at his back and demands he halt on pain of death. And all because he's carrying the rubbish to his car.'

'She doesn't carry a gun.'

'You get my drift.'

'But they needed the evidence inside the bag and the CPS

decided to prosecute, so she did the right thing, even if she went about it in the wrong way.'

Judith scrunched up her toes a few times. 'There you are then,' she said. 'My point proven. You're willing to excuse the means, given the end result. Why are you sticking up for her anyway, if you think she's a racist, maybe?'

'I'm evaluating the evidence dispassionately,' Constance said. 'Not letting my own prejudices get in the way. That's what you've taught me, isn't it?'

Judith changed the subject. 'Where's Charlie? That's what I want to know.'

'I asked Sergeant Thomas when I saw her at the station last week,' Constance said. 'She told me he was on holiday. I did say we knew he'd been ill but she wouldn't say anything else.'

'Ah. When you're next passing, maybe pop your head in, see how he is.'

'Sure,' Constance said. 'Look, I think you did well with her. I mean, she wouldn't even say what she thought the cause of death was.'

'I know. I was lucky there. I'll make sure I use it when I sum up, remind the jury that not even the police present at the scene think it's credible that Brett died from an allergic reaction –something along those lines. Although she was right with what she said. It's not her place to judge.'

'What about Andy?'

'What *about* Andy?'

Constance laughed now. 'I saw you two talking. Did he say anything about his Court TV stint?'

'You mean apologise for making two million people hate me. No, funnily enough, he didn't do that.'

'That's a bit unfair. We both saw how the things he said were... misinterpreted.'

'Oh Connie, you are always so balanced.'

'You need me that way, if you're going to be so judgmental.'

Judith scrunched up her empty crisp packet and launched it at the basket in the corner. 'Enough chat,' she said. 'We're only at the start. I hadn't pictured the bit with the kettle, as Sergeant Thomas described it. Can you run through it with Nick and see if we can defuse it, when he gives his evidence. And tomorrow we have... yes, the two celebrities: Rosa Barrera and Dr Adrian Edge. Have you watched any of Rosa's shows?'

'I caught last week's,' Constance said. 'Not a great success.'

'The jackfruit curry or the chickpea meringue?'

'The chickpea meringue. My whisk overheated and the meringue smelt...earthy. I bought a creamy raspberry one from M&S instead.'

Judith laughed. 'At least you tried. I think she's rather good. And getting the slot in the first place. It's a tough world out there.'

'You like her?'

'I like her TV persona. I think we both know that means nothing in real life.'

'Is there anything she can say to help Nick?'

Judith pulled out her hairband and wound it around her wrist. 'This case will be a war of attrition,' she said. 'Andy sending us witness after witness with hardly anything to say – just enough to hold his narrative together. We have to focus on knocking each one down, one by one. But if you can come up with anything positive we might be able to glean from any of them, something that points to another culprit, please let me know. I've been wracking my brains and I haven't thought of anything yet.'

21

NEXT MORNING, CONSTANCE watched as Rosa settled herself in the witness box. The TV chef wore a shocking pink tunic and turquoise cropped trousers, her dark hair thick and glossy, as if she was about to take part in a shampoo commercial.

Judith leaned towards Constance and spoke behind her hand. 'Do you know, if I believed in reincarnation, I think I'd like to come back as Rosa Barrera.'

'Really?'

'That look, anyway.'

Constance glanced in Rosa's direction, trying to appreciate what had so impressed Judith, Judith who never envied anyone, especially not based on their appearance or image.

'You will be able to focus on cross-examining her, won't you?' she asked.

Judith just smiled. 'Have I worried you?' she said. 'Once I get in the zone, everyone's dead meat, no matter how glamorous.'

'Ms Barrera,' Andy began, rolling his rs like a native Spanish speaker. Constance stifled a laugh. 'You are a practising vegan. Can you explain to the court what that means, please.'

Rosa turned to the judge and flicked her lustrous locks over her shoulder.

'Where to start?' she said, her eyes bright. 'I think most people know that vegans don't eat meat or any other animal products, so no milk or eggs. But veganism is a philosophy based on not exploiting animals in any way, so not wearing leather or wool, either.'

'And what is your profession?'

'I'm a chef. I own a small café in London.' She suddenly stopped and looked out over the public seating, before sighing deeply. Then she returned her attention to Andy. 'And I have a TV show in which I cook vegan food from all around the world.'

'How did you know Brett Ingram?'

'I didn't really know him – not well. I met him, ooh, around 2016, at a food fair in Bristol.' Rosa stared out into the distance again. 'He was a guest of the National Farmers' Union and he was promoting British beef, so it wasn't exactly love at first sight.' She managed a half smile.

'After that?'

'I didn't meet him again till he invited me to the event on the 13th of April but we were in touch, from time to time.'

'Why did you agree to attend?'

Rosa turned towards the judge, opened her eyes wide, then returned her attention to the jury. Constance made a note. One thing which Constance had liked about the 'cameras in the courts' pilot of two years before was that you could watch witnesses again, afterwards, in your own time, slow things down, really analyse their responses and body language. The traditional process meant she had to be constantly on her guard.

And Judith liked her to notice things like this – that Rosa had spent longer than she might have contemplating her response – and keep a record. That way, afterwards, they could try to work out what motivated a witness to give a particular answer. And given Judith's continuing and persistent alternative theory that one of the speakers might have been involved in deliberately trying to kill Brett, her close scrutiny gained even more importance.

'Heart Foods is a big player in the UK market,' Rosa said. 'Since 2019 they've been buying and promoting vegan food. I'd like to think I had something to do with that. After we first met, I put Brett in touch with some fabulous vegan food suppliers. And he promised an interesting collection of people in the food industry would be there.'

'Am I right that you and the other panellists arrived earlier than members of the public?'

'We were invited for 12; I arrived around 12.30. We had an hour or so for lunch and chat before everyone else came.'

'What did you eat for your lunch?'

'I remember sweet potato pakora and flat bread. Not bad, actually, although not as good as the ones I make myself.'

'Was the food hot?'

'The pakora were warm, the bread no. It might have been hot earlier.'

'And how was the food arranged?'

'There was a long table at the back of the hall with platters of food. I asked one of the staff to show me what was vegan.'

'Do you remember what other food was on offer?

'All kinds of things. I think Brett was trying to make a point about how diverse our diets were. There was thinly sliced beef and burgers, edamame salads, halloumi, sandwiches and fruit and an assortment of breads. Everyone left the salad. Not that it didn't look nice; just difficult to eat when you're juggling everything. I'd have preferred to sit down. How can you really appreciate food when you're worried about whether it's even going to reach your mouth?'

'Did you go into the kitchen?'

'No.'

'Did you see the defendant, Nick Demetriou, at all?'

Now Rosa shifted the top half of her body around, to fix her eyes on Nick, who was still focused on the ground just ahead of his feet.

'I don't remember seeing him,' she said.

Andy paused and drew breath. 'Think hard, Ms Barrera. You didn't see the defendant at all, throughout the meeting?' Constance suspected this wasn't the answer Andy was expecting. It probably wasn't that important, but it still seemed strange. Constance looked at the words she had typed onto her screen. 'I don't remember seeing him'. Not yes or no. Rosa's answer was equivocal. Perhaps she really wasn't sure, but then Rosa seemed to be the kind of person who was sure about most things.

'He might have served me a drink. We didn't have any conversations, any interaction that I remember.' Rosa's voice wavered as she directed her answer to the jury, but then her gaze appeared to seek out Lisa Demetriou, who was watching her closely. Their eyes met and Rosa almost smiled for a second time. Constance was confused. Did Rosa know Lisa?

'Did you see Mr Ingram over lunch?' Andy stuck with the simple questions, clearly worried now about the extent to which he could rely on this witness.

But Rosa had returned to her usual confident self. 'Of course. He was the host,' she said.

'You spoke to him?'

'And the others, yes.'

'How was he?'

'He seemed fine. He greeted me with a kiss on both cheeks, he introduced me to Mark Sumner, one of the other guests, he said he was enjoying my show.'

'Did you see Mr Ingram eat anything?'

Rosa screwed up her face and stared up at the ceiling, then back at Andy.

'Sandwiches,' she said.

'Mr Ingram ate sandwiches?'

'There was a plate close by and I'm fairly sure he took one while we were talking.'

Andy made a point of typing a note into his laptop, although it was patently obvious it was for effect. Rosa's statement had said she saw Brett eating sandwiches; it was nothing new. Constance wished Rosa had answered this question opaquely. The sandwiches were the key to the prosecution case.

'When did you first notice that Mr Ingram was unwell?' Andy continued.

'When his head hit the table next to me.'

'You didn't detect anything earlier, over lunch?'

'If he wasn't feeling well, he didn't say.'

'Then what happened?'

'Diana and Adrian looked after him. I tried to make sure I gave them plenty of space. You'll have to ask them for any details of what happened.'

'That's Diana Percival and Dr Adrian Edge?'

'Yes.'

'Well, we can ask them all about it when they give their evidence. Thank you. I have nothing more. Please wait there for Ms Burton's questions.'

***

Judith stood up and waited, watching Rosa take a drink of water and fiddle with the neckline of her tunic. Perhaps she wasn't quite as confident as she appeared.

'Ms Barrera,' Judith asked. 'Why do you think you were invited to the Tanners' Hall event?'

Rosa took a moment to answer and Judith felt the heat of her gaze, in a way she felt sure Andy hadn't.

'Brett wanted to present different views to the public about the food we should eat. I represented the vegan perspective and, well, I am on TV, so I expect he thought I would pull in viewers.'

'Viewers?'

'He was filming the event and planned to use the recording in marketing. I'm not sure how, but we all had to say we agreed. To our images being used. That kind of thing.'

'You mentioned that Heart Foods sells vegan food?'

'It has a small range, yes. I was trying to encourage Brett to expand. There's been a big push for products which mimic meat, for sensible, commercial reasons. I wanted him to go back to the celebration of vegan foods, wonderful vegetable dishes where you can see what you're eating, not some mash up of pea protein, dressed up to look like a meatball.'

'What did Brett think about that?'

'He was sympathetic, but he was a businessman and he had to

think about what would sell.'

'That's what he said?'

'Yes.'

'You think vegan food is here to stay, then, not just a fad – Veganuary 2021 and never again.'

'I'm sorry, Ms Burton, what was that you said?' Judge Linton had pushed his glasses back up his nose and was peering at Judith.

'*Veganuary*, My Lord. There was a big push by some major supermarkets to persuade the public to try out a vegan diet in January this year – vegan and January – hence Veganuary.'

'I see. I understand, thank you. Do answer the question.'

Rosa treated Judith to her trademark grimace, 'I'm insulted you would call my way of life a "fad" and I imagine four million other people in the UK would feel the same, if they were here today.'

'Ms Barrera, I'm sure Ms Burton's intentions were honourable,' Judge Linton said. 'The question was asking for your opinion in any event, which, although interesting, is not what you are here to provide. Ms Burton, next question please.'

'My Lord, yes. You told us Mr Ingram was "fine" when you arrived at the hall. I wanted you to provide some more detail of how he seemed. Was he lively?'

'Yes.'

'Talking to his guests?'

'Yes.'

'Making jokes?'

'I don't remember jokes. Not any I laughed at anyway.'

'He appeared in good health?'

'Absolutely.'

'And would you describe him – I know you said you've only

met him once before – but was he a charismatic character?'

'Yes.'

'Loud?'

'Yes.'

'Inquisitive?'

'Yes.'

'You've described the food on offer for lunch: beef carpaccio, exotic salads, gourmet burgers, your own choice of sweet potato delicacies, breads and sandwiches. Were the sandwiches all meat?'

'There was a selection, I think. All kinds of things.'

'Why didn't you choose a sandwich then? You've told us why you didn't try the salad. Sandwiches are the perfect finger food, aren't they?'

'Sandwiches are boring, however well made,' Rosa said. 'If I'm allowed to say that because, that's just my opinion, of course, My Lord.'

Judith had to hand it to Rosa. She was not going to let Judge Linton bring her down. Perhaps she had read about his last case and she was determined not to be cowed by him. Although she would be better advised to focus on just answering Judith's questions.

'I see,' Judith said. 'Are you seriously telling me then that Brett Ingram, head of Heart Foods, lover of innovation and novelty, who could have had his pick of anything on that table, chose a "boring" sandwich?'

'That's what I told the police.'

'I see. Is it what you remember now?'

'It was a long time ago. Do you remember what other people ate for their lunch in April?'

Judith paused to allow Rosa's answer, with its own embedded

rhetorical question, to hover before, hopefully, finding a place to land in the minds of the twelve members of the jury. Out of the corner of her eye, she saw Constance look up.

'This wasn't any old day, Ms Barrera,' Judith continued, to press home her advantage. 'This was a day when a man died right next to you.'

'I know. I know that.'

'We heard from Sergeant Thomas yesterday. She said that you were upset when she arrived and that you went home shortly afterwards. Is that right?'

'Mark…Mr Sumner was good enough to accompany me. I didn't want to be on my own.' Rosa looked out over the public gallery, then at the judge, then back at Judith.

'And it was, in fact, two days later, on the Thursday, that you spoke to police and mentioned the sandwiches?'

'If you say so.'

'That's the date on your statement.'

'You must be right then.'

'Were you certain *then* about what Mr Ingram ate?'

Rosa looked across at Nick now, then back at Judith. All this fidgeting suggested to Judith that Rosa was anything but comfortable with her line of questioning, which seemed strange, as it was fairly straightforward.

'I think so. I would never have said something if I didn't believe it was true,' Rosa said. Here, yet again, Rosa was hedging her bets. Judith had to press on.

'But maybe you guessed when the police asked you, before it took on any importance, when the prevailing view was that Mr Ingram had died from a heart attack, and now you don't want to admit you were wrong?'

Andy was on his feet in a flash, his mouth half open, but Judge Linton cut across him.

'Mr Chambers, I would like Ms Barrera to answer the question. Ms Burton, do take care how you address our witnesses; they aren't on trial, you know.'

Rosa's shoulders drooped and Judith, heeding the judge's warning, retreated a few centimetres from her lectern and softened her tone.

'Think hard now, Ms Barrera, as this is important. Here, today, in this courtroom, we want your recollection of what happened, not what you may have told other people on other occasions. Did you see Brett Ingram eat anything at the meeting?'

'We were talking and I was eating so I thought...'

'Maybe he didn't like to talk and eat at the same time? Many people don't.' Judith thanked Greg in her head for her quick-witted retort.

Rosa closed her eyes. 'We were next to the sandwiches. I was eating. I can't tell you now if I saw Brett eat anything at all, not to be sure. I'm sorry.' She stared at Andy, who nodded benignly but who, Judith suspected, was secretly seething at Rosa's apparent change of heart.

'No need to apologise,' Judith replied. 'That's all the questions I had for you, thank you.'

***

Judith watched the TV chef stumble down the steps of the witness box and make her way towards the exit. As she reached the door, a man appeared from outside the court and held it open for her. When she saw him, she leaped back as though she had been stung, then straightened up, nodded to him and scampered out.

Judith leaned over towards Andy.

'Witnesses, eh?' she said. 'Always forgetting their lines.'

'I should probably have moved her down the list,' he replied. 'She started OK, but once you began your routine, she became a bit distracted.'

'Was she unwell?'

'Just all that stuff about her café is coming to a head.'

'Her café?'

'Yes,' Andy said. 'The fire.'

'It's coming to a head, is it?' Judith asked, trying to sound uninterested.

Andy nodded. 'The police have dropped it. Not that surprising as most arson cases never get solved. But she's done the place up at her own expense and she's still waiting to hear if the insurers will honour the cover. If not, she may just sell up at bargain basement price and move on.'

22

DURING THE LUNCH BREAK, Judith found herself confronting the mirror in the ladies' toilet, examining the lines around her eyes. She hadn't spent much time in her life agonising over her face. She had appreciated early on that she'd been blessed with good skin and pleasant, regular features and that she could exaggerate them to maximum effect with a few dabs of deftly-applied make-up. Recently, though, she had found herself looking longer and closer and comparing herself with younger women, much as she had done with Rosa today.

Behind her the door swung open and Constance appeared. 'I thought I might find you here,' she said. She came and stood beside Judith. 'Our chef was a bit strange.'

'I thought so too, but I'm interested in your observations.'

Constance smoothed her own hair down and then turned towards Judith. 'She didn't say what we expected, that's all. First, she denied ever seeing Nick before, which must be a lie. Then she couldn't remember what Brett ate, even though it was in her statement.'

'Andy says the police have given up on finding out who set fire to her café and the insurers may not pay and that's why Rosa was so…malleable in the witness box. Perhaps she couldn't be certain that her memory was correct when it came to such an important point. I can imagine the prosecution solicitor would have explained to her just how crucial it was to establish that Brett ate the sandwiches.'

'It was still strange. Why even come and give evidence if you're not going to say anything useful?'

'Unless of course she was involved in what happened to Brett, and everything else is a smokescreen'

Constance shook her head. 'What would Rosa's motive be?'

'I don't know. Maybe she had wanted him to do more for her cause, or it might have been a failed romance? Wasn't Brett linked with a number of women over the years? Maybe their vegan collaboration was more than business.' Judith saw Constance rolling her eyes. 'Yes,' she said, 'I know you want me to focus on the evidence we have, but you did ask. I wonder if the judge was thinking about that, about the fire, when he told me to go easy on her. On the other hand, he doesn't strike me as the kind of man who reads celebrity gossip columns. She gave me short shrift when I asked about Veganuary though, didn't she?'

'That was classic.'

'I asked for it. It was useful though as a comparator.'

Constance frowned. 'What do you mean?'

Judith loved it when Constance asked her to explain her thought processes. 'Like you,' she said, 'the jury will remember that Rosa was very certain of two things: that veganism is here to stay and that sandwiches are boring. Everything else was rather vague.'

Constance nodded her appreciation, pleased that Judith was back on track. 'Did you see that she gave Lisa a sympathetic look right near the start, when she said she couldn't be sure she'd seen Nick?'

'I didn't see that.'

'I wondered how she knew Lisa, so I flicked through some online press articles and there were family photos in a couple of the papers. She might have just recognised her from those.'

Judith nodded. 'That's possible. You know I read that Rosa was married once, very young, and her husband had a nasty gambling habit.'

'I missed that.'

'Hmm. Giving away personal details in an early interview before she became media-savvy. Assuming they don't know each other, maybe Rosa was trying to be supportive – kind of solidarity for wives of husbands who mess up. Who knows? Send me those articles you read, anyway – the ones with the photos please.' Judith could see that Constance was unconvinced by her theory, but it didn't matter.

'So it went according to plan then, Rosa's cross-examination?' Constance asked.

'Pretty much,' Judith said, 'although Judge Linton was no longer entirely *on our side,* you probably saw. I suppose we'll have to expect that, after that guidance they gave judges on menopausal women yesterday.'

'What?'

'When he told me to speak to her gently. Now I think about it, it was much more likely to have been that than the arson. You didn't see it? Quite hilarious it was. All judges were reminded in the strongest terms that middle-aged women – well, pretty much any women; Rosa would probably be offended to be labelled "middle-aged" – might be suffering from menopausal symptoms – hot flushes or weak bladders – and may be too embarrassed to ask for the air conditioning to be turned on, or for comfort breaks.'

Constance laughed out loud. 'Shouldn't all witnesses be entitled to that?'

'Precisely. But it also mentioned taking account of "lack of concentration and memory problems" from what I remember. I can't be certain of course, as I may be suffering myself, and have already forgotten the guidance.'

'Stop!' Constance covered her face with her hands, but Judith had not quite finished.

'I mean, if you read the bulletin,' she continued, 'you would completely ignore all evidence of women between the ages of thirty and sixty-five for unreliability. We're back to "hysterical" women again; not being able to work because of our wombs.'

'It sounds like it was well meant.' Constance said, heading for the door and holding it open so Judith could exit before her.

'Well meant; ill spent,' Judith said. 'Anyway, whether it was because she was brooding over her café or because of her reduced mental capacity or for any other reason, who cares? Rosa didn't remember what Brett Ingram ate for his lunch! I wasn't going to ask originally, because her statement was so clear, but there we are. Just shows that no question is too stupid to ask a witness.'

As they returned to their break-out room and settled themselves down, Judith fished around in her bag, pulled out a packet of crackers and offered them to Constance.

'I planned to bring in prawn sandwiches for lunch today, but thought that might be in bad taste,' she said.

Constance took a cracker, sat back and nibbled at one corner. 'Rosa said that Mark Sumner gave her a lift home, didn't she?'

'She did.'

'I don't know if you noticed, but he was outside the door, right at the end when she left, and she didn't look pleased to see him.'

Judith paused. 'That was Mark, was it?' she said. 'Maybe she didn't like his driving – objected to being taken by tractor?'

But Constance persisted. 'He mentioned her when I was there, when I went to see him. He mentioned Rosa, that he thought Dr Edge had been rude to her. There was no hint then of bad feeling between them. It was more like he felt he had taken her side, defended her.'

'Which she might not have appreciated?'

'You think Mark read it wrong?'

Judith would not make a joke this time. She had been the one who asked Constance to look into all the panellists, even though it was outside their remit. She should listen to Constance when she drew conclusions from those enquiries. Constance didn't reply.

'What is it?' Judith asked.

'Oh...probably nothing. It's just Mark's not due to give evidence till Thursday, is he?'

Judith shrugged. 'He probably wanted to get an advance look at the layout. Or it wouldn't surprise me if the prosecution told him the wrong day. You know how disorganised they are. Anyway, back to Rosa Barrera, the woman of the moment. Despite the latter part of today's performance, she strikes me as a woman who can look after herself.'

Constance took another cracker from the packet. 'Maybe,' she said, before pushing the cracker into her mouth and munching away.

23

Sᴜᴇ ʜᴀᴅ ᴀ ʟᴏᴛ ᴏɴ ʜᴇʀ ᴍɪɴᴅ. She was on standby to attend the trial of the caterer, most likely before the end of the week, a matter she was trying to forget. And her deadline for presenting the final results of her research loomed. In addition to that, the sponsors had invited her to a Zoom call today to discuss next steps, which had only ever happened once before in the life of this project. Now, as she followed the link to the call from her laptop, seated in the lab where the WIFI was most reliable, she wondered what this was about.

'Hello Susan.' On screen, Dougie Crane's face came into view, closely followed by his sidekick, Gemma. 'We thought it would be useful to have this short meeting today, as there have been one or two developments at our end we wanted to share with you.'

That sounded ominous. Usually when people spoke of 'developments' they meant problems or cost cutting or someone important didn't like what you were doing. If so, they'd left it late in the day to tell her.

'All right,' Sue said. 'Go ahead.'

'First of all, we wanted to ask you where you are with your testing.'

'I've pretty much finished – a few more graphs to complete, but it's done. I can certainly make recommendations about the right temperature and humidity for reproduction and growth, and for food sources also. And the numbers are looking very healthy. From one batch of larvae, we end up with between three and four sacks of feed, depending on those conditions.'

'That sounds great. On food sources, which did you find were the best?'

'I'd rather wait to present everything, once it's all complete.'

'Oh come on. You can give us a sneak preview. We won't hold you to any numbers. You must know the answer, if you've nearly finished.'

Sue had anticipated that Dougie and Gemma would press her on something and she had resolved, privately, to resist. Her deadline was not yet reached; still a few more days. Contractually, she simply had to deliver the data at the appropriate time; nothing more. However, this wasn't all about her obligations. Dougie had previously made it clear that if she proved herself reliable there may be more work for her, a consideration not to be underestimated for a scientist keen to make a worthwhile contribution at the same time as making ends meet. And she couldn't see the harm in telling them in advance what her report would say, even if they shared it.

'Well,' she said. 'The best by far is the household food waste, combined with fish offal. That achieves the most growth.'

'What about the sewage?' Dougie asked, and although he had kept his voice level and maintained eye contact, suggesting that this was just a casual enquiry, Sue immediately sensed this was what he had been getting at all along, with his more open request for an early taster. What she couldn't work out yet was why this food source in particular should be the one he wanted to focus on.

'You mean the sludge from the wastewater treatment plant?' she said. 'We haven't had enough of that yet to be statistically significant, but it's down at the bottom of the scale.'

'Why haven't you had enough?' Now Dougie was leaning in, and his nose blurred before the picture returned to its usual level of clarity. And with his question, Sue also gained more insight into where the conversation was leading.

'Regulations,' she answered. 'There's a lot of paperwork associated with purchasing and transporting human waste, as well as requiring it in a form we can feed to the larvae.'

There was a pause during which she saw Dougie look up into the corner of his screen, most likely reading a message. It coincided with Gemma dropping off and then reappearing.

'When you say "not statistically significant", you're not saying it's the worst then? You're saying you need more samples?'

'Yes, but, in my experience, based on what I've seen so far, the sewage is unlikely to yield the best results.'

'Why's that?'

'I've read a few papers from previous tests in the UK and other countries. Sewage, without more nutritious additives, tends to delay development in the larvae.'

There was a silence again at the other end of the line.

'That's disappointing,' Dougie eventually said.

'Is it? I didn't realise our focus was on getting rid of sewage. I thought it was on finding the best yield from the larvae.'

Dougie shifted closer to the screen for a second time. 'Our focus has changed.'

'Since when?' she asked.

'Since now. Look, Sue. We've had the three-line whip. The clear message is that we need to put the sewage angle front and centre. There isn't enough impetus to take things forward if we're just replacing feeding chickens on grain with feeding chickens on maggots. I know we save the cost of growing the grain...'

'And we save water and use up food waste and offal. That's a pretty good thing to do in a country which throws out...'

'It's not enough. They want the fairy tale!' Dougie grinned at his own joke.

'Remember our main funder is the Sanitation Trust.' Gemma spoke for the first time, and Sue resisted the temptation to respond that she was well aware of that. The Sanitation Trust logo was liberally daubed over every piece of paper Sue received.

'I didn't think they had imposed any conditions on their involvement. You never said.'

Dougie took over again. 'Things have changed. Priorities have shifted.'

'And I thought the use of human waste was never going to get through Defra,' Sue persisted. 'I mean, will people really eat a pig fed on larvae fed on human faeces?'

'The larvae get rid of the bacteria.'

'I know that. I know how well my soldier flies do their job. But the public doesn't, and the fear has always been that they won't want to eat anything in that food chain once they know.'

Gemma chipped in again. 'Look, we might be able to get around the public knowing.'

'How are we going to do that?' Sue asked, beginning to feel

uneasy about all of this.

Gemma closed her mouth and sat very still. Dougie also said nothing. Sue waited. She could wait all day. Well, she couldn't and she wouldn't, but she was going to make them explain to her what they really wanted.

Dougie scratched the top of his head. 'Now we've left the EU, there are…less rules about how we have to describe food, and, I mean, the sewage would be two steps away, so, we have *pigs fed on solider fly larvae* and that's it. That's all we have to say.'

Sue sat back. She wanted time to take stock, time to reflect on all of this: *new focus, more testing, more secrecy.*

'So many people are in favour of transparency,' she said. 'Brett Ingram, for example, of Heart Foods, before he…' Sue faltered. 'He was absolutely clear that we needed to give consumers more information, not less, about what they were eating.'

Dougie grinned. 'Well, that sounds like quite an unpopular line Mr Ingram was taking. Anyway, our target markets lie outside the UK. No one is going to care in less developed countries, where they're happy just to have food on the table. Look, don't you worry yourself about any of the other stuff: labels or what people think. Over the next week, before you finish, we'll get you some more human waste, OK? Plenty of it. We'll do the leg work. And you…you just ensure the results look OK.'

'You're asking me to falsify my research?'

'Absolutely not,' Gemma attempted outrage, but Sue could see through her. Her only contributions had been to state the blindingly obvious and now to lie.

Dougie also raised his eyebrows, but only fleetingly. 'Do you want all of your work, all of our efforts, all of the funding from sponsors and charities to have been for nothing?' he said. Clearly, he preferred the justification technique to outright untruths.

'Of course I don't,' Sue said.

'Well, as of today, the only way we can keep their interest, their support, is if we offer it all; the clean-up of human waste plus the production of a viable foodstuff for livestock.'

'Look, there is a compromise, isn't there?' Gemma spoke again. 'Try a mix – sludge plus a percentage of food waste. I bet that will produce better results than you think. Then leave the marketing to me and Dougie.'

After the call ended, Sue went downstairs into the factory. She stood in the doorway and surveyed the containers; great big rotund glass globes, twenty-four of them, conforming to very specific measurements. To their inhabitants, they were twenty-four worlds. What would happen when the project was finished? Most likely, all the equipment would be dismantled, the room would be cleared, ready for the next scheme. All of this would be forgotten. Except to the extent that it lived on through her results and through whatever happened next because of her results.

She wrung her hands together. The conversation she had just had with Dougie and Gemma summed up her life; compromise and disappointment, not reaching the heights expected of her. OK, she was a professor and that had taken a lot of hard work, but it hadn't, on its own, led to a glorious career. She could have held a prestigious position at a university, but that would have involved a rigorous interview process and then she would have to work in close proximity with strangers, which had not been easy for Sue ever since…

A thought began to surface and she suppressed it. Anyway, the work she was currently undertaking – ad hoc work in the field she loved, generally undertaken alone – suited her better. People who knew her well, like her mother, would agree with that, tell her it was a good job *for her*. But there were two sides to every coin. And now she was taking orders from the most junior members of a local voluntary organisation who probably didn't have more than two A levels between them.

She stepped forward and checked on the flies again. All seemed quiet and there were no signs of life this time, just the regular hum of the machinery and the wriggling of the ever-fattening larvae. The return to work mode calmed her and allowed her to view things more dispassionately than a moment before.

However abhorrent she might consider Dougie's methods, was there really any harm in what Dougie and Gemma had asked? Just to run the tests. She hadn't tried all that hard to source the sludge for obvious reasons, so, although she hated to admit it, they were probably right to encourage her to give it a proper chance.

But what if the other research was wrong and the larvae didn't kill all the bacteria? It might be like mercury in tuna or, worse still, like microplastics in the oceans – a deadly killer with a lasting legacy. She was too much of a worrier, she told herself. She should just take things one step at a time. *Legacy* – that was a word she liked. It summed up what she really wanted from all this. Not for herself – she wasn't interested in personal glory, her name in lights – but Dougie had been astute when he appealed to her sense of duty and purpose.

This was a laudable project and it had been entrusted to her; the insects were similarly consigned to her care. Much better that they died as part of a successful trial that would have a positive impact than a project which was mothballed, although the farms these batches were sent to would accept them anyway. The farmers would do anything for a free lunch, especially if it really was a free lunch.

'Hey there, boys and girls,' she spoke softly to the nearest container and then laughed aloud, because otherwise there would be no response to her greeting. 'Tomorrow we're going to feed you some sludge,' she said. 'What do you think about that?'

24

ON THEIR WAY BACK TO THE courtroom after lunch, Constance and Judith walked past Dr Adrian Edge. He was sitting in the area immediately outside, engrossed in some papers, most likely a copy of his statement. He looked more serious than Constance had imagined. On his radio shows, he was relaxation personified, interviewing guests with a carefree manner, delivering opinions casually and non-judgmentally and recommending recipes with delight and without pressure.

Finding themselves the first back inside, Constance asked Judith: 'Have you ever listened to Dr Edge? You must have if you've watched Rosa Barrera.'

Judith began to arrange her papers again, ready for the afternoon session. 'Not before my research for the trial,' she said.

'I thought everyone who was anyone listened to Dr Edge; well, everyone over the age of thirty-five.'

'Then you were mistaken. I have listened to some recordings and I managed around half an hour of his live show last week.'

'You didn't like it? You like Rosa Barrera,' Constance rolled her 'r's now, to mimic Andy Chambers, 'but you don't like Dr Edge?'

'Too light and fluffy for me, I'm afraid,' Judith said.

'Isn't Rosa fluffy?' Constance asked.

'No, Rosa is luscious and luxurious,' Judith replied. 'You must see the difference.'

Constance laughed, checking over her shoulder that they remained alone and not overheard. 'If you say so. I could listen to Dr Edge's voice forever,' she said. 'He could be reading the shipping forecast and still make it sound like Adele.'

'Style over substance,' Judith replied. 'All he said, when I tuned in, was that we should eat food that makes us happy. I thought the obesity monitor would swoop down and take him off the air.'

'When I last listened, he had a guest from Egypt who was 102, said he drank a mixture of turmeric and ginger every morning and could still do press-ups. And he said that we had got things badly wrong in the West, believing we had to find a good job and a partner and settle down and only then would happiness come. He said happiness came first – it was just a state of mind.'

'Which you are supposed to maintain when alone, unemployed and destitute? I told you: light and fluffy, divorced from reality. Talking of finding happiness, how's your new man working out?'

Constance was surprised Judith would ask her outright, especially at this moment when her mind was well and truly rooted on the case.

'I am…I'm taking things slowly,' she said.

Judith nodded. 'Slowly is good. Like the tortoise, not the hare.'

Constance thumped her playfully on the arm.

'Look,' Judith said. 'I get all this mindfulness, look-after-your-mental-health focus of recent months that Dr Edge is promoting, and how he links it to food. It's a welcome antidote to the compote of bravado and machismo I endured when I was first practising, which persists even now in some quarters,' she continued. 'But I sometimes think the pendulum's swung too far the other way. I mean, if the work has to be finished by tomorrow, sometimes you just have to stay up all night. Burning lavender-scented candles, drinking chamomile tea or...listening to garden bird song – the only thing that will do for you is make you feel slightly less suicidal when you're sacked for missing your deadline.'

***

As the afternoon session began, Adrian flashed a broad smile at his courtroom audience and his bushy eyebrows met in the middle before separating again. They reminded Constance of those slinky springs she'd played with as a child: contract and expand, contract and expand, turning over and over themselves all the way down the slide of the playground near her house. Until her little brother, Jermain, had got hold of hers and distorted its shape, so that it no longer slunk. And not long after that, someone had burned a hole right through the centre of the slide, so it wasn't safe to use anyway.

Constance watched Adrian open the buttons on his jacket and settle himself into the witness box where he stood, arms spread, hands resting on its furthest edges, to encompass the whole courtroom.

'Dr Edge,' Andy began. 'How long did you know Brett Ingram?'

'A long time,' Adrian said. 'We were at school together.'

'How well did you know him?'

'Pretty well, like I said, we'd been friends for years.'

'Did you see each other often?'

'Every six months or so. We'd meet for golf, tennis or dinner.'

'On the day of the meeting, what time did you arrive?'

'Around 12.30.'

'And how was Mr Ingram?'

'He was...*himself* – confident, larger than life, a showman. Honestly, I know he loved that food empire of his, but in another life he would have been an entertainer and probably something dangerous, you know. The guy who puts his head in the lion's mouth or throws daggers blindfolded, or even catches a bullet between his teeth. But he understood that not everyone lived their life at the speed of light. I once sat in on one of his board meetings. I had an idea, a radical one, and he asked me to come and present it. Do you know what he did?'

'No.'

'He made us all sit on bean bags with headphones with Diana, his PA, taking notes. He insisted every board member closed their eyes and cleared their minds before we even began. He understood that food is not all about eating; it's an experience. He was revolutionising the food industry, single-handed.'

Constance liked this anecdote but suspected, from their recent conversation, that Judith would not. In particular, she could imagine how disparaging Judith would be about a board meeting progressing while reclining on the floor. The word 'slouch' was not in Judith's vocabulary. Andy didn't seem all that impressed either, because he moved swiftly on.

'What did you eat for lunch on the day Mr Ingram died?' he asked.

'I grazed,' Dr Edge said. 'I think I had a bit of most things. Not sure whether I was supposed to. Mr Demetriou, over there, came up one time, in a hurry and started putting labels on the food, with names – not just what it was, also who it was for. But we'd nearly finished by then. I told him it was fine, not to worry. Everyone was satisfied.'

'Mr Demetriou had some labels?'

'Little plastic sticks with a place you can slot a card in – like when you receive a bouquet. Maybe he stole them from a florist. He attached them to the food. But it was too late.'

'And Mr Demetriou was in a hurry, you said?'

'Because he'd forgotten to label the food earlier. That was what I thought at the time. Of course, I could have been wrong. Maybe he had masterminded Brett's murder and he didn't want to stick around to see it happen.'

Judith did not require Constance's dig in her back to persuade her to stand up, but Judge Linton waved her down.

'Dr Edge, please listen to me for a moment.' Judith couldn't determine if his tone was genuinely paternalistic or full of sarcasm.

Adrian turned his head in the judge's direction and his expressive eyebrows contracted again.

'This is a trial, do you understand? A criminal trial.'

'Of course I understand. Yes, sir. That's why I'm sitting here giving my evidence, you're wearing those costumes and the accused is over there.'

Judge Linton grunted, stared at Andy Chambers, as if to admonish him for selecting a witness who thought he was a comedian. Then he turned back to Adrian.

'A man is dead...'

'And he was my friend.' Adrian was no longer jovial.

'You need to answer the question you are asked and nothing more,' the judge said. 'No jokes, no quips, no clever retorts. And

I remind the jury – I suspect they don't need reminding but perhaps you do – that Mr Demetriou is not on trial for murder. No one is suggesting that Mr Ingram's death was anything other than an unfortunate mistake.'

'Yes of course, sir…My Lord,' Adrian nodded his apology. 'I must try to understand that all these…details – how long we knew each other, what the caterer was doing with the labels – they are all important, even though they don't seem to me like they are.'

Judith wrote the word 'Bolshie' on a Post-it note, underlined it and handed it backwards to Constance. The judge ignored Adrian's further protest, returned to his laptop, typed some words and hit 'enter' noisily before nodding to Andy to continue.

'When did you first realise that Mr Ingram was unwell?'

'He was talking, introducing us all. Then, he kind of seized up, all stiff, as if something hurt, maybe his chest or his stomach. He kept going and then – crash – he hit the table, hard. It was very sudden. There was a guy filming. You should watch it. That's better than me prattling on.'

'You were the first one to go to his aid, which was very commendable. What did you see?'

'His skin was clammy, his hands balled into fists, his eyes popping out of his head, it seemed like he couldn't breathe. He was gasping, gasping for air.' Adrian paused, sniffed and shuddered. He was clearly not enjoying revisiting the image he described. 'I loosened his clothes, his pulse was racing. I tried to turn him over onto his back but he resisted me. Even though he was ill, he seemed determined to stay on his stomach. Then he went limp. His pulse stopped. I rolled him over and lifted him down to the floor of the stage.' Adrian's hands tumbled over each other, simulating the actions he remembered. 'I tried CPR, kept going as long as I could, but I could see he was gone. Then the ambulance arrived and they took over.'

Adrian wiped a tear from the corner of his eye. This was good strategy from Andy, making Adrian reconstruct Brett's death for the jury, although Judith couldn't understand why he didn't also use the video shot by the cameraman. That's what she would have done.

'I'm sure you did all you could. No one is blaming you,' Andy continued. 'I want to focus on the defendant now. Did he remain in the room when you were all eating?'

Adrian sighed before answering. 'Not much. Like I said, he put out those plastic sticks, then he disappeared.'

Judge Linton looked up, pen poised in the air, opened his mouth, closed it and returned to his notepad.

'Did Mr Demetriou see what Mr Ingram ate?'

This was a strange question to ask, Judith thought, but maybe Andy was anticipating Nick saying that the sandwiches were never intended for Brett, that he'd labelled them specially so that Brett wouldn't eat them.

'Maybe?' Adrian said. 'He was certainly in and out, like I said.'

'Did Mr Demetriou remove any food from the table?' Andy asked.

'Probably. Well, when we all shifted to the front of the hall and the public started to arrive, then the food was cleared away, I think mostly by the waitress.'

'What did Mr Ingram eat? Do you remember?'

Adrian smiled and pointed at Judith.

'I understand that some of the other witnesses aren't sure,' he said, 'but I am. He ate the sandwiches. I remember it as if it was yesterday. Maybe he was just being polite and leaving the best for the guests – his mother must have gone to school with mine.'

Constance began to make a note and then stopped and looked at Adrian. Out of everything he had said so far, this comment was reminiscent of the suave and amiable radio personality, who often wove personal stories into his shows, rather than the acerbic man in the witness box. She tried to understand why his observation appealed to her, but the best she could come up with, in the limited time available, was that everyone liked men who respected their mothers.

25

CONSTANCE HAD BEEN RIGHT that Adrian's voice had a smooth quality, and it exuded authenticity. Judith's initial view had been that there was little point seeking to discredit him, particularly given his popularity as a radio presenter, not forgetting that he was also a member of the medical profession, whose stock had risen dramatically since 2019. Instead, she should find something helpful for him to say to her, something which would stick in the minds of the jury even longer than his comment about the sandwiches. But he had blotted his copybook with the judge with his distasteful joke about Nick's rushing around. Now, reflecting on his testimony as a whole, she was uncertain whether it would be better to play along with Adrian or challenge him.

And, in Judith's experience, people who put on a false face of conviviality in a public role often cracked under pressure and showed their true colours. With force applied in the right places, that could happen to Adrian today. But was that really what she wanted? Would it help Nick? Judith looked across at the jury. She took a moment to fill her glass with water and contemplate her options. She could sense, rather than hear, Constance shuffling around behind her.

'Dr Edge, just a few short questions from me,' Judith began her cross-examination, her mind made up, at least for now, on the way forward. 'Did you eat anything from the vegan tray?'

'I remember eating some pakora, also a mini burger and some sliced beef.'

'So you didn't eat any of the sandwiches, the ones you remember seeing Brett Ingram eat?'

'No.'

'Are you certain? Sometimes, if you are standing close to someone and both talking – chit chat – you might pick at the nearest food, like you said – graze.'

'I didn't eat any sandwiches.'

'And you were well afterwards?'

'I can't say I felt so well, but I think that was more down to someone dying in my arms than anything I ate.'

Judith found that, like Andy, she had no desire to smile at Dr Edge's witty repartee. The judge had been right. This wasn't a slot on his show, or even the time when you sat around after a funeral and tried to cheer up the family by sharing tales of better times. But needs must. She allowed one side of her mouth to twitch into a half smile, just for a brief moment, to feign the empathy which so often eluded her in real life.

'Now, a moment ago you described for Mr Chambers what happened when Mr Ingram collapsed on the stage. At the time, what did you think was wrong with him?'

'I thought he was having a heart attack. That's usually the case when someone collapses suddenly in my experience – not that it has happened to me very often.'

'Did anything cause you to change your mind?'

'Diana, Brett's PA. She said he had an allergy to shellfish.'

'When did she say this?'

'I'm not sure. I can't remember. There was a lot going on.'

Judith paused. It was useful that Adrian was uncertain about when Diana had shared this information, and she wanted the jury to remember that. 'If people have food allergies,' she continued, 'severe food allergies, they normally carry a device which we colloquially call an "EpiPen", don't they?'

'Yes.'

'Can you explain what that does?'

Adrian nodded. 'In severe allergic reactions, the sufferer's blood pressure drops and their airways narrow. The EpiPen helps open the airways, so the patient can breathe.'

'Did Mr Ingram carry an EpiPen?'

'I don't know.'

'You didn't look for one?'

'No.'

'Diana didn't say "he's got one in his pocket" – that kind of thing?'

'No.'

Judith's face crumpled up, as if she had found Adrian's answer totally incomprehensible. 'If you're faced with someone dying from an allergic reaction, wouldn't you ask?'

'You're right,' Adrian said, 'But I had no idea it was an allergic reaction. It must have been later on, once the ambulance had arrived, that she mentioned the allergy.'

'Later on. I see. Only once Mr Ingram's heart had stopped?'

'Probably, yes.'

'Perhaps it wasn't a severe allergy then?'

'People can be too relaxed about *other people's* food allergies. They can have very serious consequences.'

'*You're* not relaxed about that kind of thing?'

'Absolutely not.' Adrian was animated again. 'If someone tells me they're allergic, I take it very seriously.'

'You would…make a mental note?'

'And warn other people; make sure they understood the need to take care.'

Judith nodded her understanding. 'But there are mild allergies, ones you can treat with antihistamine, for example?'

'Yes.'

'And I hear what you're saying about *other people's* allergies,' she said. 'However, if Mr Ingram *had* taken it seriously, had been concerned about the potential to experience a severe allergic reaction, wouldn't you have expected him to carry an EpiPen?'

The judge intervened. 'Ms Burton. While Dr Edge is a doctor, and clearly knowledgeable, he is here today as a witness of fact.'

'Of course, My Lord. You're absolutely right to remind me. I'll approach this in a different way. When Brett tucked into the sandwiches, when you were talking to him, did he ask anyone what was in them?'

'No.'

'Did he look to see what was inside, before he ate them?'

'You could pretty much see what kind of sandwiches they were and, well, he ordered them. I expect he would have known.'

'Dr Edge, please remember to stick to the facts, even when Ms Burton here is encouraging you to…embellish,' Judge Linton growled at Dr Edge this time, then raised his eyebrows at Judith.

'Did he check…'

'No,' Adrian interrupted. 'I didn't see Brett check, specifically check, what was inside each sandwich before he ate it.'

Judith waited a moment, as Adrian had lost his cool again, although she hadn't intended to annoy him – not quite yet.

'On those many other occasions, when you had been out with Mr Ingram: *tennis, golf, dinner,* school lunches – in all that time did he never tell you that he had an allergy to shellfish?'

'I don't think so,' Adrian said. 'I don't remember.'

'He didn't tell you or you don't remember?'

'I don't remember.'

'But, surely, had he told you, you would have remembered, given that you were close friends and that kind of information was something you've just told us that, *ordinarily,* you took very seriously?'

Adrian looked at Andy, who, to his credit, gave nothing away.

'He didn't tell me,' Adrian said. 'I didn't know.'

Judith waited again. Anyone charitable would think she was giving Adrian the opportunity to change his mind. In fact, once more, the hiatus allowed his admission to register. Now Judith needed to hammer home its significance.

'When Mr Ingram ordered food in a restaurant, you never heard him checking ingredients, when he gave his order?'

'I mean, he might have asked what was in something, what it came with?'

'To see if he liked it?' Judith asked. 'Chips or new potatoes?'

'Yes.'

'I understand. Where were all the other panellists when Brett collapsed?'

'We were all on the stage. After that, I was focused on Brett. Zoe, she left quickly. I saw that, while I was giving CPR. I don't blame her.'

'And my client, the defendant?'

Adrian looked over at Nick and frowned. 'He'd been standing at the back of the hall, in the middle. Then he came closer.'

'Did he say anything?'

'He was saying "is he all right?" I think. I really wasn't looking at him. But, I mean, they were all saying that. I wanted to say "I'm not God". In fact, I think I did. I get this all the time. Just because you're a doctor, people think you can work miracles. Well I couldn't. That's the shame of it. Not this time around.'

***

After court finished, Constance and Judith returned to Constance's office and settled themselves in the smallest meeting room. Constance was exhausted. Although Judith did the talking, her role required concentration too: watching, listening, making notes, cross-referencing what she heard to the evidence she'd already seen and sifting through it all, in real time, for the tiniest of clues which might help Judith turn things around. Judith, in contrast, appeared euphoric.

'I think today must go down in history as the most supportive comment for the defence I've ever had from a judge,' she said, 'apart from those immortal words, *no case to answer*. And the most disappointed a prosecution Counsel has ever been. Couldn't have happened to a nicer person than Andy, of course.'

'Really? Which comment?' Constance asked.

'Oh come on, Connie. The one where Dr Edge made one of his bad jokes about Nick plotting, then the judge replied that Brett's death was all *one big mistake*. Andy nearly fell off his seat. I mean, if that's what it was – a mistake, a wholly innocent mistake, not negligence – then our client's not guilty.'

Constance did not want to burst Judith's bubble, but she had not understood the point to be quite so well made. 'I don't think he meant it like that,' she said.

'You're right, of course, but that's what he said and I'll use it. I have to. It's gold dust. And Dr Edge; do you still like him as much as you did before?'

Constance crossed the room, collected a bottle of water from a side table, opened it and emptied it into two glasses. 'He was a bit flippant, I agree,' she said. 'But maybe that was his way of dealing with the stress of it all. He seemed sincere when he said Brett was his friend – close friend. I believed him then. It can't be easy watching someone you care about die like that, feeling so helpless, especially, like he said, when he's a doctor.'

'You are the embodiment of the voice of reason, reminding me to be even-handed, as ever.'

'Where were you going with the EpiPen?' Constance asked.

'I hoped that was obvious,' Judith replied. 'It just occurred to me that all this allergy stuff is so convenient as an explanation. If Brett had a severe food allergy, why wasn't he more careful himself? OK, we heard, he was a great showman, a daredevil even, but no one has suggested he had a death wish.'

'So?'

'So, maybe he didn't know he had a shellfish allergy or maybe he didn't have one at all? We've only got Diana's word for it. Nobody else knew about this allergy. Although, given how self-absorbed Adrian is, you can see him having forgotten all about it and not wanting to admit it. Who stands to do well out of Brett's death?'

Constance had picked up her phone. Now she stopped scrolling through her messages and looked at Judith.

'Not Diana. She's handed in her notice,' she said. 'Says now Brett is gone she doesn't want to work at Heart Foods any more. I don't think she's getting a pay-off either.'

'What about the others?'

Judith had clearly not given up yet, privately, on investigating the others, widening the net even more, which Constance wanted to avoid, and although she had thought long and hard about Mark since her visit to his farm, she couldn't even begin to see how he might be involved. But Judith was leading her away from her original question.

'I thought we agreed on a two-pronged attack,' she said. 'First, you go for the expert, Dr Leigh, *maybe something else killed Brett.* Second, if he's adamant it *was* shellfish, we get Nick off because he didn't know about the allergy. And Adrian's evidence was really helpful on that point. No murder allegation against someone else, and no saying the whole allergy thing is made up. We don't need either of those things and we can't prove them.'

Judith was on her feet now. Constance knew how she loved to pace, but there was almost no space in this room.

'Was there any allergy recorded in Brett's medical notes?' she asked.

'No. I checked. You know that.'

'Doesn't it strike you as odd that Diana says he had an allergy but it's not in his records?'

Constance shook her head. She could see that she had not convinced Judith yet that they should stick to their plan. 'I can't see any reason for Diana to make it up,' she said. 'If she hadn't said anything at all, people would have thought it was a heart attack or food poisoning, back where we started. Brett would still have been dead. Her admitting Brett had an allergy she knew about, that's worse for her, isn't it? If she was worried people would point the finger at her, wouldn't she just keep quiet?'

'Perhaps. You've met her. What did you think of her?'

'I told you. Not volunteering much but organised and grieving. Not a murderer.'

Judith stood behind her chair, her hands gripping it tight 'All right,' she said. 'I'll focus on the other arguments for now. But can you dig around Miss Percival a little more? See if you can get me any more leads before…ah, tomorrow. Tomorrow is a big day.'

'Isn't every day?'

'Dr Leigh, our eminent pathologist. I'll need my beauty sleep twice over.'

'You'll be fine. You did well with Dr Edge, I thought.'

'Despite my diversionary tactics? Hmm,' Judith seemed unsure. 'He was very insistent that Brett ate the sandwiches, wasn't he? That's why I had to run with it. It was a shame because we did so well with Rosa on that point, but that's how it goes. Didn't stop Adrian making another joke though, did it?' Judith finally sat down again, leaned back in her chair and ran her fingers through her hair.

'Does that matter?'

'Of course, it does. Because…' Judith paused and then she reached for her notebook, flicked through it until she found what she was looking for. 'Yes,' she said.

'What?' Constance asked.

'I may be wrong, but I think you've just put your finger on something very important. God, sometimes the most fundamental things are staring you in the face, but you just look the other way.'

'I'm pleased I've got something right,' Constance said. 'Are you going to tell me what it is?'

'No, but you'll only have to wait till tomorrow to find out.'

Judith tidied her papers into her bag, emptied some boiled sweet wrappers from her pocket into the bin and then, finding one intact sweet, she offered it to Constance.

'My sister Clare is very intrepid,' she said. 'Always jetting off to faraway places. She walked the entire Inca Trail, four days, on a packet of boiled sweets. She'd picked up some awful bug and couldn't stomach anything else. I know it's not the healthiest option, but they've got me through worse days than today.'

Constance took the sweet, unwrapped it and popped it into her mouth. In the five years she'd known Judith, she had a vague recollection of her mentioning her sister once, in some disparaging way and, prompted by Greg, revealing a sibling photograph. But Judith had never shared a story with Constance, a personal memory, like this. So why now? Was it her reward for helping Judith make a breakthrough?

'Thanks,' she said, still musing on how unfathomable Judith could be sometimes. 'And I'll see if I can find anything else on Diana to help you, before tomorrow.'

26

WHEN JUDITH ARRIVED AT COURT, on the third day of the trial, she was surprised to see that the expert pathologist, Dr Leigh, was not with Andy or his team. She soon realised he was not in the building at all. As the minutes ticked by, Judith watched with mild amusement as the prosecution lawyers made hurried calls behind cupped hands, huddled together and waved their arms around, clearly concerned that the doctor would be late, but pretending to the outside world that they weren't.

Eventually, they all shifted into the courtroom itself, and took their places, Andy drinking down two glasses of water in close succession and filling up for a third time. Judith avoided his eye. There was nothing she could say or do to assist and she would not gloat; a witness running late or failing to show was low down on her list of 'things I love about my job', especially when it was a key witness.

Then Dr Leigh arrived, one minute before his appointed slot. His relaxed demeanour suggested blissful unawareness of the furore caused by his 'just in time' approach. But Judith wondered if it was deliberate. That Dr Leigh wanted them to know that he had more important things to do with his day than come to court. After all, he wasn't a forensic pathologist; one assigned to crime scenes, who might actively seek out expert witness work. He was one of the many hospital-based pathologists who carry out millions of vital biopsies and tests every year; autopsies were just one part. That also meant he was unlikely to have given evidence in court many times before.

'Dr Leigh. You conducted the post-mortem on Mr Brett Ingram?' Andy began, taking a deep breath, to calm himself.

'I did, yes.'

'Can you tell us what that showed you?'

'Mr Ingram was aged forty-one when he died, a man who appeared to be in good health. His weight was around the mid-range for his height, but he had considerable muscle mass. In summary, he appeared to have been in good physical shape. There were no underlying health conditions either, from his medical records or from my examination.'

'Then how did he die?'

'The million-dollar question.' Dr Leigh showed his teeth, in what Judith wasn't entirely certain was a smile. 'In my opinion, Mr Ingram suffered an allergic reaction termed *anaphylaxis*, after ingestion of an allergen, most likely shellfish, over the lunchtime period.'

'What is anaphylaxis?'

'It's a reaction where different organs in the body react together, with the consequence that the body's airways close and blood pressure drops. If it's severe, it can cause death.'

Dr Leigh had surprised Judith so far with his lucid testimony.

In her experience, it was difficult to explain medical issues to lay people in a succinct way, yet he appeared to be doing so, and with ease. As long as he continued, that would help when it came to her cross-examination.

'Is the body attacking itself?' Andy probed.

Dr Leigh gave that almost-smile again. 'You would think that, wouldn't you?' he said. 'In fact, the body's own immune system is stimulated, and usually this would protect it, but in this case, the immune response does the opposite: it shuts the body down.'

'What information told you that this was anaphylaxis?'

'The most obvious feature, on examination of Mr Ingram's body, was a raised level of an enzyme called tryptase in his bloodstream. I took a sample of Mr Ingram's blood from the femoral vein in the leg, and it contained just under 150 micrograms per litre of tryptase. Anything above 44.3 micrograms leans towards anaphylaxis. Separately, there was swelling around the larynx – that's in the throat – which is another potential pointer towards anaphylaxis.'

Judith underlined some words in her notebook. This was good. She would use all this herself.

'Were those the only factors?' Andy asked.

'No. What I was told by the paramedics and the police featured in my diagnosis also, which is standard for a post-mortem. As I make clear at section three of my report, anaphylaxis often comes on suddenly; sufferers have difficulty breathing, they exhibit low blood pressure and sometimes a rash will appear on the body. Based on the eyewitness evidence, all of those features were present in Mr Ingram's case. And then of course we had Miss Percival's evidence of Mr Ingram's shellfish allergy, which was passed on to me by the coroner's office.'

'Thank you, Dr Leigh. We're going to take a moment now to play a short film, which was recorded by a cameraman employed by Mr Ingram to record the event, but which, instead, catalogued his death.' So this was where Andy had decided to deploy the film. Fair enough, but Judith would have probably used it earlier. She braced herself for the fallout. 'You've seen this film before, haven't you?' Andy asked.

'Yes, and it's consistent with my diagnosis.'

The judge warned the jury and the public of the potentially distressing nature of the footage, but no one made to leave. Then the lights dimmed and the film began to play on the overhead screens. It began just a few seconds before Brett started to speak, showed his dramatic collapse and ended abruptly, shortly after Diana ran forward to tend to her incapacitated boss. Judith watched the film closely, not because she needed to – she had memorised most of it – no, it was more to illustrate to the jury, if any of them happened to be looking in her direction, that it held no fears for her in defending Nick. Afterwards, Andy returned to questioning his witness.

'Is there anything we see in the film specifically that helps you determine cause of death?' Andy asked.

'If you go in close-up on to Mr Ingram, you see him pulling at the clothing around his neck. Also, his microphone was switched on and he is clearly gasping or wheezing and…just the general suddenness of the collapse. All consistent with anaphylactic shock.'

'And there was no other obvious cause of death?'

'No.'

'Are you certain about that?'

'I'm a hundred per cent certain that there was no other obvious cause of death, yes.'

'A hundred per cent certain,' Andy repeated Dr Leigh's words. Then he allowed the film to play a second time through to the end. No one spoke. Andy's eyes travelled across the faces of every juror, checking they had all seen the footage and were paying close attention to Dr Leigh, before he moved on.

'How many people die of food allergies every year?' he asked.

'About two million people in the UK live with a food allergy. Around 1,500 deaths a year are certified as due to asthma, which could be triggered by food allergy, so a fairly substantial number.'

'Gosh, 1,500 is four people every day.'

'That's right. A not-insignificant number.'

'I had no idea it was so high. So, in your view, is it important that people are aware of food allergies?'

'It's absolutely crucial. More deaths would be avoided if people were better educated and took the relevant precautions to protect others.'

Andy shook his head from side to side to illustrate how very sad each and every one of those deaths was, adding them, by association, to the death he placed on Nick's tab, tapped twice on his lectern to reinforce his message further, then promptly sat down.

***

Judith reviewed a paragraph in her blue notebook one final time, stared out into the distance and then rose to her feet. Dr Leigh stood, hands folded in front of him, waiting for her to begin.

'Dr Leigh, just going back to your figures, before we get into the detail of your report, are you aware of a recent study by Imperial

College, London, which concluded that there are fewer than ten fatalities a year in the UK linked to food allergies alone?'

'I am, and that is correct, I mean, correct, that is what they reported.'

'You just told us 1,500 deaths, didn't you?'

'They're different things. The bigger number is deaths where asthma was listed as the cause. I am saying that often doctors stop there but, in some cases – in many cases – the asthma itself only comes on because of the presence of an allergen. The smaller number – ten – that's where people are pretty sure there was no other cause, but the number of allergen-related deaths is really somewhere between ten and 1,500.'

Judith nodded her understanding. It suited her, for now, for the jury to have confidence in Dr Leigh. 'That's all allergens though, not just food,' she said, 'so it includes pet hair or allergies to grass or pollen?'

'That's right.'

'And, even at 1,500, those are still tiny numbers. At best, less than half a per cent of the UK's deaths?'

'I haven't done the maths, but that sounds like the right ballpark.'

'Is there anything else you can tell us about that study that might be relevant to this case?'

'Hmm, yes, it focused on the figures for admissions to hospitals, which is where a lot of media interest arose. Allergy cases have generally gone up by around five per cent over the last twenty years. Mostly children and young adults are affected, and the worst culprit is the nut: peanut or other variety.'

'Isn't it also correct that the study referenced the number of EpiPens prescribed, which has increased by more than four times, and that may be one of the reasons why, despite more people having allergies, fewer people have been admitted to hospital and fewer people have died?'

Dr Leigh nodded. 'That's true. They've had a sizeable positive impact.'

'Would you go so far as to say that EpiPens save people's lives?'

'Yes, they do.'

'Thank you. Returning then to *your* report and *your* findings, it's true, isn't it, that no EpiPen was found among Mr Ingram's clothes or belongings at the hall or in his car?'

'That's right.'

'And there is no reference to Mr Ingram's food allergy in his GP's notes either, is there?'

'No.'

'Can you, with the benefit of your experience, put forward a sensible explanation for this?'

Dr Leigh opened his hands, as he weighed up the question. 'I can deal with this, perhaps, more by omission,' he said. 'If Mr Ingram had suffered an allergic reaction previously and had gone to his GP, it would have been recorded in his notes. Equally, if he had undertaken any food allergy testing, even if this were done privately, it would be in his notes.'

Judith raised an eyebrow to illustrate to the jury how credible Dr Leigh's account was. 'You mean the fact it wasn't in his notes,' she continued, 'suggests that he had not been tested for allergens and that he had not previously suffered an allergic reaction or... or, at least, consulted his GP in relation to a food allergy?'

'Yes. Look, I can see that an otherwise healthy man – maybe on one occasion he's eaten something – let's say, mussels – he's felt unwell. He's self-diagnosed, you know, had a look on the

243

internet – sickness, stomach cramps, maybe some blotchy skin – and decided he *might* be allergic. He decides, instead of going to the doctor – he's busy, he doesn't take it too seriously, he takes an over-the-counter anti-histamine, feels better – he'll just avoid mussels in future, to be on the safe side. That, to me, is a plausible explanation.'

'Thank you. I see that as a possibility too, although not helpful to us in our quest for what *actually happened*.' Judith paused. Now it was time to begin to turn the screw. 'Tryptase in post-mortem blood; the main indicator you mentioned to Mr Chambers, which led to your conclusion of anaphylaxis. I read a paper which came out only last year on the unreliability of tryptase. Do you know it?'

'I'm not sure I know which paper you mean. It's not my speciality, but I accept that it's not a test routinely used in post-mortems.'

'But you tested for it?'

Dr Leigh nodded. 'I did. Once I received the message about the food allergy.'

Judith took a moment to look at her notes again. She had to make sure she addressed all the issues they were discussing, in the right order, for maximum effect.

'Is it correct that tryptase levels in the body change?' she asked, 'including after death, and so it's important to conduct the post-mortem quickly, if you are to have anything like an accurate picture of what was going on at the time of the death?'

'Ideally you would test in the first twenty-four hours, but that's hardly ever possible.'

'When did you conduct your post-mortem?'

'On the Friday. Mr Ingram had died on the Tuesday.'

'Perhaps as much as seventy-two hours later, then. Not *ideal*, you've just said. Is it also correct that you would normally prefer to have a comparison rate? There might, for example, be a reason why a person has a high rate of tryptase in their blood on a day-to-day basis, without any allergic response. When you test post-death, you can't know that.'

'That's true, but Mr Ingram's levels were pretty high.'

'In the study I've referenced, it says, "post-mortem tryptase levels must be treated with caution". Why is that?'

Dr Leigh gave Andy a look which communicated that he had not been prepared for such a difficult ride. 'Other factors can raise tryptase levels,' he said, 'but the majority of those factors were not present here.'

'You choose your words carefully, doctor. Isn't one of those factors, which can elevate tryptase, any form of CPR?'

'Yes.'

'And you know that Dr Edge performed CPR on Mr Ingram, as did the paramedics? The film we just watched stopped around that stage, but that was his evidence yesterday.'

'I know that. But I took the sample from Mr Ingram's leg, rather than directly from the heart, to compensate for that.'

Judith consulted her notes. Despite Dr Leigh's apparent annoyance that he was being pressed so hard, most of her thrusts were being parried calmly and expertly, even though he was, quite candidly, accepting the limitations of his diagnosis. This wasn't enough to save Nick. She had to convince the jury that Dr Leigh's conclusions were totally wrong. She had to challenge him even more, but she must do this in a simple way everyone would understand.

'When a person suffers an allergic reaction,' Judith said, 'is it right that a *specific type* of immunoglobulin E, an immune response, *which is different for each and every allergen*, is secreted by the body?'

'Yes. Immunoglobulin E or "IgE" is a type of antibody found in mammals. If it is present in skin or blood, it *can* confirm a specific allergy.'

'Then, there is a specific IgE antibody which would confirm that Mr Ingram was allergic to, say, crab?'

Dr Leigh nodded again. 'It exists, but I didn't test for it.'

'Why not?'

'It's not routine. There's general agreement that people with allergies may well already have raised IgE levels, or that you can have anaphylaxis without an IgE response.'

Judith turned to the jury and treated them to a broad smile, a smile which told them, even if they had not yet followed every twist and turn of her argument, that it had produced the desired result. One woman even smiled back.

'So,' Judith elongated the word, 'even if this *was* an allergic reaction, your post-mortem provides no evidence of the *specific* antigen, that is, the specific substance which caused the reaction to occur?'

'That's right.'

'It might have been…a bee sting, as much as any food ingested?'

'In theory, but I checked the body carefully for signs of any bites or stings and I didn't find any.'

Judith had to stop herself from grinning from ear to ear. Now this was good.

'You checked Mr Ingram's body for signs of bites or stings?' she asked.

'Yes.'

'Why would you do that?'

'To be sure...'

'Because you had your doubts, I see that, and that's OK to admit. Even with that raised tryptase level you described (albeit you'd done the post-mortem much later than the recommended twenty-four hours and Mr Ingram had received CPR) and the breathlessness, you, the pathologist conducting the post-mortem, with Mr Ingram's body right there in front of you, you had *no evidence* that shellfish was the cause, did you?'

Dr Leigh swallowed and gave a shallow nod. *Success* Judith thought. But no time to rest on her laurels.

'Let's move on to where the shellfish was found in the food served at Tanners' Hall,' she said. 'I'm not interested in the part of your report which mentions traces in the kitchen. The defence accepts that's accurate but it proves nothing, because the kitchen was used for many consecutive events. I mean, where in the food served by Mr Demetriou?'

'That's easy. It was in the sandwiches.'

'And how do you know that? It's right, isn't it, that the sandwiches had meat or vegetable fillings, but no obvious fish or shellfish?'

'The label said it contained shellfish.'

Judith had to hand it to Dr Leigh. He'd been knocked down, but he was content to get back up and fight on. 'Ah. I'm pleased you brought that up,' she said. 'Usher, can you pass to Dr Leigh exhibit two, which is a copy of a label from Costco taken from a platter of sandwiches. Dr Leigh, you can take your time to read through, but do you agree that there is no fish or shellfish listed in the ingredients?'

'Yes, I do.'

'Can you read out the last line, below the ingredients?'

'Yes. It says "traces of nuts and shellfish. This product has been made in a factory which manufactures products containing nuts and shellfish".'

'So, that tells me – a lay person – that the sandwiches themselves contain no shellfish, but they might have been contaminated in some small way by shellfish products elsewhere in the factory.'

'Yes.'

'Thank you. Can you also tell me what date is on the label?'

'Um, it says 13th June 2021.'

'What does that say to you?'

Dr Leigh frowned, then he scratched his chin. 'Um, this isn't the label from the sandwiches Mr Ingram ate.'

'Precisely. The prosecution has appended this label to your report, but you didn't have it to hand when you conducted your post-mortem, did you?'

'No. I didn't.'

'In fact, no one tested the actual sandwiches Mr Demetriou bought for traces of shellfish, did they?'

'Not as far as I'm aware, no.'

Judith held her copy of the label tightly in her right hand and used it to point at Dr Leigh as she spoke. It was a tactic she had used before to good effect. Any kind of physical activity helped the jury focus, at a time they might be dropping off and scrunching up the document communicated how little respect she had for it. 'It was only when asking you to prepare a more formal report, in preparation for this trial,' she said, 'that the CPS, that's the Crown Prosecution Service, appreciated that this critical test, to check if the sandwiches really did contain shellfish, had never been carried out. Of course, the original sandwiches were long gone.

So they bought some new replacement sandwiches and sent them for testing. Isn't that right?'

For the first time, Dr Leigh frowned. 'I'm not sure,' he said.

'I can take you to page 32 of your report…thank you, it's on the screen just to your left – can you see that the test on the sandwiches is also dated 13th June 2021, the same date as on the label?'

'That must be right then.'

Judge Linton held his hand up and coughed. 'Mr Chambers, is Ms Burton correct? Were the actual sandwiches served to Mr Ingram never tested for shellfish?'

Andy rose with little enthusiasm. 'My Lord, the test was conducted on the same trays of sandwiches, but purchased in June, and there were traces of shellfish, sufficient to cause anaphylaxis, which I will ask Dr Leigh to confirm, when I re-examine him.'

Judge Linton typed some notes into his laptop. Then he took his pen and wrote something heavily on his pad, before looking across at the pathologist.

'Well, let's do that now, shall we?' he said, 'while we're on the topic. Dr Leigh, these sandwiches which were made in June 2021. Were the levels of shellfish in them sufficient to trigger an allergic reaction?'

'They are small, My Lord, but yes, in my opinion, sufficient, for some people.'

'But you accept, and Ms Burton has helpfully drawn the court's attention to this, that this was a completely different batch of sandwiches, manufactured two months later?'

'But the same line of sandwiches, same factory, same shop.'

Judge Linton continued to make notes and he pursed his lips to emphasise he was giving the matter considerable thought.

'You see,' he said, 'there is a possibility that Costco changed its practices between April and June 2021 and introduced shellfish into its production line, which was simply not there in April. You do see that, don't you Dr Leigh?'

Dr Leigh nodded. He could not do anything else. Even so, Judith's heart sang. But Andy, if pressed, could bring evidence from Costco that their practices remained the same. Judge Linton waved at her to indicate his intervention was over. Judith had one more argument though, far simpler than immune responses and antibodies, or even than the small print on labels, to complete her cross-examination. It was the point Constance had, unwittingly, flagged for her last night. Assuming it went in Nick's favour, it would be a good place to finish with the accomplished Dr Leigh.

'Here's one thing I find confusing, but I may have missed it,' Judith tipped her head to one side and screwed up her face to reinforce her misunderstanding. 'Where, in your report, does it say that Mr Ingram had *consumed* any shellfish?'

'It doesn't.'

'Is that not something you could have determined from his stomach contents, perhaps?'

Now Dr Leigh's bottom lip drooped and his eyes narrowed. 'I didn't check the contents of Mr Ingram's stomach – not thoroughly,' he said, and he sipped at the water next to him, spilling some down his shirt. *I have him*, Judith thought.

'Why on earth not?' she said. 'Isn't that the first thing to check, if a person has died from a suspected food allergy?'

'Look. I didn't know about the food allergy at first, when I was undertaking the post-mortem. I concluded, independently, that this was most likely anaphylaxis…'

'How?'

'From the swelling in the throat, the police reports and Miss Percival's evidence, which confirmed my diagnosis, and there was also the rash mentioned by the paramedics, although that had faded by the time of the post-mortem. And then, later on, the tryptase levels confirmed things. But....' he hesitated.

'Do go on, Dr Leigh.'

Judith snuck a peek at the jury, but everyone was listening very carefully now. Dr Leigh was silent.

'Am I right that the guidance given to pathologists about post-mortems in suspected food allergy cases recommends testing stomach contents?'

'It doesn't recommend *testing*, but it does say you should check.'

'I don't understand. What's the difference?'

'We don't usually send stomach contents away for testing – some kind of analysis – not unless we think someone might have been drugged or ingested alcohol; those kind of things. Checking is...well, it just means having a look.'

'All right. What did you see when you "checked" Mr Ingram's stomach contents?'

'I...' Dr Leigh looked across at Andy and his head shrank down as his shoulders raised up. 'I had collected the stomach contents, but my assistant was cleaning up and disposed of them before I could take a really good look.'

Judith's mouth fell open and remained open for a few seconds before she continued. She wanted the jury to share her shock at Dr Leigh's answer. 'Your assistant disposed of them?' she said.

'Yes. But look, stomach contents is just one element. I would never, like I said, have sent them off for testing for traces of shellfish. I wouldn't even know who would do that kind of test. At best, I might have been able to see, myself, if there was anything like bread in the stomach, but that all depends on how long ago it had been eaten, how much it had been chewed. It's quite basic, I'm afraid.'

Now was the time then to demonstrate Dr Leigh's limitations to the jury. 'Dr Leigh. You're not a forensic pathologist, are you?' Judith began.

'No. I'm not.'

'You were asked to conduct this post-mortem, because it was thought to be death by natural causes. Is that right?'

'Anaphylaxis counts as natural causes. I was perfectly well qualified to do so.'

'But your day-to-day work, your bread and butter. Ah…excuse the poor choice of words, your general approach to this work doesn't involve crime scene investigation, that kind of thing.'

'That's true. I don't go to the scene and I don't deal with obvious crimes.'

'Is that why you don't know where you would send stomach contents for testing? If your assistant hadn't thrown them away?'

'Yes. I suppose it is. But it wasn't…'

'Dr Leigh. You accept, then, that, without testing or even checking stomach contents, you have no evidence that Mr Ingram actually ate any shellfish, there is no evidence there was any shellfish in the sandwiches offered to Mr Ingram and, without the IgE test – as a reminder, that's the test that identifies a specific allergen – and, again, assuming it was an allergy, which is also not certain, you have *no idea* which allergen brought on anaphylaxis – one hundred per cent no idea?' Judith couldn't resist the last comment, and she sensed, rather than heard, Andy grinding his teeth.

'You're misunderstanding what I do,' Dr Leigh said. 'The post-mortem examination is only part of the story. In this kind of death, there are many other factors which play a part.'

'Yes, I know, you relied on Diana Percival and the police and the paramedics. You've said that. Well, we'll be hearing from Miss Percival soon enough. How many post-mortems have you carried out, during your career as a pathologist?'

'A lot. More than four thousand.'

'That is a lot of post-mortems. In how many of those did you suspect a food allergy was to blame?'

'I *concluded* that death had been caused by anaphylaxis in three cases.'

'In addition to this one?'

'Including this one.'

'It would be good, from a CV perspective, for you to have more experience of deaths caused by food allergy, in a world where allergies are increasing.'

'I don't know what you mean,' Dr Leigh said, leaning out over the witness box and raising his voice for the first time. 'I report on what I see. I don't tailor results to suit my CV and I don't tout for work. Believe me, I don't need to.'

'Of course not. I apologise if that was how my question was interpreted. Thank you, Dr Leigh. You've been most helpful.'

Dr Leigh left the court without looking at Judith or Andy, and Judith turned her head through ninety degrees to feel the heat of Constance's gaze of admiration.

27

ZOE ARRIVED AT COURT AHEAD of her appointed time, while Dr Leigh was still giving evidence. She hung around outside, waiting to attract interest, carrying a placard bearing the printed message 'Revenge of the Vegetables'. She was keen to take advantage of any public appearance even when, like today, it was one to which she was not looking forward. After about five minutes, a group of tourists came past and asked if she would photograph them. She lowered her sign and obliged and, impervious to her agenda, they simply thanked her and left. Then a man walking a dog encouraged it to pee against a lamp post only centimetres from where she stood.

But she was rewarded twenty minutes later when two women approached, one of them stopped, made some welcome enquiries, asked to take her photograph and agreed to post it online, with some appropriate narrative. At this point, Zoe removed her jacket to reveal a t-shirt with a print of an aubergine, sitting in a pool of purplish liquid which could have been blood. Finally, just as she was about to go inside, a journalist, who confessed he was covering another case, gave her two minutes of film time, which he said might make it onto BBC London, so she headed for the entrance to the court building on a high.

When she had finally made her way inside, without the sign – the security staff had confiscated it at the door – she'd caught sight of a young, smartly dressed woman and approached her, to ask the way to the courtroom. It hadn't surprised her to find out that this woman was Constance, the lawyer who had called her back in April and a couple of times since. Clearly, Fate had driven them together, an omen Zoe would be unwise to ignore.

She apologised for ignoring Constance's calls. That seemed the polite thing to do in the circumstances, and certainly now that destiny had placed Constance in her path. Then she decided to dive right in and ask something which had been bothering her for a while. 'If I'm giving evidence for the prosecution, does that mean I think the caterer is guilty?'

She waited for a response, doing her best to continue to look contrite for having snubbed Constance previously.

'No,' Constance said. 'It means the prosecution believe your evidence will help them, but it doesn't matter what you think. You just have to answer the questions you're asked. Don't worry about anything else.'

Zoe was reassured by Constance's open smile and dulcet tones. She decided then and there that she should confide in Constance. 'There is one thing I wanted to say, though,' she began, 'in case they don't ask me about it. I think it's important. Can I…'

But Constance cut her off. 'I'm sorry,' she said firmly, 'but, now you're a prosecution witness, it's not appropriate for me to discuss the details of your evidence with you. Talk to Mr Chambers or the prosecution solicitor. They'll advise you.'

This was no good. This wasn't what Zoe had planned. OK, she was prepared to be able to talk about the stuff in her statement – what Brett ate, what happened when he collapsed. And she had prepared lots of material about her blog, just in case people were interested. Her horoscope this morning had predicted 'Fortune will come from an unexpected source'. What could be more unexpected than a criminal trial?

But she had all sorts of other things she wanted to tell, including everything which had happened since that fateful day. Brett wanted her to tell them, she was sure of it. And now Constance was saying it was too late. Why hadn't she talked to Constance earlier, before she became 'a prosecution witness'? And even though Constance said that didn't mean Zoe thought the caterer was guilty, didn't want him to go to jail, it certainly sounded like it did.

Constance smiled at her again and Zoe sensed a connection. Maybe, with Constance at her side, she could get people to understand some of the other things she had to say? The CPS solicitor hadn't even wanted to meet her, had asked her to write out a statement and send it by email, and that's what she'd done. And then Zoe had a brilliant idea.

'What about afterwards?' she asked.

'Afterwards?'

'Can I talk to you today, after I give my evidence?'

She saw Constance's puzzled look, but that just spurred her on. This was it. She knew more than ever that she had to talk to Constance afterwards. It wasn't too late, after all.

'If you want to speak to me afterwards, that's no problem,' Constance said.

'Good. I think Brett would like that,' Zoe replied.

Zoe saw Constance do a double-take then, her eyes narrow, as if she wasn't quite certain what she had heard, but she didn't scoff or turn away. Another sign that Zoe had chosen wisely – again.

By the time she was called into court, Zoe felt calm. She had practised her lines over a few times. *It all happened so quickly. I didn't have a very good view. I tried not to look.* That stuff should be easy. And then she would do as Constance said, just answer the question, nothing more. She would be fine. Zoning out all those people watching her, she walked across the wooden floor and climbed up into the witness box.

'Miss Whitman. Can you tell everyone what you do for a living, please,' Andy smiled at her. Zoe relaxed and remembered her plan, but Andy had given her a dream start.

'I write a blog about the dangers of eating vegetables. It's called Meat and no Veg,' Zoe said. She saw Judith turn in Constance's direction and Constance nod in response and then smile at her.

Judge Linton stopped tapping away at his keyboard. 'The *dangers* of eating vegetables?' he said.

Zoe kept her head and voice very still. Slowly, slowly.

'My Lord, yes,' she said. 'There is so much scientific evidence that many of the vegetables we eat are bad for us, particularly staples like wheat, rice and potatoes. I make sure I give people that information on my blog – Meat and no Veg.'

She waited. The judge was clearly mulling over her words, but he stopped short of asking more questions for now. Instead, he made a note and nodded to Andy Chambers to continue.

'Is that why Brett Ingram wanted you at his meeting?' Andy asked.

'I can't say for sure, but he knew that was what I would talk about.'

'How well did you know Mr Ingram?'

'I'd never met him before. We'd traded messages and he read my blog.'

'You know that?'

'He used to comment on some of the posts.'

'Comment in a positive way?'

'In a questioning way. If I explained, for example, that walnuts contain phytic acids, an anti-nutrient which robs the human body of essential minerals like iron and magnesium, leaving us anaemic and nauseous, he would ask me how that occurred. I would provide the science and a link to a study.' Zoe paused. She had practised those lines over and over and they had come out perfectly.

'I see. But Brett Ingram sold all kinds of food, including vegetables, including vegan food.'

'And plenty of meat too.' Zoe smiled at Andy. He smiled back. 'When he messaged me, he said he would try out my diet.'

'And did he?' Andy asked.

'He had some other products to try first and then he said he would let me know when he started. That was only maybe two weeks before he died, so I don't think he had got around to it yet.'

'I see,' Andy smiled again. 'When did you arrive at the meeting?'

Now, here was all the stuff in her statement. She'd try to stick to it, as much as she could, but taking advantage of any opportunities to talk more about her blog – obvs. 'I think I was the first,' she said. 'I like to be on time. Brett was there with Diana, his assistant.'

'How did Mr Ingram seem?'

'Like I said, I don't know him, but he was friendly. He asked me about one of my latest posts, about seeds and the possibility of a lectin attack. He was very interested in it.'

'A lectin attack?'

'Lectins are a plant's defence mechanism. When the plant is attacked, like when we harvest it, it takes its revenge. Then, when we eat it, lectins stick to our gut wall and they prevent vitamins and other nutrients from getting through and being digested. If that's not enough, then they make these enormous holes in the gut, allowing bacteria in. Anyway, there's a whole load of other bad consequences which we talked about. Brett was really interested and asked for more information.'

'What did you eat? Presumably nothing containing seeds or walnuts?'

'If I was there first, there was no way that beef was going to anyone else. Not till after I'd had some.'

'And Mr Ingram?'

'He had the beef too, when we were talking. I can't say what else he ate.'

'And what did he drink?'

'There were some bottles of orange juice. And beer. Water on the table. I don't know.'

'Did you see the defendant, Mr Demetriou, at all?'

'Only at the end, when I was leaving.'

'We'll come back to that, then. So, sticking with the meeting, you all sat down at the table at the front of the hall. What happened then?'

'We sat down. I was right next to Brett. He stood up, started to speak. He said some pretty nice things about me, about all of us. Then, he just fell onto the table. It was so quick. I…'

'What did you do?'

Zoe hadn't bargained on being asked a question here, right in the middle of her pre-arranged answer. Even so, she swallowed, re-calibrated. She could do this, just answer the questions, like Constance said. 'I…I jumped back,' she said.

'Why did you jump back?'

'I was scared. I'm not really sure now. At the time, he was kind of waving his arms around and I didn't want to get hit.' Ah. That wasn't what she had rehearsed. Even so, it was all right, wasn't it? To say what she'd seen.

'And then?'

'I called 999, waited, told them where to come.'

'After that?'

'Adrian, Dr Edge, he tried to help Brett. The rest of us, we gave him space. I…I didn't really see much. It was all very quick.'

'And then you left?'

'When I realised it was for real, I was in shock, I suppose. I just wanted to get away.'

'You said you saw the defendant when you were leaving?'

She nodded at Nick. 'Yes.'

'What was he doing?'

'It took me a while to get out. All the people from the hall were blocking the way. Then I saw the defendant, just ahead of me, going through this other door. I thought it might be another way out. Turned out it was the kitchen.'

'What did you see in the kitchen?'

'There was a waitress, packing up the food. The…defendant shouted at her to leave everything and to go.'

'He ordered the waitress to leave?'

'Yeah.'

'Do you know why he ordered her to leave?'

'He just said to go quickly. To get out.'

'And what happened then?'

Zoe sighed. She had no clue why they were interested in any of this stuff. Still, the sooner she answered, the sooner they'd be done. 'She left,' Zoe said. 'She didn't even take off her apron. Then he started tipping food into a black bag, like a bin bag. And he was talking to himself.'

'Did you hear what he was saying?'

'Just kind of muttering.'

'And then what?'

'Then I left, through the back door. That's it.'

'You entered the kitchen?'

'Entered and left as quick as I could.'

'Did you speak to Mr Demetriou?'

'No.'

'Did he react when he saw you?'

'He stopped what he was doing and stared at me. He looked kind of guilty, like *hands in the cookie jar*, you know.'

'As if he had something to hide? What did you do?'

'Like I said. I walked through as fast as I could and I left. I wasn't hanging around any longer.'

Zoe smiled at Judith. Then she smiled at Andy. She shifted in her chair and fanned herself with her hand. The usher came over and passed her a glass of water. She thanked him and opened her jacket, revealing a substantial portion of aubergine, but not the caption.

'Thank you,' Andy said. 'Wait for Ms Burton, please. She will ask you some more questions.'

Zoe saw the other lawyer in the wig, the one defending the caterer, turn around and whisper to Constance, who was seated behind her. Constance crossed the floor of the court and talked to the caterer. He seemed quite excited and when Constance left him to return to her place, she wrote a note on a piece of paper and gave it to the other lawyer. Zoe wasn't sure what any of that meant but she knew she wasn't done yet. She had to answer more questions. She closed her eyes and took two deep breaths. And then the prickling sensation in her fingers began.

28

JUDITH WAS NOT PROPOSING to spend long with Zoe. She would do what she must to neutralise any damage done by Zoe's description of her encounter with Nick in the kitchen. But that must begin by at least a hint that her evidence was unreliable, something much easier to achieve with a young person with a trivial profession.

'Hello Zoe. I just have a few questions for you... Miss Whitman?'

Zoe registered Judith's address with a low murmur, but she kept her eyes closed.

'Did you take any photographs over your lunch at Tanners' Hall? Maybe using your mobile phone?' Judith's question had the desired effect of forcing Zoe to focus.

Zoe opened her eyes. 'Photographs?' she said.

'Selfies, something for your blog?'

'I...I might have done.'

'You mean you haven't checked back in all this time?'

'It was a day I prefer to forget. I…I didn't post anything from the meeting. It didn't seem right.'

'You didn't post anything at all?'

'No…well, no.' Judith read from her notes. 'Twitter, Tuesday 13th April, 13.30 from @Meatandnoveg aka "Zoe". "Here is me at public meeting with @HeartFoods @DrEdge @RosaBarreraChef #ProfMills about to talk #food" and there's a photo of you at Tanners' Hall.'

'OK. That was before anything happened, wasn't it?'

'It's still a picture you posted of you, Dr Edge, Rosa Barrera and Professor Mills.'

'Well, the professor was like, quiet and a bit shy. I was trying to "break the ice". It's a nice picture.'

'Twitter, Tuesday 13th April, 17.05 from @Meatandnoveg aka "Zoe". "Just had big shock. With Brett Ingram today @HeartFoods #breakingnews #heartbroken". That message was posted together with an emoji of a broken heart. Same day, 19.00. "Feeling shaky, send love, no writing tonight #Iwasthere" posted together with a link to a local news story about Mr Ingram's death. Should I go on?'

'OK. I posted a bit,' Zoe said. 'Not about what actually happened though. I was feeling pretty awful, you know, so I shared it. My followers sent me support and it really helped.'

'Did you gain any new followers as a result of this activity?'

'I don't know. That's not why I did it.'

'And you coming here today – you could write about that also. That might interest your supporters.'

'Not really.'

'Perhaps you're right. It doesn't seem to me that you have anything relevant to say at all. I'm not really sure why Mr

Chambers invited you along.'

'My Lord. This is unhelpful commentary from Ms Burton,' Andy half stood to administer his rebuke.

Judge Linton tutted and raised his eyes, without moving his head, as if he was being forced to intervene in a fight between unruly children.

'My Lord, I will need only a moment to illustrate why Miss Whitman's evidence is irrelevant. I should add that I'm not for a moment directing any criticism at Miss Whitman.'

'All right,' the judge muttered and Judith knew she had used up most of her good will with him now.

'Thank you. So, two other short areas I wanted to revisit.' Judith glanced at Constance's note again, just to reconfirm its contents. 'You said that you followed Mr Demetriou into the kitchen, where he asked the waitress to go home. Then he started tipping the leftover food into a black bag, I think you said.'

'That's right. Not just the food. He was throwing away the trays, the cups – everything – into this black sack and he didn't want the others to see.'

'He told you that, did he?'

'He...he asked the girl to leave, so that's what I thought.'

'Because he suggested to his server that she might like to go home?'

'It wasn't like that. He shouted, like, "Don't touch anything. Just go, now!"'

This wasn't good. It might have been better for Judith to leave this well alone. Too late now. 'Where were you standing, when you saw this happen?' she continued, keen to salvage something.

'I was in the hallway, just outside the kitchen?'

'Were you visible to Mr Demetriou?'

'I was kind of half behind the door post, but he was more interested in what he was doing.'

'Do you agree, now you think about it, that you were not visible to Mr Demetriou?'

'Yes.'

'How many people would you estimate attended the meeting, in the audience?'

'At least a hundred. Maybe more.'

'And things were pretty hectic, you just told us, when everyone tried to leave. A hundred people – more, perhaps – you say, were piling out of the hall, immediately behind you, into the hallway and towards the main exit. It would have been quite noisy. Do you accept that?'

'Hmm.' Judith decided that was probably agreement from Zoe.

'You're still certain that you heard *exactly* what Mr Demetriou said, each and every word, sifting it out from that disorderly crowd behind you, in the corridor?'

'Yes,' Zoe said.

'All right. I'm going to ask the jury to remember what you said just now, as we'll be revisiting it with the waitress who worked for Mr Demetriou. Would you like to say anything else, now you know she will be giving evidence?'

'I…maybe it wasn't those exact words,' Zoe said, her confidence waning a little, when faced with the prospect of someone else commenting on what she heard, 'but it was definitely like an order, telling her to go, and she did.'

'The things that you saw Mr Demetriou tidying away into the rubbish bag, were they all disposable items; plastic trays, cling film, silver foil, that kind of thing?'

'I think so.'

'He wasn't putting glass or solid, reusable serving dishes in the bin?'

'I…I don't think so. But pretty much everything was disposable.'

'And Mr Demetriou had just left the hall directly in front of you, so, like you, he had just witnessed Mr Ingram's unpleasant death?'

'Yeah.'

'And it appeared to you that Mr Demetriou was…in a hurry to clear up and leave?'

'That's what I thought.'

'And you?'

'What?'

'What did you want to do, at that moment, having just seen this awful sight, the one you Tweeted about, the one that made you feel "shaky" and "#heartbroken"?'

'I wanted to get out of there as quick as I could.'

'Is that what you did?'

'Well, yeah but, like I said, it took a minute, going through the kitchen.'

'When you walked through the kitchen, past Mr Demetriou, on your way out of the building, did either of you speak?'

'I just wanted to get out.'

'You said. So there was no opportunity for Mr Demetriou to explain to you that he was, similarly, keen to conclude his responsibilities and leave, just like you.'

Zoe said nothing now.

'Miss Whitman. There's no real basis for you to attribute a guilty motive to Mr Demetriou's actions, is there? Wasn't Mr Demetriou only doing exactly what you were doing? Finishing what he had to do, so that he could leave that place where something awful had happened and get home as quickly as possible?'

Zoe looked at the judge. 'I wanted to get out and I did,' she said. 'And I went home and ran a bath and had half a bottle of wine. I don't know what the caterer wanted to do. I'm just saying what I saw.'

***

'Like a cracked record,' Andy said, leaning over to speak to Judith, once the court had emptied out.

'What?' Judith didn't want to engage with him, but she couldn't completely ignore him.

'Two witnesses, so far, have testified they saw your client acting strangely and your response, each time the same, is to try to discredit them.'

'I'm testing their evidence. It's called "cross-examination". Have you heard of it?'

'That's not what you're doing,' Andy said. 'You're attacking them personally, when they've come voluntarily to tell us what they saw. If every lawyer treated witnesses like you do, we wouldn't be able to persuade anyone to come.'

Judith opened her mouth to respond but Constance touched her arm and gestured to her that they should leave.

***

'Do you think they each *paid* Andy to ask them to recite their résumés?' Judith began, once Andy had gone and she and Constance were finally alone.

'What?'

'The panellists; Rosa, Dr Edge, Zoe. I mean, they're not contestants on Mastermind. We don't need to know their specialist subject.'

'It sets the scene,' Constance replied.

'Tax payers' money is being wasted allowing them to spout their propaganda. I mean, we got a rendition of the "best of" Zoe's blog. All that nonsense about lectins.'

Judith could see that Constance was unsympathetic to her comment.

'I can't see the harm,' Constance said. 'And you can't have it both ways.'

'What do you mean?'

'Maybe, instead of being so dismissive of the witnesses, you should listen to what each of them has to say and use it to your advantage – Nick's advantage – especially as you think one of them might have killed Brett. Have you thought of that?'

Constance had switched on her phone and, having read a message, she got to her feet in a hurry.

'What is it?'

'I have to go somewhere.'

'Right now?'

'Yes.'

'Is everything all right?'

'Yes, yes. I think so. I'll…I'll call you later.'

Judith was left alone to reflect on their conversation. Constance was smart but didn't realise just how smart she was. Perhaps that was a result of her upbringing, which Judith knew had been modest, although she was careful not to probe too much. From the way Constance spoke about family, on the rare occasions she did, Judith was sure Constance had been loved, but she doubted whether the people around her had appreciated her many gifts, had made her aware of them and how exceptional she was; the quiet way she worked through the maze represented by every case to its centre, the emotional intelligence which allowed her to pick up clues Judith sometimes missed and her ability to remain grounded, every step of the way. And she did this despite the undoubted challenge of being a young woman of colour in a white man's world.

Constance was right. Every word a witness uttered had meaning. She should not discount whole speeches, sentences or even phrases, because they didn't answer the questions she was posing. She had listened to the prosecution witnesses, but only for mistakes, chinks in their armour that would let her in. She hadn't paid much attention to the rest. After she had prepared for tomorrow, if time permitted, she would look back over the peripheral evidence, the material that was not important for the questions she had asked, including the mundane. Perhaps there would be something there of value, after all.

But she couldn't accept that Andy was right about her treatment of witnesses. With the exception of Sergeant Thomas, where perhaps she had pushed things a little far, she had only followed her usual routine of applying pressure, in order to uncover the truth. And Sergeant Thomas was a police officer who, she was certain, would have lost little sleep over it. But the very fact that Andy, whom she considered a pretty good lawyer, despite their recent exchanges, should suggest that witnesses must be revered purely for deigning to turn up and should not therefore be challenged, worried her far more than her preparation for the following day.

29

WHEN JUDITH ARRIVED HOME that evening, Greg was seated in her favourite armchair. She set her briefcase by the door, removed her jacket, then bent down and kissed him. He rose and gestured for her to take his place. 'How's the trial going?' he asked, perching himself on the arm of the sofa.

'It's going well,' she said, after some deep breaths. 'I mean, Dr Leigh, the pathologist, admitted that he'd never even checked what was in Brett's stomach, which must almost get us home and dry on its own, although Dr Edge was certain Brett ate the sandwiches. And then Leigh couldn't tell which allergen sparked off this allergic reaction, the one I don't believe ever happened. He isn't even a forensic pathologist. God knows why they didn't insist on one, if they were going to bring a criminal prosecution. Oh, and alcohol is fine on the all-meat diet. Zoe said she had some after Brett died. You remember we talked about it.'

'It all sounds really positive then, particularly the alcohol part. Why do I sense some doubt?'

'It's just that there's so much else going on, which I don't know about or understand. I'm wondering if I'm out of my depth on this one.' Judith sat down and allowed her head to fall back against the cushion.

Greg frowned. 'That isn't like you,' he said. 'And I'm sure you're not. Maybe you just need to wind down a little.' He went to the kitchen and returned with two glasses of red wine. He handed one to Judith. 'I've had some more thoughts myself…about the case,' he said. 'Can I share them with you?'

'That doesn't sound much like the winding down you just promised.'

'You can do that after I tell you. I think you'll be interested.'

'That's what I'm worried about,' Judith said. 'Oh, why not? I have so many different theories; a few more can't hurt.'

'It's about the crew on the stage – the panellists. They're a mixed bag, aren't they? But there's only one of them, really, who's a proper heavyweight in the food industry and that's Mark Sumner. Think about it. You have a TV chef and a man who talks about food on the radio and a blogger and a scientist – all a bit flimsy. But Mark, he's a farmer. He's the one with real skin in the game.'

'I see that.'

'I've been looking around online and I reckon that he and Brett didn't see eye to eye on a number of things. Nothing specific, but there's loads of potential for them to clash.'

'Go on.'

'Brett is all about quality products, I get that, and so is Mark, on the surface, but Brett was outspoken last year on the ritual slaughter issue – you know kosher, halal.'

'Brett was against ritual slaughter?'

'Not exactly, but he might as well have been. To be fair, he was forced into a corner by the animal cruelty brigade. He'd always been massively pro full ingredients on products, information about source, country of origin, all those things. That's pretty much Heart Foods' motto, so it was hard for him to row back from when he was pressed to answer questions in a *Sunday Times* interview on whether he would include details of method of killing.'

'And Mark Sumner is against it?'

'Ritually slaughtered cows are not stunned before they're killed. If you label beef as *not* having been pre-stunned, which is what the pro-animal lobby want, because they say that's cruel, then, the argument goes, you have to label *all* beef; *shot, throat cut, electrocuted, gassed.* Hardly the best strapline for your product. The beef farmers hate it. It's enough they're having to deal with the massive push towards vegetarianism. It's a big issue for them, and Brett is on the other side of it with powerful friends...or, he was, until April.'

Judith had closed her eyes and she sat very still. She knew what Greg was telling her was fuelling her desire to investigate the other panellists more and would put her in conflict with Constance again.

'Connie must have been given access to Brett's diary and phone calls at some stage,' Greg continued. 'You two have too much to do. Let's ask her if I can take a look through. I could check how much interaction he was having with Mark. I bet there was a lot, and not all cordial.'

Judith remained silent.

'Have I put you to sleep? I mean, I know it's not riveting but...'

She opened her eyes. 'Thank you,' she said. 'It's very good. It's just... Connie and I wondered what the speakers were doing there in the first place, why they were selected. Connie asked Diana, the PA, and she came up with some flimflam about Brett wanting to keep his ear to the ground. It doesn't ring true to me. Maybe they weren't all firm friends. If you say Brett and Mark were in conflict, I wonder about the others. Remember I mentioned that someone set fire to Rosa Barrera's café in May. And you thought Zoe might have been forced offline.'

'You think there's a connection?'

'I don't know. I don't know what I think. We've got Diana tomorrow morning, but I'm not sure how much to ask her in court and how much to leave for another private session, if she'll agree to have one. Either way, she must know more than she is letting on so far. PAs – good PAs – which I suspect she was from Connie's description, they know everything about their bosses.'

'It was just a hunch, about the farmer.'

'No, I want to see what more you have,' Judith said. 'I want to see everything. And I've had another thought. Did you say you had seen the messages which were sent to Zoe, just before she paused her blog?'

'Like I said, the website was taken down and even I couldn't recreate it but, unsurprisingly, she does have a few critics and they'd screenshotted some of the content on Twitter, so I have copies – probably the best bits.'

'Good. Something else you can help me with, then. I understand there are "tools" out there which can analyse text and find out its likely origin?'

'You can check if material is plagiarised. You just type it into this programme and it measures the similarities, effectively tells you if it's been published elsewhere. Is that what you mean?'

'Nearly. That's a start. Look, I'm going to change and eat and clear some space in my mind. But all this does mean no rest yet for either of us – perhaps no rest at all this evening.'

***

At 9pm Judith was still at the dining table, her paperwork spread out around her unfinished salad. When her mobile rang, she knew it would be Connie.

'Hi,' she said, downbeat, the word sliding from the corner of her mouth.

'Uh. Is this a bad time?' Constance asked.

'Yes, no, maybe. What did you really think of the farmer, Mark? You went to see him, didn't you?'

Constance didn't answer straightaway. Maybe it was so long since she'd interviewed him that she didn't remember him well. 'He's...he's...rough around the edges, I suppose is what I'd say,' Constance began, 'you'd probably say something like *unrefined*. But, if you mean, do I think he's a murderer? That wasn't the first thing that crossed my mind when I saw him feeding his cows, no.'

'Greg has this theory. And it's not totally outlandish.'

'OK.'

'He says that the British beef industry is anxious about changes which would force them to describe how animals have been killed, and that Brett, for various reasons, was firmly in the other camp.'

Constance was quiet again. Judith had predicted that widening the scope of her theories might be unwelcome to Constance.

Eventually, Constance said, 'I've just spent half an hour with Zoe and then more time researching Diana. But, if you want me to tear up everything I found and begin again with Mark, that's just fine. I have all night.'

Now it was Judith's turn to keep quiet. She picked at some sunflower seeds from her leftover salad. She was tired. She didn't want to have to waste valuable time bringing Constance around to her way of thinking, but she did need to keep her onside. Sometimes, an apology was necessary and appreciated, even if it was insincere.

'I'm sorry,' Judith said. 'Tell me what you've discovered from Zoe. It will all help, I'm sure.'

And it had the desired effect on this occasion. 'No, I'm sorry too,' Constance replied. 'Look. Since April, I kept trying to get to talk to Zoe and she wouldn't. Then she texted me, immediately after court today. That's why I disappeared in a hurry.'

'She texted you?'

'Long story. When she arrived at court this morning, she asked me for directions to the courtroom, probably thought I was security, or the cleaner…then, once I introduced myself, she started spouting this stuff about whether she was allowed to talk about things that were not in her statement. I explained I couldn't speak to her before she gave her evidence.'

'And she accepted that?'

'She seemed pretty upset, so I said it would be fine afterwards.'

'Ah.'

'I never thought she would follow through, but she wanted to talk. We had a drink – she had tap water, before you ask. She's a mess, psychologically. She…she thinks she's seeing Brett's ghost.'

Judith cackled down the line, 'You're just saying that to corroborate your theory.'

'I'm being serious. Zoe says that immediately after his death Brett appeared to her and told her to keep quiet.'

'Keep quiet about what?'

'Not to talk about his death online, that kind of thing, but since then she's seen him a number of times. She even thought she saw him in the courtroom. She says he's restless, trying to communicate something.'

Judith suddenly felt even more exhausted. There was so much to do and Connie was wasting time on a girl who saw ghosts. 'That's it?' she said. 'Well, you're right about something. She does sound unreliable. If I'd known, I could have used it to discredit her evidence even more.'

But Constance was persistent. 'She wants to share something with me, from her phone. She'd left it at home, said she couldn't risk security taking it away on the way in. Although she kept checking for it the whole time we were talking. Talk about addicted. Anyway, she said she thinks that's what Brett wants her to do. I'm to go over to her flat in the morning, first thing, to see what's on there.'

Judith realised that Constance was serious about pursuing this lead, that dismissing it was probably not the right way forward. She would try a different tack to dissuade Constance. 'Are you sure it's safe?' Judith asked. 'If she's so…disturbed. Maybe you shouldn't go inside?'

'I'll be fine. She's harmless.'

'Really? Did you see that t-shirt she wore?'

'I wish you wouldn't be so disparaging about things you don't understand. My aunt had psychic powers.'

Judith said nothing now. She could sense that Constance was sinking her feet into the ground, that nothing and no one would move her from her point of view.

She decided to change the subject. 'Did you ask her about her website closing down?'

'No. I didn't think it was important.'

Was that really what Constance had thought? Or was it more that Constance was determined to clip Judith's wings, to keep her focused on a narrow case theory. Anyway, she probably had enough material from Greg for what she required. No point starting an argument now, when they had just made up.

'OK,' she said. 'I agree that it's definitely worth checking out whatever she has on her phone. Then get back to court as soon as you can afterwards. You know how much I value you being there. Greg is offering to help review anything Brett received on the Mark Sumner stuff. So that shouldn't distract you. You do have something you could send over for him this evening, don't you, so he can get started?'

'Give me a few minutes and I'll dig out what I have.'

'OK, thanks.'

As she hung up, Greg appeared with a cup of coffee and she suspected the timing was not accidental.

'OK, you're on,' she said. 'Connie's going to send you whatever she has from Brett's files so you can begin on that, straight after the other query I asked you to research. You're probably going to need a coffee too then, I expect.'

30

SUE WAS NOT LOOKING FORWARD to her time in the witness box. She knew how lawyers could twist your words, make it sound like you had said things which were the opposite of what you meant. And, as they had told her she wouldn't be required before 2pm and perhaps not at all today, she had come to work first – there was no way she could take a full day off – and she'd have to try not to think about it. Although it was really all she could think about: wooden benches, black cloaks, curly wigs and everyone's faces upturned towards her own.

As she went through the first part of her handwashing ritual, she paused and sniffed the air. Something was different this morning. She couldn't say precisely what; she just knew. She grabbed the towel and rubbed it around her hands, then thrust it back in its holder. When she tried to enter her code, she tapped the keys so hastily that she missed a digit, then had to repeat the sequence, and that only served to exacerbate her feeling of unease.

Once inside the factory, instead of the customary muted drone of the pumps, she heard an unfamiliar high-pitched whine, as if her babies were crying out to her. Taking a step forward, she sensed, rather than saw, something unusual in the nearest container. Nothing specific or focused – not even shapes – more that something was present there, inside and moving, where there was usually absence, space and relative inactivity.

She ran forward and pressed her hands against the glass, spying straight away that the flies had hatched, not just one or two rogue defiers of science this time; this was all of them. She checked the temperature control, but even as she did, she knew that it would be high, too high for the larvae to maintain their semi-slumbering state. Had the thermostat malfunctioned or overheated? But as she raced from one container to the next, hardly drawing breath, she saw that each and every one sat above 40 degrees Celsius. Only when she had finished her assessment and all the dials were returned to their preferred positions, did she survey the damage.

In every vessel, the flies had hatched – hundreds, thousands, clambering on top of each other, struggling to breathe, their new, unfamiliar bodies pressed hard against the glass, their discarded pupae piled high, their unfurling wings crushed before they had even taken their first flight. It was carnage. A sea of black death wherever she looked.

If only she hadn't dithered about her clothes – what she would wear for court – if only she'd got here earlier. But even as she chastised herself, she knew this had not happened in just the last half hour. It was as she had been lying down last night, with her glass of Aldi Sauvignon Blanc and her copy of *New Scientist*, dreaming of the glory which would come from the successful completion of the project and the publication of the various academic papers it would spawn, that her dependants had begun to choke and writhe and gasp for air.

Sue took her phone from her pocket, without knowing who she should she ring or what she would say. The last thing the sponsors wanted was anything other than good news. That had been apparent from yesterday's call. Their priority would be to get rid of the mess, clean out the containers and start again, as quickly as possible, and that should probably be Sue's way forward also, especially as a consignment of sludge they had arranged was arriving at 10am. No time for sentimentality or mourning, then.

She took photos, so she could always follow things up, then called two technicians down from the lab and asked them to bring some large sacks – the kind they usually used to transport the larvae. She made sure they saw the problem first-hand then, biting hard on the inside of her cheek, she turned all the temperature dials down again, this time to zero. There was no other option. Even if any of the flies were still alive and intact, she couldn't set them free, so a quick death was the best option. It should only take a few minutes and the technicians would dispose of them.

Then, feeling tearful but doing her best to hold it back, she rang security and first asked them to give her a list of everyone who had been in or out of the lab since she had left yesterday, and then to check the overnight security cameras. Finally, once she had delivered all those instructions and the technicians had gone away to find the next batch of eggs about to hatch, she leaned her face against the nearest dome and wept.

31

Diana walked stiffly to the witness box on the morning of the fourth day of Nick Demetriou's trial. She wore a black trouser suit and a black blouse, like a widowed matriarch twice her age. Andy had flashed Judith a gleeful glance before standing up, a look which said to her 'now watch this'. Judith would never do that, never give away to the opposition what she was thinking or planning, or her hopes for a particular witness. But some people – people like Andy, who loved to play to the audience – couldn't help themselves.

From what Constance had told Judith, Diana would be a challenging witness for the defence to crack: strong, steady, not easily ruffled. Constance had said she thought Diana and Brett had been a couple, although she had accepted this was a guess based on instinct. That was no reason, in itself, for Diana to lie about Brett's death, although it would make her keen to see someone punished.

And while Judith understood that Constance needed to follow

up with Zoe, she wished she'd hurry up. It wasn't easy conducting cross-examination without back-up and Judith sensed the void behind her, gaping and deep.

'You were Brett Ingram's PA?' Andy began.

'Yes.'

'What did that entail?'

'Keeping his diary, setting up meetings, arranging events, reviewing his mailbox to prioritise mail, attending events with him, including the one at Tanners' Hall.'

'It sounds like you were indispensable.'

Diana's jawline softened with a sad smile of recollection. 'I didn't take much holiday in five years, but I enjoyed my work.'

'How were you involved in the meeting in April?' Andy asked.

'I contacted the hall and made the booking. They put me in touch with Mr Demetriou. I emailed a list of the food we wanted and we spoke a couple of times before the event.'

'Did you tell Mr Demetriou about Brett Ingram's shellfish allergy?'

'I did, yes.'

'And what did he say?'

'He acknowledged it. Said he would make sure there were no shellfish in the food.'

'That's not true.' Judith heard Nick's shout and all eyes turned towards him.

Judge Linton, who had been focused on his laptop screen, looked over at Nick. 'Mr Demetriou. You will have your turn to speak later. Please remain quiet while the witnesses are speaking.'

Diana's cheek twitched at the cold rebuke, as if it had bounced off Nick and on to her. Then she recovered her poise. In the front row of the public gallery, Lisa Demetriou, still wearing her twinkling necklace, gestured to her husband to keep calm, and when the eyes of the jury turned on her Judith regretted not having asked her to leave the showy jewellery at home. Nick muttered something incomprehensible under his breath and then returned to his impassive state.

Andy ignored the interruption. 'Can you walk me through what happened, on the day of the meeting?'

'I arrived with Brett by car – his car – around 11.45. Our cameraman was due to be there much later – at 1.30 – and I spoke to him during the journey to check everything was arranged. When we arrived I went into the kitchen and met Mr Demetriou. Then I checked the layout in the hall.'

'Was Mr Demetriou alone in the kitchen?'

'He had a girl with him; late teens, early twenties. They were preparing food, heating it up, taking it through to the main hall. At one stage, I remember Mr Demetriou bringing bottles of water in from his car. That might have been later.'

'Did you have a conversation with him?'

'I checked through the list of food and drink, and everything was there. Brett introduced himself. Then he left to take some calls. Always busy. It was hard for him to take even half a day off for an event. That was because he was CEO of such a large company, not like some of the others who pretend they're busy.'

'And then?'

'We went into the hall together and talked about when to serve the food. Mr Demetriou returned to the kitchen and I waited in the hall for the guests to arrive.'

'You didn't go back into the kitchen?'

'I…popped my head in once or twice, later on. I remember Rosa Barrera had arrived, the TV chef, but the vegan food wasn't out yet, so I went in to hurry that along.'

'Did Mr Ingram tell you, at any time, that he was feeling unwell?'

'He never said, but I could see he wasn't right.'

'How?'

'He'd disappeared to the toilet two or three times. Then one of the panellists, I think it was Mark Sumner, asked me where Brett was. He said he particularly wanted to speak to him before the talk began, so I sent him outside to where Brett was making some calls. A few minutes later they came back in together, but Brett didn't look well. He leaned against the wall, took deep breaths.'

'Deep breaths?'

'Like when you're not feeling good.'

'Did you ask him what was wrong?'

'I did. And he said it was nothing, but in that way when you know it really is something. I said should I cancel the meeting and he said of course not. I can't tell you how difficult it had been to co-ordinate everyone's diaries. The meeting had taken months to arrange.' She scowled at the recollection.

'What happened then?'

'Brett waved me away, said he would be fine.'

'When did the public begin to arrive?' Andy asked.

'Shortly before 2pm, right on time. The panellists moved to the front, the food was cleared away and Brett headed up onto the stage. I was sitting on the front row, keeping a note.'

'Then what happened?'

'Brett began his introduction. He was only a minute – maybe even less than a minute – into his speech, when he collapsed, very suddenly. Adrian…Dr Edge ran to help him. Everyone else started screaming and panicking. And then…he stopped breathing and…

he died.' Diana frowned, her top lip crumpled and she stared at Nick with an expression of supreme sadness. Then she cleared her throat. Judith watched her and followed her gaze but, whether or not Nick sensed Diana's focus, he did not respond.

'I'm sorry,' Andy said.

'He was a very good man, you know,' Diana continued. 'All this is about what happened and you deciding whether Mr Demetriou did anything wrong – legally, I understand that. I think we must protect people from someone like Mr Demetriou, who doesn't take care with customers' health, because they forget or they can't be bothered to check, or it's too expensive to do what they promised. Whatever happens here, Brett was a very good man; a good businessman and employer, a good person. He was a visionary in the food industry. He wanted to make a real difference. He was involved in every food-related initiative you can imagine, always keeping consumers as his focus. The world is a darker place without him.' Diana threw her shoulders back and stood taller.

Judith contemplated interrupting; it was clearly inappropriate for a witness to opine that the public required protection from her client, but the jury was likely to be sympathetic towards Diana, and Judith would gain little by asking the judge to admonish her, even if he would oblige. Better not to draw attention to what she had said.

'Thank you for reminding us of the human side of this case.' Andy hovered halfway between standing and sitting as he acknowledged Diana's powerful words but, to his credit, he did not try to take unfair advantage. He didn't even sling Judith another triumphant sideways look, but perhaps he did not need to do so. The performance of his star witness had been everything he had hoped for, without any embellishment from him.

32

CONSTANCE WOULD BE LYING if she didn't admit to some reluctance associated with visiting Zoe at home. Perhaps surprisingly, it wasn't because of Zoe's admission that she had seen Brett's ghost. As she had said to Judith, although she was a pragmatic person, she could not totally disregard the value of spirituality. No, it was more that Zoe had communicated this perceived need to speak to her rather than anyone else, and she worried where it might end. Perhaps Zoe would find her inadequate and make a formal complaint or, worse still, would want to continue the relationship after the case was over.

With all those thoughts bothering her, she rang the buzzer of Zoe's apartment and climbed the stairs to the second floor.

'Right on time,' Zoe said, gripping her arm and pulling her inside. 'I knew you would be.'

Constance entered a modern, neatly-kept flat and Zoe led her through to the one living room and promptly sat down on the sofa. There was no other seating, so Constance sat next to her.

'You said you had something to show me,' she began.

'I'm good at seeing things,' Zoe said. 'That's why I knew Brett was ill, even before he collapsed.'

'You knew Brett was ill. How?'

'Little things, you know. He was holding on to his stomach, he was making faces like he had pain somewhere. And I got this tingling in my fingers, so I knew it was bad. That's how it usually happens. No one else saw – just me.'

'Sounds like you're very perceptive.'

Zoe was silent for a moment and Constance sensed she was making a decision about how much to share.

'Your lady lawyer, who asked the questions, she asked about me taking pictures on my phone.'

'Yes. I'm sorry about that. I can see that...'

'I took a video too.'

'A video?'

'At the end. It was supposed to be of the speeches, you know? Brett said it was OK. But then...'

'Can I see it?'

Zoe hesitated again.

'That's why you invited me, isn't it?' Constance said. 'To show me?'

Zoe remained silent and Constance wondered if she should remind her that Brett had wanted her to share the video. She suspected Judith might have done so but for Constance that felt like a step too far. Instead, she folded her hands in her lap, fixed her eyes on Zoe and waited. And this time she was rewarded.

After a moment, Zoe removed her phone from her pocket, scrolled through some screens, pressed 'play' and handed it to Constance. Constance watched the video through once and then a second time. Zoe sat quietly next to her.

'Have you shown this to anyone else?' Constance asked.

Zoe shook her head. 'I was going to at the beginning. But Brett said I shouldn't. Or that was what I thought. But now I'm not sure. He's been here every night since the trial started. I think he wants you to have it. Can you use it?'

Constance was silent. It appeared she couldn't avoid addressing the 'seeing Brett's ghost' issue after all, as clearly Zoe wanted to talk more about it.

'I know what happens when a soul is in torment,' Zoe explained. 'It happened with my nan. She haunted us for weeks, banging cupboards, turning on the kitchen tap, knocking over the cat's bowl, until we discovered that the cleaner had stolen her favourite brooch. My mum saw her wearing it in Asda. She denied it, naturellement, but she gave it back, and the minute we returned it to Nan's jewellery box, everything stopped.'

Constance's expression remained calm. She didn't mock. 'I see,' she said. 'You think that giving me the video will…put his mind at rest?'

Zoe nodded and Constance focused on the video again. She knew it had no value on the key defence issue of what Nick knew about Brett's allergy. And playing the film would evoke sympathy for the prosecution, which was one of the reasons Andy had played the Heart Foods' version in court. But this video covered so much more and, most of the time, in close-up – Zoe had zoomed in on the action – and the more Constance reflected on those details, the more she felt sure it would be useful. One thing she was certain of was that Judith would want to see it.

She heard a ping on her phone. 'You want it, don't you?' Zoe asked.

Constance nodded. 'I knew you did. I've just sent it to you,' she said.

Constance checked her phone. 'Can I ask you something else,' she said, 'about the other panellists?'

'Sure.'

'I just wondered how you'd all been selected in the first place. Did you know each other?'

'It was just like I said in court,' Zoe said. 'Brett liked my blog. I suppose he liked things the others did too. I hadn't met any of them before. But we were going to make a film together.'

'A film?'

'That's why the cameraman was there.'

'Of course. Diana mentioned it.'

'I…I don't know if you need to know this but…Dr Edge wanted us to make the film anyway.'

'Did he?'

'He messaged us afterwards, set up a call on Zoom, even though everyone knows Teams is heaps better.'

'And what happened on this Zoom call?'

Zoe shrugged. 'Sue just went mute, Mark didn't hang around – said he had better things to do – and Rosa got really cross.'

'Why did Rosa get cross?'

'It was a while ago. You should ask her. It's hard to explain. I think…Adrian started off asking us to do the film, like I said, "Brett tribute band" kind of thing. Mark didn't believe him. Then Rosa started saying stuff in Spanish. She got angry, said Adrian wanted the film for himself.'

'Why did she think that?'

Zoe bit down on her bottom lip, engrossed in thought. Then she smiled. 'I've remembered. He said this stuff about "confidentiality" – that he had an idea, but his lawyers said we all had to sign something before he could tell us. I couldn't see the problem, but Rosa didn't like it one bit.'

'You don't have a recording, of the Zoom call?'

'No. Not this time. Couldn't see the point. I've probably got the invitation still. I'll send that on.'

Constance rose to leave. 'Thank you,' she said. 'You've been very helpful, but I need to get back to court.' Then, her good heart intervening, she looked around the room and then back at Zoe. 'Are you going to be OK?'

Zoe laughed. 'I feel better already,' she said. 'This is what Brett wants. It will all be fine now.'

As Constance stepped forward, she trod on something small and hard on the floor and almost turned her ankle. She bent down and picked up the offending item - a scrabble piece. She handed it to Zoe. 'Here you go,' she said. 'Are you any good?'

Zoe looked confused.

'At Scrabble,' Constance added.

Zoe laughed again. 'I've never tried,' she said. 'Doesn't it take, like, hours to play?'

'Depends how good you are.'

Constance was almost at the door when Zoe called her back. She was turning the tile around in the palm of one hand and rubbing at her neck with the other.

'Wait,' she said. 'I…I think he wants you to see this too. I thought he might. That's why I kept it.'

Zoe walked towards the window where a low coffee table sat, with a tea towel draped over it. Constance followed her. Zoe gave her an apologetic look over her shoulder. Then she removed the tea towel with a quick tug, like a magician revealing the disappearance of an assistant. Except on this occasion, there was something to see; a small pouch with a drawstring, to one side of the scrabble board on which six letters were laid out, horizontally, across its centre.

Constance read the words aloud. 'The Boy,' she said.

33

JUDITH SPENT A MOMENT running through her notes, focusing on what Diana had said in opening, when she had listed the many tasks she had completed for Brett. She would use that information this time, just not yet. She still had, at the back of her mind, the feeling that Diana had something to hide; that no one could be quite so loyal after five years of knowing all the company secrets, and maybe that had been the catalyst for Diana's speech of a moment ago. When she was ready, she stood up and found Diana regarding her attentively.

'Miss Percival,' she said. 'I want to take a look at the email you sent to Mr Demetriou, confirming the food choices for the "light lunch" you ordered. I'm using that term very specifically, because it was a term in the booking, wasn't it?'

'Yes. We could have ordered "hot lunch" or "sit-down lunch" or "light lunch" as I remember.'

'And "light lunch" was the least expensive option?'

'Yes.'

'Based on what?'

'Based on the food on offer. It was supposed to be finger food, cold food or small plates – that kind of thing, like a buffet.'

'Was there a suggested menu?'

'When I booked, the hall did send me a menu.'

'How did they provide it to you?'

'By email. We spoke on the phone and then they emailed me everything.'

'Did you order from that menu?'

'Mostly, no.'

'Why not?'

'It…it wasn't very appetising. And we had some unusual tastes to cater for.'

'Why didn't you source the food yourself?'

'To be honest, I nearly did. That's when I asked to speak to Mr Demetriou and he persuaded me that he could provide whatever Brett wanted. I did suggest a few suppliers to him, though.'

'So, you could have contacted the food suppliers you knew, but you preferred to let Mr Demetriou do it. Wouldn't that cost more than doing it yourself?'

'Probably. But the people at the hall were comfortable working with Mr Demetriou and I didn't have the time to run around after the food. It would have been an enormous headache on top of everything else I had to do.'

'I see. Let's take a look, then, at the email you sent, setting out the food you required. It will come up on the screen to your left. There you are.'

'I see it.'

'It is very clear, if I may say so. Bullet point one, you want a tray of beef only. Point two, the salads. Three, mini burgers etc. I have read through the email quite a few times now and I couldn't see any reference to any allergy of any kind. Have I missed it?'

Diana spent a few minutes deliberately reading through the email, although Judith was certain Andy would have provided it to her before, for her review. Judith resisted the temptation to raise her eyes to heaven as Diana read on and on.

'I didn't mention it then,' she said, finally.

Judith was careful to keep her voice even, although clearly this was a crucial point in Diana's cross-examination. 'You sent a second email three days later,' she said. 'Let's take a look at that one. It's much shorter. Here, you ask for a gluten-free plate for Professor Mills, and Mr Demetriou writes back, referencing the salad that is already on the menu and the meat dishes. Why didn't you mention Mr Ingram's allergy then?'

'I had already told Mr Demetriou about Brett's allergy. If you see, at the beginning of the email, I reference our phone call. We had spoken in between the two emails and I told him then.'

'So you informing Mr Demetriou about Brett's allergy – there is nothing in writing. It's something you told Mr Demetriou over the phone?'

'Yes.'

'And you are certain he heard you correctly and understood you correctly?'

'Yes, certain.'

Judith looked at Diana. Her face might be a little flushed, but no more than you would expect from someone giving evidence in court. 'Why do you think Tanners' Hall sent you the menu by email rather than, say, taking you through it over the phone?'

'I suppose it was easier.'

'Any other reason?'

'So nothing was missed out. I could see everything and it would all be clearly listed.'

'To avoid any misunderstandings?'

'Yes.'

'And you were sent the contract, also, by email for the same reason?'

'Yes. And I had to sign it and send it back.'

'And you chose to send Mr Demetriou an email with the food you required – that's the first email we looked at earlier – again, so it was there in black and white; no misunderstandings. Perhaps you were also thinking, if Mr Demetriou gets it wrong, if he doesn't supply the burgers on the day, I can point to the email and say he'd agreed to provide them – kind of an insurance policy. Put it in writing.'

'I think that's fair, but there's nothing unusual in that – setting important things down in writing.'

'I agree with you entirely, and yet you didn't mention that important thing – perhaps the most important thing – Mr Ingram's food allergy, in any email, did you?'

'I didn't think I needed to, because I'd already told Mr Demetriou.' Diana's whipped response impressed with its speed and clarity, but to Judith it smacked of justification after the event. She couldn't be certain everyone else would view it that way though.

'How bad was Mr Ingram's allergy?' Judith asked.

'I don't know what you mean?'

'Let's go back a stage, how did you discover that Mr Ingram had a food allergy in the first place?'

'He told me.'

'In what circumstances?'

'I think, the first time I arranged food for him, around five years ago. He said something like "make sure there's no shellfish; I'm allergic".'

'He wasn't more specific? He didn't say what kind of shellfish: lobster or mussels maybe?'

'Just shellfish.'

'Or tell you what had happened to him previously?'

'No. It was like I said.'

Now was the time for Judith to remind everyone of Diana's earlier testimony, to put things into context. 'From what you said to Mr Chambers,' she said, 'you've spent a lot of time with Mr Ingram over the last five years. Is that a fair assessment?'

'Yes.'

'Taking messages, fielding calls, booking meetings, accompanying him to events, typing up notes, sending letters?'

'Yes, all of those.'

'How many hours a week, roughly, do you think you put in?

'At least forty, sometimes more like fifty.'

'Fifty hours a week, allowing for some holiday, forty five weeks a year for five years. That's just over eleven thousand hours.'

'Yes.'

'In all that time, those eleven-thousand-plus hours, did you ever hear Mr Ingram ask anyone whether a particular dish contained shellfish?'

Diana hesitated for the first time, which suggested she was thinking long and hard, but Judith was certain she knew the answer immediately. She just didn't want to say it aloud. 'I don't think so,' she said after a while. 'But he knew I would check in advance, like I did with Mr Demetriou.'

'Did you ever see Mr Ingram have an allergic reaction to any food?'

'No.'

'Did he ever tell you that he had been unwell, as a result of something he had eaten?'

'No.'

'Did he carry an EpiPen? You know what that is?'

'I know, but I don't know if he carried one.'

'Based on what you've just told me, that Mr Ingram didn't ask about ingredients when he was out, never mentioned any issues to you other than that one time five years ago, didn't carry an EpiPen, I can only conclude that, if he had an allergy, it was a mild one and not life threatening.'

'Then why is he dead?'

Judith gulped. She had walked right into that one. She should add 'insightful' to the list of adjectives Constance had used to describe Diana.

She took a moment, then said: 'The defence will show, if it hasn't already done so, that it cannot be proven beyond reasonable doubt that an allergic reaction killed Mr Ingram.'

'Then what killed him?' Diana stood very upright in the witness box, again, and her indignation radiated outwards to fill the room.

Judge Linton stepped in. 'Miss Percival. Can you answer Ms Burton's questions, please, not ask your own?'

'I'm sorry. It's just I don't understand what she's saying to me,' Diana said. 'The doctor was clear, in the post-mortem, that it was an allergic reaction.'

Diana was proving to be a truly formidable adversary. 'Miss Percival, I understand your frustration,' Judith said. 'It's my fault entirely for not making my question clear. Let me approach this in a different way. Did you ever get the impression from Mr Ingram that he was worried about his health?'

'No.'

'When he told you about his allergy, five years ago, did he say it was a life-threatening condition?'

'No.'

'Did he lead you to believe that he was worried that, if he ate the wrong thing, then his life might be in danger?'

'No.'

'That, then, is my point. How can we expect other people – strangers like my client – to take *more* care regarding Mr Ingram's health than he did himself? That isn't a question for you to answer. Moving on, I wanted to ask you about Mr Ingram's diet.'

'His diet?'

'Zoe Whitman, one of the panellists, told us just yesterday that she recommended her carnivorous diet to Mr Ingram, but he said he was following a different regime. Do you know anything about that?'

'Brett liked to try things out. If he bought a new range, he would sample the products.'

'Like what? Did he do Veganuary, for example?'

Diana smiled briefly. 'He didn't, no. He'd been trying out something else.'

'Do you know what?'

'Smoothies, I think.' Diana's cheeks flushed pink. 'Kale smoothies. I could look for you. He had it all set out in a diet plan.'

Judith tried not to look too smug, as another avenue of defence opened up before her, courtesy of a past edition of Zoe's blog. Would Andy cotton on? He was no fool, despite his desire to swap the rigours of a life of advocacy and paperwork for the relative leisure of the small screen, but she doubted he engaged in her level of research.

'My Lord, perhaps this would be a convenient moment to take a break,' Judith suggested. 'And Miss Percival could revert with details of what Mr Ingram had been eating in the weeks leading up to his death?'

Mr Justice Linton took a moment to check the time and fiddle with his laptop before rising to his feet.

'Twenty minutes then,' he said, and hurried out.

***

Judith needed some fresh air to help her reflect on the morning's evidence. She headed out of the building via a back exit, and out to a paved area. She sat down on a bench, checked her phone and found a message to call Greg. She ensured she was not being overheard, then rang him back.

'It's me,' she said. 'What have you discovered about Brett and Mark Sumner then?'

'Nothing about Mark yet,' Greg replied, 'but quite a bit more about this Ambrosia project, like you asked, and it could be something.'

'Go on.'

'As far as I can make out, Brett wanted to co-opt celebrities and influencers to denounce ultra-processed food.'

'Wait a minute, I need you to unpack that for me.'

'Ultra-processed food is junk food, food that comes in plastic containers and is full of chemicals. It's been on the news a lot recently. I found the notes of a Heart Foods' board meeting, not long before that AGM we talked about a while back. It was headed "The Ambrosia Project" and Brett was trying to persuade the board to mount a public campaign against it: *Heart Battles Junk*. You can imagine the strapline. The board supported him in principle, but they worried about taking on the big guys – you know, the McDonalds of this world. Told Brett that Heart Foods should stick to promoting high standards in its own food, not rubbishing everyone else.'

'OK.'

'But Brett wouldn't give up, so they agreed he could keep it on the agenda but they asked him to keep quiet about it in the meantime. That's probably why he was all coy about it when he was asked a question at the AGM. Anyway, there's this throwaway comment, at the end of the board minutes, about how the best way of making young people take notice is if you get the ear of someone they respect.'

'This is all very interesting but…'

'I know, it's not evidence. But this Ambrosia thread has come up twice now in my research and, like I say, it sounds pretty controversial. You've got his PA on today, haven't you? You could ask her about it. I mean, we're talking serious money here.'

'All right. I need time to think about it and I only have five minutes now. Look, I appreciate you calling and all the time you've spent. I really do.'

Judith crossed her legs and mulled things over. She had planned on raising only one point with Diana when they returned – Brett's diet – so there would be time to ask about Ambrosia if she wanted to and it did sound promising, even if it only hinted at an alternative anonymous suspect. But Constance had been right to remind her previously that it was dangerous to enter uncharted territory in the witness box. And despite making light of it then, she had no idea what she might unearth, what Diana might say. If only they'd followed the Ambrosia lead up months before, when Greg had first uncovered it. She was about to go back inside when she saw Constance running towards her along the road.

'What?' Judith said, as Constance threw herself down on the bench, struggling to get her words out.

'Zoe took a video on her phone,' she managed, in between gasps for air.

'A video?'

'Of Brett dying. That's what she wanted to show me and I think you need to see it.'

'Is it very different from the one we've already seen?'

'She was up on the stage, at the same level as Brett. And she didn't stop filming when…when he collapsed. Why don't I show you and you can see what I mean?'

34

WHEN COURT RECONVENED, Judith was feeling more positive about her cross-examination, although Diana stood before her, just as poised as before. 'Miss Percival. Did you have an opportunity to look into what Mr Ingram was eating in the weeks leading up to his death?'

Andy Chambers interrupted. 'We don't see how this has any relevance whatsoever to the case before this court,' he said.

'My Lord, we won't know until Miss Percival answers the question.'

Judge Linton looked from Judith to Andy and back to Judith. *Yes, you're going to have to make a decision on this one,* Judith said, inside her head.

'Go ahead then,' Judge Linton said, with a scowl which suggested to Judith he had read her mind. 'Miss Percival. Can you do your best to reply please.'

'He was interested to see whether eating kale would improve

his health,' Diana said. 'He had read that it boosted your immune system. He was having a kale and spinach shake for breakfast every day and then various meals with kale through the week. I have the daily menus if you would like to see them.'

'Thank you...'

'That won't be necessary,' Judge Linton barked and Judith swallowed the comment she had been about to make. It would have been useful to draw out quite how much kale Brett had been eating, but she could manage without.

'Did Mr Ingram report any particular changes to his health, as a result?' she tried instead, after a short hiatus.

'He lost a couple of pounds in weight. He told me he didn't much like the taste or the texture – said it reminded him of all the things he'd been forced to eat as a child – but he was going to persevere for a few more days.'

'Thank you.' Now for the new evidence, courtesy of Zoe via Constance. 'Were you in court yesterday,' she asked, 'when the film from your cameraman was shown?'

'No.'

'But you have seen that film previously?'

'I have. The police showed it to me.'

'Here's a very similar piece of film, shot by Zoe Whitman on her mobile phone. It isn't as good quality as your cameraman's, but it's taken from a different angle; Zoe was first sitting and, later, standing on the stage and behind Mr Ingram, whereas the cameraman was on the floor of the hall and in front, like you. I'm going to play the film on the screen next to you and then I have a few questions. I apologise in advance as I know it will most likely be upsetting. If, at any moment, you need to take a break, do please indicate.'

'All right.'

The video played in the packed courtroom and Diana watched, through half-closed eyes. Judith fast forwarded so that the film began with Brett already lying on his stomach on the table, his head thrown back, nostrils flaring, staring out across the hall. Then, as Dr Edge had described, he manhandled Brett onto his back and he and Mark supported Brett's weight and lifted him down to the floor of the stage. Meanwhile, Diana could be seen clambering up and crawling underneath the table to sit at Brett's side. Then she bent over, close to his face and appeared to say something and his hand closed around her arm for a few seconds, before falling limp to his side. The film finished with Diana shouting and Adrian straddling Brett's body and pumping at his chest.

Judith watched Diana throughout. At the sound of her own anguished cry, she had shuddered and turned her head away. Judith allowed a moment to elapse before continuing and, in that time, Diana collected herself.

'In the video, you lean over Mr Ingram. Why do you do that?'

'Dr Edge had pulled back, I think, to see if Brett was breathing. I wanted Brett to know I was there. I thought if he could hear me, feel my touch, it might help bring him back.' Her voice cracked and a tear began to roll down her cheek. She wiped it away with the back of her hand.

'You did speak to him, then?'

'Yes.'

'What did you say?'

'I'm not sure now. I think I said his name and then "stay with us" – that kind of thing.'

'And what did he say to you?'

'What?'

'I can take you back to the film again, if you like, but there's definitely a moment when he speaks to you. Isn't there?'

Diana looked up at Judith. 'It was nothing,' she said.

'Nothing?'

'He kept saying the letter J.'

'J?'

'Well, the hard *juh* sound, like *jus*t or more like *jaw*. I couldn't work out what he meant, and that frustrated him, I think.'

'He does seem quite insistent.'

'He'd grabbed my wrist, just for a second, and he wouldn't let go. Not until...'

'You're sure you couldn't understand more of what he said to you?'

Diana's hand went to her face again.

'I didn't mean to distress you,' Judith said. 'We can...'

'We'd argued, you know, just before. And then, I was thinking all those hours you added up, the hours we spent together over the years. I knew him better than anyone, but there, like you can see, he wanted to tell me something, something important, what turned out to be the last thing he ever said, and I couldn't understand what it was.'

Judith allowed Diana to compose herself again.

'You and Mr Ingram had an argument, you said?'

'A disagreement. That's all. There had been this silly incident with the food. Because everyone had different diets, I'd asked Mr Demetriou to make sure all the trays of food were clearly labelled with what they were and who they were for, but he'd forgotten. I'd made a fuss. I said we should withhold part of the bill and Brett... disagreed. I just thought it was a simple ask and it was important to the guests and Mr Demetriou had not bothered to do it and I said so. Brett made out I was being mean and it upset me. I'm not a mean person. I just expect people to do as they are asked. In fact, Brett and I were still not really talking when...'

Diana looked across at Nick again. Judith couldn't discern if he was aware of the heat of her gaze or in a world of his own, as he remained expressionless, head down, his eyes to the floor.

'Take your time,' she said.

'I was cross about the labels and it was so stupid. I keep thinking that the last thing we talked about, before he went up on that stage, was him telling me not to be angry any more.'

'Mr Ingram's last words to you – last intelligible words to you – were to ask you not to blame Mr Demetriou?'

'For the labels. That's all.'

'Yes, of course. For the labels. Thank you. That's all.'

***

'That was brilliant,' Constance said to Judith, as they snatched a few moments together over the lunch break. And she really meant it. Judith could weave so much cloth from the tiniest of threads. 'I can't believe I was worried about whether to bring you the video.'

'I can see why you might have hesitated, but it worked well. Although it reminded everyone in that courtroom that someone had died, it reinforced what the witnesses have said so far, that Brett's death looked like a heart attack right to the very end. Granted we're not medical experts, except Dr Edge – and Dr Leigh – but to the rest of us, it appeared just like the heart attacks we've all seen on TV dramas, and that's so useful. It also reinforces that it was a non-violent death, a spontaneous death I'll say, a natural causes death. I mean even Dr Leigh called it a natural causes death. And it brought all that personal information from Devoted Diana about their final argument. Very touching. Who knows if any of it was genuine? Who cares?'

It was great that Judith was also feeling so positive now. 'Why did you ask Diana about Brett's diet?' Constance asked.

'Something to explore with Dr Leigh, when I call him back. I'm pleased you weren't here for the earlier session, though,' Judith said. 'It was not my finest hour. Granted Diana accepted she didn't send Nick an email setting out his allergy and that was stupid of her, but she was so solid when she maintained she had told him over the phone. Even I believed her when she said it.'

This was not good news, although Constance knew Judith could be unduly harsh on herself. 'Maybe she honestly thinks she did tell him,' Constance said. 'It's a known phenomenon – "false memories" it's called. Or something like that.'

Judith snorted through her nose. 'Can you imagine what Judge Linton would say if I even began to explore that in his courtroom? He'd call it "psychobabble" or "mumbo jumbo" – or something equally derogatory. Ah. That's why, overall, I failed with Diana. Calm, collected and totally sure of herself. Anyway, I'm not ready to tell you yet precisely why I asked her about Brett's diet, but I'm hoping it will be plausible enough to raise yet more doubts in the jury's mind. Then just maybe they will remember her evidence as tinged with uncertainty. We can't hope for anything more than that, after today. Do you think Nick has appreciated any of the nuances of the last three days?'

'I'm not sure Nick is appreciating much of anything. Are we still planning on calling him?'

'I really don't know. We'll have to decide tomorrow; Monday at the latest,' Judith said. 'One more thing. Is there any way we can work out what Brett was trying to say in the video – his actual last words?'

Constance had thought about this herself already. 'I doubt it,' she said. 'It's not like it's something faint, where we can use technology to make it louder, or to lip read even. Diana said he was trying to say something, but he couldn't get the words out.'

'He gripped Diana's arm, did you see? He didn't want to let her go.'

'Maybe she's the killer,' Constance said, 'and he wanted to tell everyone.'

Judith laughed. 'Now you're thinking just like me, although I suspect she would have had a million opportunities to bump him off in private. Is there not something you can do to the sound, where you remove background noise? I saw it on a film once. It might be worth trying.'

Constance was non-committal. 'I'll see what I can do.' Did Judith really think she had the resources of MI5 at her fingertips? 'Oh. Did Greg reach you? He called me when I was on my way back from Zoe. Said your phone was off.'

Judith frowned.

'What's wrong?'

'I chickened out on the Ambrosia stuff, that's all – with Diana. I didn't want to divert attention from the good work we'd done, especially with the video.'

'Ambrosia? You mean the four million in the company accounts?'

'Greg discovered more from those emails of Brett's which you forwarded; board minutes evidencing a campaign against ultra-processed food. It would have made Brett unpopular with some very important people. Greg will be disappointed I didn't use it, especially after all the hours he worked to find it.'

Constance frowned. 'Can you really see any of those very important people coming to a public meeting in a run-down hall in Haringey on a Tuesday lunchtime to bump him off?'

'That's Greg's point, I think. That Tanners' Hall would be perfect cover for a murder. Like you say, it's so incongruous.'

Constance had to hand it to Judith. Once she had formulated a theory, it was almost impossible to persuade her to give up on it, even when she was basking in the wake of a successful cross-examination. 'So, a hitman, paid by…Pepsi, shot Brett with a poison dart, when no one was looking. Is that what you think happened?'

Judith smiled. 'You're right,' she said. 'I'm getting over-excited about nothing. That's why I didn't ask her. Stick to what we know and can prove. Was there anything else Zoe said that I should know about?'

Constance thought back to the two words spread across Zoe's improvised Ouija board. Would Judith mock her the same way she'd belittled Zoe, if she mentioned them? And even if she had any idea what the words meant, it would only distract Judith even further from their agreed strategy and her ever-growing 'To Do' list. 'No,' Constance said. 'Nothing else.'

'I thought not,' Judith said. 'But the video was good, really good, Connie. Well done you.'

And while Constance was happy to accept the praise, she had a momentary pang when she reflected that, albeit for justifiable reasons, she now had two secrets she was keeping from Judith.

35

As SUE APPROACHED THE courtroom that afternoon, she noticed Mark sitting in the waiting area, reading a newspaper. He wore a white shirt, open at the neck, dark jeans and desert boots. Sue thought he hadn't dressed up sufficiently for court, then she wondered if she had overdone things, herself. She'd ensured she wore a suit and some shoes with a kitten heel. She hovered by his elbow, until he looked up and noticed her.

'Is it all right for me to sit next to you, do you know?' she asked.

Mark shrugged. 'Why wouldn't it be?'

'We're both witnesses, aren't we? I was told you're on before me. I thought, maybe we weren't supposed to speak to each other.'

Mark frowned. Sue wondered if she had overdone it – the formality. She hadn't wanted to just plonk herself down, especially if he was nervous. Some people wouldn't have cared. She bet the Rosa Barreras of this world would have dived straight in. But if Mark thought her starchy, he didn't say.

'I'm sure it's fine,' he said. 'If you're worried, you could sit over there.' He pointed to a row of seats across the corridor.

That wasn't what Sue had wanted or expected. Now she'd put herself in a difficult position. If she sat next to Mark, it would appear as if she didn't care about thwarting rules, important rules to prevent *perverting the course of justice*. But, if she sat over the other side of the corridor, he would think she was a pedant or, worse, that she had something to say about Brett's death which might compromise him. Why hadn't she just sat down without saying anything?

'I'm sure it's fine, here too,' she said. 'This is where they told me to sit. That's what I'll say if they ask.'

She wondered if Mark shifted just a few centimetres as she settled herself down next to him. Perhaps he was being courteous, not wanting that awkwardness which could come when you accidentally brushed against the arm – or worse still, the leg – of a friend or work colleague. That was what men – yes it was usually men, she wasn't being sexist, just telling it how it was – gave as an excuse, when you complained about them.

'How have you been?' she asked Mark.

He stopped reading.

'All right. You?'

Sue gave a half smile. 'Not so great, actually. We had a break in overnight, at my lab.' Her eyes rested on Mark's face, longer than she would normally have dared.

'Was anything stolen?' he asked, withstanding her scrutiny without turning a hair.

'No. It's just…someone turned up the temperature. All our larvae hatched.'

'Is that bad?'

'The animal feed is larvae-based. Once they hatch into the

adult flies, it's no good.'

Sue had told herself to put the episode behind her, at least for now, when she had to focus on the court hearing. She applied pressure to her right leg, to prevent it from shaking. She didn't tell Mark how the glass containers had similarly vibrated, as her quivering progeny fought for survival; the equivalent of a mass stampede in a kindergarten, the life being squeezed from them, before they even took one breath of real air.

'You mean it was all wasted,' he said, his words indicating a modicum of interest, but he still had one eye on his newspaper.

'We had to switch everything off, clean out all the tanks and bring in some newly hatched larvae,' Sue said. 'It's set us back, but it's not just the cost. I'm not sure if I'll be able to get all the test results in in time. If I don't, all my research over the past six months will have been for nothing.' This, of course, was untrue, but it could have been true if Sue hadn't been so well organised and cleaned up so quickly. Other, less determined people might have failed, faced with this kind of setback.

Mark looked at her now, full on. 'That does sound bad. I'm sorry to hear that,' he said. 'Do they know who did it?'

'The police came. They didn't seem interested. But I've asked them to come back again and check all the cameras.'

'Are you sure it was a break-in? Maybe someone just got the temperature wrong, got distracted? Someone made a mistake, most likely.' Mark continued to look at Sue and held her gaze for a second or two more than she thought was normal, as if he was certain that he was right and wanted her to know that. But Sue was less bothered by the look and more by his words.

A mistake? she bristled. Another *mistake.* Did he think she was so incompetent that she would change the temperature on twenty-four separate containers *by mistake*?

'We're all very careful,' she said. Then she picked herself up and sat herself down for a second time, in the chairs on the opposite side of the corridor.

Mark's eyes followed her again, over to her new perch. He frowned. Then he returned to reading his paper.

***

Andy called out to Judith from behind as she headed down the steps towards court after the lunch break. 'Judith, can we have a word?'

She waited for him to catch up.

'You may have noticed I didn't say anything about the film.'

'Film?'

'The video you showed Diana Percival. From Zoe Whitman's phone. No one has verified it as genuine. I could have objected...'

'You'd have lost,' Judith said.

'I would have been allowed an adjournment to review it...'

'Which would have wasted everyone's time for no good reason.'

'Which is why I didn't. But that doesn't mean I'm a pushover.'

Judith wondered what Andy was really getting at with his protestation. Was he just vain, worried what she thought of him, what she might say if asked to provide feedback on his performance: *sloppy, took it for granted that he would win, unprepared to graft*, or was there something else at play?

'Of course not,' she said. 'You were being pragmatic, which is admirable.'

She began to move off, but Andy drew level again.

'I hope you'll do me the same courtesy, if the opportunity

arises,' he said.

Ah, so that was it. *Tit for tat. You scratch my back* and all that, which had never been Judith's scene. Andy was laying down a marker, stacking up favours, or so he hoped. 'I can't promise,' Judith said, 'you know that. But your...expectation is duly noted. That's the best you'll get from me.'

***

'Mr Sumner, you are a farmer?' Andy began in familiar mode, and Judith had to fight the temptation to comment to Constance that the public was to be treated to yet another witness CV.

'Yes, Lee Way Farm in Hertfordshire,' Mark replied. 'I also work closely with the board of the sustainable beef campaign.'

'What were you doing at Brett Ingram's meeting?

'If you mean, why was I invited, then it was to talk about my work. There was a report out earlier this year, by the Food Farming and Countryside Commission, endorsing everything we do. Explaining that the carbon impact of beef livestock is less than we all thought and reinforcing that our pasture-based system of farming is nothing like other countries. Essentially, grass grows here in the UK without much help and cows take that grass and convert it, very efficiently, into beef – a pure source of protein. And, with a few tweaks here or there, we could be carbon-neutral by 2030. The clear message was that no one is forcing you to eat beef, but don't give it up for climate reasons. Your t-shirt from Boho probably had a bigger impact on the environment than your T-bone steak.'

'Is it true that Brett Ingram was a supporter?' Andy asked.

'Brett was interested in good-quality food, whatever it was.

That's what's most important. We don't want imported chlorinated chickens or hormone-fed beef. We want local beef fed on lush grass, watered by rain. And I'm not against people substituting vegetables for meat, like I said, even if that's for a number of meals. But we can't get away from the fact that a vegan diet can leave many people deficient, particularly in iron and vitamin B12. Red meat is also high in potassium and zinc. You also have to ask what we would do if eight billion people decided they wanted to give up meat and dairy and only eat plants. And in the UK alone we import around forty-seven per cent of our food already. If we were trying to feed our entire population on nuts and soy – products we don't produce here – that would have an enormous impact on carbon footprint, leaving aside the demand for new arable land for farming.'

Judith found her fingers tapping lightly against her notepad. She knew what Mark and the beef brigade said to justify their stance. Mark was simply repeating the material emblazoned across the National Farmers' Union website, and this was rapidly turning into some kind of campaign speech. But given that Greg had not found anything among Brett's emails which supported a specific falling out with Mark or the NFU, if she was going to hint at conflict, it would be based wholly on conjecture. Constance dug her in the ribs. 'He hasn't answered the question,' she whispered, loud enough that Andy turned around and frowned at her. Judith obliged by half-rising to her feet.

'My Lord, it might be helpful to the court if Mr Sumner indicated whether, as my learned friend asked, Mr Ingram supported this local, grass-fed beef initiative that he has so eloquently described.'

'Of course he did,' Mark replied. 'British beef is quality beef and that's what he wanted in stores.'

Andy began to take Mark through the events of the 13th of April, but there was nothing new, although he corroborated Adrian's evidence about Brett eating a sandwich. By the end of his evidence, Judge Linton was twisting a loose thread on the sleeve of his jacket around one of his buttons, his lips drawn together in concentration. Although she had sympathy with the judge, given that she felt Mark had little to add, Judith allowed one of her books to fall from her lectern onto the desk with a low thud, as she stood up to take over, and this was sufficient to attract the learned judge's attention. She had already decided that she would grasp the nettle with Mark and try to find out what he and Brett had really been discussing at Tanners' Hall. At worst, it would allow the jury a whiff of her murder-by-a-competitor theories.

'Hello Mr Sumner,' she began. 'I understand that during the course of lunch at the 13th of April event, you particularly wanted to speak to Mr Ingram about something.'

'Well, not anything special… I was a guest like everyone else. We all wanted to talk to the main man.'

'Miss Percival said you were quite insistent that you speak to Brett before the public part of the meeting. You asked her to find him, if she could. She eventually located him outside, in the car park and you joined him out there. Does that jog your memory?'

Mark's face seemed to grow to double its usual size and he ran a finger around the inside of his open collar.

'It wasn't anything about…nothing about…'

'What wasn't it about?' Judith asked.

'I'm not sure I remember now.' He frowned and shook his head.

'Brett Ingram was in favour, as I understand it, of giving consumers as much information on packaging as possible, regarding what was inside, including its precise source and, in the case of livestock, that included how the animal had been killed.'

'If you say so,' Mark said. His face reverted to its usual size, but he fidgeted again, adjusting his shirt, at the cuff. 'I wouldn't know.'

'That's not what you were talking to him about that day?'

'No. I mean… No. I don't know anything about that.'

'Were you aware of any enemies Brett might have made, because of his stance on food quality? It sounds like you are in favour, but clearly not everyone shares that view.'

Mark held Judith's gaze. 'If you're in business, you can't please everyone,' he said, eventually, 'but "enemies" sounds like you mean something really serious, like someone who would want to hurt Brett. I don't know anyone like that.'

'All right. What were you talking to him about, then?'

'Just what I said a minute ago, about supporting beef farmers, promoting us, that kind of thing.'

As Mark was sticking to his story, Judith decided to move on. 'Before Mr Ingram's collapse, did you see anything to indicate that he may be feeling ill?'

Mark hesitated. He looked at Andy, then over at Judith and behind her to Constance, who obliged by leaning over so that she was not in Judith's shadow.

'I didn't know the man well, OK? But when she took me to him, Diana took me out to him in the car park, he didn't look all that great. I can't say what or why, but I just had the feeling at the time.'

'Was there anything in particular…'

'I…he was kind of leaning back against his car, he had his phone in his hand. At the time I thought he'd had a difficult call with someone – that sort of thing. Then, when we got talking, he seemed OK. We went back inside together. Now you're asking, he might have felt ill and he'd gone outside for some fresh air. I left him talking to Diana.'

'We saw a video earlier today of Brett's collapse, filmed by Zoe on her phone. At one point, he said something to Diana. Do you have any idea what that was?'

Mark shook his head. 'I was there at the beginning when he collapsed, but then I tried to keep the audience away and Diana sent me off looking for a defibrillator. It was just those two left with Brett then: Adrian and Diana.'

Judith reflected on how all roads seemed to lead back to Diana. But none of this took her any further with Nick's defence. She nodded to Mark. 'That's all from me, Mr Sumner, thank you,' she said.

Judge Linton checked his watch. It was hardly 3pm but he closed his laptop with an air of finality.

'I'm not sitting tomorrow,' he said. 'You should have been informed.'

Judith exchanged a glance with Andy which confirmed to her that neither of them had known this was the case. Judge Linton frowned.

'And Mr Chambers, I see you have *another* two witnesses. You do understand how precious court time is, don't you?'

'Yes, of course, My Lord.'

'How we're desperately trying to clear our backlog.'

Judith thought, but did not say, that taking a Friday off during a trial was not going to assist that objective.

'Yes, I'm aware, My Lord.'

'So, I suggest you use the interval wisely, to think really hard about whether you need those two witnesses. At least two of those you've brought before me so far have had nothing of any real value to add. If it happens again, I shall have something more serious to say. Back Monday then. Thank you.'

As Judge Linton stood up, everyone rose to their feet, and he left the court without another word.

'And just like that, he was gone,' Judith quipped to Constance, who smiled, but Judith could see she wasn't entirely sure of the reference.

'*Usual Suspects*, wasn't it?' Andy chipped in, although it was clear he was trying to be chirpy when he felt anything but, after his telling-off. 'I had to watch it twice before I got it,' he admitted. 'Great film. One of Kevin Spacey's best, if we're allowed to say that any more. I imagine you worked it out first time though,' he said to Judith.

'I'm not sure I remember now,' Judith said. 'See you Monday.'

36

JUDITH AND CONSTANCE waited behind until the courtroom had emptied. Once they were alone, Judith slumped down in her seat. 'Well that was hopeless, wasn't it?' she mumbled. 'Not exactly hitting the target…or should I say "hitting the Mark"?'

Constance frowned. Perhaps now was the time, finally, to disclose what she had overheard at the farm, if she could only find a way to do so without revealing her transgression. 'I don't think he really helped the prosecution much either, except when he confirmed Brett ate the sandwiches,' she began. 'But he was definitely lying about talking to Brett, what they talked about. I wonder what it really was.'

'I was hoping you might know, seeing as you spent that day out with him, back in April.'

In normal circumstances, this would be unfair criticism. But Constance felt it even more keenly, given she knew Mark had held things back from her. 'I was with him for half an hour, with his cows,' she protested. 'I told you. I didn't get his life story.

You wanted him to admit to all the labelling stuff, so you could uncover some conspiracy to kill Brett.'

'You have been listening, then.'

Agh! Why was Judith so condescending? No way was she going to tell her anything now. 'There's no evidence that Mark killed Brett or even that they argued with each other,' she said. 'You said Greg found nothing specific.'

Oblivious to the offence she had caused, Judith tapped her pen against her lip. 'Can we, at least, find out who Brett called from the Tanners' Hall meeting?' she said.

Constance nodded. Both Diana and Mark had mentioned Brett making calls, so that was all out in the open. 'I can check.'

'And we've got an extra day off now, unexpectedly. Go and see Mark again, on his farm. Maybe he'll tell you whatever was on the tip of his tongue just now, that I was incapable of obtaining.'

'What? When?'

'What he really talked to Brett about, like you said. I owe it to Greg not to give up on that one yet.'

Now Constance had the opportunity to do what she had wanted – to go back and quiz Mark again - but she wasn't sure she wanted it any more. 'Why on earth would Mark tell me?'

'Zoe confided in you, didn't she? And Mark was looking at you when he was talking, seeking you out. You…you have a way with people. They trust you. There, that's three reasons to go.'

Constance almost laughed. Why was it that when Judith gave her even more work and found fault with her, she mixed it all in with some compliment, which made it difficult to be cross with her, after all? 'All right. I'll see what I can do,' she said, finally deciding that she was pleased, after all, that she could try to put things right with Mark.

She glanced at her watch. 'Come on,' she said. 'I've asked Nick and Lisa to wait for us, and we're already late.'

***

Judith and Constance met Nick and Lisa outside the court building, in the paved pedestrian area, where Judith had spent a few minutes during her morning break. Nick sat on the same bench Judith had occupied earlier, staring out at nothing, and Lisa perched next to him, her hand resting on top of his.

Constance felt a pang of sympathy for them and she knew that, despite her confident words with Judith, Nick was still at risk of a guilty verdict. The jury only had to find him negligent, that he was careless, his behaviour fell below the standard expected. That was all. It was not outside the realms of possibility they would decide this was the case, especially if he admitted to not checking the ingredients in the Costco sandwiches. And, faced with the death of an otherwise healthy man, there would be pressure to find someone to blame.

'Nick, did you have anything for us on today's evidence?' Constance said. 'I saw you writing notes early on.' This wasn't entirely true. Nick had, for one brief moment, lifted his pen and made some marks on the page, but it had looked very much like aimless scribbling, rather than anything meaningful. Then there had been his one outburst. Nick acknowledged Judith and Constance but said nothing.

'There was what that Diana said,' Lisa prompted him, 'about telling you he had an allergy. You told everyone that wasn't true.'

Nick swallowed and moistened his lips before he spoke.

'She *never* told me anything about shellfish,' he said. '*Never,*

never, million years, never. You saw what she's like. The woman drove me mad with this and that, but never an allergy.'

'And it's very helpful that she didn't tell him, isn't it?' Lisa looked from Constance to Judith.

'Yes, it's helpful,' Constance said, thinking to herself that Lisa also didn't seem to be keeping up with the evidence. 'What about the food labels? That was Dr Edge's evidence too?'

Nick turned his palms outwards. 'I couldn't find them. When I arrived, I was cross about the fridge and then I got distracted. I found them later on, in the car. I saw her looking at me when I brought them out. I knew she was cross, but I can't believe she wasn't going to pay me, because of the labels! You know I made zero profit after all the things she wanted. Zero.'

'Well, it sounded like Mr Ingram didn't agree with her.'

'I never got paid. You know that.'

Judith and Constance exchanged glances. 'I think that's understandable in the circumstances,' Judith said.

'I still had to pay my waitress. And Tanners' Hall gave my contract to someone else, two days after. *Two days.*'

Lisa nodded in sympathy with her husband and their sorry plight.

'Is there anything else you wanted to say about today?' Constance asked.

'No.' Nick's clipped response indicated his return to caginess.

Judith nodded once, to acknowledge Nick's contribution. 'I have one question then,' she said. 'It's just thinking ahead to your defence.'

'Go ahead,' Lisa said.

Constance wondered if Judith would insist on Nick answering but she seemed content, for now, with Lisa taking the lead. 'When we first met,' Judith continued, 'you mentioned the restaurant Nick and his sister Maria ran, in the West End. I just wondered, if it was so successful, why did it close down?'

'It was…just one of those things.'

'Did anything happen…'

'Oh no, nothing like that,' Lisa said. 'It was just hard, that's all. Nick and Maria, they shared the cooking. But Maria was more in the restaurant too. What do they say: "front of house"? She was very popular. I helped with the admin, once I was part of the family. But then…'

Lisa looked back at Nick and then continued. '…Maria was newly married and…she didn't have so much time for it, day and night and weekends, no break. I had Michael, our eldest. He was always ill at the start. Nick struggled to manage it alone. We kept it going for six or seven years, then we sold up.'

'I see,' Judith said. 'Thank you. So you heard the judge. We won't begin again till Monday.'

Judith took two steps away, paused and spoke over her shoulder. 'Lisa, just a small thing, but could I ask you to leave the necklace and ring at home next week?'

Constance had seen Judith staring at Lisa more than once during the trial, but she hadn't realised that Lisa's appearance had bothered Judith. What was the problem? Lisa's fingers went up to her necklace and wrapped themselves around it.

'It's just that the prosecution have noticed,' Judith said, 'and they're making a big point about it. Saying it's very…glamorous.'

Surely Judith wasn't serious. But Lisa clearly believed she was, as she stood up and released Nick with a loud grunt. 'What? I'm not allowed glamorous?' she said angrily.

Judith ignored her outburst. 'We'll be in touch if we need you

325

before Monday.'

Lisa took Nick's arm again and pulled him to his feet. 'Come on, I'll take you home,' she said.

'Do you think they were like that before?' Judith asked, after Nick and Lisa had gone.

'What do you mean?'

'Lisa wearing the trousers.'

Constance frowned. What did it matter? Nick was clearly in need of support and his wife was prepared to provide it, at least in public, which was a large part of the battle. But comparing the broken Nick of today with the man Constance had first met in the police station back in April, the garrulous man who had told her proudly about his 'light lunch', Constance wondered if he would ever recover from this ordeal, whatever the jury's verdict.

***

Rosa sat in her car, parked in a lay-by at the side of the country lane, her window open, staring at a cluster of field poppies dotted around the remains of someone's tyre. Part of her wanted to forget what had just happened, but the other part, the part which loved to punish her, to chastise her for poor decisions of the past, could not resist forcing her to revisit every word, every glance, every nuance of what had just happened.

It had begun well enough, in the sunshine in the Sumners' beautiful walled garden, where she had sat, drunk tea and chatted with Rachel. And she'd pretended that this was a perfectly ordinary visit. She'd drawn the usual 'town versus country' comparisons favoured by city dwellers, praising the latter for a myriad of desirable features: space to grow whatever produce you wanted – not just a few pots in a back yard; the elaborate parties you could host and the ability to breathe the freshest air from morning to night.

She'd held back some of her reservations, mostly related to the facilities she'd viewed as she drove at a snail's pace – behind a combine harvester – along the high street. True, it was picturesque, with plenty of trees and grass and old buildings, and she'd noticed a wine bar professing to serve food. But the other food establishments, an Indian and Chinese restaurant – the staples of any village fayre – appeared jaded and tired.

Then Rosa had explained to Rachel that she'd come unannounced because she was 'just passing' and Rachel had understood, had said how she was amazed Rosa could find the time in her busy schedule and had not asked her what she, a vegan TV chef, might actually want from Mark.

As the minutes slipped by, and just when Rosa was thinking that she might have to leave the idyllic setting without seeing him after all, that she would have to come up with an alternative plan, she heard a door open in the house and then slam shut.

'There he is,' Rachel declared, as footsteps and a further door opening announced Mark had well and truly returned. Rosa turned around to face him.

'Hello Mark,' she'd said.

Now, in the rural rest area, she squeezed her eyes shut and tried to erase it all. She should never have gone to his home. What was she thinking? Any momentary pleasure she had experienced from being close to him again had been quickly dulled by his vehement rejection. She could imagine him now, brooding on her visit. Maybe he'd driven his fist through a wall or stamped on some of those lovely, trailing plants in his garden. She hoped he

327

hadn't taken things out on Rachel, who had been so hospitable. But she must have known what marrying Mark entailed; that the veneer of respectability their union gave him could not change what he was.

She'd seen the suspicion in Mark's eyes even before he spoke, although he'd kept it in check until Rachel had left them alone together. A tiny part of her had wanted him to explode, to precipitate a scene. Sometimes that was the best way. Then, once it was over, you could move on. But this time, especially as she was on Mark's turf, at least at the beginning, she had reined herself in.

'Why are you here?' Mark had said and she'd noticed his left hand, close to his side, tensing up.

'That's not a very nice welcome,' she'd replied, flicking at her hair. 'If only you'd answered my messages...'

She saw that left hand rise up to waist height and for a moment she wondered if he would grab her. Then he lowered it again. 'If I'd only answered your messages, what?' he said.

'You just ignored me?'

'I didn't think there was anything to say. We were both shaken up by Brett's death. That's all. I thought you agreed.'

'You never asked.'

'I...look. All right, I'm asking now. What is it you want?'

Rosa looked past the garden, to the fields beyond.

'It's a beautiful place you have here,' she said.

'Rachel does most of it... I was sorry to hear about your café.'

Rosa wondered if he really was sorry or just saying that. Then it just slipped out. 'Thanks,' she said. 'You know, I thought for a moment that you might have...been involved.'

'What?' Mark leaned forward, both palms pressed on to the table.

Why had she said that? Even though it had crossed her mind more than once that the fire might have been Mark's message to her to keep her distance, she should never have said it. Not here, like this, when they were alone together. And if she really believed that, in her heart, she wouldn't have come today.

'We don't know who it was,' she said, rowing back. 'The police say it could have been kids. I…I know it wasn't you.'

Mark said nothing.

Maybe talking about the café, about the worry it had caused her, might help them return to an even keel. 'Anyway,' she continued, 'we're almost ready to reopen and the insurance paid up, eventually. We only found out for certain today. It's been such a worry. Couldn't sleep, couldn't eat. Couldn't cook. It was just so awful to see it that way, you know. And the smell. When they talk about smoke damage, you think it's nothing, but it's all pervading.'

'Look, Rosa…'

'No, you look. You men – all the same: so vain, so self-centred. You think this – me coming here – you think it's all because we fucked, that I'm some sad rejected woman who's going to make your life a misery, take away everything you have. Is that what you think?'

She saw him then, really looking at her, sizing her up, that it was dawning on him, she hoped, that she wasn't here to shop him or to blame him for the incident at her café.

'You telephoned here three times, four even. I answered and you didn't speak,' he said. 'How'm I supposed to know what you're going to do?'

'I came here to warn you, that's all.'

'To warn me?'

'Zoe came to see me. You remember Zoe? The carnivore with

the pink hair.'

'What about?'

'She came under attack, had to take her blog down, for weeks.'

'And who was it?'

'If she knew, she wouldn't say but she's been so affected by the whole thing – Brett's death, I mean. Then there was my fire. She thinks someone's targeting us all, the ones who were with Brett when he died.'

'That's quite a theory,' Mark said. 'You came all the way out here to tell me that some girl who gets trolled online, like everyone does these days, thinks we're *all* in grave danger?'

'Yes. I did.'

Mark laughed. 'And what's going to happen to me? Someone's going to put a banana in the exhaust of my tractor. Is that it?'

Rosa had predicted this. 'It's not a joke. My café was badly damaged,' she said. 'And people live above it. But it doesn't matter. I can see you're not interested.'

'You could have told me all this over the phone,' Mark said.

'You didn't answer my texts.'

'When you called me at home and then refused to speak.'

'I could have, but...'

'You thought instead you'd come out here and remind me that one false move and you can bring my whole life tumbling down around my ears. That's what you thought, isn't it? That you would show me what you *could* do, if you wanted. Perhaps you planned this all along. Perhaps it's not the first time you've done it. Perhaps you torched your own place and now you want to hold it over me. Does it make you feel powerful? Is that it?'

Rosa stood up then, picked up her bag, walked back into the house and through the kitchen. She heard Mark following her.

She anticipated that at any moment she might feel his fingers around her neck. She was relieved to reach the front of the house unscathed.

'Grow up,' she told him from his doorstep, where the immediacy of her escape emboldened her. 'Like you said, we were both shaken up that day. We needed each other. We don't need each other now. I hope for your sake that you're right, and that this is an end to all the bad things. Goodbye.'

And she walked the seven or eight paces across his driveway to her car, climbed inside and drove off, feeling his eyes boring into her back all the way.

37

SUE SAT IN HER LOUNGE on the sofa in the dark. All was quiet. She had no idea how long she had been sitting there – just that when she had first sat down it had been light and now it wasn't. Her body ached all over, her head throbbed, her eyes would hardly focus. She knew she should move, do something, go and get a drink or something to eat, watch TV, read a book, go to bed. Instead she sat.

Was she grieving and, if so, for what? For the insects: suffocated, squashed, trampled? Was she worried about the project? – six months of work spoiled, like she'd told Mark – or Dougie and Gemma's disapproval? Or not being able to get more funding? It was none of those things. The insects were always destined to die and the technicians had been brilliant at cleaning up; one hour on and you wouldn't even have known that a massacre had taken place in that white-washed, sterile, high-ceilinged hangar. And the sludge arrived on time. In any event, her research was pretty much there, even with this setback.

No, it was something else bubbling up, something she'd suppressed for so long. She'd been to Yellowstone National Park last year; the trip of a lifetime. She'd hiked and camped and embarked upon early morning and late night treks, seeking wildlife. She'd seen bears and otters and herds of bison, bald eagles and moose. But what had fascinated her most were the geysers, super-heated water below the Earth's surface, biding its time, waiting for the right moment to force its way up and out into the light. She'd sat by Old Faithful for the best part of an afternoon, making her own predictions about when it might break the surface.

And so it was with Sue, deep down inside – her own geyser, about to blow; the *mistake*, being *mistaken*. Why did people say that to you? Tell you *you* were wrong when they knew you were right and they were the ones at fault. Why couldn't they be honest? Why couldn't they say: *We know you're telling the truth, but it's your word against ours.* Or: *We know you're telling the truth, but we have too much to lose.* Or: *We know you're telling the truth, but it won't help anyone.* Or: *We know you're telling the truth, but sometimes it's better to keep quiet and move on.* Any of those things would be better than what they did say; that you were *mistaken*. And why? They did it to belittle you? To make you doubt yourself, doubt your own sanity? To validate their own behaviour and diminish yours?

She hadn't been *mistaken* about what she'd seen and heard all those years before – another life snuffed out too early, another person gasping for breath – and she bitterly regretted her silence.

She hadn't been *mistaken* about the deliberate sabotage of her project either. The police, accepting there was an additional, unaccounted for sign-in to the building overnight, telling her that, if it was unauthorised, that was her problem. There was no forced entry, they said. And no damage to any equipment; nothing stolen. It was an internal matter, they said. Someone had a security pass left over, hadn't handed it in, had asked for a duplicate and forgotten to cancel the first. It could be anyone, they said. And why would an intruder want to mess with her project, when there were plenty of valuables in the lab to steal?

It was funny how they had put her last out of the panellists on the prosecution witness list for Nick Demetriou's trial. There was no logical reason. If they'd listed everyone alphabetically, even by last name, she'd have come ahead of Zoe. Or age; she sat in the middle. Or gender; they'd taken the two other women panellists first. It was significance. They considered Sue's evidence insignificant. First mistaken, now insignificant. Were you mistaken because you were insignificant to begin with or did your mistake consign you to a future of insignificance?

And then now, this afternoon, the final straw, the lawyer walking past her on his way out of court, without so much as a glance in her direction. The one who'd been so charming when he wanted something. *You just come to court and say what you saw.* No thought for how anxious that might make her feel, how exposed, how vulnerable. So she'd conquered her fears, she'd reminded herself it was her civic duty, she'd arranged her schedule to take off the time, she'd had the stupid conversation with the farmer.

I thought you needed me, she'd said, when everything had gone quiet and she'd been left sitting there outside a locked courtroom and she'd called the lawyer and been put through by his secretary. *No thanks* had been the response. *We think your evidence has been covered by other witnesses after all. We don't want to trouble you any further. Our mistake.* At least it was their mistake and not hers. But this time, it was a really big mistake. Because Sue did have something new to say, something to tell them all, which no one else had covered or was likely to know. Something connected to that boiling water under pressure, bubbling and seething and almost breaking through.

Sue's phone rang, somewhere far away, in the depths of her bag. She ignored it, but the sound roused her from her reverie. She registered properly now, for the first time, that darkness had swept down and enveloped the room. She rose, rolled back her shoulders, leaned over and switched on the lamp. Then she grabbed the remote and turned on the TV.

38

CONSTANCE RETURNED TO SEE Diana on Friday morning. Today the office smelled of gingerbread, which Constance was determined to disregard, by doing her utmost to inhale through her mouth as shallowly as she could possibly manage, even though privately she thought the scent rather pleasant. One thing in life she understood was the importance of sticking to one's principles.

Diana saw her in the same meeting room as before, but this time she poured herself a coffee and didn't offer one to Constance.

'I want you to know that I agreed to see you only as a professional courtesy,' Diana said. 'Apart from the fact that I genuinely believe your client is guilty, I also want to put this behind me and move on with my life. I have carved out twenty minutes from my day for our conversation, but that's all I can spare. And I won't see you again, afterwards.' Diana had delivered those words almost without drawing breath and with a forcefulness that made it clear her terms were non-negotiable.

Constance nodded. She was surprised she had been granted

this audience at all, in the circumstances.

'I completely understand and I'm grateful,' she began. 'But there are two new pieces of evidence I need to ask you about. And they should both be quick.'

'All right.'

'The first is about Mark Sumner and why he wanted to talk to Brett.'

Diana's face creased up. Evidently, reliving Brett's last moments was painful. 'Go on,' she said.

'We think it was about changes to the rules on the packaging of beef, to include more information. That Mark was anxious about how it might impact sales, but he denied that when he gave his evidence in court. Said he just wanted general support from Brett for British beef. Do you know anything about that?'

'I'm sorry. I don't know what they discussed and I've no reason to believe that Mark would lie to you.'

Constance was disappointed that Diana was sticking to that line, but she wouldn't give up yet. 'You said that Mark was desperate to speak to Brett. You also said that you knew every part of the Heart Food business. You must know what it was about?'

'I don't have any knowledge of what you just mentioned; labelling of beef in our shops,' Diana said, but Constance sensed she was choosing her words carefully.

'Maybe if we knew who Brett called when he was outside, that would help. The police released to me the numbers he rang that day. There's only a few. If I send them to you, would you see if you can match them to Brett's contacts?'

'I told you. I'm very busy.'

'Don't you want to find out how Brett died?'

Diana stared at her then. 'If it's the only way to satisfy you, I will see what I can do, but can I ask you why you are so interested in Mark suddenly?'

'We can see from material we've reviewed that food labelling was a big issue. We wondered if, well, if someone might have deliberately targeted Brett.'

'That's ridiculous,' Diana said, but even as the words came from her mouth, Constance could see her already beginning to mull it over, weighing it up, re-winding to that fateful day to see if it might fit what she had seen and heard. 'No,' she said, after a few seconds. 'I'm not saying it's impossible but if it was Mark, how did he do it and why didn't Brett say anything to me? I saw him just after the two of them spoke.'

'And you said Brett looked ill, leaned against the wall?'

'And he insisted he was fine. No. I don't believe it. If you knew… it doesn't make sense.'

Diana sat back in her chair and stretched her long legs out in front of her.

Constance took a deep breath. If she didn't say something now about what she had overheard at the farm, there may well not be another chance.

'What produce does Mark grow?' she asked, 'and why is it secret?'

Diana shuffled forward and tucked her legs back in underneath her seat. 'OK,' she said. 'There are other things going on at Mark's farm that I haven't mentioned before. I don't want to say anything more, because it's not my place. But I can absolutely reassure you that it's all things Brett knew about and supported. Mark would never harm Brett.'

Constance nodded. Diana was still not budging. She decided she had gone as far as she could on that line of questioning.

Perhaps Mark himself would tell her about the 'other things' with a gentle nudge, like Judith hoped. 'All right,' she said. 'Here's my second question. What's "Ambrosia"?'

Diana lay her spoon down on her saucer. 'What?'

'There was a big payment, more than £4 million, in the company accounts, titled *Ambrosia*, and the company didn't want to tell shareholders what it was for.'

'I'm not sure that's...'

'And there was a board meeting where Mr Ingram...Brett, made it clear that he wanted to take on some of the fast food giants. Some of that £4 million was used to pay people to take a stand against junk food, wasn't it?'

Diana's jaw slackened. 'You have been busy, haven't you?' she drawled. 'Perhaps your energy would be better spent trying to get your client off the very serious charges levelled against him.'

'I can carry on digging.'

'Not for much longer you can't. Look. You're barking up the wrong tree. You really are. The Ambrosia Project was something special – Brett's gift to the world. It had a number of different strands to it. That's why there was such a big spend. And one of them was, I accept, about opposing junk food – we can all see the enormous cost of obesity in health terms – but it's not just that. Brett commissioned research which found that processed food affects our brains. It rewires them so that they crave more and more of the food which is going to harm them. We make fun of obese people, blame them for their condition, reel off all these figures illustrating how much the NHS spends on them, threaten to withdraw their access to healthcare if they can't lose weight, but it's not their fault. We tell them to control themselves when they truly can't. The only way to treat the problem is to remove the cause, and that was something Brett was passionate about.'

'And he wanted celebrities to help? Is that why you had Rosa and Dr Edge there?'

'Heart Foods is a successful company, but it's dwarfed by the junk food giants. Brett knew about the power of social media and influencers. If we'd found someone really big to support us, that could have made a real difference – not someone like Rosa. His hope was to find a famous sportsman who would speak out; Anthony Joshua, Lewis Hamilton – someone people really look up to. It sickened him that these companies would seek legitimacy by sponsoring the biggest sporting tournaments.'

So Greg had been on the right lines after all. Constance thought for a moment. 'If Brett wanted to attract attention from superstars, why did he hold the event in Tanners' Hall in the middle of the day, and why not be up front about it all?'

'What they kept out of the board minutes you saw, deliberately, was that they asked Brett to share his findings with the government first instead, quietly, and to lobby for change that way, rather than making big enemies. To push for government-imposed restrictions on advertising, rules on lower salt and sugar content in foods, removal of the worst additives. And they wanted Brett to get feedback from "ordinary people" to evidence the need. That's why we chose that venue.'

'That doesn't sound like enough.'

'It was a start. Every initiative starts somewhere.'

'But it can all continue now, can't it, the Ambrosia Project?'

Diana stared out of the window and said nothing.

'Is that why you're leaving?' Constance asked. 'Because it's being shelved?'

'You're very astute, aren't you?' Diana said. 'I suppose it's all those years of legal training. I may not be leaving now, not straightaway, anyway. The board have asked me to stay on, just for a while, and I thought about it and I've agreed. Even so, they will need a lot of persuasion to support novel projects without Brett to power things forward. That was your second question wasn't it?'

'Dr Edge?' Constance said.

'This sounds like a third.'

'Were he and Brett really so close?'

Diana stared out of the window before replying.

'I don't like Adrian,' she said. 'I should tell you that, as it may colour my views. I couldn't understand how they remained friends for so long; they were so very different. And I couldn't see any good reason for him to be at that meeting, although I suppose it came in handy, when Brett's heart stopped.' Her nose quivered her discomfort.

'You didn't like the fact he and Brett were so close?'

'In my experience, some people in life are content with their lot or, if they're not, they take sensible steps to change things and are thankful when that happens. Others are simply never satisfied, even when they achieve success they probably don't deserve and they use every opportunity to try to make others feel guilty.'

That was a fairly comprehensive assassination of Adrian's character, Constance thought, although she had to remember that Judith didn't trust Diana either. 'Was Dr Edge part of the Ambrosia project?' she asked.

'No. He certainly wasn't. Was there anything else? If not, I'm afraid your time is up.'

39

ON SATURDAY MORNING, Constance called in to see Judith. Greg buzzed her into the building and she was only halfway up the communal staircase when she heard the door open and he appeared on the landing to welcome her in. He was wearing only his pyjama bottoms. He kissed her on both cheeks and gestured for her to pass by him and enter the flat.

'What a nice surprise,' he said.

Judith was clearing a space on the dining table. 'Blimey, Connie,' she said. 'You don't look like you've had much sleep.' She gestured to one of the chairs. Greg returned with a half-empty cafetière and a mug and set them down on the table.

'That's because I haven't,' Constance said, sitting down. She ran her fingers over her hair.

Judith poured her a coffee. 'What have you found? she asked. 'You could have called.' Constance sensed her excitement. She wanted milk, but that could wait.

'Your mobile was off...again. Anyway, I needed to see you. It's easier to explain face to face.'

Constance removed her jacket and smoothed down her t-shirt. She sensed Greg watching them, watching her, then she heard him mumble that he would take a shower and they should call for him if he was needed. That was better. She preferred him not to be there. It was better if it was just the two of them.

'I saw Diana again,' Constance began.

'Good. And?'

'She confirmed all the stuff about Ambrosia that Greg found out, said it was part of some big crusade, Brett's "gift to the world". She accepted he wanted a high-profile figure to help campaign against junk food but he also privately lobbied the government. She said the board probably won't continue his work now, and that's partly why she was leaving, except now she isn't. Well, not for a while, anyway.'

'She isn't leaving. Interesting.'

'She hinted that there was something going on at the Sumners' farm, something unusual, but she was absolutely clear they were on the same side, that Brett supported Mark in whatever he was up to. And I don't think it was the labelling stuff that Greg was talking about. Maybe it's something he's growing there?'

'Did she say anything else useful?'

'I asked her to check everyone Brett called from the meeting, like you asked. She's going to send me the names to match the numbers. Oh, and she really doesn't like Dr Edge.'

'A woman close to my heart.'

'Said she didn't understand why he and Brett were still friends, or why he was even at the meeting, that he was never part of Ambrosia, hinted he had invited himself, put some pressure on Brett even.'

Judith was alert now, her elbows on the table, her head in her hands. 'All right,' she said. 'And have you been to see Mark also, the man with most to lose?'

Judith could be very exacting. It was only 9.30 in the morning and she'd spent most of yesterday doing more research, even before her session with Diana.

'He didn't answer my calls,' Constance said. 'I'll try again today.'

Judith stood up and began to pace the room. Constance tried not to laugh, as Judith had a grave look on her face, totally incompatible with her pyjamas and slippers.

'It's all linked,' Judith said, after at least ten circuits.

'What?'

'Brett's death, Zoe getting trolled and Rosa's café.'

Constance sipped at her coffee, even though she still wanted milk. Judith remained silent, but her eyes were darting left and right.

'What?' Constance said, after a while.

Judith stopped walking. 'You didn't say anything.' She poured herself the last of the coffee. 'I expected you to say something. The fact you didn't say something means something.'

Constance rose, went into the kitchen, opened the fridge, added some milk to her mug, then took a mouthful. Better now. She couldn't see Greg, but she could sense him, on the other side of the bedroom door, listening in to their conversation. She returned to the living room.

'All right. The reason I didn't say anything is that you don't listen when I do. It's just back to where you keep going – that one of the panellists killed him; Diana's the favourite, closely followed by Mark. I think you're making links that don't exist.'

'What about Susan Mills, the scientist?' Judith said.

'What about her?'

'Zoe said she was quiet, didn't she? Never trust the quiet ones. You haven't spoken to Susan, have you?'

'She didn't answer my calls either.'

'So we don't have the faintest idea what she's like or what she might be capable of,' Judith said. 'There were six people on that stage and three incidents we know about, one of them fatal. I think there are three more things still to happen. I'm hoping none is as bad as the first.'

Constance was determined to fight her corner. 'Or there's no connection,' she said, 'and nothing else will happen.'

'Maybe they've happened already, but we just don't know about them.' Judith finally rested her hands on the back of the chair.

'All right,' Constance said. 'I'll go and see Mark and I'll find Susan. Does that satisfy you?'

Judith gave a gentle nod. In the silence that followed, they both heard the shower switch on in the nearby bathroom and then the sound of a door open and close and a shuffle of feet. Constance felt suddenly hot and she found herself moving over to the sash window and thrusting it upwards, to allow some air into the room.

'Am I right that Dr Edge lives round here?' Judith said suddenly.

Pleased to have something to occupy her, Constance checked her phone. 'England's Lane,' she said. 'And I've just remembered. He messaged all of them after Brett's death, wanted to meet up.'

'Dr Edge messaged each of the panellists?'

'Zoe told me.'

'And what happened?' Judith's question was accompanied by the kind of look that suggested she considered it extremely remiss of Constance to have forgotten to pass on this information.

'They had a Zoom call. Adrian said he wanted them to make a film together, in memory of Brett, but then Mark and Rosa challenged him, thought he wanted the publicity for himself. That pretty much confirms what Diana said about Adrian. Like I said, the kind of person who is never satisfied.'

Judith walked over to the open window herself and pressed her hands against the glass. Constance knew how Judith's mind worked, that she would consider all these tiny pieces of information about Adrian to be crucial, or at least potentially crucial, and that she was holding back words which would express to Constance how she must pass everything on, no matter how insignificant. And Constance knew that Judith was right. It's just that there had been so many things to do and she had wanted to keep Judith focused on what really mattered, and Zoe's video had taken precedence. And Judith had Greg to bounce ideas off, to keep her sane. While Constance had to do everything alone.

'Did anyone make a recording of their Zoom call?' Judith asked. 'Most likely it would have been Zoe.'

'Zoe didn't. I haven't a clue about the others.'

Judith marched off towards her bedroom. 'All right,' she called over her shoulder. 'Let's pay Dr Edge a visit, shall we? On the way over there, you can tell me all Zoe told you about the Zoom call. Don't miss anything out. And I'll tell you what Greg has discovered about the offshore shareholding in Heart Foods. Better warn Adrian we're coming, though. You can do that while I get dressed. He said he and Brett went back a long way. Maybe he can shed some light on all this darkness.

40

ADRIAN EDGE LIVED IN A raised ground-floor flat, less than half a mile from Judith. He greeted them warmly and hurried them past an airy living room into a small office with a view of the garden. As he sat down, he reached for a mug of watery green liquid.

'It's matcha,' he said, noticing Constance's grimace. 'Would you like some?'

They both declined.

'Really? It does wonderful things for you: flushes out liver toxins, boosts brain function, fends off the slightest whiff of a carcinogen. I recommend it to every patient now, regardless of age, gender or medical symptoms.'

'We'll bear it in mind for another day,' Judith said.

Constance noticed a framed photograph on Adrian's desk.

'Is that you and Brett?'

He picked it up and handed it to her.

'Yes,' he said. 'It was a wonderful day. One I'll never forget.'

In the photograph, Adrian and Brett stood on board a boat,

either side of a dazzling monster of a fish, its snout a treacherous spike, its scales shimmering in the sunlight. To Adrian's left, two young women stood smiling and pointing

'Where was it taken?' Constance asked.

'The Canaries, 2012.'

Judith leaned across now to take a look.

'Is that a marlin?' she said, and Constance wondered if there were any limits to her general knowledge.

'Yes.'

'Did you catch it?' Judith asked.

This time Adrian hesitated before answering. 'Actually, no. It was Brett. I reeled in a substantial tuna.'

'But you have the photo?'

'Brett didn't want it. Said he was ashamed to admit he enjoyed the adrenaline rush which accompanied their epic battle. The girls wanted the photo, you see, and it took a few minutes to compose the shot. In that time, the creature thrashed around, sliced a rope clean through. Brett was upset he might have injured it. Of course, when we released it, it swam away completely unaffected.'

'You don't have a photo of the tuna?'

'No. It was rather dwarfed by this magnificent beast. Anyway, it's a nice reminder for me of happier times.'

Judith gave a half smile and Constance knew she would be squirrelling that story away, ready to reel it out at an opportune moment.

'What do you know about the Ambrosia project?' Judith said, replacing the photo on the desk, as Constance opened her tablet to make notes.

Adrian blinked twice and, if he was at all surprised by the question, it didn't show. 'Not much,' he said. 'I mean, I'd heard

Brett mention it, if we were out and someone from the office called him, but that's it. I don't know any details.'

'Really? There was quite a hullabaloo at the Heart Foods' shareholders' meeting last year about it.'

'Why would I...'

'Which you attended.'

Adrian was silent, clearly mulling over how best to respond.

'Before you say anything else,' Judith continued, 'I know about your thirty per cent shareholding in the company. It's well hidden, but not well enough. I have no interest in shopping you to the tax man, if that's what all the secrecy is about, but in return, I don't expect you to lie to me. So – are you denying you were at that meeting?'

Constance did not think she had ever heard Judith talk to someone quite as directly as this, outside the witness box. Clearly, she was angry with Adrian and fairly sure she was on solid ground with her questions. Even so, Constance was relieved when Adrian did not prevaricate any further. 'I was there,' he said. 'I remember now.'

'Was the Tanners' Hall meeting part of the Ambrosia project?'

'Yes,' he said eventually. 'It all was.'

Judith continued in a more even tone, but Constance knew she would press Adrian until she got something more from him. 'Bringing together people from different areas of the food world, with vastly different opinions, but with the professed aim of producing high-quality food. Was that what Ambrosia was all about? That's what Diana said. Was she wrong?'

Adrian looked out of the window and didn't reply.

'Out of everyone at the meeting, you and Brett had known each other the longest. Was the Ambrosia project something you hatched together?' Constance tried now, hoping that Judith was happy with her intervention. 'I have the transcript here, from court. We could...'

'No,' Adrian said. 'Ambrosia came from Brett.'

Constance was not to be deterred. 'You talked in court though, about a presentation you gave to the Heart Foods board.'

'Bean bags,' Judith said, 'headphones and something about our brains, as I remember.'

Adrian ignored her obvious sarcasm. 'That was something different. I had a brilliant idea. A way of bringing together people from across the spectrum. If you look at how everyone is now, they're tearing each other apart; if you're not vegan you're some kind of savage. Even then, if you consume a product containing palm oil, you're killing orangutans, you eat truffles you're exploiting pigs.'

'What was the idea?'

'It's confidential.'

Ah. Just as Zoe had remembered. Judith leaned forward conspiratorially. 'We won't tell,' she said.

'All right.' Constance saw Adrian's eyes light up. Perhaps he had been waiting for the opportunity to share, after all. He waved his hand at eye level, with a flourish, as if he could see the words written up on a banner or across a screen. '*Food for your mood,*' he said.

'Food for your mood?' Judith repeated his words.

'A whole new concept. When you go into a supermarket now, everything is arranged in categories: fruit and veg, meat, fish, dairy, vegetarian products. That engenders conflict.'

'It does?'

'Of course. Because there's no interaction. Brett loved my idea, was itching to set it free on the public, on the world,'

'I can see why it might appeal to you, to your listeners,' Judith said. 'You're always talking about how food makes you feel, as well as lauding its health benefits. What I fail to see is why it would appeal to Mr Ingram.'

'That's what I'm trying to explain. Everyone wants more and more information, OK? How many calories does a product contain or grams of protein or vitamins? That's been around for decades. More recently, where's it from? How's it sourced? Were the people who harvested it paid a fair wage? How was it killed? What was it fed on? You name it, on and on and on, and Brett knew there was no point trying to fight it. This quest for more and more information couldn't be stopped, like an unquenchable thirst. Then came the beauty of my original idea; the synergy between the two.'

'Go on.'

'You change the narrative. You focus on how eating the food is going to *make you feel*. Are you going for a job interview? You need food that's going to give you confidence? Are you at the end of a long week and you want to put your feet up? You need food that's going to help you relax. A romantic evening for two – you get the message. If that's how food is presented to people, how it's badged and packaged up, the other stuff gets forgotten. Sure, have a list of ingredients on the side, in the small print, or any of the other stuff, but shift the focus onto mood, mental health, wellness, what everyone is talking about. Pure brilliance.'

Adrian sat back in his chair, beaming from ear to ear.

'And that was the substance of your presentation to the Heart Foods' board, the one with the bean bags?' Judith said.

'Yes.'

351

'But that was some time ago. Constance has the date, I'm sure. So, why wasn't the initiative already being rolled out?'

'Brett said to give the board time. They had lots of other things going on – this Ambrosia thing you're talking about, for one. We'd agreed to pick up the conversation again, towards the end of the year.'

Now Judith sat back and Constance could see the cogs whirring behind her eyes. She worked so fast, taking in what Adrian said, processing it, thinking how to get him to give more away, including things he would not normally volunteer.

'You don't really believe that, do you?' Judith asked.

'What?' Adrian said what Constance was thinking.

'I mean, a man like Brett Ingram had the board eating out of his hand. It sounds to me like he thought your idea was nonsense, but didn't want to hurt your feelings.'

Adrian threw himself back in his chair and then catapulted himself forwards to lean over his desk, elbows splayed.

'That's not true,' he said. 'We spent a lot of time working on it together. Brett wouldn't have done that if he didn't support it. He was a busy man, that's all.'

'If you say so.'

Adrian's eyes flashed his anger at Judith's words. 'I do.'

Constance remembered the other part of their agenda. 'Why did you send a message to the other panellists after Brett died?' she asked.

'What?'

'You messaged all the other panellists, wanted to meet up?'

'I…I wanted to get in touch.'

'Why?'

'I just… Brett was my friend, my oldest friend. I wanted to

make contact with the others. We didn't know when the funeral was going to be.'

'And you all met on Zoom?'

'Yes.'

'What did you talk about?'

Judith inclined her head towards Constance's laptop and pointed to something on the screen. Constance understood that Judith wanted Adrian to think they might have a recording of the Zoom call, when of course they didn't. She played along by nodding and shifting her screen a fraction in Judith's direction, as if she was sharing an image.

Adrian said nothing. Then he picked up his phone. Then he put it down.

'You wanted the other panellists to help you promote *your* idea, because the Heart Foods board wasn't interested,' Judith said. 'Brett had put you off and now you had lost your opportunity to talk about it at the public meeting.'

'I called them because I wanted to fulfil Brett's legacy. I thought we could still make the film he wanted, promote his aims.'

'And they weren't interested?'

'No.'

'I'm not surprised. They didn't owe you anything, or Brett.'

'You're so wrong,' Adrian said. 'They owed everything to Brett; they just didn't appreciate it or they didn't care.'

'How did they owe everything to Brett?' Judith asked.

Adrian tapped his fingers against his mouth. Then he turned back to Constance and Judith.

'All right. Ambrosia was everything you said, but Brett was using the money, the Ambrosia pot, to support them all financially in some way. Even Zoe, the blogger. He sponsored ads on her site, although God knows why. I think it amused him. And when he replied to her posts, it got noticed. They all owed him, big time.'

'I see. People can be ungrateful sometimes, like you said.'

'They don't have to be disparaging though, do they, or just downright rude?'

'No, you're right. That sounds like reprehensible behaviour.'

'Look, I've answered lots of your questions now, haven't I?' Adrian crossed his hands in front of him. 'Can you answer one for me? Do you still think your man wasn't responsible for Brett's death? That he didn't ignore the warning Diana gave him, leaving my best friend dying on the floor, like a rat in a sewer?'

'Yes,' Judith said.

'We are investigating the possibility that someone else may have deliberately targeted Brett,' Constance said.

'Investigating? I thought that was what the police did.'

'A poor choice of words. We're evaluating the evidence we have,' Judith corrected Constance.

'All right,' Adrian said. 'For what it's worth, I think that's a load of crap. I'm a hundred per cent sure, just like Dr Leigh, that your guy is guilty as hell. He knew about the shellfish, but either he was too stupid to realise what it might do to Brett or he just didn't care. But if you're insisting it was someone else, and it was…well, murder, like you say, then my money would be on the farmer.'

'Why do you say that?' Constance asked, feeling the heat of Judith's gaze, hoping she wasn't thinking *I told you so.*

'Brett liked misfits and enjoyed helping them. It wasn't kindness. He found it thrilling, exciting. I decided someone had to look after his interests. So I did some digging around on him, the farmer,' Adrian said. 'Mark has a criminal record, *ABH*, served six months and came out with a nasty drug habit. Sure, he's married now and has responsibilities, but the farm only came to him because his father dropped dead one day – a bit like Brett, now I think about it. He's the one who could most easily have been bribed, say, by a competitor, to get Brett out of the way.'

***

'What do you make of all of that?' Judith asked, as she and Constance walked back up Haverstock Hill.

'I think you were right about Dr Edge, after all,' Constance said.

'I was only criticising his voice on the radio, not his integrity. Honestly, matcha tea and marlins. I knew he hadn't caught that fish. I just knew it! I bet he tells less discerning guests it was him. That's the only reason he's kept that photo.'

Constance agreed with everything Judith said on this occasion, but she wanted to keep her focused on the case. 'You don't think he had anything to do with Brett's death, though?'

'We got him to admit that he was the odd one out, didn't we?' Judith didn't answer Constance's question. 'That the others were all part of Ambrosia, all funded and supported by Heart Foods, even if it was under the radar – all except for him. That must have made him very angry and bitter.'

Constance sighed. She was going to have to participate in Judith's post-mortem of the session with Adrian after all. 'He didn't like it,' she agreed, 'when you suggested Brett was stringing him along.'

'Not one little bit. But would he kill his oldest friend because of it? And in such a public way? I mean, if he's guilty, he only pretended to try to save his friend's life with the CPR. It would be…unusually callous. And more importantly, much as I dislike our oily friend, I can't see him bumping off his mate when there was still a chance Brett would come good and fund his "brilliant idea". But we should re-evaluate whether he had a hand in trolling Zoe.'

'Or burning down Rosa's café.'

Judith stopped walking and faced Constance. 'Ah, so you do see a link now,' she said. 'Interesting how one second his idea was "confidential" – no doubt that's why he couldn't just announce it on his radio show – and the next he was giving us the hard sell. I had the feeling he spouted that nonsense just to get rid of us.'

'I thought he enjoyed telling us. He wanted to see our reaction.'

'Perhaps – yes. He couldn't help himself. So, what did you think of his idea then; *food for your mood*?'

'I thought it was quite good.'

'Really?' Judith laughed and Constance had the feeling that she was about to be treated to another lesson in why her views were unsustainable. 'Tell me this,' Judith pointed a finger at her. 'You have an important exam, you buy the meal called, "brain food" – probably oily fish and wholegrain rice with a handful of blueberries. You take the exam and you fail. You're hardly going to endorse the product.'

'Oh, come on.'

Judith began walking again and Constance joined her. 'Or... you have a romantic evening planned – with your new man, Chris, for example – so this time you choose the "won't be able to resist me" menu or something much catchier. Then...'

'I get the message. I still think it's good. People will like it. It fits with, you know, what's going on at the moment.'

'Does it? I must be so out of touch.'

Constance resisted the temptation to agree. 'Why do you think

Adrian might have trolled Zoe? Would he do that if he was trying to get her and the others to make the film?'

'We should look at the timing, but I suspect it was after they all rejected him. And there's something Greg has drawn to my attention. An algorithm. There. I never thought I would ever say those words. Remember this day. Today, I, Judith Burton, prepare myself to rely on something as flimsy as an algorithm to help solve a mystery.'

Constance ignored Judith's overacting. 'You thought something might have happened to the others too. We didn't even ask Adrian. Then there's Mark and Susan.'

'Yes. Well, they're on your list. You can ask them, if you ever get round to seeing them.'

Constance gritted her teeth. She had already agreed to go and see the other two panellists. Why was Judith such a hard taskmaster?

'Look,' Judith said. 'Why don't you leave the trolling and the other related incidents to me. I have an idea of how to deal with them; one which may help me build bridges elsewhere.'

'All right,' Constance replied. 'Are you giving up on Ambrosia as a reason for Brett's death then? You said murder was all about money and Ambrosia was all about money – big money.'

'I never give up on anything, you know that. But I may be near the end of the line, this time around.'

Now they were level with Belsize Park Underground station and they hovered by the entrance.

'What now?' Constance asked.

Judith shrugged. 'Who's left for the prosecution?'

'Their solicitor messaged me to say they're not calling Susan Mills now, probably a result of Judge Linton's warning about time-wasting. So there's just the waitress, Eleni Pallas. Then it's over to us.'

'And I want Dr Leigh back, to talk about smoothies. One last trick up my sleeve for the eminent doctor.'

As Constance pushed through the barriers at the Underground station, she looked back over her shoulder. Judith was still outside but was calling someone on her mobile phone. That was unusual; something which couldn't wait till Judith got home. With that thought in her mind, Constance continued on her way.

***

'Hello, is that Sergeant Thomas? Hello, yes, it's Judith Burton here, representing Mr Demetriou.'

Judith, with her phone to one ear and her finger wedged in the other to blot out the passing traffic, paused for a response but none came. She had not expected Sergeant Thomas to be delighted to hear from her, given her robust attempts to challenge the Sergeant in the witness box. But a few days had passed now and, hopefully, the officer had moved on.

'I…this is a little awkward,' Judith continued, taking advantage of the silence, 'but I have some information you may be interested in. It relates to some unsolved offences, and some that may not have been committed yet.'

Judith waited, imagining the officer running the gamut of emotions, from displeasure at hearing from Judith, to impatience, to having her interest piqued.

'All right,' Sergeant Thomas said, albeit sulkily. 'Wait on the line and I'll go get a pen.'

41

CONSTANCE MET CHRIS for a pizza that evening. He'd been overseas for the past two months and this was the first time she'd seen him since his return, although they had exchanged messages and a few, hurried calls. She didn't normally socialise during a trial, but it was the weekend, he'd been keen and she had to eat.

When, after twenty minutes, their pizza hadn't arrived and her mind turned to her long 'To Do' list, she began to think this had been a bad idea.

'You've checked your watch six times now,' he said, refilling her glass with fizzy water.

'I'm sorry. I…I'm a bit preoccupied.'

'It was my fault. I pushed you. We can just leave if you like. I can make you something quick at my place or we can just call it a day. I won't be offended.'

Constance smiled for the first time since she'd arrived. Chris hadn't pressed her that hard to come out with him; he'd asked and she'd accepted. It was nice that he understood though. He was probably the first man she had dated who so openly accepted that her work was important and might distract her, even before he knew much about it. And he was willing to take the blame for the failure of the evening. Both attributes were refreshingly attractive. But he had now given her the choice as to what to do next and she wasn't in the mood for decisions. The only thing she was certain of was that she didn't want to mess things up with him.

At that moment, the waitress appeared from the kitchen and set their plates on the table. Constance picked up her knife and fork and began to saw her way through her pizza crust and Chris followed suit. Thirty minutes later and she found herself accepting an invitation to join him for dessert in his flat, which he said was only around the corner. She told herself not to pass up the opportunity to see where and how he lived; personal space could reveal so much about a person.

Chris' flat was at the top of a Victorian terraced property and the sun was just beginning to set behind the rooftops opposite, so that a yellow glow bathed the lounge.

'I have ice cream,' he said, waving two different tubs of Ben & Jerry's in Constance's direction, 'or strawberries, or both? And I can offer a hot drink or a dessert wine.'

'Dessert wine?'

'A gift from a client. It looks expensive.'

'You get presents from clients?'

'Not often. But we installed this special drainage system for their hotel.'

'I'm pretty full from the pizza, actually,' Constance laughed. 'I'll just have coffee, white no sugar, if that's OK. And I can't stay too long.'

'I know. You said. Relax. I'll put the kettle on.'

But Constance found herself far from relaxed. She didn't want to sit down and wait for her coffee, she wanted to explore, to dig around, to delve below the surface. That was why she had come, wasn't it?

The one adornment on the otherwise white-washed walls was a large black-and-white photograph. It showed eleven men – she counted them – sitting on a huge iron girder, each one wearing an oversize cloth cap, their feet dangling over the edge and a gap of hundreds of feet to the tightly-packed skyscrapers below. Only the man on the furthest right, who was holding an empty spirits bottle in his hand, appeared to have even noticed the camera. The others were all otherwise engaged: smoking, chatting or eating, completely unaware of the danger they were in. And she'd been afraid of a few cows.

'I know it's a bit of a cliché, but I've always loved that picture,' Chris had returned with her coffee.

'Where was it taken?'

'Manhattan. They were building the Rockefeller Center in the early 1930s, part of a programme to revitalise the area. Apparently it was staged – the photo – but you wouldn't know it. It's why I decided to become an engineer.'

'How come?'

'I saw the photo in the window of a shop when I was a kid and I loved it. And I woke up one day and thought I wanted to make buildings. I know that's not quite what's happened, but that was what started me off on this path. And I said to myself that as soon as I got my own place I would hang a copy of the picture on the wall, to remind me. So there you are.'

'A man who keeps his promises,' Constance said.

'I hope so.'

As Chris didn't seem to mind Constance's snooping, she approached the narrow shelf above the radiator, where a model of a windmill sat, made entirely from matchsticks. Although they must have been glued together, it was impossible to see any joins, so neatly had each piece been attached to the next. Constance inserted her little finger into one of the four tiny blades and spun it around.

'Is this your work, then?'

'You've picked up on the theme. 'It's... I'm not a train spotter, before you ask. I just... I like making things, that's all.'

'Making things is good,' Constance said. 'I have a friend who's a carpenter, but he gave it up to sell life insurance. You might be my only friend who makes things now.'

Chris smiled. 'My last girlfriend told me I'd be useful in an apocalypse. That's when I first noticed things going wrong.'

Constance smiled at him and he looked away. Then he sat down on the sofa. She finished examining the model and then replaced it carefully in its appointed space. There was a silence then, aching to be filled.

'Connie, look. I don't want to mess things up with you,' Chris said. 'I...I really like you. I thought about you loads when I was away. You're clever, you're beautiful, you have a great sense of humour, you care about your work. That's what I know so far and I want to get to know you better. But I'm not sure how you feel about me and I don't want to make an idiot of myself, you know. I probably already have. So...if you want me to just be the friend who makes things, that's really OK, but I was hoping for something more, you know?'

Constance looked through the window at the sinking sun, then at the coffee sitting waiting for her, neatly positioned on a coaster.

Chris was not like other men she'd dated. Maybe because he was already established in his career, had his own place, understood where he fitted in the scheme of things. And he was certainly much tidier than Mike had ever been. And she liked him – she knew that already. Who would have thought that anecdotes about water pressure and dams and sewage treatment could be entertaining? It was just…

'I think I'll skip coffee,' she said.

Chris' shoulders slumped and he looked away again. She picked up her bag and walked towards the door and then she paused, one hand on the latch.

'I had a really lovely evening,' she said. 'And I'm not used to people coming out with what they think, especially when it's so flattering. But my head's all over the place with this trial. If you can wait for me, just a few days, then…please. I missed you too, when you were away. I missed you a lot.'

As Constance left the building, she wondered at her reticence. Chris was the best thing to happen to her, on a personal level, for years, maybe ever. And as her mother delighted in reminding her, she wasn't getting any younger. But at the moment when Chris had told her how he felt, had opened up his heart to her, and she'd been on the point of responding, Greg's face had flashed before her eyes. How could that be?

Even as she asked herself the question, she knew the answer. Because her embarrassment that morning at Judith's flat had been for the same reason. She had spent months encouraging Judith to take Greg back, not saying anything too obvious; outright praise for Greg would almost certainly have raised Judith's hackles. Instead, every now and again, she'd drop his name into the conversation, mention thoughtful or clever things he had done, draw Judith's attention to how his businesses were flourishing. And of course, she had kept in touch with him herself; the odd drink or dinner, which she'd enjoyed more than she wanted to let on. And that was the problem. She'd been there to advocate for her friend, her partner in crime, but she couldn't help but succumb to Greg's charms herself.

She realised now, in this moment, that she loved the way Greg looked; his unkempt, curly hair, often neglected so it grew long, his over-large frame, simultaneously full of latent power and grace, his voice, low and even and soft. When she thought of him, her heart rose up in her chest. But Greg wasn't hers to love. He belonged to Judith. If she hadn't known that for certain before now, it had been confirmed to her, twice over, this morning, as he had hovered with the coffee pot, his devotion to Judith blatantly on show. She must bury any feelings other than friendship for Greg and never let them surface.

42

As CONSTANCE APPROACHED Lee Hill Farm on Sunday morning, she was aware of activity outside the farmhouse – vehicles on the driveway, harsh noises, doors opening and closing, voices raised and receding – but the thick hedge which ran along the roadside impeded her vision. As she turned the corner into the lane, the shapes and colours resolved themselves into an old-fashioned Land Rover, an open backed truck and a police car drawn up close to its front bumper.

While the police car was empty and she saw the figures of two uniformed officers disappearing along the lane, Constance could hear rustling coming from the far side of the pick-up, suggesting that someone or something was in there. She bypassed the door of the house, continued beyond the police car and around the truck. It took her a moment to process what she saw.

Mark sat cross-legged in the back of the open trailer, his face stained with tears. An olive green tarpaulin had been draped over a great, sprawling, lumpy mound. Mark held something in his lap, his hands supporting it, his fingers spread wide. As she peered in closer and her brain finally made sense of what she saw, she felt her late breakfast rise into her throat; it was the head of a cow.

The door of the farmhouse opened and Rachel emerged. She stood beside Constance, who had turned away and was taking deep breaths, trying not to think about what she had just seen.

'Mark,' Rachel called out to her husband. 'Enough now. Come inside.'

Mark sat where he was. He didn't move or appear to register her words.

'What happened?' Constance whispered to Rachel.

'Someone let the cows out,' Rachel said. 'I was shopping, Mark was working on the other side of the farm. First thing we knew, the police called, said the cows were running around on the road and two of them had been hit. The other dead one was taken off somewhere. I think it was really mashed up. We got three of them back safely. Mark insisted they bring this one back here. It's Klara, his favourite. Lucky no one was killed, really. Mark might have preferred that to the cows, though.'

'How did it happen?'

'Kids, maybe? I mean, cows can't open the gate themselves, can they? Although Mark's been a bit edgy recently. I don't know if he argued with someone and this is the result. He's not always the easiest person to talk to.' Rachel's fingers clawed at her neck. 'Help me get him down, will you? He can't sit here all day.'

Rachel clambered up onto the back of the trailer, edged around the carcass and rested her hand on Mark's shoulder. He finally focused on her.

'Come on,' she said. 'Come inside. You can't do anything for her now.'

Constance helped them both climb down and she followed behind as Mark was led into the house, through the hallway and into the kitchen. He slumped down into a chair and didn't move. Rachel put the kettle on and set out a teapot and some mugs. Then the doorbell rang.

'That's probably the police,' she said. 'They went to look at the field and the gate. Can you keep an eye on Mark while I'm gone? I don't want to leave him.'

'Sure,' Constance agreed, although she would have preferred not to be alone with him in this obvious state of distress, especially now that she knew a little of his background from Adrian.

She poured Mark some tea, pushed it towards him and sat down herself. He didn't speak at first. He kept staring back out of the window towards the trailer and the dead cow. Then he took the tea and looked at Constance.

'I know people think they're only cows,' he said, 'and you'll say they were going to end up on the plate anyway, but it was such a cruel thing to do. They must have been terrified out there on the road, with the cars and lorries whizzing around them, lights flashing and horns hooting.'

'Do you have any idea…'

'I know who it was,' he said. 'I know exactly who it was. Rosa. It was that bitch, Rosa.'

'Are you sure…'

'She even came here to tell me, well not *what*, but to expect something. So much for being a vegan.'

'Whoever it was probably didn't realise they'd get hurt.' Constance wanted to say something conciliatory, without giving too much away just yet. But it was rapidly dawning on her that this latest awful event couldn't be a coincidence.

Mark stared at her then, wide-eyed. 'I'm no lawyer,' he said, 'but I know, if you do something really stupid, because you don't think about the consequences, that doesn't get you off. I'm right, aren't I?'

'Yes you're...'

'I mean, if that's wrong, then someone should sue your colleague who defended me when I was a kid, 'cos that's what he told me, that's what they all said. That being young, being impulsive, being "reckless" – that's the word they used – none of that would help. She warned me, Rosa did, that something was coming, but I never expected this.'

'Will you tell the police you think it was Rosa?'

Mark gave the shallowest shake of his head. Constance was about to ask him why he wouldn't report Rosa, if he suspected her, and then she thought back to the courtroom and Rosa's testimony, how she had looked unsettled when she told everyone Mark had driven her home from the meeting. She and Judith had joked about it. And Mark coming to court two days early on the day Rosa was giving evidence, and how Rosa had reacted when she'd seen him at the door. Should she say something? Judith wouldn't hold back. And Judith had sent her to probe and poke around.

'Did something happen,' she said, 'when you took Rosa home?'

Mark stared at her again and colour flooded his cheeks. Then he looked towards the window, although this time Constance saw him look around the truck, most likely checking to see where Rachel was. Then he stared at his hands. Constance didn't need him to answer.

'Look. She came here on Thursday. Rachel made her tea, like this, like she does for everyone. Served her cake even...'

'I don't think it was Rosa who did this,' Constance said.

'What do you know about any of it?'

Mark had raised his voice and Constance was anxious to calm him. She glanced out of the window. Rachel had now reappeared, talking to two police officers – a woman and a man. The woman pointed along the track towards the field where the cows were usually kept, while the man made notes. She looked again. The first one was Sergeant Thomas, which was surprising, as they were so far from her patch.

'I…I can't say,' she said, 'but I think it was someone else – the same person, in fact, who torched Rosa's café, and when she came here, Rosa really *was* trying to warn you.'

Mark's face clouded over.

'Whoever it was, we're…taking steps to make sure they will be punished,' but even as Constance said this, she was anxious not to raise expectations too high. How could they possibly prove who let Mark's cows out, unless… She started to formulate a theory which involved Sergeant Thomas, but didn't get very far before Mark intervened.

'It wasn't just us – me and Rosa,' he said. 'Susan, the prof, she told me someone killed all her flies.'

'Killed her flies?'

'Turned up the heat, made them all hatch, spoiled her research. She was pretty upset.'

'Oh.'

'You won't tell Rachel that…you think they're all connected, the things you told me about,' he said, eventually.

Constance marvelled at how obvious it was that Mark was skimming around the edges of what had clearly happened with Rosa. 'It's not my business to interfere,' she said. 'I'll wait till she comes back in and then I'll go.'

Mark stumbled over to the sink and began to wash his hands, rubbing at each palm with the thumb of the opposite hand. Then, as the water gushed out of the tap, he began to splash it over his face, then on to his neck and arms and all over his t-shirt, until he was soaked through. He switched off the water, pulled his sodden shirt over his head and stood, arms either side of the sink, his chest heaving up and down.

Constance stared too. Instead of pale skin – the indent of the vertebrae, the ripples of a few muscles – Mark's back was covered in an image of an oak tree, majestic and stately, sprouting from splayed roots, which began their journey just above the line of his low-slung joggers. But it was no ordinary tree; its trunk was replaced by a twisting, double helix, snaking and meandering and thrusting its way upwards either side of his spinal column. A veritable tree of life.

He turned and saw Constance staring at him. He pushed past her, shuffled to his room and returned a moment later wearing a clean t-shirt. He sat down and finished his tea.

'Why did you come here today, anyway?' he asked. 'Isn't the trial almost over?'

Constance was pleased to return to polite conversation, but she could not forget what she had just seen and it confused her. She'd noticed the inking on Mark's wrist the first time they'd met but had not viewed it as reflecting any strong sentiment; she'd interpreted it as humorous. Given he was clearly not religious, she'd seen it as Mark's idea of a joke. And the stylised cow's face staring out from his forearm, readily apparent on Zoe's version of the video – another light-hearted picture.

But the tree was different; it was sprawling, urgent, vital. It told her that Mark Sumner was not a clown or a man who skipped through life lightly. That all of this, the cows, the land, the farm, was his lifeblood too, so fundamental to him that he had etched it permanently on his body. He had told her that, when he gripped her hand and made her engage with Klara, back in April. He had explained it again, when he referenced the sacrifice he felt he made, with the slaughter of every cow. He had said it a third time, in court on Thursday, but she hadn't really been listening. She hadn't understood. Not till now.

'I had some questions, about the Ambrosia project,' she said, berating herself, as she spoke, for so underestimating Mark. His past history of violence, his devotion to his livestock and now his obvious allegiance to this higher calling – all of those things told her he was capable of killing Brett Ingram, if he had a good enough reason. And she knew he and Rachel had a secret, a secret that, in Mark's own words, might benefit from Brett being out of the picture. 'Diana told me all about it,' she continued, her heart leaping into her throat.

'She did? So why come to me, then?'

Constance heard loud footsteps on the flagstones outside, then the front door opened and slammed shut and, a moment later, Rachel appeared in the kitchen.

A wary look descended on Mark. 'Have they gone?' he asked.

'It's the strangest thing,' Rachel said, shaking her head in disbelief. 'You'll never guess.'

'What?'

'You remember those old CCTV cameras they put in a while back, when we had that spate of fly tipping?'

'I didn't think they worked any more.'

'Me neither, but the woman police officer said they were

371

serviced only yesterday. Now they've taken away the film. She's almost certain they'll have something. That's good, I suppose.' She stared at Constance, waiting for her to speak. 'I'm pleased you were here to help out,' she said, when Constance didn't volunteer anything, 'but I'm sure you must be very busy and want to get back.'

Constance looked across at Mark. She didn't know what Rachel knew about Ambrosia. She wanted to ask more questions, but she didn't want to betray his trust. Then again, she knew something that he really didn't want Rachel to know about. That might just make him more talkative than he might otherwise have been.

But Mark answered her question for her. 'Constance here was asking about Ambrosia,' he said, his voice flat again. 'I think she's bluffing, pretending she knows more than she really does. Because if Diana had told her everything, there'd be no need to come and ask us, would there?'

Constance stood up. This was all getting too much. She'd survived all week on little sleep, she'd run herself ragged following endless leads which had gone nowhere, and while the dead cow in the trailer outside had almost floored her, it was Mark's tattoo and the raw energy she sensed throbbing inside him which made her fearful for her own safety. She did want to know their secret, what they grew in those greenhouses out back, but not enough to put herself at risk. She'd just have to admit to Judith that she had failed. Only Rachel stood between her and the door.

'Brett was good to us,' Rachel said, raising a hand to hold her back. 'Mark inherited the farm, but it was failing – the beef side of the business is not so lucrative...'

'Rache, we don't have to tell her anything...'

'We owe it to Brett to get it all out there. I never wanted secrets anyway.' Rachel turned to Constance again. 'Mark was in prison. When he came out and inherited the farm, you can imagine that people weren't exactly falling over themselves to give him credit. Brett gave us a wonderful opportunity, to be involved in a global project. We'd receive government funding and there was the potential to be at the forefront of something new and exciting.'

Constance hesitated. With his wife at his side and fully clothed, Mark did not seem quite so menacing. And she was finally getting the answers she wanted.

'What was it?' she asked, struggling to keep her voice strong.

'Gene-edited crops,' Rachel said.

Constance sat down again. 'Is that like...'

'It's not the same as genetically modified,' Rachel explained. 'With genetically modified crops, you mix species, you "mess with nature", and that's why people don't like it. Gene editing is completely different, much safer, much more natural. You just snip little bits of DNA out and that changes things. It makes plants more resistant to drought or pests, or they produce three times as much fruit. Imagine: the same dusty plot of land you've always farmed can suddenly grow more food, with less water and no pesticides. Replicate that a few times over and you could eradicate world hunger.'

'It goes further than that, though,' Mark joined in now. 'There are enormous health benefits too. They're working on a strain of wheat with reduced gluten, oil without saturated fats and vegetables with additional vitamins.'

'Is this all public knowledge?' Constance asked. She'd never heard of gene-edited food, but she wasn't always on top of every new development.

'The tools have been around for a few years and they're legal in the USA and other countries,' Rachel explained. 'But the European Court decided a couple of years back that gene-edited food should be treated the same as GMO, so that meant it wasn't allowed anywhere in Europe. It was a huge blow to all of us and we almost gave up. But Brett told us to persevere. We'd already had the Brexit vote, so he said to wait. Because if we're not part of Europe, that case is irrelevant. And now it looks like it's going to be made legal here, after all.'

'Is that what you wanted to talk to Brett about so urgently?' Constance asked.

'There was a Defra consultation which closed in March and Brett had his ear to the ground,' Rachel said. 'I wanted to know which way it was going to go. Mark was meeting Brett anyway, so I asked him to find out how the wind was blowing. Our future depended on it. It still does.'

Constance began to appreciate the significance of what she was being told and she could hardly contain her excitement and relief.

'Are you saying this was the real Ambrosia project then? Diana said it was about boycotting junk food, although she did also say you were involved.'

'It was all part of Brett's plan for a radical shake-up of what people eat, to guide them to make properly informed choices. The junk food was one strand – and an important one. But that was about stopping what other people did. This – the gene-edited food – this was what Heart Foods itself was going to take forward. It would have been the main focus for the future of the company. Brett's real, positive contribution to feeding the world. If it happens – if it's approved – it will change everything. Corn with more starch, lettuce which never goes brown. It can be used on animals too; cows producing more milk and with no horns so they can't injure each other, pigs resistant to diseases which kill hundreds of thousands of piglets every year, super-sized salmon. And it's all natural. It's all products which we could achieve by traditional farming – just speeded up.'

'And you're growing these crops here?'

'We are. We have three fields set aside. You saw the greenhouses out the back, the first time you came. We're not allowed to sell the crop to retailers, but the government buys it from us at a commercial rate and checks it out. If…when we go live some time this year, they want to be able to reassure consumers that it's all safe.'

'Do you think any of this had anything to do with Brett's death?' Constance asked them both.

Mark looked at Rachel before answering. 'That's what your barrister was asking me in court. Did he have enemies? You think someone bumped him off because of this – food wars, like in some Colombian drug cartel?'

'You both seem to have known Brett well, better than I understood. I thought you might have some ideas.'

'Food is big money. We all know that.' Rachel took Mark's hand as she spoke and squeezed it affectionately. 'Everyone has to eat. And people will make and lose fortunes if we get the approval we want. But I'd still like to think that in this country we don't kill people just because we don't like what they say or believe in. Maybe I'm just an idealistic fool.'

43

CONSTANCE TEXTED JUDITH from the train. 'You were right!' she wrote. 'Two more events. Mark's cows let out and Susan Mills' larvae got boiled.'

Judith surprised her by asking for the address of Sue's lab, which she provided. And nothing more. So she followed up with 'will call later', although she was not sure she had the strength to tell Judith the details of what had happened at the farm. Not yet, anyway.

Constance arrived home at 3pm and called Sue. She had tried her before she left for the Sumners, without success. She knew she mustn't harass her, but as Sue hadn't replied, or blocked her, or messaged her to tell her to stop, she told herself that she could justify one more attempt. She crossed her fingers behind her back, and after only two rings, this time Sue answered.

'Professor Mills, it's Constance Lamb,' she began, unable to believe her luck. 'I'm the solicitor representing Nick Demetriou in the case...'

'I know who you are,' Sue replied.

'I've called you before, but not managed to catch you.'

'I've been working all weekend. I'm still working. I have a deadline Monday afternoon.'

'Is it possible for us to meet?'

'As I said, I have a deadline.'

'It's important. And it really won't take long. Just a few minutes of your time.'

'I'm sorry. I came to court last week and you sent me away. I've devoted enough time to this unpleasant experience and I really have to ask you to leave me alone now.'

'Wait! Just one more thing. If you say no, then I'll hang up and you won't hear from me again.'

Constance took the silence at the end of the line to mean she was at least permitted to continue.

'Something bad has happened to you recently at work, hasn't it? Something associated with your food project.'

Constance waited, and this time the fact that the call was not cut short emboldened her.

'You're not the only one. Zoe had to close down her blog, Rosa's café was set on fire. And...' She couldn't tell Sue about Mark; not like this. 'Look, I'm going to switch to video, OK? It's easier to talk, I think, if we can see each other.' She pressed the video button on her phone and waited. After a few seconds, Sue's pallid, drawn face appeared across her screen.

'Hi.' Constance smiled her warmest smile.

Sue said nothing but she didn't leave the call.

Constance decided to take a step back, begin with some less personal questions to try to build Sue's trust, start where she had left off with Mark. 'Do you know anything about the Ambrosia project?' she asked.

'Nothing,' Sue said. 'What is it?'

'It was part of Heart Foods' plan to improve food quality.'

'OK. I still don't know anything about it.'

'Brett inviting all of you to the meeting was part of that long-term plan.'

'Maybe. I never heard that name. But, I mean, all of us who were there, we want to produce good-quality, sustainable food.'

This was good. Sue was talking now and she seemed more relaxed. 'How does that fit with your research?' Constance asked.

'My research is about feeding livestock on soldier fly larvae. It's the way of the future.'

'I thought it was about making people eat insects, like on *I'm a Celebrity*.'

Sue smiled, just briefly. Constance had made a connection. 'Bush tucker trials?' Sue said. 'There's no reason why we shouldn't eat insects, though. They're very nutritious. But no, my insects are fed on things we want to get rid of, like food waste or even human waste. They grow and then they're fed to pigs and chickens.'

'And someone sabotaged your work?'

'They turned the temperature up on all twenty-four containers on Wednesday night. The flies hatched and then suffocated. It looks like someone got in with an old security pass, but we haven't been able to trace it.'

'I'm so sorry,' Constance said. 'It must have been awful.'

'I was very upset.'

This was even better – Sue sharing her feelings. Time now for Constance to move on to more relevant questions. 'Can I take you back to the Tanners' Hall meeting, just for a moment? I know it must be painful, but I promise not to keep you for long. When you arrived at the meeting, how did Brett behave?'

'He was charming, very welcoming.'

'What about the others?'

'They were mostly fine. Dr Edge was – I don't know – impolite, a bit restless, like he wanted to pick a fight with someone.'

'Did you see anything unusual or suspicious which might lead you to believe that someone might want to hurt Brett?'

'I didn't see anything like that, no.'

Constance had told herself before this call that she was to listen – really listen – to Sue. Now she had listened and she had heard Sue answer her question, but with a precision that suggested she had something more to say.

'Did you hear anything?'

'No.'

'But you know something about his death, don't you?'

Sue said nothing and Constance knew she was almost there. Sue fiddled with the top button of her blouse; her smile had faded.

Constance would row back a little, a second time. 'Did you join a Zoom call with Dr Edge after Brett's death?'

'Yes.'

'Why?'

'It was easier than not turning up. I got the feeling Dr Edge could be very persistent.'

'What did he want?'

'He said he wanted us to do something together to honour Brett, but I didn't think that was it. Rosa told Dr Edge what she thought – what we all thought – that he was trying to use Brett's death to advance himself. She told him he should be ashamed.'

'Anything else?'

'He was upset and we all rang off. That's it. Is any of this, I mean, is this going to come out in court? He is on the radio, after all.'

'The prosecution aren't calling you as a witness any more, are they?'

'They said my evidence wasn't needed.'

'How do you feel about that?'

'Relieved, I think. I wasn't looking forward to it much. But it's nice of you to ask. It's not often I'm asked that kind of thing – anything about myself at all. Maybe it comes with the job.' She smiled and then she looked away.

Constance smiled back and waited. She had a feeling that, if she was patient enough, Sue would reveal more, but she was also conscious of running out of time. 'Where were we?' she asked, when Sue was silent.

'You were asking if I was coming to court.'

'That's right, and you were worried you might be asked about Dr Edge. You don't like him?'

'He…he reminds me of boys at school, kind of class idiots, making jokes at other people's expense to cover up their own inadequacies.'

Constance nodded. She thought that a shrewd assessment of Adrian.

'I mean, it could have been much worse. I shouldn't complain really.' Sue looked away again.

Almost, Constance thought. We're creeping towards something. If only she was Judith. Judith would find the right words.

'Has your research been successful?' Constance asked.

'I think so. I can say that, now it's just about finished.'

'And how did you get into food science in the first place?'

Sue's eyes flickered and then focused on Constance for the

first time and then she knew that she had finally asked the right question.

'It's funny,' Sue said. 'I suppose it was all because of Brett Ingram.'

'Why's that?'

Sue stared at Constance then. She opened her mouth, then she closed it again. Then she looked incredibly sad. 'I'm sorry,' she said. 'I really have to get on.' And, with a smart tap of her finger, the call came to an end.

***

Judith received the long-awaited update from Constance at 5pm. She sounded truly exhausted. Not surprising, once Judith had heard about her day. Constance had also forwarded the phone numbers and names received from Diana. These were the people Brett had phoned from the meeting, with two calls, made in quick succession around 1.30pm, highlighted. Both were to a Simon Fogarty, Heart Foods' Chief Finance Officer. Judith Googled the name and smiled when she found an image of him on the Heart Foods website. Although he appeared younger than the man she half-expected to see, by at least ten years, his prominent nose remained unchanged.

Then she spent a few minutes staring at an online image of a building she'd found earlier – the laboratory where Sue was currently working. Following up Mr Fogarty could wait a bit longer. With the information Constance had provided earlier in the day, and Greg's suggestion bearing fruit, the more urgent matter was to pay another visit to Adrian Edge.

44

ADRIAN DID NOT SMILE WHEN he found Judith on his doorstep for a second time that weekend, at 6pm on a Sunday evening, but to his credit, he invited her in.

'Were you just passing?' he asked, leading her through to his sitting room. She wondered if he hoped the relaxed setting might spare him any difficult questions. She settled herself down, plumping the cushions behind her, and refused the offer of any refreshment.

'You were so hospitable last time,' she said. 'I've come back for more.'

'You're too kind.'

'I'm here because I reflected on our conversation and I'm an inquisitive person – that's all.'

'I see.'

'After Brett's death, you contacted the other panellists?'

'We've been through that.'

'We talked about their negative response, but I didn't appreciate you would take it upon yourself to punish their ingratitude.'

Adrian's eyebrows twitched but he didn't speak.

'Oh come on now, Dr Edge. As soon as I read those caustic missives sent to poor Zoe, I realised an educated man, of around your age, must have crafted them. Then there were those distinctive turns of phrase used by the troll. And this might surprise you, but there is some wonderful technology out there these days which traces the provenance of pieces of text. You just input one source – for example, what a radio presenter might say on their regular show – and compare it with your chosen article, and it gives you a result on how comparable the two are. More than seventy per cent correlation and they almost certainly share the same birthplace. Are you really going to deny it was you?'

'There's an easy answer to all that.'

'Is there?'

'*There are three kinds of lie: lies, damned lies and statistics.*'

'You're saying I don't have any evidence.'

'That's what I'm saying.'

Judith smiled, then crossed and re-crossed her legs. Adrian's cheek muscle twitched just once.

'Do you remember that wonderful photo you showed me and Connie when we were here yesterday morning – the one with the marlin?'

'Yes.'

'My memory isn't as good as it was, but I recollect now that you and Brett were wearing matching t-shirts, white ones with a logo on them in black lettering.'

Adrian looked out of the window.

'Yours said – what was it? – "truth warrior" and Brett's said "son of truth warrior". Presumably some private joke you were sharing. I'm right, aren't I? Now, some people would say it was a coincidence that the first two trolls who upset Zoe shared those usernames. I would call it…evidence.'

'It didn't stop her for long,' Adrian said slowly, 'and when I last looked, debunking total nonsense wasn't a criminal offence. Anyway, since she's been back up and running, she's been much more cautious. Not that I'm admitting anything.'

'It impacted her business, she lost valuable revenue from her blog and it affected her mental health, which you understand all about, as you are a health professional. Do you know she's been seeing Brett's ghost?'

Adrian shrugged. 'It's hardly my fault if she's so… impressionable.'

'Ah. I sense a modicum of guilt for poor Zoe, given what you now know. But not for Rosa Barrera, I suspect. We both know Rosa is made of sterner stuff. She told you where to go on that Zoom call, and you didn't like it, did you? Maybe you even thought you might have had a chance with her, that she might have succumbed to *your* charms. Instead, she told you to sling your hook. Burning down Rosa's café. That *was* criminal, though.'

Adrian opened his mouth and closed it again.

'Although I suppose you could say no one was hurt, insurers paid up, it has had a well-needed lick of paint.'

'This is crazy. Again, you have no proof.'

'Ah, that's where you're wrong. You see I've recently befriended Sergeant Thomas of Hackney police. I'm not sure whether you saw her in court, but she impressed Constance and me with her thoroughness and foresight. She tells me that they have an eyewitness now, saw someone outside the café. They're planning a line-up; tomorrow at 3pm. She'll be in touch with you shortly, if she hasn't already.'

Adrian shrugged again, but Judith sensed his nerves.

'So we've discussed trolling and arson, but I never thought, having taken the Hippocratic oath, that you would stoop to murder.'

'Oh come on. I don't have to...'

'You're absolutely right. You don't *have to do* anything. But you must be curious to know what I know.'

Adrian had stood up; now he sat down again. 'Not really,' he said, but it was half-hearted.

''There was a break in at Susan Mills' lab on Wednesday night. Someone killed all her flies. Except it wasn't really a break-in, as that same someone had an old security pass.'

'You're calling *that* murder – isn't it rather "insecticide"? And those are freely available in most reputable retail outlets.' Adrian smiled at his attempt at a joke.

Judith didn't smile back. 'I understand that in January 2021 for a six-week period, the building where she is conducting her project was used as a vaccination centre against Covid-19.'

'If you say so.'

'I've looked up where your practice is located. You boasted on your website that all your staff volunteered to be part of the vaccination programme. It will take me five minutes to confirm that you were based there. Granted it was along with other medically qualified staff, but it was your local centre, wasn't it, and you had a pass?'

Adrian said nothing, again.

'All right, let's accept, as you are implying that flies don't have feelings, that they're not *sentient*. How about cows?'

'What?' Adrian tried incredulity. Judith was not sure he

succeeded.

'I'm interested in what you think about CCTV?' she asked. 'Are you one of those people who are in favour, think it's a deterrent against crime and a valuable tool in the police armoury, or are you in the privacy camp – a brave citizen who wanders around with a placard shouting about infringements of your God-given right to behave in an antisocial way, at all times free from the risk of being caught?'

'That sounds like a loaded question.'

'Ah. You're right. You see, in the UK, there are not many surveillance cameras outside the big cities, apart from speed cameras on roads. That's what Sergeant Thomas tells me, anyway. But, what a stroke of luck for Mark and Rachel Sumner! They have not one, not two, but three hidden cameras in fact, situated at various strategic landmarks around their property. And so, when someone trespassed on their land in the early hours of this morning, opened the gate and let their cows out, they captured it all on film.'

Adrian's face had drained of all colour.

'We can continue this pretence for a while, but it won't save you,' Judith said. 'Sergeant Thomas will be calling you in for the identity parade and interviewing you about the cows, and if she decides it's a worthwhile use of police time, also about the lab break-in and Zoe's blog. Actually, you know how hot the police are on internet safety these days, so the blog may get top billing after all. Like I said, you certainly don't have to tell me anything. But I am interested – one professional person to another – in understanding what might have driven you to commit these nasty, vindictive and, yes, criminal acts. Was it all because Brett was popular at school and you weren't?'

'What?'

'Or because you chose to invest your family money in his business. Not for nothing – of course not. You took your shareholding, that was only right and proper. But then, when Brett wouldn't support your big idea, your *food for your mood*, you were angry. You felt he was supporting waifs and strays: a blogger, a chef, a convict even, but you were out in the cold.'

'I can't see how any of this is relevant, unless you're trying to link it to Brett's death, and we already know that your client killed him.'

'You still maintain that none of this has anything to do with you?'

'Of course not.'

'You know,' Judith went on, 'What I can't understand is why *you* were at the Tanners' Hall meeting at all. You see, Diana told Connie quite candidly that Brett had issues with the board – they were cautious – you confirmed that yourself. They wanted public feedback on all the Ambrosia initiatives before they would allow him to go live. That's why the panellists were assembled, representatives of the different strands of Ambrosia. But you weren't one of them, you had not been granted any money by Heart Foods. We discussed this yesterday. They didn't like your idea. So why were you there?'

'I'm a celebrity. Brett thought it would draw people in.'

'You were doing it for your friend, then, and your thirty per cent shareholding too – I'd forgotten. Diana says it was more than that. She says you had a hold over him, that Brett agreed to all sorts of things when you asked. I'm wondering why that could possibly have been.'

'This is all ridiculous.'

'Maybe you didn't even have to say it. Just one flick of your eyebrows and he'd fear you.'

'Really,' Adrian said, 'you have it all wrong. First of all, Brett was not scared of me. We were friends. And second, my idea is brilliant. The board are a bunch of Neanderthals. All right, I asked Brett if I could be at the meeting, even though I wasn't included in the Ambrosia spend, but it was a good idea. That's why he agreed. Not because he was frightened of something I would say. We were going to sound the public out on all the different aspects of Ambrosia, plus my vision, when we asked for feedback. It was win, win. Brett had no problem with it.'

'What a shame for you then, that you hadn't yet achieved board support by the time he died. And the other panellists weren't interested in helping you out. If only Brett had lived for another few weeks – time for the public feedback to come in; time to vindicate his support for your project.'

Adrian's mouth settled into a grim line. 'That's how things work,' he said. 'I've been around long enough to know that when one door closes, another one opens.'

He rose now and gestured towards his own front door. Judith smiled at him, considered offering her hand, but decided against it. And without prompting, she found herself whistling the theme tune to his radio show as she walked off down the road.

45

ON MONDAY MORNING at 9.30am Andy called Eleni Pallas, the waitress employed by Nick, to the witness stand. She was to be the last prosecution witness. Judith estimated her age at around twenty years old. Last night, Constance had messaged to say she wanted to follow up some more leads first thing and would be late. Judith had thought about calling her to find out what the leads might be, but then her preparation had taken over and she trusted Constance to come to court as quickly as she could.

'Miss Pallas, can you tell us what time you arrived at Tanners' Hall?' Andy began, and Judith noticed the lack of an invitation to recite her life story this time around. He had the bit between his teeth. He wanted to finish things soon. Or perhaps he had taken the judge's words about time-wasting to heart.

'Mr Demetriou asked us…me to be there for 11.'

'Was there any problem you found, when you arrived?'

'Mr Demetriou opened up and the fridge didn't look clean. I said I'd clean it, but we needed to get things set up and we were warming up food and had to cut the fruit up fresh. There wasn't much time. He told me not to put the food in the fridge.'

'Mr Demetriou told you *not* to put the food in the fridge?'

'That's right.'

Andy nodded sagely and mumbled his approval, as if Eleni had confirmed some complex scientific theory. 'What did you do with the food instead?'

'I helped bring it in from Mr Demetriou's car and we left it in bags in the kitchen until we served it.'

'You didn't put it in the fridge?'

'No.'

'Were you told of any special dietary requirements of any of the guests?'

'I remember Mr Demetriou said there was a vegan and someone else who only ate meat, so we had to keep the food on separate trays. That's all. But it was already separate. It wasn't a problem.'

'He didn't mention anything else – any allergies or anything like that?'

'No.'

'Do you know that it's a breach of health and safety regulations, to serve food which has not been sufficiently refrigerated?'

'The fridge was dirty, so we couldn't put the food in there. But we kept it in freezer bags, with ice packs.'

'Do you know how long the food had been in those freezer bags *before* it arrived at Tanners' Hall?'

'No. But I trusted Mr Demetriou. He caters lots of events. And he doesn't live that far away. Even with traffic it was probably only half an hour.'

'That's assuming he came straight from home?'

Judith noticed Eleni stick out her chin. Clearly, she didn't appreciate Andy's challenge. 'Why should I think he did anything different?' she said.

'All right. No one is suggesting *you* have done anything wrong. And when did the food go out on the table?'

'Not long before 12.30. And we started clearing it away at 1.30. Mr Demetriou says one hour is the limit. We took the fruit and the salad away last, because that's not such a problem.'

'So at the very least, some food – for example, the beef carpaccio – was not refrigerated from 11am to 1.30pm, but most likely longer, say 10.30, because Mr Demetriou had packed it into his car, earlier in the day?'

'Yes, but in freezer bags with ice packs.'

Judith was pleased to see that Eleni was expanding her answers in a way which suggested support for Nick. She hadn't asked Nick how he and Eleni had got on and she regretted that now, but she did have some useful material she could use when her turn came. But Andy didn't seem bothered by Eleni's answers. 'Did you see what Mr Ingram ate?' he continued.

'I was too busy warming up the food, making salads and taking it out and serving the drinks. It was a lot of work.'

'Mr Demetriou was also helping?'

'Yes…yes, he was.'

Eleni looked over at Nick, then back at Andy. Andy had clearly noticed the look, but he couldn't decipher it. Judith wondered what it might mean, but with Eleni having spoken for barely two minutes, she could not possibly understand. Constance might have interpreted it better, but Constance was not there.

Andy sat down and coughed lightly when Judith failed to respond. She acknowledged him with a nod of the head and then stood up to begin her cross-examination.

'Miss Pallas,' Judith began. 'I just want to focus on one thing, which relates to evidence given by another witness called Zoe Whitman. She was a guest at the event. She's a young woman and, that day, she had some pink colouring in her hair. Do you remember who she was?'

'I think so,' Eleni said.

'Miss Whitman says that after Mr Ingram collapsed, she was watching Mr Demetriou speaking to you in the kitchen. Can you tell us what you remember?'

Once again, Eleni looked over at Nick. That was interesting. Judith scribbled a note down in her pad to record it, just as she had done the first time Eleni had done so.

'I was just clearing up,' Eleni said. 'I didn't know what had happened. Then I heard everyone coming out of the hall. Mr Demetriou came in and he was very upset. He said Mr Ingram was ill; there was an ambulance coming. He said I should go home and he would finish clearing up.'

'Did Mr Demetriou raise his voice to you?' Judith continued.

'He was upset. I could see that. His voice was shaky, his hands too. Not shouting so much.'

'Had you finished what you were doing?'

'Almost. I'd put the leftover food into Tupperware, put the glasses in the dishwasher.'

'There wasn't much more work for you to do?'

'And he pays us by the hour, so there was that too.'

'I understand. He was being thrifty.' Judith paused for a second, staring at the note she had just made. 'Us?' she said. 'You said "he pays us by the hour". Was anyone else there?'

'Me,' Eleni corrected herself. Judith waited. 'There was

supposed to be two of us. That's what I meant.'

Judith knew this, of course, but it was helpful to have Eleni volunteer it. 'You were expecting a second helper that day?'

'His name's Andrew. But he was ill and we couldn't find a replacement. That's why we were so busy – more than usual. There was a lot for us to do.'

'I can imagine it was stressful for you and for Mr Demetriou.'

'It was.'

'What *language* does Mr Demetriou speak to you in?'

Eleni blinked twice. 'English, I think.'

'Do you speak Greek?'

'Yes.'

'Does my client ever speak to you in Greek?'

'Maybe, sometimes.'

Judith hoped to put to rest Zoe's evidence that she'd understood every part of Nick commanding Eleni to leave, with the implication being that Nick had something to hide. 'Why might he do that, switch to Greek?'

'I don't know. You'd have to ask him. Habit maybe, or he just forgets.'

'Do you think he might have spoken to you in Greek when he asked you to leave?' This was the point on which Nick had perked up and called Constance over when he heard Zoe's evidence. He had been adamant that he spoke to Eleni in Greek.

Eleni smiled; not an expression of happiness – more as if she wanted to be obliging, to give the right answer, but she didn't know which it was. 'You know, it's hard to remember. I would say yes, but I'm not sure now, maybe.' If that was the best Eleni could do, despite Nick's absolute certainty on the point, then Judith would have to accept it and move on. But she sensed something else, something the young woman was holding back, something that might not assist Nick. She should wrap things up quickly.

'Did you see Zoe Whitman, the young woman with the pink hair, when you were packing things up?'

'No.'

'You didn't see her at all in the kitchen?'

'No.'

'What happened then?'

'I…I took off my apron and I left. It was only the next day when the police came around that I knew what had happened.'

Eleni slipped out of court and Judith felt certain that she would go straight home and up to her bedroom, where she would reproach herself for the half-truths she had told in the witness box.

46

JUDITH SPENT THE TEN-MINUTE break before Dr Leigh's return musing on Eleni's testimony and wondering why Constance had not arrived yet. She checked her mobile but there had been nothing from Constance since her cryptic message at 10pm last night.

As with the first occasion he had been called, Dr Leigh arrived in the building only seconds before he was due to appear. This time, as he crossed the floor of the courtroom and returned to the witness box, he scowled at Judith.

'Dr Leigh. I'm so grateful to you for making time for us, again,' Judith began, keen not to allow his animosity to derail her. 'I apologise that you've had to return, but it picks up on the evidence given by Miss Diana Percival, Mr Ingram's personal assistant, regarding his eating habits, leading up to his death.'

'All right,' he said, although his demeanour suggested his irritation had not yet passed.

'Miss Percival told us that Mr Ingram had been eating large

amounts of kale.'

'Kale?'

'The leafy green vegetable. Perhaps you can tell us about its potential health benefits?'

'You've called me back to talk about kale?' Dr Leigh looked at Andy, then at the judge. Judge Linton stared at Judith.

'It may sound a little left-field, My Lord, but bear with me for five minutes only. It's an important line of questioning.'

'It had better be,' the judge said, his expression grave. Then he turned to the pathologist. 'Dr Leigh,' he said. 'Much as I share your surprise and scepticism about this topic and, I have to add, I would rather die than frequent any establishment with kale on the menu, I'd appreciate you humouring Ms Burton and answering this question, which, she assures me, is important.'

'All right. If that's what you want. Kale is high in vitamin C and calcium and I know there are studies being conducted to confirm it can help reduce cancer. That's the sum total of what I know about kale.'

Judith smiled at him. 'Miss Percival gave evidence that over the three weeks leading up to his death, Mr Ingram had been eating very large quantities of kale. He consumed a kale and spinach shake every morning and included kale in his midday and evening meal. Now, I want to refer you to a blog written by Zoe Whitman, one of the witnesses in this case. It's up there on the screen to your left. I'm going to read out one section to the court. "Kale is a cruciferous vegetable – part of the cabbage family – it contains two chemicals, glucosinolate and myrosinase." Let's hope I pronounced those correctly. "When you eat kale, the two chemicals react and form sulfurophane." Then there's a comment about how you smell that sulphurous smell when you cook kale or other cruciferous vegetables, particularly broccoli. Now, to continue, "When you eat kale, you absorb the sulfurophane and it causes damage to all cells." Can you comment on that?'

'If you had prepared me for a grilling on the dangers of eating cabbage, I might have been able to speak with more authority.' Dr Leigh flashed a further look of annoyance at Andy and then at Judge Linton. Judith wondered if the judge might end things there and then, but he was silent. Perhaps, notwithstanding his earlier comments, he disliked Dr Leigh's irritability as much as he professed to dislike kale.

'I can read on, if you like,' Judith said. "Sulfurophane can damage structures inside cells, like mitochondria. Mitochondria produce ninety per cent of the chemical energy which we need to survive. When mitochondria go wrong, we go wrong."'

Dr Leigh huffed his annoyance. 'It's not as straightforward as that.'

'"Another side effect of kale consumption is interference with the uptake of iodine in the thyroid gland, causing goitre." What is goitre, Dr Leigh?'

'It's a swelling of the thyroid gland.'

'Which is where?'

'The front of the throat, just below the Adam's apple.'

'Am I right that a large goitre can make it difficult to swallow or cause breathlessness?'

Dr Leigh pushed himself back so that he hung from the front of the witness box by his fingertips and his eyes widened. 'Brett Ingram didn't die because his thyroid gland was enlarged!' he shouted.

Judge Linton removed his glasses and held them out in one hand towards the witness, like a peace offering. 'Dr Leigh,' he said.

'I understand your frustration with the line of questioning, which is – just about – within the parameters of relevance, but please answer the questions as best you can. If you would prefer a short adjournment in order to brief yourself more on these specific issues, your Counsel should address the court.' Judge Linton looked across at Andy. Andy remained silent.

'I just mean that the human body is complex,' Dr Leigh replied, evidently deciding not to take the judge up on the offer of a postponement. 'You can't blame all its problems on eating cabbage.'

'I understand,' Judith said. 'You are accepting, then, that kale can be bad for *some people?*'

Dr Leigh uttered an enormous and prolonged sigh, as if he were being forced to address the most tedious subject ever, but he did answer. 'Just looking at this article,' he said, 'if you read on, we're talking about very large quantities having a relatively small impact. I'm not aware of anyone ever dying from eating kale.'

'But it would be much better to eat things in moderation, wouldn't it? When you gave evidence last week, you told us that, had you understood from the start, that Brett Ingram might have had a food allergy, you would have conducted the post-mortem differently – that is, you would have examined his stomach contents. Isn't that correct?'

'Yes.'

'Is it also true that, if you had known that Brett Ingram was eating as much as 500g of kale every day, plus unknown quantities of spinach, broccoli, spring cabbage, you would have conducted the post-mortem differently then also?'

'I might have taken a look at his thyroid gland, but only out of interest, that's all.'

'To see if the claims made in the article we just read out were correct, those claims that it could cause swelling?'

'Look. I still can't believe this is what you've called me back for. I have four post-mortems waiting for me, all urgent. I'll keep it simple. There's no way, in my opinion – no way, zero percent – that anything in Mr Ingram's diet caused his death.'

Judith paused and allowed Dr Leigh's words to sink in again and watched him closely as Andy stared at the ceiling and Dr Leigh suddenly appreciated the significance of what he had just said and, like the true professional, acted quickly to recover. 'Except for the traces of shellfish, of course,' he added.

Judith gave what she hoped was a supportive, but not wholly genuine smile.

'Ah. Except for those…yes, of course,' she said.

Andy had now recovered from his soul searching, Judith noted, as he stood up and began to speak. 'My Lord,' he said. 'As Dr Leigh has been re-called, there is one useful area he can assist the court with, now we have heard from Miss Pallas, the waitress. I was going to ask for this evidence to be allowed *after* Mr Demetriou testifies, but I believe the facts are not in contention, and given that we have already troubled Dr Leigh to attend a second time…'

The judge turned to Judith. 'Ms Burton?'

Judith hated to be ambushed but she remembered Andy's words about how professional courtesy was a two-way mirror. 'I'm not sure what Mr Chambers is referencing,' she said, 'but if it's not contested…'

'Is it about kale or spinach or…brussels sprouts?' Judge Linton asked.

'No, My Lord, it relates to refrigeration and the important health and safety offences with which Mr Demetriou has been charged. Not as serious as manslaughter, but still grave breaches which deserve sanction.'

'Something relevant then, at last. Very well.'

Andy turned back to the witness. 'Dr Leigh, we heard evidence from Eleni Pallas, who served the food at Tanners' Hall, that the sandwiches which contained traces of shellfish were not refrigerated. They were kept in freezer bags from at least 10.30am to 12.30, when they were served to guests, and then the food stayed on the table till at least 1.30pm. Can you comment on how non-refrigeration might have impacted the traces of shellfish we now know were in the sandwiches?'

'Cold slows things down. Bacteria is never killed by refrigeration, but it slows down the rate of reproduction, so that food remains safe to eat for longer. If that food is then cooked at a sufficiently high temperature, then most bacteria will also be killed.'

Judith stood up. 'My Lord, is Mr Chambers now coming up with a new hypothesis? Unless I've not been listening for the past five days, the prosecution are not claiming that Mr Ingram died from any kind of food poisoning caused by bacteria.'

'Ms Burton, you've put forward a whole host of theories over those past five days – enough to sink a battleship. I'll allow Mr Chambers to at least explain where he's going with this one.'

'But the prosecution can't be allowed to make up an entirely new case right at the end...'

'I'd like Dr Leigh to answer the question, please. And you will have the floor for the rest of the week, in any event.'

'All I'm saying,' Dr Leigh said, with what Judith considered might be a smile of minor triumph, 'is that if the sandwiches were not cold, were taken from the fridge during the morning and left at room temperature for two or more hours, then there was a risk of bacterial growth. And that, in turn, could have made Mr Ingram unwell.'

Judith protested. 'My Lord, this is completely new evidence, with no formal connection to Mr Ingram's death.'

Judge Linton smiled at Judith, but without any warmth. 'That didn't stop you putting forward your "death by kale" theory a moment ago.'

'I must, at least, be allowed to ask Dr Leigh about the basis for...'

'No, thank you, Ms Burton. No more questions about refrigeration of sandwiches or any green vegetables. Dr Leigh's a very busy man. That will be all.'

As Dr Leigh marched out of court, Judith looked across at Andy. He mouthed 'sorry' to her, behind his hand, but she couldn't be bothered to respond.

***

'Hello, Mr Fogarty. Judith Burton here. I'm representing Mr Demetriou in the trial resulting from Mr Ingram's death.'

Judith had finally made time for the call she had prepared for last night. She sat in the small breakout room at the court, having checked there was no one in earshot outside the door. There was an intake of breath and a short pause, before the person on the end of the line spoke.

'Listen. I'm very busy,' Simon Fogarty said. 'If you'd like to speak to my secretary, I'm sure she'll be able to find a slot for you next week.'

'Oh this won't take long. I'd've chatted it through with you after court, except you only came that first day.'

Another silence confirmed to Judith that she was still pressing the right buttons. 'Listen, it's just a tiny thing you can assist with, but quite important, I think. You see we now know that Mr Ingram called you – twice in fact – from Tanners' Hall on the day he died. Isn't that something you should have told the police?'

'If you're going to make insinuations about my conduct, aren't I entitled to a lawyer?'

Judith gave an exaggerated sigh. 'If that's the way you want to do things, that's perfectly fine. Sergeant Thomas will bring you in for questioning – you'll remember Sergeant Thomas from that first day. She's awfully efficient. And you can have your lawyer, of course. But it would be so much simpler to tell me why Brett called you from Tanners' Hall. We know he was keen to speak to you and he didn't much like what you told him.'

'Maybe I'm too busy for police questioning,' Mr Fogarty said, although Judith heard the fear in his voice. She knew she had him.

'Then I'll ask the judge – Judge Linton: firm but fair – to order your attendance and you can tell us all in court what Mr Ingram wanted. We used to call it a "subpoena" – the court order demanding you come – but that's a bit dramatic-sounding, isn't it?'

Judith waited. She could hear Simon Fogarty's breath, but more than that she could sense him weighing up his next move.

'All right,' he said. 'It was about something which happened twelve years ago at the factory. I didn't have the answer straightaway, which is why we had to speak twice.'

'Twelve years ago?'

'Yes. It was about a boy.'

47

Constance had waited almost twenty minutes before she saw Sue crossing the street at the pedestrian light. She was smaller than Constance had imagined from the video and yesterday's call, a slight figure, whose briefcase dwarfed her. As Sue placed her foot on the bottom step, leading up to the entrance to her place of work, she saw Constance in the doorway.

'Professor Mills, I'm so sorry. I would never normally do this – ambush someone like this. I'm Constance Lamb. We spoke yesterday. Listen, time is running out. The prosecution finishes today and then it's over to us, the defence. Can we just get a coffee? Fifteen minutes, please? I think you know something which might really help my client. He's a good man, with a family. Please?'

Sue stared at Constance, then she checked her watch. Then she turned around and pointed at the Greedy Pig café two doors away. The two women entered in silence and sat down. Constance ordered them two cappuccinos.

'You said something happened to Zoe, and I heard about Rosa's café,' Sue began, her tiny hands clasped before her on the shiny table.

Constance wondered if this was a deliberate attempt to divert her from where they had left off yesterday, but if that was where Sue wanted to start, she would roll with it. She could manoeuvre the conversation where she needed once they got started.

'Someone let Mark's cows out of their field on Sunday, on to the road. Two of them were killed.'

Sue gasped and one hand went to her mouth.

'We think it was all the same person – your break-in too,' Constance said. 'If you know something, you should tell me.'

Tears sprang into Sue's eyes. 'I don't understand any of this,' she said. 'Why anyone would do these things.'

'We think it's linked with Brett's death, but we don't know how. You knew Brett before, didn't you? You told me that yesterday. You said he was the reason you became a scientist.'

As the waitress delivered their coffees, Sue wrapped both hands around hers, as if she needed the heat to sustain her.

'I'm probably overstating things. I never even met him – Brett Ingram. I got some holiday work with his company, straight from school,' she began. 'Quite basic, in the lab, testing for salt and sugar content and other similar stuff. But we were also allowed onto the production line to see all the things they were making. That was amazing. I realised that food was my thing. I wrote a paper on the impact of flavourings on rise and consistency in bread and I was set on the road that led me to where I am now.'

'So Heart Foods gave you your first job?'

'Yes, but the company had another name then; um, *Kwality Foods*, it was called. No, *Hi Kwality Foods*. There was a problem there, that summer, and they changed the name.'

Sue looked away again.

'Do you remember what the problem was?' Constance asked.

Sue's hands began to shake so violently that she spilled her coffee and was forced to return her mug to the table.

'I can't,' she said, 'I can't talk about it.'

'Can't or won't?' Constance asked. 'A man is dead.'

'I have to go now.'

'Wait!' Constance caught Sue's arm, gently but firmly, as she began to rise out of her seat.

'I think you want to tell me,' Constance said. 'You want to tell me what happened at Brett's company, before it changed its name. Please. I might be able to help.'

'I've never told anyone,' Sue said. 'Well, that's not true. I told them when it happened, the supervisor and a lawyer. They said I was mistaken. But I know what I saw. I was prepared to do it, be brave; *whistleblowing* they call it nowadays, don't they? The lawyer advised me to keep it to myself; keep well out of it. Said Brett's company had deeper pockets, said they had evidence I was mistaken. Told me to move on. So I have, all these years. I'd buried it. But when Brett died, just like that, it brought it all back.'

'What were you advised to keep to yourself?'

'It was the boy,' Sue said. 'The poor boy.'

Constance was conscious that her own pulse was racing. The boy? Was Zoe's phantom right and she'd been too embarrassed to follow it up? Had Sue held the key all along?

'Who was the boy?' she asked, hardly daring to breathe, in case it caused Sue to clam up again.

'George,' Sue said. 'His name was George. He was my age, nice-looking, kind, funny. He worked with me that summer. And then…and then he died.'

***

As Dr Leigh's evidence had been disposed of quickly, Judith had time to check on a few leads in addition to reviewing the prosecution evidence. First she called Greg, gave him two names and asked him to find out more about them. Then she rang Constance. No reply. She allowed the call to click to voicemail but hung up without leaving a message. What could be taking her so long?

Finally, she opened up the transcript of witness evidence on her laptop and began to skim through it all, from the beginning of the trial.

Two hours later, Judith was on her way back to the courtroom, when she saw Greg waiting for her. As she greeted him, Andy appeared in the corridor and stepped between the two of them.

'Hello again.' Andy stretched out his hand to Greg and then saw Judith's enquiring look. 'I don't want to interrupt, I just saw you and wanted to say hello.'

Greg nodded to Andy. 'Nice to see you again,' was all he managed.

'Are you recruiting Judith too?' Andy went on. 'I have to say, that *would* be a surprise.'

'Not today,' Greg replied.

Andy accepted Greg's response with a raised eyebrow. He folded his hands one on top of the other and, when he saw that nothing more was forthcoming from either Greg or Judith, he nodded amiably and walked on.

'What's he talking about?' Judith asked, once Andy had disappeared into the court.

'It's nothing. We met a couple of years ago. I'll tell you all about it later.'

'I'd prefer now.'

'It's too long to explain.' He kissed her cheek. 'Look, Connie called me because she knew I was nearby. She'll be here in half an hour, tops.'

Judith watched Greg closely for any giveaway sign of what business he and Andy Chambers had transacted two years ago. Maybe Greg had been an expert witness in one of Andy's cases, like he had been for her. That still didn't explain the curious 'recruitment' comment though.

'I've been ringing her and she doesn't pick up,' she said.

'She's probably on the Underground. She said to ask to adjourn till she gets here. She says it's big news and you have to wait for her.'

'Well then,' Judith said, sneaking a glance which followed in Andy's wake. 'I'd better do as she says, don't you think? Are you sticking around?'

'I can't. I have a presentation to give shortly. Look, you asked me about those names. Maria and George Doukas. I…I didn't want to put into writing what I found.' He stood close to her and whispered in her ear.

Judith drew back with a frown. 'I understand,' she said. 'Thank you.'

'Must run,' Greg said aloud. 'I just came over to pass on Connie's message, as it was so important. I'll see you this evening.'

As she watched his receding back, Judith took a moment to process what Greg had told her. The key now was to buy a little more time. She turned around and stared at the door leading into the court. The simplest thing. *Just ask for a short adjournment* she told herself. *Go on in there. You can't lie, but just say your solicitor has been delayed and you need her.* If that doesn't work? Then she smiled, as she knew what reason she would give and why the judge would be forced to agree.

After Judith had engineered a further two-hour adjournment, she sat alone, closed her eyes and reflected on the day's events. She had the feeling that although some of the others might have provided clues, it was in Eleni's testimony that something of real significance was lurking. She looked back through Eleni's answers. After the third reading it clicked and she chastised herself for not working things out sooner. Now, at last, everything was clear.

48

Constance ran the last half mile to court, and by the time she reached Judith, she could hardly breathe and her clothes were sticking to her. She burst into their break-out room.

'You haven't opened the defence yet, have you?'

Judith appeared remarkably relaxed. 'I persuaded Judge Linton to wait for you,' she said.

'You didn't?'

'No. I...I was rather naughty, actually. I just reminded him of that guidance I mentioned, for women of a certain age, said that I was suffering and asked to be allowed a rest to recover my equilibrium.'

Constance laughed, despite her excitement at her own news. 'You didn't? You did. And what did he say?'

'His face was a picture, as was Andy's. I mean, he knew it was total rubbish, but there was no way he could object, especially with his track record. We have another forty minutes still to regroup. I thought of going round the corner and buying everyone choc ices. What?'

Constance had stripped off her jacket and drunk down half a bottle of water.

'You were right,' she said. 'Brett Ingram was murdered. And I know who did it. I got the answer from Susan Mills – and Zoe helped, but it took a while.'

'Good,' Judith said, picking up her blue exercise book. 'I do too. Shall we compare notes?'

***

Judith and Constance found Nick and Lisa waiting outside the building, sitting next to each other on a bench in the sun. Lisa, arms folded, was leaning her head back against Nick's shoulder and her eyes were closed. In different circumstances, they would have been an ordinary couple, at ease with each other, enjoying the beauty of the day. Constance hesitated, but at that moment Lisa's eyes blinked open, she noticed them and beckoned them over.

'Hello there,' she said.

'Hello there,' Judith replied. 'Nick. Constance and I need to speak to you. Is it possible we could find somewhere to talk to you alone?'

Nick regarded his lawyers blankly. 'Whatever you want to say to me, you can say in front of Lisa. You know that already.'

'I understand that we've discussed your case with both of you up till now but, really, if we could have a moment, just with you. It's important.'

Lisa frowned. She took hold of Nick's hand in her own and gripped it tightly. Nick put his free hand on top of hers, in a clear sign of their unity.

'All right,' Judith said. 'There's no easy way to say this, but we have to withdraw from representing you.'

'What?' Lisa released Nick and one hand went up to her neck. That was brutal, even by Judith's standards.

'But you can't,' Lisa protested. 'It's the middle of the trial. Isn't Nick giving his evidence today?'

'I'm sorry,' Judith said.

'He's been practising and he'll be very good. I know he will. He'll explain about the fridge and the clearing up and he remembers he talked to Eleni in Greek – all those things you said.'

Judith was silent, unmoved by Lisa's protest.

'We don't have any choice,' Constance added, hoping that might end the matter.

'Why?' Lisa said.

Judith took over again. 'I'd rather not say,' she said.

'That's it! You're not going to explain. Is it because you're not getting paid enough? We have some savings – not much, but you can have it all. You can't leave my husband now. He needs you.'

Constance looked at Judith but said nothing. They had agreed they should say as little as possible. That it was best for Nick, but Constance could see that it might look to Lisa as if they were just deserting him.

'You know, when Nick said you were his lawyers, that time you came to our house, I wasn't so sure,' Lisa continued. 'But when I met you, talked to you, I said to him, "these are clever women. They will help you".'

Judith frowned. She was clearly unimpressed by Lisa's sycophancy. 'We have discovered some evidence which makes us believe that your husband has not told us the entire truth,' Judith said. 'If that is the case, the rules say that we are not able to defend him. We can make arrangements for another defence team to come in, but we have to stand down.'

'We'll tell the judge and the prosecution that we're withdrawing,' Constance joined in, pleased that Judith was providing a little further explanation, 'and ask for a short adjournment, a break, for new lawyers to get up to speed. We'll pass on all the papers.'

Lisa stood up and faced Constance. 'We engaged you to defend Nick. You can't just stop half way through.'

'Mrs Demetriou, I've explained the difficulty.'

'No, I don't accept it. If you withdraw, what reason will you give the prosecution?'

'We'll say the minimum, but...they'll draw their own conclusions.'

'You mean they'll think it means that Nick's guilty?' Lisa said, and Constance thought how quickly she had grasped what they were saying, despite Judith talking in riddles.

'They might suspect something, but we can't tell them what it is.'

'But they'll *know* there's something and, if *you* found it, whatever it is, then they'll find it too.'

'Maybe, but the trial is nearly over. Although there might have to be an adjournment, like I said, for a few days, to allow the new lawyers to come in.'

Nick still didn't speak, but a tear squeezed its way out of one eye.

'You can't do this,' Lisa began to cry also. 'You can't leave us like this. I'll complain. I'll go to the newspapers. You'll never work again!'

'It's over,' Nick said suddenly.

'What? No. Don't be silly,' Lisa grabbed Nick's arm. He shrugged her off.

'They're trying to tell us it's over,' he said. 'Don't you understand? It was really over the moment that man died.'

Judith tried to correct him. 'Mr Demetriou. That's not exactly what I'm saying. With a new legal team...'

'I don't want a new legal team. We'll end up in the same place and I'll only have put Lisa and my family through even more of this.'

Lisa stepped back now and her eyes flashed daggers at her husband. 'Now,' she said. 'Now you're thinking about me. You didn't think about me then, did you? You only thought about one person. You and your sister. You did for her what you would never do for the rest of us.'

'Enough,' Nick shouted, springing to his feet, and Lisa cowered away from him. 'Bring Maria to court.'

'What are you talking about? Are you crazy?' Lisa kept her distance. 'You saw Maria,' she appealed to Judith now. 'She's on all this medication, for anxiety. She can't even sit still. She'll make a terrible scene. Then you'll lose.'

Nick drew himself up to his full height. 'I'm not asking you for anything else,' he said. 'I may not ask you for anything else ever again. Do this one thing for me.' Then he turned to Constance. 'When Maria arrives, then I'll give my evidence.'

'Mr Demetriou, we can't...' Constance began.

'No,' he said. 'Either I do it with you, or I do it without you. I don't care which way. But when Maria arrives, then I will explain.'

49

JUDGE LINTON ALMOST SMILED as court reconvened, at a little after 3pm. 'Ms Burton, are you sufficiently refreshed now, to continue?'

'Yes, thank you, My Lord,' Judith replied, but she was unable to appreciate his gesture, as she fought hard to preserve her usual mask of neutrality. In the public gallery, next to Lisa, sat Nick's sister, Maria. She wore a yellow blouse, with a bow at the neck and her hair had been trimmed to a neat bob. But her eyes were constantly in motion, wandering the room and she kept whispering to Lisa and raising and lowering her hands.

Nick crossed the room and entered the witness box, covering the ground in three long strides. Judith could see Andy watching her closely. From the running order, Nick was not supposed to be called for another two days, so he knew something had happened. He could have complained, said he was not prepared for Nick's cross-examination, but he didn't. She suspected he was relishing the opportunity to question Nick, even if it arose earlier than expected.

'What will you do?' Constance asked Judith, as they had hurried back inside.

And the truth was that Judith was not entirely sure, until she sat down in court and took a moment to stand back from recent events. But she realised, once she did, that Nick had made things easy for her.

'My Lord. I know this is rather unusual,' she began, 'but Mr Demetriou has indicated to me and my solicitor, in the break, that he no longer requires our services. He now wishes to conduct his defence himself and…he will be giving a statement to the court. I suspect it will not be a long one.'

Judge Linton sucked on the end of his pen and looked pensive. This was not what he was expecting, although the prospect of speeding things up was always welcome.

'Are you content that this is perfectly proper?' he asked.

'I believe what my client is suggesting *may* be the most appropriate way to elicit his evidence, on this occasion,' Judith said. 'The other options are to adjourn until new representation is found for Mr Demetriou, but he has asked me to tell you that he will not accept any new legal team or, I suppose, you could declare a mistrial.'

'Mr Chambers?'

'I'm in Your Lordship's hands. I would be content to go ahead. I am thinking, primarily, of the costs already incurred in this not insignificant trial.'

Judge Linton stared hard at Nick. Clearly, he did not want to answer for the potential waste of a valuable week of court time. But on the other hand, there was the concern that a renegade defendant in his courtroom would set his return to favour back even further. Even so, all credit to him, he decided to take the plunge.

'Very well then, Mr Demetriou,' he said. 'Please go ahead.'

Nick looked at Lisa and Maria. Lisa was stony-faced, her hands clasped tightly together in her lap. Maria raised her head and smiled at him. Then Nick turned to the jury and he began to speak.

'My sister, Maria, had a son,' he said. 'My nephew, George. Well, he was Giorgios, named after my father, but everyone called him George. He was a good boy; tall, good with his hands. Maria was a widow, her husband died when George was only four years old. She never had the good luck my mother hoped for. But Maria knew George would do well, would look after her, and for a while he did. Then, like lots of teenagers, he got in with a bad crowd, stopped going to school, his grades dropped and he left without qualifications.

'This was 2008; he was just seventeen years old. He looked for jobs so many times, but nothing.' Nick held his hands out, palms turned upwards. 'Then he applied for a position at Hi Kwality Foods. That was what Heart Foods was called, then.'

Judith looked at the jury. If they had not been totally engaged until now, this last revelation changed everything, and every eye was fixed on Nick. They could suddenly appreciate that they were not listening to the minutiae of Nick's family history, but to material evidence inextricably linked, in a way which was most likely to be shortly revealed, with Brett Ingram's death.

'He didn't hear nothing for a week, maybe two,' Nick continued. 'Then he got a call. They said Mr Brett Ingram had a special scheme to take on young people – "underachievers", they said – to give them a chance to show what they could do. George went for an interview. He got the job. We went out to celebrate. We ate and drank and laughed. We were all so happy for him.'

Maria let out a low moan. Nick noticed, waited a moment in deference and then continued.

'George was there for a few weeks, working in the lab. He loved it; said the people were nice, the work was interesting, said he'd even met Brett Ingram one time and he'd been friendly. And then...'

Judith looked at Lisa. She had lowered her head into her hands. Maria remained silent and unexpectedly still, her eyes fixed on her brother.

'Maria, my sister, got a call,' Nick said. 'It was the hospital. They said George had collapsed at work, in the canteen, and died. They said he had eaten biscuits containing peanuts. A girl who worked with him had used his EpiPen, but it wasn't enough. Seventeen years old, tall, nice-looking, good with his hands, his mother's only child; dead.'

'Oh God.' Next to Judith, Andy had uttered the curse aloud, without realising.

'They had an enquiry, the company, and we got a lawyer to help us. George had eaten biscuits they made. He'd bought them in the canteen. I know George. He would have checked the label; he always did. But the label didn't mention peanuts or nuts or anything. They said he must have eaten something else, something he brought from home, which was stupid. First, we had no peanuts at home. And if he had biscuits from home, then why would he spend money buying their biscuits?'

Nick checked to see that everyone was following his logic.

'They wouldn't let us into the factory. They swore there were no peanuts; they got all the people who worked there to say so.

But they never let us in to look inside. That said everything to me. Then, just to make sure we really understood, they sent us all the statements from all the people who worked with George: *confidential, for the purposes of the enquiry.* But at least then we had some names, and I found them and I called them, each of them, one by one. When I got to the girl – Susan, she was called – the one who was with George when he died, the one he trusted with the EpiPen, then I knew Hi Kwality/Heart Foods – it doesn't matter what they're called – I knew they were lying.

'She told me – Susan – that she'd shared the biscuits with George just twenty minutes before he died, that she thought she'd seen peanuts on the production line when she went around the factory. Sometimes they tried new products, moved things around, didn't always clean up all traces of what was there before. Then she checked again, after George died, and the peanuts were gone. She said it had been explained to her that she must have been mistaken about what she saw.'

'Mr Demetriou. I am going to stop you for a moment just so that I am clear,' Judge Linton interrupted. 'You are telling this court that your nephew, George, died of an allergic reaction to peanuts at Brett Ingram's factory in 2008. And that the company denied responsibility.'

'Yes, sir.'

'You do understand that you are on trial for causing Mr Ingram's death, don't you, and that you have pleaded not guilty?'

'Yes, sir.'

'All right. Continue.'

'We tried to get our lawyer to make them admit it, that George had done nothing wrong, that it was *them* all along. But Susan disappeared and her statement, the one she signed, said the same as the others. Then they came up with all these clever arguments like George never having said he had an allergy on his application form - as if it would have made any difference. We went to the police but they weren't interested in the death of a Greek boy named Giorgios - not the same way they were interested in Brett Ingram.

'Our lawyer said we could go after the ambulance crew if we really wanted to blame someone. It had taken them over an hour to reach George. The coroner said if they'd got there inside thirty minutes he would still be alive. But it wasn't their fault either. There had been an accident on the road; no one could move. They sent someone on a bike, but they arrived too late.'

Nick stopped his monologue, filled his glass of water with a shaking hand and gulped it down.

'After George's funeral we talked - our family - about what to do. Maria was all alone and she was unable to work. She was... on lots of pills, hardly knew what day it was. We decided to go and talk to him, to Brett Ingram - Maria and me. We made an appointment and we went to his fancy office, where he sat by the window in his fancy chair, spinning around. We told him that George was all Maria had. And he listened. And he could see how Maria was. He spoke to someone on the phone. Then he said to us that if we would sign an agreement to say that they were not to blame, he would pay money to Maria, to help her, now George had gone. And that's what we did.'

Maria groaned again, this time more visceral than the last.

'He paid Maria two hundred thousand pounds, half straightaway, the rest over the next two years. Very generous, our lawyer said. We used the money for Maria to buy her house and put some away for her. She seemed better. It took a while, but she went back to work and life went on, without George. And then, around a year ago, I saw on the News a report that a girl, fourteen years old, had died from eating nuts, just like George. But this time they went to jail – the chef, the director. And Maria saw it too. And she told me we had done things wrong. That I had done things wrong. That we should never have signed the agreement, that the money we took was *blood money*. She wanted to give it all back and go to the police. I explained it was too late for that. She…she became very unwell and had to go into a hospital for a long time. She only came out in the spring.'

Nick stood with both hands gripping the lectern. One of the jurors wiped at her eyes with a handkerchief.

'Are you going to tell us about the 13th of April, Mr Demetriou?' Judge Linton asked.

Judith looked at Lisa. She was staring at her husband and shaking her head from side to side. So she knew. She had always known. Nick ignored her.

'When the booking went in the diary,' he said, 'I didn't know at first that it was them, the same people who had killed George. But as soon as I spoke to Diana and she said his name, *Brett Ingram*, then I knew. How could I ever forget? And then I began to think about how I could make things right for Maria, for George. This Diana, she told me he had an allergy, to shellfish. Him, Brett Ingram, big cheese, CEO, swivel chair. He had a food allergy, just like poor, nobody-cared-about-him George. She said to make sure there was no shellfish, not even tiny amounts, in any of the food.'

Judge Linton spoke softly. 'Is that what you did?'

'I went to lots of shops to see what was in their sandwiches. I wasn't going to serve shellfish – that would have been too obvious.

When I got to Costco, I could see they had sandwiches – beef, chicken – the label mentioned "traces" of shellfish. I bought those and threw away the wrapper.'

'You knew the Costco sandwiches were labelled to mention shellfish?'

'Yes. I did. But I couldn't be sure it would be enough. What did "traces" mean and, if they were on another production line, maybe there wouldn't be any in these sandwiches. So…I had fish sauce at home, for Thai cooking, mostly. I like to add it to my dishes. It contains shrimp; that's what the label says. The bottle was large, but I found one from vanilla essence, much smaller, only around this high.' Nick showed a height of around ten centimetres between finger and thumb.

'I washed it out, poured in the fish sauce and hid it in my sock. Even then, I thought, if he says something, if he comes to me and tells me how sorry he was, if he asks how Maria is, then I won't do it. I won't. But that's not what happened. He got out of his expensive car and came into the kitchen. He looked at me and I saw in his eyes that he remembered me, he remembered everything. But he said nothing.'

'What did you do, Mr Demetriou?'

'I served the sandwiches and I poured the fish sauce in his water, just small amounts, a little at a time. I'd tested it at home. It has a brown colour in the bottle but it doesn't show, if you're careful and it doesn't taste. You know, it was funny, because Brett kept drinking the water to help himself feel better. And Diana made it worse, because she wouldn't let me serve bottled water, even in glass. She said I had to use tap water, in jugs. I did as she asked, just with a little extra something.'

'You're saying you intended to kill Mr Ingram?'

Now Nick was silent, weighing up the judge's question.

'I didn't mean to hurt him badly,' he said. 'I never thought those drops of fish sauce in his water, the "traces" in the sandwiches, would kill him – a big, fit man. He looked like he played lots of sport. I thought he would be ill – a headache maybe, bad stomach – like he had at first. I wanted that to happen. And I wanted him to remember George. I…I think that I wouldn't have cared if he had been scared also, wondering that his body was letting him down, worrying what was wrong. George would have been scared, would have been terrified. I…I wouldn't have minded if Brett had felt something like that. But I never thought he would die. I never imagined he would die.'

Nick looked around him. Lisa was staring at the floor. Maria sat alert, silent and still.

'I'm sorry,' Nick whispered to his sister. 'I wanted to make it all right, but, instead, I messed it all up again.' Then he sat down. He had nothing more to say.

PART THREE

50

Two hours later, Judith and Constance sat in the Magpie and Stump, with two glasses of lager in front of them on the table. In the light of Nick's revelations, the judge had stopped the trial and dismissed the jury, so that the CPS could decide how best it wanted to proceed.

'Poor Nick,' Constance said.

Judith clucked her tongue against the roof of her mouth. 'Oh no,' she said. 'Don't say that. I know how he dressed it up, like he was the victim, but you know as well as I that if you want to hurt someone and they end up dead, you may as well have planned their murder.'

Constance had known Judith would disagree. 'He was stuck in the middle, though,' she insisted. 'He loved his sister and she blamed him, when he'd tried so hard to do the right thing.'

'He could have confronted Brett, not killed him.'

'I bet Lisa encouraged him. It was obvious she knew.'

'I agree she knew about it afterwards,' Judith said. 'That much was clear. And how cleverly she played the part of the concerned spouse. She had us fooled. I bet she even speaks Greek. But her outburst about Maria; the bitterness. That was real. He never shared with her what he was planning. Or with Maria. Of course, Maria must also have known, once Brett died, that her beloved brother was responsible. So both women found themselves aligned in a pact of silence. Whether the police want to look into that too is really up to them.'

'What a mess.'

'Diana must blame herself now,' Judith said.

Constance thought that an unusual leap. 'How do you mean?'

'She chose the venue. And Nick came with it.'

'She couldn't have known about what happened to the boy, though. She's only been working for Brett for five years.'

'I'm not saying she *was* to blame,' Judith gulped down her beer. 'Just that she might regret her decision. But the CFO knew, and probably a few others in senior positions at Heart Foods.'

'Was that how you worked it out? You talked to the CFO?'

'That was the last piece of the puzzle. The first was Lisa's jewellery.'

'What?'

'One of the things which bothered me was Lisa's jewellery, the lavish necklace she wore every day to the trial. Actually, Andy tipped me off, inadvertently, of course. He saw it as a sign of Nick's cavalier attitude to work, that he must be sourcing food on the cheap, if he never made much profit but indulged his wife's expensive tastes. Apart from that being stupid, chauvinistic nonsense, it still resonated with me – but differently. It just seemed so flippant for Lisa to be wearing that shimmering necklace if she truly felt bad about what had happened.'

'Is that really what made you suspect Nick?' The sun was streaming in through the window and Constance put one hand up to shield her eyes.

'You think I should keep that one to myself, do you?' Judith laughed, 'if I'm ever asked to share the secrets of my success?'

'I think it's one to bury in a deep hole.'

'You're right. She probably just liked wearing it, hadn't had many opportunities to bring it out during lockdown. And I mean it's not every day your husband goes on trial for gross negligence manslaughter, is it?'

'What else? You said the jewellery was first.'

'The waitress, Eleni. You weren't there this morning. Nick had told us very little with any conviction, if you remember, but he insisted that he had spoken to her in Greek, when he asked her to leave. If he was right, then Zoe's evidence, that he ordered Eleni out, to enable him to race around and destroy all the incriminating evidence, was, at least to a small degree, discredited.'

'So?'

'Eleni kept looking at Nick when she was speaking. I couldn't be sure, but my instinct told me she was suspicious of how Nick behaved that day too, but she was too loyal to say. She certainly didn't remember what language Nick spoke in and I could see she might not. The very fact that Nick was so certain made me think he was making it all up. And she'd insinuated that Nick was no help serving the guests – she had to do things alone. That made me think he might have been preoccupied with his plans. And then there was the Tupperware.'

'The Tupperware?'

'Eleni said that they usually kept leftover food – that she'd packaged it up – but this time Nick threw it all away. That suggested more cover-up, but I had no idea why Nick would want to hurt Brett. Then came the CFO.'

'Simon Fogarty?'

Judith nodded. 'It had bothered me, from the start, that there was no one obviously at the trial for Brett. I couldn't work out why that might have been. I mean, I know Brett had no immediate family, but you'd have thought the company would have sent a representative, or found a more distant relative, made a public statement or something. I wondered if they had something to hide. Then I thought I was over-thinking; maybe they felt it was inappropriate to comment while the trial was ongoing. Afterwards, they'd make a statement. You get the picture.

'And then I had noticed two men in court, on day one. They seemed pretty interested, were talking a lot to each other, but they didn't come back. They might have been nobodies. I checked those photos you sent me early on, the ones the press published, with Lisa and other family members and some of Brett, but neither of the men featured. Then, as soon as you got his name – Simon Fogarty – from Diana, I Googled him and his photo is on the company website.'

'Simon Fogarty, the CFO, was in court on the first day?'

'With some underling.'

'And when you called him, he told you everything?'

'At first, no. Then I said I would subpoena him to give his evidence in court.'

'Oh.'

'He was a bit chattier then. He told me that a "Giorgios Doukas" had died at the factory in 2008 and an agreement had been reached with the mother, Maria Doukas, and that he had passed that information to Brett on the call. I asked about the circumstances of the boy's death and he refused to say. I decided I'd pushed my luck and left it there. I had my suspicions, of course, given the names, but I had to be sure. Greg did the necessary checks on the names – mother and son, the address, confirmed Maria was Nick's sister. He came to court in the break this morning and told me.'

'So you knew it was Nick?'

'I was pretty sure. And then you arrived, of course, and filled in most of the gaps.'

'Wow. I can't believe you worked it out like that. You are truly brilliant.'

'Hardly.'

'No, I mean, I got there, but only because Sue told me. She's still very affected by it. Says that she tried to forget it for so long, push it out of her mind. I think she truly buried the memory. And then it happened a second time, with Brett, and it all came flooding back.'

'Did she not make the connection with Nick?'

'Different names, years apart. And she never met any of George's family. She just knew it was the same nightmare happening again.'

'Shall we toast Susan Mills, then?' Judith said. 'One of those people who try to do the right thing but whom life tends to overlook.'

Constance obliged and they drank a toast to Sue, clinking their glasses together.

'If Simon Fogarty knew about George,' Constance asked, holding up her glass to the light, 'then he must have known about Nick. Why didn't he say anything?'

'Like I say, I asked all that was necessary for our purposes and the rest remained unsaid. But I suspect he preferred to keep anything which happened with George twelve years ago out of the public eye. The company had rebranded, and the unfortunate episode had been forgotten. And he certainly would not have wanted the payment to Maria to become public knowledge – or his role in it. No. I think he came to court and was satisfied there was a good team prosecuting Nick. Maybe if it had looked like Nick would be acquitted, he would have found a way of helping out behind the scenes. We'll never know.'

Constance shook her head. 'Out of all of this, what surprises me most, I think, is that Brett tried to cover up George's death. It doesn't sound like the kind of thing he would do.'

Judith knocked her glass against Constance's a second time. 'That's because you have such a trusting nature,' she said. 'You see the best in people. Don't ever lose that. But you might be right this time. I have a little theory of my own.'

'What is it?'

'It's hardly more than a hypothesis. And I warn you, it could be defamatory.'

'Just tell me. I'm not going to tell anyone else.'

'All right. Who, out of all the panellists, do we dislike the most?'

'Well, that's an easy one. What, you think Adrian did it – the cover-up?'

'In 2008, he'd just invested £100,000 of family money in his best friend's business. You can see why he might have wanted to persuade Brett to keep things quiet.'

Constance mulled things over in her mind. 'You think that's why Brett stayed friendly with him over the years, humoured him over his new idea – because Adrian knew about what happened with George Doukas?'

Judith's eyes were shining now. 'That would be an even better motive to keep Adrian's mouth well and truly shut than the one we attributed to Simon Fogarty. And, if that's right, then you could say that Adrian was responsible for the death of his friend, after all.'

'Oh come on.'

Judith shook her head. 'You know, as well as I, that these things all begin somewhere with something small and then they grow, just like Nick's resentment. Adrian prevailed upon his friend to clean up the production line and pay off Maria, and it came back to bite him in the worst way possible. Anyway, sounds like you don't want to hear my crazy theories any more. I'm interested in the gene-editing research you uncovered at the Sumners. Now we have a little more time, you can spill the beans.'

Constance placed her glass down in the centre of her beer mat. Now, finally, she could tell Judith about Mark and Rachel's secret. 'It's revolutionary,' she said.

'I've heard that before, somewhere.'

'No, really. It could change everything. There's this special technique they use to cut out bits of DNA they don't want from plants. Then the plant takes over and replicates the change in all its cells. Like magic really. Suddenly, your tomato plant grows eight branches instead of three and it only needs half the water.'

'And why so hush-hush?'

'It's all the stuff associated with genetically modified food which everyone got excited about a few years back. Concern that it's just not safe. Interfering with nature. Causing irreversible changes.'

'Playing God. And you were worried about Brett making his employees smell bread. This went so much further. Although that's what they said about the first test-tube baby, as I recall, and now it's completely normal. I suppose that's why the Ambrosia tag was such sublime marketing. Gene-edited food: the perfect product. It may not make you immortal, but it's still ambrosia: food fit for the gods. It sweetens today's bitter pill, just a tad. To know that something good may be coming soon that will help us feed everyone in a cleaner, more efficient way, whatever you choose to eat.'

'Diana knew,' Constance said. 'She just strung me along. She didn't volunteer anything on Ambrosia at the beginning. Then she only told us about the junk food aspect when she had to. She did give me hints about Mark, but even that was right at the end. *Something secret going on at the Sumners farm* kind of thing.'

'But why should she offer us anything? It was all a massive sideshow,' Judith said. 'Diana was completely right. And I was the one who encouraged you, encouraged us to be so monumentally diverted by it all. I'm the one to blame for all this. Not you. Or Diana. Me. The queen of the red herring. I could hear Andy laughing even before we knew Nick was guilty.'

'Don't say that. You were brilliant, Judith, really. The way you took apart the pathologist's evidence was just...sublime.'

'Well, yes, that's one way of describing it, I suppose.'

Constance thought hard. 'Oh,' she leaned forward in her seat. 'I can't believe I forgot to tell you. I saw Sergeant Thomas, out at Mark's farm.'

'Really?'

Constance eyed Judith suspiciously. 'You knew?'

Judith finished her drink and waved at the barman for two more.

'Let's say that after our joint session with the illustrious Dr Edge, I tipped her off that something nasty might happen at the farm and it may have something to do with this investigation.'

'Our session with Dr Edge?'

'And I was right about her, she is the most diligent police officer. I cannot even begin to imagine how many hoops she had to leap through to ensure that some obsolete cameras were back up and rolling, within hours, in an area completely outside her own jurisdiction. I suspect the process wasn't entirely authorised in the way it should have been, but no matter.'

'And what happened? Did they catch…whoever did it – let the cows out?'

'I think we'll have to wait and see. I have another question for you now. I was meaning to ask and then everything else happened.'

'Is it the last one? I'm not sure I can do this for much longer, today.'

'You said Zoe helped you out. What did you mean?'

'Zoe?'

'When you told me you knew Nick was guilty. You mentioned Zoe had helped, as well as Sue.'

Constance took her second beer from the barman and ran her index finger around its rim. Maybe, after all, some things were better left unsaid. 'I don't know why I said that,' she said. 'Unless I meant the video. No, there was nothing else important from Zoe.'

51

Zoe was at home, researching a new article on quinoa. She'd already discovered it was an ancient grain, dating back at least three thousand years, to the area around Lake Titicaca in Peru. That might have put some people off further investigation, given her agenda, but not Zoe. She could still work around that. The people living then had fed it to livestock first, and once she'd read that its seeds have a bitter inedible coating, she had to find out more.

***

Rosa sifted through the post at the Sweetpea Café, while greeting customers like old friends. She'd invited a camera crew along for the reopening, and whether that was the reason for the hoards, or whether the café had been genuinely missed seemed unimportant as the tables filled up and chatter spread out across the room. There had been a moment when a customer had asked if there was any mango and she'd remembered Brett popping the lump of sweet orange flesh into his mouth, his smile enveloping the room over lunch on that fateful day, but then she'd pushed away the memory, explained that they didn't serve mango because of its carbon footprint and moved to take the next order.

***

Sue sat in the lab, checking through her final table of results. Everything seemed in order. She thought about Brett and then she thought about George and how she had failed him twelve years ago. Constance, the solicitor, had been kind, had said that she'd been very young and that she'd done exactly the right thing, had confirmed that probably whatever she'd said would not have made any real difference. And it couldn't bring the boy back.

Sue knew all of that was probably true. Even so, it bothered her that she had been so powerless, that she had had no voice at all. Knowledge was supposed to be power, but only if you were prepared to harness it, to use it for your own ends or to help others. Perhaps it was all her mother's fault, bringing her up to believe that the best way to get on in life was to toe the line, keep your head down, stay below the radar. And that she, Susan, was the kind of person who, even if she was given a pair of oars in a rowing boat, would not ever be able to produce even the smallest of waves.

A few hours earlier, immediately after she'd returned from coffee with Constance, she'd marched around the lab for the last time. All the glass containers had been removed, but the power sockets and heating apparatus remained. And she'd known then, as she knew now, that there was no point fighting how things were, especially if they weren't that bad. She wasn't that kind of person. It wasn't how she lived her life. So now she checked again on her laptop that using sludge – human waste – to feed the larvae, was flagged as viable in her conclusions. She addressed her covering email to Dougie and Gemma and various other eminent people at the Sanitation Trust, took a deep breath and then pressed send.

***

Mark was out in the barn. He lifted forkful after forkful of hay and delivered it into the stall where one of his cows was recuperating from a minor illness. Airpods in, he sang along as he worked. As the cow turned its head in his direction and then ambled forward to eat, he stopped what he was doing and ran his hand along the length of her flank.

'There's a good girl now,' he said.

***

Adrian opened up his presentation and shared his screen with the CEO and marketing director of Supreme Foods. The words "Food for your Mood" were emblazoned across the top, each letter a different colour, as he had envisaged from the first time he had shared his brilliant idea with Brett, many months before. The two men seated across the table from him exchanged glances which Adrian couldn't decipher, but which he hoped signalled their excitement. After all, they had forked out a grand in legal fees for a lawyer to oversee the confidentiality agreement he had insisted they sign before he would allow them access. It would be stupid not to get their money's worth.

'That's the essence of it,' Adrian said at the end. 'You can imagine how fast it will take off – whoosh, like a rocket.' He made the noise and waved his arm in a diagonal, upright motion. 'Everyone will want a piece of it. I can guarantee.'

'That's it?' the CEO said, with a flick of his eyes to his left, where his marketing director sat. Again, Adrian tried to decode what he saw, but the CEO's tone clearly hinted at irritation. They had to like it. Maybe he'd run through things too quickly for them?

'In summary, yes,' Adrian stammered. 'But, what I've presented, it's only the bare bones of the idea. If you'd like me to…flesh out any areas for you, I'd be happy to do so.'

The CEO stood up.

'We got your drift, Dr Edge, thank you, and that's sufficient. We'll talk it over internally and let you know if we're interested.'

Adrian's smile almost left his face and his eyebrows knitted themselves together. This wasn't what he'd expected and it wasn't good.

'When do you think…'

'If you haven't heard from us in ten days, you'll know we're not interested.'

The CEO moved towards the door. Adrian stood up now, collected his laptop and shook both men's hands. 'Thank you,' he said. 'Ten days. I appreciate the opportunity to share my vision with you. I'll wait to hear then.'

As he closed the door behind him, he heard one of the men – it sounded like the CEO – burst into fits of laughter. Were they laughing at him and his idea? Had they really not understood how marvellous and ground-breaking his initiative would be? Of course, he might have been mistaken and they'd loved it and it was all an act to keep him keen. He knew how these things worked.

Or perhaps the marketing manager had just told the CEO a very funny joke.

***

Diana stood in Brett's office, running her hands over all the surfaces, trying to remember what it had felt like when she came in every morning and Brett was sitting there, opposite her, smiling broadly, with a list of things for her to do. Sometimes, he'd wait till she was leaving and then he'd call her back, just as she reached the door, to impart something he'd forgotten first time around. It had become a standing joke between them, that the moment she thought she had everything down, he'd add to the list. But it had always been such fun, that was the best word to describe her years at Heart Foods: long hours, hard work, but fun, and she doubted she would find the same enjoyment elsewhere.

She was there to clear out his room. The CFO, the others – they'd been very kind – said she could take a memento – although she suspected the offer was a crude attempt to remove the bitter edge from her mission. Now she was standing there with a cardboard box in her hand, she couldn't bear to disturb anything. Somehow, if she left it all exactly as it was: his chair angled to the side, as if he had just got up and gone to the fridge for some iced water, the photo of him with his late parents and beloved dog, taken in Cornwall when he was a child, up close to his PC, his copy of 'how to make your first million' near where his left hand would have rested, bookmarked at chapter one. He'd joked to her that, only twenty pages in, he'd realised he already knew everything in there, but he'd keep it, just in case.

But Diana had to start somewhere and it must be better for her to be the one to rummage through Brett's personal effects. She sat down at his desk and, after a deep sigh, she opened his top drawer. There was little of interest: an ancient fountain pen she'd never seen him use, some dogeared business cards, a discarded phone, a pack of chewing gum. She pulled each item out and dropped them into the box. But the drawer would not fully extend and, as she wrestled with it, something rolled forwards from the back, where it was concealed, into the light.

At first Diana thought it was a marker pen, but it was too big and, with its pale blue end and bright orange tip, the colours were all wrong. Then, as she brought it closer to her face, she saw what it was. *EpiPen 0.3mg Epinephrine auto injector*, she read.

Brett's parting words to her most days came suddenly into her head. 'You take care,' he'd say, as he waved her off, with a smile that made her knees weak. And as she clasped the EpiPen to her chest – the EpiPen which might have saved Brett's life – she thought then of how little care he had taken of himself.

52

JUDITH HAD RETURNED HOME from her debrief session with Constance and then headed off, straight away, for a long walk on the Heath. In the grounds of Kenwood House she'd stopped to rest on a bench. Ten years previously she'd been here with Martin, at a concert of choral classics. They'd sat on a blanket on the grass and watched a firework display, synchronised with Elgar's *Pomp and Circumstance Number 1*. It had been uplifting, rousing, soul enriching. Perhaps not everything she had done with Martin had been forced and miserable, after all. On the way home, as she passed by Hampstead Heath station, she'd checked out the *Evening Standard*; Nick's case hadn't made it onto the front page yet, but this may not be the last edition.

Back home, when she came into the living room, Greg removed his headset. 'I heard the news about your client,' he said. 'They said he'd changed his plea to guilty to poisoning and the CPS was going to accept it.' He waited for a response from Judith. Of course, the online press would always be one step ahead of the print version.

'You're better informed than me, then,' she said.

'So you were right to get me to check those names – his sister, his nephew.'

'I wasn't right about anything. I got things totally and utterly wrong,' Judith said, with a gasp of exhaustion, sitting down and pulling off her shoes one after the other. 'I insisted the panellists were suspects, but I never really listened to any of them, what they were saying – *Brett ate the sandwiches, Brett felt unwell, Brett had a shellfish allergy, Brett developed a rash, Nick was jumpy, didn't label things, filled up Brett's glass with water, tried to hide the evidence.* They all told the story of what happened, but I didn't listen – not till the very end, when the damage was already done.'

'To be fair, the other panellists were all colourful characters.'

Judith had a sudden urge to shout at Greg, to tell him that he'd been the one who'd distracted her in the first place, with his theories about ritual slaughter and junk food, but she knew she had already been going down that road when he'd offered to help, that she had been more than content to spread the net wide. She ran her fingers through her hair.

'And the last clue – oh I didn't even tell Connie this one. I couldn't destroy the last vestiges of her faith in human nature, not so early on in her career. She feels sorry for Nick. When Brett went down, face first, Adrian said he tried to turn him onto his back, but Brett resisted him. Zoe said Brett's arms were flailing around. Even Adrian said he noticed Nick – that during Brett's introduction, Nick stood in the central aisle, towards the back of the hall. But once Brett collapsed, Nick came forward, right to the front. To watch.'

'You think he was gloating?'

Judith hesitated. 'No,' she said eventually. 'Even my twisted mind won't allow me to believe that of Nick. But he could have said something then. And I should have worked it all out earlier. It was there in Zoe's video – Nick at the front, on the edge of the screen. When Brett threw his head back, it must have been to stare directly at Nick, his assailant. Brett's arms? He must have been trying to point to Nick. That's why he struggled against Adrian so hard. He was trying to tell them it was Nick. And they spun him around and Nick ran off, and the opportunity was lost.'

'Brett tried again, though, didn't he? He tried to say something, even though, like you said, no one could understand him.'

'I understand him now. *George.* That's what he tried to say. The name of the boy who died was George. How ironic. You see Nick said in court that if Brett had acknowledged him, had showed him he remembered the boy, even in some small way, he would never have hurt him. Of course, that may all be justification after the event, but I'm not certain. So there we are. Brett did try to tell him he remembered, after all. It was just all too late by then.'

'What will happen to Nick?'

'If they've accepted his plea, like you said – although I'm surprised they're not pushing for a murder conviction – then they'll adjourn for sentencing. Connie will do what she can in mitigation, if he allows her, but the prosecution will use words like "premeditated" and "revenge" – you can imagine. Andy will love it. Either way he'll go to prison. It's just a question of how long a sentence.'

'That's sad.'

'Not you too. I got the same sob story claptrap from Connie. It's sad that the boy died and the mother has no son. But you can't go running around poisoning people. I should have known. I was trying to be so clever with the pathologist, belittling his experience, making fun of him for his diagnosis, tearing it apart. And he was right all along. Even without the stomach contents, he'd discovered it, how Nick'd done it. I was so blinkered. I... disrespected him, another professional.'

'That's your job.'

'It's my job to defend my client, but not to the extent that I make everyone else look stupid or, worse than that, I'm so narrow-minded, so arrogant that I genuinely believe that everyone else *is* stupid and I'm the only one with the answers. The saviour of the world and all the little people in it.'

'I think you're tired and you need to rest.'

'Oh, but then I forgot the best bit.'

'What's that?'

'I even got the Ambrosia project wrong.'

'How do you mean?'

'It wasn't just about regulating junk food, like in the meeting minutes you found, or labelling meat. Ambrosia was all about gene-edited food and whether we should eat it, and the Sumners are growing it.'

'So I was right then,' Greg's face lit up. 'Mark Sumner *was* the one with the most to lose.'

Judith opened her mouth and then closed it again. Then she shuffled over towards the window and closed the curtain, even though it was brilliant sunshine outside. 'I think I might just go straight to bed,' she said. 'It's been quite a week.'

'I'll run you a bath?'

'No...thank you. I...don't need anything else from you, just now.'

Judith's hands trembled, as she removed her jacket. Greg stepped forward to help her and she pushed him away.

'Is there something else wrong?' Greg said, as Judith stood with her back to him. 'I mean...something wrong with us?'

'I'm not sure. Should there be?'

'I have this feeling, like before last time you...asked me to leave, without giving me any reason. I'm telling myself that I'm being stupid, that it's just all the other stuff you've mentioned. God knows that's enough reason for you to be upset. But I have to ask. Are you going to wake up tomorrow morning and tell me to go, again?'

Judith didn't turn around. 'I honestly don't know,' she said.

Greg sighed. 'This is about Andy Chambers, isn't it? What he said. I can explain, if you'll let me.'

'Andy Chambers – quite the chatterbox, when he wants to be.'

Greg's hands went to his mouth. He reached out towards Judith again, but then retreated.

'You're entitled to do whatever you want in your business affairs. It's nothing to do with me,' she said, her voice brittle and low.

'Don't be like that. Look. Graham Hendricks and I go back a long way, to high school. *Court TV* was his baby. He had to be out of town for a few days, just after the launch and he called me, out of the blue, asked me to keep an eye on things for him. I was there less than a week, providing input on content mostly. I could've said no, but I'd like to think that I did a good job managing the show for a couple of days, kept things running smoothly and on the right side of the law and common sense. If I'd said no, he'd've asked someone else, and things might have become really tough for you.'

'As opposed to the total media circus that prevailed.'

'That's not fair.'

'Isn't it? You sacrificed yourself then, for the common good. How noble.'

'I helped a friend out and, at the same time, I was looking after your interests.'

'You can't possibly have thought that I would have been happy for you to do that job.'

'You're right, but I thought hard about it and, like I said, I believed it was the best option. *Then,* during Debbie Mallard's case, with all the media attention and the pressure, if I'd told you, you would have been livid. *Now,* now it's in the past and you saw that the Court TV coverage was balanced. Now, I'm hoping that you'll give me a fair hearing.'

'You were always going to tell me?'

'At some stage, yes. I was waiting for the right moment.'

Judith heard the words Greg was speaking and they filled her with dread and disappointment. She could just about accept that his description of the work he undertook for Court TV was accurate, that he'd striven to be fair with the coverage and commentary which accompanied Debbie Mallard's trial. And she knew Greg hated to let anyone down, so it rang true that he had agreed to help out his friend, without necessarily thinking through the consequences. But if Andy had not alerted her, she did not believe for one moment that Greg would have volunteered anything about his involvement.

'Look,' she said. 'Maybe I made a mistake. We should never have tried this – tried again.'

'Oh no! I'm not going to let you do this, not a second time.'

'If I think our relationship isn't working, I'm perfectly entitled to say.' Now Judith had turned around and she had thrown her shoulders back.

'And I'm perfectly entitled to disagree with you,' Greg said. 'Our relationship is just fine. And that's a problem for you. It's more than fine. It's good. It's great, and that scares you, doesn't it?'

'I'm so tired, Greg.'

'Last time, I let you push me away. I respected your wishes even though I didn't have a clue what I'd done wrong. This time, you need to tell me. If you want me to leave, to back off, you have to tell me what's going on. Because I love you and I want to be with you now and always and I'm not going quietly this time.'

Judith sidestepped him, went into the kitchen, poured herself a glass of wine and then returned and sat down on the sofa. Greg perched on the arm, next to her.

'There was a day, in the summer; you won't remember,' she began, eventually. 'We sat on a park bench and this mother went past with her kids and you waved at one of them – the boy, I think.'

'OK?'

'I watched you. You smiled at him and your face lit up. More than that, something inside you came to life. A strange child, a stranger's child, and you reached out to him like that. If he had tripped, you would have leaped up out of the seat we shared and helped him up. If he'd dropped his ice cream, you would have abandoned me and offered to buy him another. If he'd cried, you would have hugged him tight. That little boy took you away from me, into another world.'

'I think you're over-analysing.'

'No. I felt it. Your connection with the boy. It was real. I never wanted children. I mean, I never actively craved them. I didn't feel that a piece of my life was missing. When friends were pregnant or had young children crawling around, I was pleased for them, but I never felt it was something I wanted for me. But I wasn't totally against the idea. If Martin had been keen, I suspect I would have conformed, performed – whatever and I think I might have liked it, being a mother, or at least some aspects of it. Not the baby stuff, maybe the things which come later on. It's far too late for me now, but it isn't for you. You could find someone younger and still have a child, someone with whom you could build models and fly kites and stamp in puddles. A mini you. Two mini yous. Five mini yous. Someone who'll be left here when you're gone.'

Greg stood up, turned towards Judith and leaned back against the table. 'Wow,' he said. 'You left me because I smiled at a boy in a park. And I thought it was my snoring.'

'I'm being serious. I wish you would be.'

'I am. I am trying to be. Judith, I love you. I love everything about you. I love the way you look and smell and taste. I love the way you dress, except for that purple scarf you sometimes wear. I love the way you tell a story. I love the way you think you know everything and when you realise you don't, you still pretend that you do. I love the way you judge other people fast and furious, but then you're always willing to reconsider, like tonight. Other people don't see that side of you; they don't always stick around for long enough. I like kids. But the kids I like are other people's kids. I'm a good uncle. I'm not sure I'd be such a great father. I have so many other things I like to do with my time.'

Judith sipped at her wine.

'Look, in some ways people who have kids are mercenary, don't you think?' Greg continued. 'I mean, leaving aside the issue of the need to keep the human race going, instead of devoting their lives to serving the wider community they, selfishly, spend loads of time and energy on their offspring. Doctors could be treating more patients, but instead, they're at home playing with their own kids or helping them with their homework. You've done some pretty wonderful things with your time Not just the people you've defended – people who could go back to their lives with their heads held high – even the ones who you advised before you did the criminal work, whose lives were better because they avoided some long dispute which would take all their money and rattle their belief in human nature. If you'd been busy with your own kids, you'd have had less time for others.'

Judith was not sure Greg meant any of this. He could so easily be saying what he knew she wanted to hear. Still, it was nice of him to go to the trouble.

'I accept, I might have liked to have kids if Andrea hadn't left me, or if you and I had met earlier,' Greg continued. 'If, if and if again. But I don't live my life looking at what might have been. And I'm certainly not going to throw away something wonderful, something remarkable with the woman I love, on the off chance I might be able to father a child or two some day.

'And, yes, you're right I should have told you about the Court TV stuff. I should have told you straight after Debbie Mallard's trial was over. But I was desperate to get you to see me again and telling you would have been fatal. Then I was so over the moon that night, when I brought the takeaway and you let me in, I couldn't bear the thought of jeopardising something so precious. I get a lot of satisfaction from my work, from mentoring some of the kids we get through the door. That's really enough for me.

Now I need to stop talking and hear from you.'

Judith rose slowly and kissed Greg on the cheek.

'I'm not good at talking about these things,' she said. 'You know that already. I…I agree with a lot of what you said. I shouldn't push you away every time something happens that I don't feel comfortable with. It's just that, since Martin, I haven't wanted to rely on anyone for anything, in case they let me down again. It's easier to make excuses for not making a commitment – to blame it on you, or on what you might want – than to appreciate that I am the one at fault. Ah. There I can't say anything else tonight. Don't make me say anything more. I need to stop talking now. Shall we go to bed?'

Greg followed Judith into the bedroom, turned back the covers and fished around for his pyjamas. And even though it was hardly 7 o'clock, he settled himself down beside her, as she drifted off to sleep. In the night, she awoke. She'd dreamed that Greg had packed a giant suitcase and left. She expected to find the bed empty but there he was, lying next to her. She stretched one arm around his shoulder, her fingertips reaching for his heart.

***

Constance met Chris for dinner. He'd brought her some flowers: tightly bound pale pink peonies with fuchsia edges. His face lit up as she approached.

'Did you win?' he asked.

Constance sat down, took the beautiful flowers from him and placed them on the table. She'd rather not talk about anything associated with what had just happened. She would tell Chris the absolute minimum. And she couldn't really believe he didn't know; it was all over the News. Maybe he knew already but didn't want to hurt her feelings. If so, why had he even mentioned it?

'Actually, we lost,' she said.

'I'm sorry. You don't look too down, though.'

'Don't I? Well, maybe that's because our client was guilty.'

'Wow.'

'Yep. Pulled the wool over our eyes.'

'It can't be the first time?'

That was more than a little insensitive, even if it was true. And she was going to have to say something just to satisfy Chris' curiosity. Maybe she shouldn't have come out tonight, after all.

'There's loads of times when you can't be sure and you do your best with what you have, you know?' There, she had kept it general and non-committal and not revealed the personal disaster, the betrayal, the professional embarrassment she felt Nick's guilt really was. 'I'd like to talk about something else, if that's OK. It's been a long eight days.'

'Sure. I was just interested. What would you like to talk about?'

'What have *you* been doing since we last spoke?'

'You really want to hear about the proposals to upgrade the Thames Water barrier?'

Constance sat back. She didn't. 'Yes, I really do,' she said.

Chris waved to get the barman's attention. Constance allowed her hand to brush against his, when he returned it to the table. He noticed and smiled. Then he leaned forward and kissed her on the cheek.

'That's nice,' she said.

'I thought so too,' he replied.

But when she started reading her way through the cocktail list and she reached the Negroni, her mind wandered of its own accord to Greg's face on that night, almost two years ago, when they'd met in Coal Drops Yard and he'd recommended she try one. He'd made her laugh over and over and only asked about Judith in passing.

And then, as she forced herself not to think about Greg, her mind flitted to the other men to whom she had been exposed over the last week or so. Mark Sumner, ruled by his passions, which, at least for the time being were heroic and worthwhile, but which, Constance sensed, could change at any moment to something less laudable and more dangerous. Nick Demetriou, demonstrating tremendous family loyalty and devotion, wracked by guilt for the events of the past – guilt which led him to kill another man. Adrian Edge, side-lined, maligned, jealous, prepared to trample all in his wake to achieve his dream. And of course Brett Ingram, whom she had only encountered through the eyes of those who knew him, but whom she could visualise now; entrepreneur, adventurer, visionary.

Then Constance thought about Chris, sitting opposite her, who was generous and kind and good-looking, who talked about artesian wells and desalination and flood defences, a man who made things with his hands and who wanted to become an engineer because of a ninety-year-old black-and-white photo he'd seen as a boy. From what she knew so far, Chris was not impetuous or threatening, and would never be inclined to take anything by force or without justification. This was, after all, Chris, who had asked for permission to love her.

And then her eyes alighted on the cocktail right at the top of the list, which she had skipped over in her haste. It certainly packed a punch and would obliterate the events of recent days in the first mouthful; a potent mix of Cognac, Calvados, fresh lemon juice and Brut Champagne.

'I'll have an Ambrosia,' she announced to the hovering waiter.

Then, her choice made, she focused all her attention on Chris, who was looking at Constance as if she was the only woman in the world. And in that moment, she felt that she was.

ACKNOWLEDGEMENTS

I called *The Midas Game* my 'lockdown book', never imagining similar restrictions would be imposed on us all at various stages throughout 2021. And while it is true that time spent alone is necessary for the writing process itself, I thrive on the comings and goings of normal everyday life to keep my characters and ideas fresh. So completing another book during this extraordinary period feels particularly special.

There are other reasons, too, why this book has been on a marathon journey to reach you. First, its subject matter – the food industry, with its many and continually shifting moving parts. No one could have failed to be moved by the death of Natasha Ednan-Laperouse in 2016, after she inadvertently ate a product containing sesame. This tragedy brought home to many people the life-threatening nature of allergies, particularly those related to food, and it has remained with me ever since.

Then, in early 2021, I read an online blog about the dangers of eating vegetables. And shortly afterwards, I came across an interview in *New Scientist* (my 'go to' read for education and inspiration) explaining the way trees actively collaborate with each other. All I could think of was what these revelations might mean for vegetarians and vegans in particular, who clearly laud the health benefits of their diet and wish to avoid consuming or interfering with sentient life. These ideas, milling around my head, sowed the seed (sorry!) for the idea of basing the plot of my sixth Burton & Lamb novel around food.

And then the serious research began, with which, as usual, I required an awful lot of help.

Thank you, first and foremost, to Professor Jason Payne-James, specialist in forensic and legal medicine and consultant forensic physician, for chewing the fat with me (apologies again for the pun) regarding the potential for Brett Ingram to have been killed by poisoning, food poisoning, anaphylaxis or something else (I always like to keep my options open) and explaining how any of these causes of death might (or might not) be revealed in a post-mortem examination.

Thanks again to my dear friend, Dr Suzannah Lishman CBE, consultant histopathologist and former president of the Royal College of Pathologists, for enduring and answering yet more questions on post-mortem procedure, including drawing my attention to a real-life case featuring an apparent suicide in prison, caused by ingesting peaches (there's no way that ending would have made it through the edit).

Thank you too to my brother-in-law, Keith Solts, Assets Standard Manager for MEICA at the Environment Agency, for everything he passed on to me regarding sanitation, flooding and flood defences.

There was also a particularly poignant moment for me when,

in October 2021, around the time I was completing my first draft, the *UK Food Information Amendment* – known to most as Natasha's Law – finally came into force. As a result, all food products, including those produced on UK shop premises, must now be labelled with a full list of ingredients.

Thank you, as always, to all the team at Eye and Lightning Books. Eye Books (the non-fiction arm) has just celebrated its twenty-fifth year with a plethora of remarkable titles, and the fiction list (I was one of Lightning's first four fiction writers) now boasts more than seventy books. I am enormously grateful to Dan Hiscocks for his continued support and belief in my abilities.

This time around I have a new editor, the wonderful Jane Harris (also an award-winning author), who has really put me through my paces and made me dig deep, and I know this book has benefitted from her considerable skills and attention to detail. Thank you also to Simon Edge for reading the final draft and for providing such insightful comments.

Thanks (again) to Simon Edge for his novel and highly creative publicity and marketing strategies, to Hugh Brune for his enthusiastic sales campaign, to Nell Wood for the fabulous cover design and to Clio Mitchell for meticulous copyediting and typesetting.

I must, of course, also acknowledge the enormous contribution of my late parents, Jacqie and Sidney Fineberg, both inspirational teachers, who encouraged me and my sisters to spend all our waking hours reading.

Finally, a gigantic thank you goes to all my readers for their support and feedback, to everyone who reviews my books and recommends them to friends and family, and to all those who have hosted me on their blogs and websites. Not only is it incredibly thoughtful of you, in a world where we are always stretched, it also helps spread the word, at a time when the crime fiction market is an incredibly competitive place.

ABOUT THE AUTHOR

Yorkshire-bred, Abi Silver is a lawyer by profession. She lives in Hertfordshire with her husband and three sons. Her first courtroom thriller featuring the legal duo Judith Burton and Constance Lamb, *The Pinocchio Brief*, was published by Lightning Books in 2017 and was shortlisted for the Waverton Good Read Award. Her follow-up, *The Aladdin Trial*, featuring the same legal team, was published in 2018, with *The Cinderella Plan* following in 2019, and *The Rapunzel Act* and *The Midas Game* in 2021.

If you have enjoyed *The Ambrosia Project*, do please help us spread the word – by putting a review online; by posting something on social media; or in the old-fashioned way by simply telling your friends or family about it.

Book publishing is a very competitive business these days, in a saturated market, and small independent publishers such as ourselves are often crowded out by the big houses. Support from readers like you can make all the difference to a book's success.

Many thanks.

Dan Hiscocks
Publisher
Lightning Books

The Pinocchio Brief

A fifteen-year-old schoolboy is accused of the brutal murder of one of his teachers.

His lawyers – the guarded veteran Judith Burton and the energetic young solicitor Constance Lamb – begin a desperate pursuit of the truth, revealing uncomfortable secrets about the teacher and the school.

But Judith has her own secrets which she risks exposing when it is announced that a new lie-detecting device, nicknamed Pinocchio, will be used during the trial. And is the accused, a troubled boy who loves challenges, trying to help them or not?

The Pinocchio Brief is a gripping courtroom thriller which confronts our assumptions about truth and our increasing reliance on technology.

A first-rate courtroom drama
Daily Mail

Silver's taut thriller provides ample food for thought as the defence team confront the implications of machines dispensing justice
The Times

A good read and an excellent first novel
Literary Review

A quirky and charming debut novel that combines modern technology with a good old-fashioned courtroom drama
Irish Independent

A *Sunday Times* Crime Club Pick
Longlisted for the Waverton Good Read Award

The Aladdin Trial

When an elderly artist plunges one hundred feet to her death at a London hospital, the police sense foul play.

The hospital cleaner, a Syrian refugee, is arrested for her murder. He protests his innocence, but why has he given the woman the story of Aladdin to read, and why does he shake uncontrollably in times of stress?

Judith Burton and Constance Lamb reunite to defend a man the media has already convicted. In a spellbinding courtroom confrontation in which they once more grapple with all-too-possible developments in artificial intelligence, they uncover not only the cleaner's secrets, but also those of the artist's family, her lawyer and the hospital.

A new Burton and Lamb legal thriller with an AI twist from the author of the acclaimed *The Pinocchio Brief*.

An intense and compelling legal drama – quite wonderful
Geoffrey Wansell

An ingenious and compelling whodunnit
The Times

A sparklingly clever and entertaining mystery with a juicy helping of courtroom drama
Daily Telegraph

Burton and Lamb's exploits will appeal to those who like courtroom dramatics; it makes for great fiction
Crime Review

A *Sunday Times* Crime Club Pick

The Cinderella Plan

James Salisbury, the owner of a British car manufacturer, ploughs his 'self-drive' vehicle into a young family, with deadly consequences. Will the car's 'black box' reveal what really happened or will the industry, poised to launch these products to an eager public, close ranks to cover things up?

James himself faces a personal dilemma. If it's proved that he was driving the car, he may go to prison. But if he's found innocent, and the autonomous car is to blame, the business he has spent most of his life building, and his dream of safer transport for all, may collapse.

Lawyers Judith Burton and Constance Lamb team up once again, this time to defend a man who may not want to go free, in a case that asks difficult questions about the speed at which technology is taking over our lives.

A tense thriller wrought from a cutting-edge subject
The Times

Who will be to blame in the event of an accident? The person inside the car? The car manufacturer itself? The software engineers? All these questions and more are bought into sharp focus
Daily Telegraph

The Burton and Lamb series always provides excellent courtroom moments and a thoughtful exploration of an area of life where technology is likely to make a big difference in the not-so-far-off future
Crime Review

A *Sunday Times* Crime Club Pick

The Rapunzel Act

When breakfast TV host and nation's darling Rosie Harper is found brutally murdered at home, suspicion falls on her spouse, former international football star Danny 'walks on water' Mallard, now living out of the public eye as trans woman, Debbie.

Not only must Debbie challenge the hard evidence against her, including her blood-drenched glove at the scene of the crime, she must also contend with the world's prejudices, as the trial is broadcast live. For someone trying to live their life without judgment, it might be too much to bear.

Legal duo Judith Burton and Constance Lamb feel the pressure of public scrutiny as they strive to defend their most famous client yet. Another thought-provoking courtroom drama from the acclaimed author of the Burton & Lamb series.

A gripping mystery sensitively told
The Times

Thought-provoking...the trial is genuinely enthralling. Silver's real achievement is in making issues that fascinate lawyers transparent, accessible and entertaining to readers
Jewish Chronicle

Sparkling courtroom exchanges
Crime Review

The fourth in Silver's series has its fingers hovering over quite a few hot-button issues... Under her assured hand, Rapunzel manages to address perceptions of trans women, the morality of eco-warriors and the wisdom of television airing of ongoing court trials without falling over itself
Shots Magazine

A *Sunday Times* Best Crime Fiction Pick

The Midas Game

When eminent psychiatrist Dr Liz Sullivan is found dead in her bed, suspicion falls on local gamer and YouTube celebrity Jaden 'JD' Dodds.

Did he target her because of her anti-gaming views and the work she undertook to expose the dangers of playing online games? And what was her connection with Valiant, an independent game manufacturer about to hit the big time, and its volatile boss?

Judith Burton and Constance Lamb team up once more to defend JD when no one else is on his side. Just because he makes a living killing people on screen doesn't mean he'd do it in real life. Or does it?

Superb, clever, contemporary, utterly gripping
WI Life

Another consuming read from Silver: a great addition to the series
A Knight's Reads

Once again Abi Silver writes an enjoyable and believable courtroom mystery which kept me guessing till the end, with some brilliantly thought out twists and red herrings
Babbage and Sweetcorn